SURRENDER YOUR HEART TO LOVE

By

Jel Jones

PublishAmerica
Baltimore

© 2009 by Jel Jones.
All rights reserved. No part of this book may be reproduced, stored in a retrieval system or transmitted in any form or by any means without the prior written permission of the publishers, except by a reviewer who may quote brief passages in a review to be printed in a newspaper, magazine or journal.

First printing

All characters in this book are fictitious, and any resemblance to real persons, living or dead, is coincidental.

PublishAmerica has allowed this work to remain exactly as the author intended, verbatim, without editorial input.

Hardcover 978-1-4489-8684-2
Softcover 978-1-61582-215-7
PUBLISHED BY PUBLISHAMERICA, LLLP
www.publishamerica.com
Baltimore

Printed in the United States of America

Chapter One

It was a clear spring day on a quiet Sunday afternoon. Miserable thoughts danced in my mind but they bared no reflection of the perfect forecast that covered the serene, peaceful sky. The thoughts that stormed inside of my head were heavy with confusion and deafening with pressure. I had to make a decision whether to pack my bags and head back home. The loneliness had mounted and on this particular day, I felt more restless than usual being cooped up in my small hotel room. I was lying on my bed with my head propped on two pillows staring up at the ceiling. All my enthusiasm about city living had quickly faded. Suddenly, I felt like I didn't belong in the place that I was calling my home. My uncertainty about remaining in Chicago had caused me to rethink my lifelong fantasy of graduating from one of its colleges.

During high school, most of my classmates knew of my plans to leave Alabama and attend a university up north. It had always been my childhood dream to leave the farm and settle in Chicago. But now that it had come to past, the grass wasn't greener and my life wasn't perfect. Other than a sense of independence that I got from working as a clerk, in a chic fragrance boutique in the loop, earning a somewhat decent salary, beside my new best friend and boss, Katie Huntley, I felt like a square peg that had been placed in a round hole. Not even fast-talking Katie could keep my mind from wondering toward home. She had pretty much kept me sane among the bright lights. She had been a rock.

A fair skinned, medium built lady with coffee brown eyes. She wore her thick dyed auburn hair pulled back in a French roll. A very savvy woman who was fifteen years my senior at thirty-six. She was not the most tactful person, but she was the most generous. She was boldly straightforward but could be quite kind and caring to those she loved. And even though, Katie and I were quite different in terms of our personalities and lifestyles, we were very taken with each other and got along great together. She was somewhat wealthy, had worked for years in management and had made some good investments. She had left her roots, living high on the hog, only visiting Montgomery and her grandmother, Mrs. Fanny Huntley, once or twice a year. Katie was Mrs. Huntley oldest grandchild. But along with Katie and her two brothers, Duane and Casey, Mrs. Fanny Huntley took the three of them into her home and care after their parents were both killed in a car accident. The youngest, Casey, was my best friend until he had a mental breakdown and kidnapped me.

Aunt Haddie and my father had mentioned in many discussions about how much determination Katie had about giving up farm life and seeking a more profitable way of living. As my babysitter, she shared with them her hopes and dreams for the future and how she had plans to one day make something of her life: something that would take her many miles from the fields of her hometown. They said she left Montgomery and moved to Chicago less than four years after her high school graduation. It was after she had gotten frustrated with nickel and dime jobs—one after another. She moved away at the age of twenty-two with just a high school education and made a good life for herself. I was just seven when she moved away. From time to time while growing up as best friends with Casey Huntley, I had often heard him speak of his rich sister in Chicago. I had often heard Aunt Haddie and Dad mention the financial success of Mrs. Fanny Huntley's granddaughter. I had a vague memory of Katie, if that. Vague memory or not, when I packed up to leave home, Aunt Haddie and Dad were determined that I attach myself to Katie's hip. It made them feel more comfortable and at ease to know I would be in the company of someone from home. They gave me her address and phone number and stressed heavily that they wanted me to get in touch with her as soon as I arrived. Feeling anxious about calling Katie, I waited a couple weeks before I got in touch with her. I wasn't sure if she would want to hear from me. Maybe she still held a grudge against me about the incident that sent her brother to a mental institution.

When I finally got the nerve to call her, she was friendly on the spot and said she had actually been expecting a call from me. Her grandmother, Mrs. Fanny Huntley, had informed her of my move and that I would be calling her. And before I could mention the incident about her brother, Casey, she told me right off that she didn't hold any of that against me.

"It's not your fault that Casey is locked up in that place. He lost it. He needed help. Believe me, I'm not carrying around any animosity toward you. I don't blame you at all. It's not like the incident with you is what sent him off to that Oak Ridge Institution. You only came forward with the whole story about the kidnapping after he had that two days cooling off period in the city jail and went back to his office and walked around in his underwear. I think that incident pretty much let us all knew that my little brother needed some professional help," she assured me. "Nobody blamed you one bit for giving the statement you gave."

It was something in her voice that made me wonder if she really meant that or was she deep down upset with me about the incident. Yet, by the time our conversation was finished, I believed she didn't blame me. During that conversation she gave me a job at the boutique where she managed. After giving me a job, I explained that I was staying in a hotel paying through the roof for room charges. She then took pity on my fading bank account and me and rented me a room in her home. I rented the room for two hundred and seventy-five a month until mid-April when she asked me to move so her boyfriend could move in. Having nowhere to go at such short notice, I took another room back at the Westin Hotel. It was a neat room on the eighth floor with a nice view overlooking a portion of the city. This time I was given a student's discount, but the room charge still took most of the weekly salary I earned at the boutique.

Some time passed and I was still restlessly lying on my bed with both hands under my head, trying to think of a good reason not to pack my bags and take the first train home. Doing so would disappoint my father, who was a deeply kind, exceptionally handsome man. A 57-year-old, six-foot, medium built man with model features. He influenced me and gave me unrealistic ideas and expectations about city life. Expectations, that was basically in his head, since he had never lived in the city himself. It was his dream to move to the big city and pursue his painting career when he was a young man, but he got stuck on his father's farm that turned into his farm. He didn't want that to happen to me. In an unconscious effort, he wanted me to live his dream.

Shaking my head lying there, looking up at the beige ceiling, I wiped away a tear that had rolled down the side of my left eye. I hadn't been away from home long. Yet I missed my family and friends. I missed waking up in the mornings to the smell of breakfast already laid out on the kitchen table. I missed going down to the fields to visit my father during his lunchbreak. I missed taking walks in the woods behind the house, watching the birds and animals at play. I missed the Alabama warm summer evening, sitting on the front porch watching Ben Drake drive by. He never noticed me sitting there, but I always noticed him dressed in his fine clothes as he drove pass our house everyday heading to downtown Montgomery to the hospital where he worked.

Suddenly, I missed all the little things that I had never really thought of before. I missed playing with our big white Collie, Bud, who was friendly with everybody. Most of all, I missed my old room, which was nothing fancy like the one I now occupied for $300 a week. It didn't take much for me to miss all of that. It was now late spring of 1998. I had only been away from home for two semesters of college, majoring in business administration at the University of Chicago. Two dull semesters was all it took and now I was ready to pack my bags and head back home to Montgomery, Alabama.

Aunt Haddie was strongly against the encouragement that my father constantly instilled in me about city life. Up until the day I actually packed my luggage and they put me on a plane to Chicago, Aunt Haddie had relentlessly bickered with my father about encouraging me. Under no circumstances did she want me to leave the farm. She preferred sort of keeping me under her thumb. She had raised me from an eight-month-old infant and I loved her deeply, but at times she could be extremely loud and rude and when she wasn't being loud and rude, her basic viewpoint toward everyday life seemed over-the-top bitter. She was my mother's older sister and only sibling, but from the portrait my father had painted of my mother, which hung over the fireplace, I could see that Aunt Haddie looked nothing like her. My mother had soft brown tea-colored eyes with an abundance of long, flowing light brown hair similar to mine. Her petite size and features were similar to mine as well. Aunt Haddie had hazel eyes with deep yellow, grayish hair. She was almost as tall as my father and they were the same age. She was sturdy built with similar features as the U.S. Attorney General, Janet Reno. When I was growing up I wondered why she bore no resemblance to my mother. My mother had fair light skin as myself, but Aunt Haddie had pale extremely light skin with no coloration to her complexion at all. She was an albino with pink looking eyes that always made her look like she was under the weather. At the time, I thought maybe, Aunt Haddie was the product of an adoption by my mother's parents. When I turned twelve, Aunt Haddie showed me a picture of an average looking man with pale light skin, thick white, sandy hair and told me that he was her father. It didn't surprise me because I could see that she looked just like the man in the photo. She proceeded to tell me that she had a different father from my mother, explaining that Grandma Susie Mason was six months pregnant with her when she married Grandpa Jett Mason after Aunt Haddie's father had been killed in the war three months prior. Aunt Haddie was given the Mason name and never knew much about her biological father or his family except that they were natives of Birmingham. She never looked them up.

As much as Aunt Haddie wanted me to stay put and go to college in Montgomery or at least the state, my father's words influenced me more. I wanted to make him proud. He was the one who had always been in my corner with an understanding ear. This was the one thing he wanted me to do. He had never tried to run or control my life as Aunt Haddie had. He talked me into moving to the city and made it sound like a dream come true. He explained that living in the country all his life with barely a high school education had held him back. He said he had worked hard all his life just to get by, only making a fairly decent living for his family. He wanted more for me. He wanted his only child to go to a big time fancy school to become a businessperson. "One day you're going to work in one of those big elite offices in downtown Chicago," he would say. "You are going to be a business lady." In his mind, I could get a better education in a big city college.

His determination to give me a brighter future caused him to work long hours in the hot sun, putting aside two dollars a day in an old foot locker that he kept tucked away in his closet. He did this from the day I was born and labeled the envelope, "Paulene's college fund." On the day I turned twenty-one and moved to Chicago to start college, he handed me the envelope which contained fifteen thousand dollars. He felt that sending me to the city away from the farm and away from the creek area would better my life. He had big dreams for me and wanted me to do something with my future, other than farming.

Chapter Two

When I stepped off the elevator on the 24th floor, just a couple doors down from Katie Huntley's condo, I could here the music even before I reached her suite. It was obvious her party was in full swing. I felt a bit awkward being unescorted and quite unsure about what I would encounter at one of her parties. But I grabbed the gold-plated doorknob and opened the door very assuredly. But when I stepped inside of her elegant three-bedroom home that Friday evening, I was taken aback by the vast crowd. The suite was packed with guests, which was surely over its legal capacity. I ended up standing against the wall next to the front door for several minutes, not ready to pry my way through the crowd to be bumped, pushed or stepped on.

Still standing against the wall, I looked about the room for as much as I could see. And what I did see was a lot of unfamiliar faces. People stood mingling in close groups, sipping champagne and talking about whatever it was that people gathered in groups talked about at big city parties. I had no idea that Katie knew so many people and had so many sophisticated looking friends. And I couldn't help but to admire everybody's outfits as I was trying to spot Katie. They were all wearing pricey looking clothes and fine jewelry. Some were wearing expensive watches and blinding rocks on their fingers.

Finally inching my way through the crowd, I glanced at the diamond shaped clock above her fireplace and only fifteen minutes had passed since I walked through her front door. I found no fun in the overly crowded room—being pushed and hovered; and I was tempted to leave, when suddenly I caught a glimpse of Katie in the crowd. She spotted me too.

"Paulene, there you are. You finally got here," she said sounding like she had finished off one too many glasses of champagne. "A few of my friends are waiting to meet you," she shouted above the music and chatter. And as I was making my way toward her, she said something else that I couldn't make out, and by the time I reached the section of the room where I had spotted her, she wasn't there.

Then as I headed in another direction hoping to spot her again, I anxiously accepted a glass of champagne from a tall server. He was squeezing and inching his way through, trying to keep his tray out of harms way—but he was having difficult time. He was barely getting his tray through without having it knocked out of his hands. It was standing room only and I needed to find another wall to lean against or a chair to sit on. But before I could make two steps toward the nearest wall, another server took my full glass of champagne and handed me a tall glass of something that looked like chocolate milk with ice in it.

"Wait a minute," I said. "I didn't even try the champagne yet." I reached back for the champagne glass. But the server had stepped away, saying over his shoulder. "I'm sure you'll enjoy the Black Russian."

I shook my head and smiled to myself. "Real good service, Katie. They don't even let you finish one drink before they give you another one. One you didn't even ask for."

But I had to admit, as much as I loved champagne and was looking forward to a glass or two, the chocolate drink looked quite inviting and would do to calm my nerves, since I felt somewhat awkward in a room filled with people I didn't know—and the one person that I did know, I couldn't find. I took two quick sips of the chocolate drink and decided to head back in the direction of the front door. My movement through the mass and shifting crowd was slow. Katie simply had too many guests in her condo. I was being stepped on and slightly pushed, and then suddenly someone sharply elbowed my arm and I could only shake my head when I realized that the cocktail that had been in my glass was now covering the top of my right socking foot and Katie's thick gray carpeting. Looking down shaking my head at my soaked foot and her carpeting, I noticed another set of feet in front of mine that were also soaked from my drink: A pair of leather burgundy expensive looking men shoes. Slowly I lifted my eyes, noticing not only had I spilled on his shoes and my foot, but also the front of my long peach dress had a big wet chocolate spot on it. But it wasn't as big as the spot that dripped from his white suit coat all the way down to his nice dress slacks. I began to apologize, feeling like a complete klutz. I already felt uneasy, now I really felt out of place. My heart sunk deeper into my throat when I looked up into the face of this tall, good-looking man who had radiant ocean green eyes. I stopped in mid-sentence; stunned by my overwhelming awareness that he was the most handsome man I had ever seen. He was so stunningly attractive until I thought I would melt right through Katie's plush carpet. I had just bumped into a walking Prince who was no other than my fantasy guy from down home: Young Dr. Ben Drake of the rich Drake family. What a small world I thought? Never in my wildest dreams did I ever expect to be in attendance at the same party as a Drake. I had caught a glimpse of him on many occasions as he drove past my house. I had heard so much about his family from Aunt Haddie and none of it was good.

All I could do was to stand there speechless with my mouth open as he flagged a waiter. He placed his drink on the waiter's tray and took the cloth napkin that draped across the waiter's arm. Finally, I managed to find my voice.

"I'm really sorry. I really am…"

"Don't sweat it," he answered, glancing at the wet chocolate spot on his white suit jacket. "This room is packed! Everybody is bumping into somebody," he said calmly without looking at me, wiping some bits of ice from his coat sleeve. He continued talking. "Maybe I'll go on and ditch this outfit now and the shoes too." He smiled. "Without a doubt that's probably what I'll do." He shook his head. "It's too weird! Whenever I'm in this outfit, I usually leave with a portion of my dinner or drink on it. This is not the first time, for sure." He glanced at my dress as he fussed with his jacket. "Sorry about your dress."

"I'll just throw this old thing in the washer." I smiled. "Besides, no need to apologize to me. I'm the one who spilled my drink on the both of us. I'm the one who's sorry."

"Calvin asked for this. I'm sure I'll let him have it now," he mumbled.

"I beg you pardon?" I asked, but he wasn't really talking to me, it was more like he was having a conversation with himself.

I watched awkwardly as he took the cloth napkin and began to wipe the front of his jacket. "Never mind me, I'm blabbing on because I knew better than to throw on this jacket. Wearing this coat is like wearing a neon sign tacked to it that says: here I am! Come and dump your drinks on me." He kept talking, but not looking my way as he tried to wipe the spot off. But no matter how he wiped it, the spot was still noticeable since it was a dark stain from chocolate and cream: the product of a Black Russian cocktail that fate had put in my hands to destroy any chance of getting to know Ben Drake.

"Believe it or not, this is not the first mishap with this outfit. It has shown me up before, by being dumped on, spilled on or rained on. You name it," he explained in an irritated voice.

"I know what you mean. I seem to have the same problem with this dress. It's my best, most expensive piece of clothing and every time I wear it—you can bet I end up getting something on it. But at least this can go in the washer." I stopped going on and on about my dress and apologized again. "I'm really so sorry."

"It's okay. Think nothing of it. There's nothing wrong with this garment that the dry-cleaners can't fix," he said and begun to make his way through the crowd.

My heart was racing now, feeling less awkward. I felt light as my heart felt hopeful. Suddenly, I felt like being at Katie's party was a Godsend. No way did I want to stand against the wall or leave the party after looking into Ben Drake's eyes. I was hoping to get another opportunity to hold a conversation with him after a couple glasses of champagne to fade some of the layers of my reserve. And it didn't matter to me one bit that I had a big wet spot on the front of my dress. Sometime in the course of the evening, it would dry. In the meantime, I would just hold my purse in front of it. But before I could finish that happy thought, catch my breath and continue my slow journey across the huge room to find Katie, I glanced in the direction he had headed through the crowd and I swallowed hard as I watched him leave out of the front door. Just like that, he had lit up the entire room with his incredible good looks, now he was gone. Being just inches away from him I was able to see just how gorgeous he was. Watching him tear through the crowd and head out the door broke my spirit. .

So overwhelmed by the incredible beautiful effect that he'd had on me, without stopping to say hello or one word to Katie, I quickly pushed my way through the crowd and slipped out of her front door and left the big bash.

As I was waiting for the elevator to take me down, groups of people were still going into Katie's door. I felt like I should have at least said hello and told her I was leaving, but she had so many quests she wouldn't even notice I had left.

When I got down to the lobby and asked the doorman to call me a taxi, I noticed more people pouring in that were probably headed to Katie's party. She knew enough people to hold a fund-raiser.

"Miss, you may want to wait outside," the doorman said to me. "The taxi will pull up in front of the building.

"Thank you, sir. I'll wait outside. How long of a wait did they say?," I asked.

"Not long, just a few minutes." He smiled.

Dragging along with no reason to smile, but when I walked out of the building to wait, my heart pounded in my chest loud enough for me to hear it. My eyes lit up when I saw Ben Drake standing there, also apparently waiting for a taxi. I was staring at him when he glanced my way. But he wasn't really looking my way; he kind of glanced down the street in the same direction that I was standing. A few seconds went by and I still hadn't taken my eyes off of him. He glanced at his watch and looked in my direction again. This time his eyes caught mine and my heart skipped a beat. We looked at each other and he nodded my way casually as if he had no idea it was me who had dumped a cocktail all over his clothes and shoes. He looked away and pulled his cell phone from the inside of his suit coat.

"Hello, Mom," he said. "I'm calling to see how Mr. Barnes is doing. Did he come back to Dad for his follow-up?" he asked and paused, listening. "Okay, Mom. That sounds good. I'm still not sure. I'll give you guys a call back soon when I know something more definite." He paused, listening. "No, I got to go. My taxi is here."

The taxi pulled right in front of where he was standing. He swung open the door and was about to get in, but he hesitated and looked at me with what seemed like a frown, but then it could have been from the high wind pushing against his face.

"Where are my manners?" He held the door open and waved his hand toward the inside. "Ladies are first in this country, right?" He smiled. "You can take this taxi." He glanced back down the street as if he was looking to see if another taxi was coming.

"Thank you, but that's okay. You have been waiting for a while just like I have. I'm sure another car will pull up in just a little while. Thanks for offering."

He beckoned his right hand for me. "You are not from here, are you? On a busy Friday night like tonight, you could be standing on this corner all night. So, if you don't mind riding with a stranger with a wet suit on, we can both take this taxi," he said teasingly and smiled.

Suddenly my legs felt like jelly, I had stood there hoping he would say something to me. Anything. Now that he had offered me a ride in the taxi along with him, my feet felt glued to the sidewalk. How would I be able to walk those few steps to the cab? In a love struck daze, I found the strength to walk to the taxi as he held the door for me. It felt like I was walking in slow motion. Anxious thoughts of him getting into the cab and pulling off before I reached the car popped into my mind. But finally I reached the car and hopped in the back seat on the driver's side, then Ben walked around the back of the car and hopped in on the other side. The moment he closed the door and the driver pulled off, the bold, fresh scent of his cologne had the back of the taxi smelling like an expensive cologne factory. His fragrance was not overbearing, it was just the right hint of sensuous. Sitting there in the far left corner, my mind begin to wonder would this just be a ride to my hotel room, which was coming up fast or would he at least talk to me.

It was the heavy voice of the taxi driver talking to his dispatch that brought me back to earth. Then I vaguely heard the driver say," Where to young lady?"

By now I was so overwhelmed by Ben Drake's presence until my mind was in a daze. I heard the driver, but I wasn't responding.

The next masculine, very sensuous voice came from the right side of the back seat.

"What's your street address?" Ben Drake asked.

But still in a daze—looking out of the window, I didn't response. Then in the corner of my eye I noticed him lean forward and I glanced around right before he was getting ready to tap my shoulder. He pointed to the driver who was glancing through his rear view mirror at me. "The driver just asked where do you want to be dropped off? He didn't get your street address."

Lost in his radiant eyes, I stumbled with my words, looking wildly around like I didn't know where I was for a moment.

"The Westin Hotel on…." He cut me off.

"It's only one in this city. I know where it is," the taxi driver said.

After what seemed like the longest silence, he said, extending his hand, "Excuse me, there goes my manners again. My name is Ben Drake," he said, looking in my eyes.

"I'm Paulene Dawson," I looked in his eyes and shook his smooth hand. I immediately glanced away from that glow in his eyes as beautiful sensations instantly flooded my body like nothing I had ever felt before. I thought I would melt right through the car seat.

"I want to apologize again for messing up your night. I'm sure you know that I'm the klutz that messed up your outfit and caused you to have to leave so abruptly. I'm sure you hadn't meant for your evening to end like this," I said, not looking in his eyes, fumbling with my hotel room key, which I had taken out of my purse.

"Like I said, don't sweat it. It was just an accident. I'm sure I wasn't the only person who got a drink spilled on them at that party." He shook his head. "It was just too many people there." He pulled a note pad from the inside of his coat pocket and my heart got lodged in my throat. Was he getting ready to ask for my phone number?

"You didn't mess up my evening, just this dreadful outfit I'm wearing," he said, jotting something on the pad. "It cost a nice penny but I haven't gotten my money worth, that's for sure." He kept jotting notes on the pad.

This let me knew that the pad in his hand was for business purposes only. He had no intentions of asking for my number. The only way he would get my number was if I were to open my mouth and offer it to him. Being my reserved self, I just didn't have the courage and boldness to offer up my own phone number.

"I'll let you in on a little secret, Paulene. If the truth were told, I was looking for a reason to hightail it out of that madhouse. A roomful of drunks stepping on everybody toes." He shook his head and smiled. "I think that about sizes up Katie's parties."

"This was my first time attending one of her parties,"

"Well, if you have seen one—you have seen them all." He grinned. "Katie is a woman of habit with her parties. Same food, same drinks and same crowds, and usually too many." He paused.

"So, I take it. Her house is always packed with guests all over the place?"

He nodded, writing something on his pad. "Always, wall-to-wall." He quickly glanced at me, what was so quick it almost wasn't a glance at all. "Always! That pretty much sums up any party she gives. "I had no intentions of making an appearance this evening. Katie invited me and I told her I had a former engagement. It cancelled, and I just decided to swing by at the last minute. If I had followed my first mind and stayed home and took care of these notes I'm working on, this outfit and my shoes wouldn't be soaked right now." He kept his eyes on his pad busy writing. Saying what he was saying to me was just a casual pastime. "So you see, Paulene. It's not your fault, it's my own."

The driver was getting ready to pull in front of my building and I wondered if our chance meeting had anything to do with fate. He had just mentioned that he had no intentions of coming to Katie's and I had no intentions of coming to her party either, until she called me up at the last minute and kept asking me to throw on something nice and come anyway.

The cab stopped at the front entrance of the Westin Hotel. My hand trembled with nerves as I passed the driver my five-dollar fare, plus a dollar tip. I opened the door and stepped out of the car. Shutting the door, I glanced at Ben and said goodnight and without glancing back at me, his eyes still buried in his notes, he said goodnight casually as if he was saying goodnight to a stranger that meant nothing to him. I guess that's what I was in his eyes: a stranger that he had no interest in getting to know.

Chapter Three

Somehow I made it to my room and found myself leaning against the closed door and staring into the dark. After collecting myself a bit, I flipped on the light, threw my wrap on the sofa, kicked off my high heels and threw my purse on the bed. I didn't have the mind or the strength to pull off my dress to soak the stain out.

My evening had been embarrassing, but most exciting that I had finally officially meet Ben Drake. He had been a dream fantasy of mine for the past couple years, but only from afar. Flopping down on the sofa, I just wanted to spend some time thinking about him and relive every word he had just said to me. I couldn't seem to get the image of his face and the sparkle of his eyes out of my mind.

Sitting there in thought, the room felt a bit warm so I stepped across the floor to the east window to lower the thermostat, but as the warm air circulated in the room, it was not nearly as warm as the warmth spilling throughout me. It was as though a love bug had bitten me. Quickly I stepped over to my one window, opened it and the cool night air rushed into my room. I stood there at the open window with both of my hands pressed heavily on the windowsill as I tried to catch my breath. No man had ever affected me the way Ben Drake had. I probably would have fainted if he had kissed me goodnight or even if we had shaken hands. What in the world had happened to me tonight? And what was wrong with me acting this way? I'd had my share of dates since arriving in Chicago, but no one had really excited me. In fact, quite the opposite!

Most of the guys I had dated since moving to Chicago had fallen in the category of the looking for one thing type of guy, so it seemed to me. Since sooner or later, and usually sooner, they all got around to the same old line. "I did this for you, now what are you going to do for me? It seemed like most of the guys that I had gone out with expected me to go to bed with them just because they had purchased my meal or taken me out. One date went as far as taking me down some isolated road and said the dinner he had just paid for entitled him to at least a kiss from me. And maybe he would have gotten a kiss if he hadn't been such a jerk about it. Then if everything seemed okay and you got to the second date, they poured on the compliments, which was usually followed with my place or yours? The come-on lines were constant and predictable, and all the men so pushy and desperate about getting you into bed. It was a turn off how they were totally lacking in their concern to get to know anything about me beyond what they could see or could get out of me. The two guys I had gone out with made me feel like an object. I began to think that all men were just like Aunt Haddie had said.

"They are out for one thing, Paulene," Aunt Haddie would say. "Remember that, and that one thing, it doesn't include getting to know you better."

She had preached those words to me for so long, until they had become a part of my physic. So exhausted by my efforts, while living on my own in the big city, trying to fend off men in a polite way, I had sort of decided to put dating on hold. Yet, I wasn't without certain knowledge about certain things, because even for an innocent unworldly type like myself, I knew about sex. The opportunities that had been offered me had never been with someone who made my heart sing, and so far I had never made love with a man. Aunt Haddie had always preached at me from the time I was fifteen years old about the dos and don'ts when it came to boys and men. Mostly the don'ts! She would say, "Paulene, you got to think of a man in the sense of a wild animal. He wants every fresh kill, but once he has gotten his stomach full, it doesn't look as appetizing. And he soon walks away. A man needs to crave his just dessert before he can totally enjoy it. So in a nutshell, young lady, keep your dress down no matter what and just remember that no boy has any business putting his hands on you unless you want him too. And if you want him to put his hands on you, make sure he's someone very special and make sure you have exchanged your I-do's first."

With her words embedded in my head, I had saved the experience for someone very special. Somehow I had the feeling that that someone might be Ben Drake. Perhaps it was because be hadn't come on strong like all the others. For that matter, I reminded myself, he hadn't even noticed me, much less made a pass or asked me out. But somehow I knew that he would. He had to. The more I thought of him, the more my feelings went into turmoil. At the moment, at least, nothing for the deep warmth that had washed over me except a shower.

After my shower, when I hopped into bed and slipped between the cool sheets, the warmth of his outstanding presence was still lingering within me. I had never felt so much longing and needing for another human being. I rolled over on my side listening to the sounds of the city rushing through my bedroom window. I pushed the sheet off of me, got out of bed and went over to the window. The sounds that were always vague and unimportant to me before, now listening, somehow brought Ben Drake closer to me. Somewhere out there in this big city he was listening to the same sounds. Wrapped up in my thoughts, I could barely notice the glimmering light throughout my bedroom: the courtesy of the moon, which I got a full view on clear nights, casting lonely shadows across the dark beige walls.

Standing there looking out, my tears kept falling. I stepped back over to the bed and slipped between the covers. I rolled to the right side and I rolled to the left side, but sleep would not come. I threw the bedspread back, hopped out of bed again and sat on side of the bed holding my face. What I was doing was silly. Why couldn't I get this man out of my thoughts? I hopped back in bed and lay on top of the covers, staring at the ceiling.

Minutes and hours passed and I was still wide-awake. Ben Drake was heavy on my mind. I couldn't shake the thought of him, and I was pleased that I could not shake thinking of him, and I was also pleased that I couldn't shake the beautiful feelings that thoughts of him left lingering in me. It was around two am in the morning. My eyes were becoming heavy as I lay there on my pillow, now under the covers. I could feel the fresh night air rushing in from the window as I could hear the rushing sounds of cars coming and going.

My hotel room was dark and quiet and the only light that was still noticeable was the moonlight shinning through my window. By now I was drifting off to sleep, feeling more and more exhausted with sweet thoughts of Ben as tears dripped slowly from my eyes. I was praying that Ben Drake and I would meet again and would somehow find our way into each other's life. As I closed my eyes, they blinked opened again from a shadow that crossed over my room. My head jerked up and there he stood with his radiant eyes looking down at me.

"It's me, Paulene," he whispered.

"Ben, what are you doing here?" I softly whispered back.

Having him that close, gave me goose bumps. I couldn't believe my eyes. He had been on my mind most of the evening. Now he was somehow in my hotel room. I was speechless, waiting to hear what he had to say on his cleverness to enter without my awareness. Would he confess the same feelings for me that I felt for him?

He dropped to his knees beside my bed, looked me in the eyes for a second, and then kissed me passionately. The kiss was everything I had imagined and more. But suddenly he stopped the kiss and stood over the bed, looking down at me in silence for a few seconds before slowly taking a seat on the edge of the bed next to me. He placed his lips against my neck and kissed me softy.

I sat anxious with anticipation of my most special moment. He treated me like a delicate flower as he trailed kisses upward toward my face. With the blink of an eye, he kissed me again. I was bewildered in the most wonderful way. He stood to his feet again and still hadn't said one word, as he looked down at me with desire in his dreamy eyes. He stood back and started unbuttoning his red silk shirt. Slowly with great ease, he removed his white suit coat and draped it along with his shirt over the back of the chair next to my bed. With the same patience, he removed the rest of his clothes and crawled into bed next to me. He reached over and pulled me next to him and held me tight as we lost ourselves in a passionate kiss.

"Paulene. You have been on my mind since you stepped out of that cab tonight. You are the finest, most exquisite female I have ever laid eyes on. I want to hold you next to me like this for the rest of my life," he whispered against my neck.

Breathless with the sweetest sensations flooding throughout me, I lay in his arms with a feeling of weightlessness wondering how was it possible that he was in my hotel room and in my bed? How did he get in my room when I hadn't opened the door to let him in? Maybe it wasn't lock. Maybe I had left it opened with the hopes of him finding my room and sneaking in just as he had. It didn't matter I thought. He had, and that's what counted.

Ben raised himself on one elbow and smiled at me and whispered in my ear.

"I adore you, Paulene. I lost my heart to you tonight."

"I adore you too, Ben," I uttered tearfully happy.

"Paulene, I would like to ask you a question."

"Sure, Ben, you can ask me anything."

"I know we just met and don't really know each other that well. But I know all I need to know, and that is how I feel. I don't need to spend a hundred more days with you for my heart to tell me the same thing that it's telling me now: that you are the only woman for me. Will you be mine?" He whispered against my neck and kissed me.

Just as I caught my breath to shout yes, I was interrupted by the sound of an airplane flying over the hotel. I jerked and my eyes blinked opened, staring up at my lonely dark ceiling. It had all been a dream. I softly said, "Yes" to myself as I rolled over on my side and smiled. Despite the realness, I should've known it was too wonderful to be true.

Chapter Four

    After tossing and turning in my bed most of the night and barely completing three or four hours of sleep, the loud sound of a fire siren outside my hotel window shook me out of a peaceful dream, and then suddenly I was completely awake. I turned on my right side and glanced at the bedside clock. It was only six in the morning, and another empty Saturday lay ahead of me. And, one thing was sure, I didn't plan to lie in bed all morning and fantasize about Ben Drake. I had broken a record on doing just that from the moment my head hit the pillow, not to mention the beautiful dream that had just filled my night.

    Quickly, kicking the pink flowered bedspread to the foot of the bed, I sit up in bed and wrapped my arms around both knees and rocked back and forth a couple times. Then I stretched my arms above my head and held them there for a few seconds. After which, I hopped out of bed and stretched and twisted my arms as I walked to the bathroom. And whenever I entered the small bathroom I always dim the lights because it had dreaded snow-white walls and those walls were almost blinding to my sensitive eyes, especially on mornings after a glass or two of champagne. I lingered in a warm bubble bath scented with *Wind Song* bath oil and fantasized some more about the incredible handsome Ben Drake. And with a thick white bath towel wrapped around my waist-length light brown hair, I went back to the bedroom and dressed in a pair of white jeans and a olive green cotton blouse. I removed the towel from my hair and pulled my hair back, putting a rubber band around it, making a ponytail. I then took some money from my purse and placed it in the pocket of my jeans. After that, I grabbed my keys and left my room.

It was barely 10:00 a.m. when I walked outside into the fresh morning air. It was a warm, sunny morning. The first week of May and I could smell spring in slight breeze that carried wonderful fragrances of blossoming trees and bushes. It was a perfect day to be out. Not one single cloud in the clear sky. Three blocks down after leaving the building, I stopped at Denney's restaurant. I walked inside and they were quite busy but seated me right away at a small table near a window. I ordered dry toast and apple jelly, one fried egg and a small orange juice. Sitting there near a window, I noticed the deep blue sky and how the weather was perfect for two people to take a walk in the park or window-shopping. And of course, the person I wanted to walk with or window shop with was Ben Drake.

When the waitress placed my plate of food in front of me, I tried to focus on my meal, but I only managed to eat two bites of my eggs and one bite off my toast before my mind wandered back to the incredibly handsome Ben Drake. I visualized him as he lay in bed, his three inch healthy-looking dark brown hair which was naturally straight with finger waves all over his pillow, his sparkling ocean green eyes shut with a slight smile on his face, and his trim, well-built body stretched out under the sheets. In my fantasy I saw him getting out of bed, stretching away the last trace of sleep as he yawned. Now he had dropped every piece of nightwear and was stepping quickly into the shower, letting the smoothing warm water pour against his lean, firm body. Now he was taking his hands and spreading soap all over his body and allowing the water to rinse it off each time. His eyes still close as he enjoy the warm, soothing water pouring against his body. After his shower, he takes a large towel and ties it around his waist, then steps across the spacious bathroom to open the bathroom door to allow the fresh air in that cleared the steam and his bathroom mirror. Then he steps up to his bathroom vanity and place rich, thick Gillette foamy lemon-lime shaving cream on his face, takes his razor and shave.

Feeling refreshed and ready to face the day with a clean scent of Ivory soap on his skin, with a large blue bath towel wrapped around him, he walks into his spacious kitchen, open the refrigerator, pulled out a bottle of grapefruit juice and a carton of two percent milk and sit it on the kitchen counter. He then reaches up on top of the refrigerator and grab a box of corn flakes. He opens the cabinet and takes out one glass and one bowl. He pours himself a tall glass of grapefruit juice and fills his bowl to the brim with corn flakes, pours milk and one teaspoon of sugar in the cereal and takes it to his small table and eats his breakfast. After eating his cereal and finishes up his juice, he pours more juice in his glass and takes it back to his living room, where he opens the front door, bend over and pick up the Chicago Sun Times that's laying in front of his door. He then takes a seat on his living room sofa and glances through the pages as he sips at his juice. But after only a few short minutes, he throws the paper aside and decides to dress and face the day. But first he made his bed, placed the juice glass and bowl in the dishwasher and stacked the paper neatly on his coffee table. He now steps into his bedroom and dresses in a pair of Levi's 505 jeans and a neatly pressed white shirt and leaves his apartment. He's in route to where on a beautiful, sunny day like today? Too many possibilities to pin down one: a museum, the library, a bookstore, work or maybe the park? Lincoln Park was more than possible. Why not? Saturday and Sunday mornings were the only time to get out into the fresh air after a long week in a stuffy office building. The more I dwelled on it the more logical the fantasy became.

After draining my juice glass, I got up quickly, leaving half of the toast and most of the eggs untouched, paid the check and asked the manager to call for me a taxi. Shortly the taxi showed, I hopped in and had the driver proceed toward Lincoln Park. Once inside the park my mind was flooded with a dozen fantasies and thoughts, which were all negative. How in the world would I find him, if this was where be would be going? The park was a gigantic section of land. And the park itself was only one in a hundred places that he could have gone. And of course, while I'm strolling around Lincoln Park for him, he still could be resting comfortably in his bed. So, realistically, was it really possible that I could accidentally bump into him? Probably not, but I desperately wanted to run into him so I didn't want my fantasy to die. I grabbed my face for a moment and reminded myself again: "Paulene Dawson this is just a daydream in your mind, remember? It's wishful thinking on your part. Not more than a whopper of a fantasy in your head. I kept reminding myself of that. But there was an urge that felt like a driving force that had somehow pulled me out to the park. And I did believe in fate and destiny, just like we both had ended up at a party that we both had not intended to attend. Don't be ridiculous, I told myself. Fate sounds romantic, but things happen unrehearsed there was no way I could just imagine up his itinerary for the day. Life was not a stage play or a movie script, where you could change the script and write in your own fairy-tail endings.

By eleven that morning I had given up, feeling sad and happy at the same time. Happy that I felt the way I felt about him, but sad and helpless that I couldn't run into him again. I knew nothing about his hangouts or places he liked to go. If I knew those things, then maybe there would be a chance of meeting him again.

Slumping down on a weather beaten park bench, I told myself, "Well, when you headed out to the park hoping to bump into him, you knew it was all just a fantasy with a one in a million chances of it really happening. In fact, you already knew it wouldn't happen. But it made you feel hopeful and good inside just to imagine that it could. Now the fantasy is over and you see that wishing something to happen will not make it come true."

I was still sitting there thinking to myself when a young kid around the age of eleven stopped his pushcart in front of me. He was a nice-looking little boy with bright eyes, but from the torn clothes and rip shoes he was wearing, he appeared to be from a very poor family.

"Would you like to buy an ice cream cone? I'm selling them for $1.50 each." He smiled with such friendly eyes.

"What flavors do you have?" I asked, smiling, getting up off the bench to reach into my pant pocket for some money.

"I only have three flavors, strawberry, vanilla and banana," he said, looking through his selection. "I just sold out of the chocolate cones," he said smiling.

Passing the kid a buck fifty. "I'll take a banana cone."

He pulled a banana cone out of his cart that was packed with ice and handed it to me. "I don't sell many banana cones." He grinned. "But this makes two in a row. I just sold one to a man who said he was a doctor, and that I shouldn't push this cart around in the hot sun without wearing something on my head. He said I could get a sun stroke." He ginned, placing the money into a money belt across his thin waist.

"A doctor?" I asked, my fantasies taking over again.

The short, thin boy grinned, shaking his head as he pushed his cart along. "He said he was a doctor, but he was no doctor if you ask me. That dude was too young looking to be a doctor. Doctors are older than that."

There were hundreds of young doctors in Chicago, but now that this little kid had sold a banana ice cream cone, the same flavor that I just bought to a young doctor, the first thing that came to mind was fate. That Ben had been at the park and we both had just missed each other but ran into the same little boy selling ice cream.

Walking right along side the kid. He looked up at me with puzzled eyes; probably wondering why was I walking alongside him asking him about some strange man.

"Young man, I don't mean to bother you, but was this doctor African-American or white?" I asked with my fingers crossed.

"He wasn't white. This was a black doctor. But I'm telling you, this dude was no doctor. He was too young to be a doctor. Anybody can call himself or herself a doctor when they are trying to tell you what you should or shouldn't be doing. I have been selling ice cream in the hot sun for the past two years and I haven't had any sunstroke. That dude was lying."

My heart started racing. Could it have been Ben? Of course it probably wasn't, but just the fact that it sounded like a possibility, a young black doctor, I had to keep asking that little kid questions. I would think it was Ben until the kid said something that voided out that possibility.

The little boy stopped in front of another park bench about half a block down from where I was sitting and asked an old gray haired man, who appeared to be in his mid-seventies did he want an ice cream cone.

"Would you like to buy an ice cream cone, Sir?" he asked.

The old man waved his hand, being grouchy with the kid. "Get out of my way. I'm not paying a dollar and a half for a fifty-cent ice cream cone. You probably stole those ice cream cones anyway. I'm not going to buy no stolen goods," he grumbled.

"No, Sir. I didn't steal this ice cream. I bought it." The little kid stressed.

"Well, if you bought it, you darn sure didn't pay a buck fifty for each one! Now did you, young man?" He waved his hand again. "So go on and find yourself another sucker!" The old man grumbled.

The little boy put on a brave display, but I could see a slight hint of water in his eyes. I knew it was none of my business, but I could not stand idly by and allow some old grouch to hurt a little kid's feelings.

"Excuse me, Sir, but there's no need to insult the kid. He's out here working, making an honest living. Why put him down and accuse him of stealing his products?" I said in an unfriendly tone.

The old man looked up at me from his park bench with his mouth open, probably wondering who in the heck is this woman?

"Miss, I don't know who you are, but I don't think you're his mother…"

Cutting him off, I propped one hand on my hip. I was offended that he assumed I wasn't the little boy's mother. "How do you know I'm not his mother? You don't know that, Sir? And further more…"

He cut me off. "And you don't know it either!" He barked. "I don't know who the hell you are or where you get off trying to give an old man advice on these little hustlers out here!" He pointed his finger at the kid. "But woman that boy is no more your kid than he is mine."

"I beg you pardon, Sir?"

"You don't have to beg me pardon!" He shouted. "I'm just calling it the way I see it. You're not going to stand there and tell me that's your son. If you want to speak up for the kid that's your business, but he's darn sure not your son!"

"Sir, why are you being so rude?" I asked. He was not letting up off the fact that I had stated the possibilities of the little boy being my son.

"Call me rude if you want to, but if that's your son, you must have had him when you were about nine or ten." He pointed to the kid. "Woman you are lighter than Michael Jackson and that kid is about the color of those sandals you're wearing! So if that's your son, who is his father, Tar Baby?"

"No, he's not my son! But you didn't know that! I don't care if I'm green and he's orange!" I paused, shaking my head. "But I was trying to make a point to you. It's not nice to be grouchy and go around hurting people feelings. I would be proud if he was my son. He seems like a wonderful young man. If you didn't want his ice cream, Sir, all you had to do was say that, and not accuse him of stealing."

He waved his hand at me. "Why don't the two of you make tracks," he barked. "Don't stand here and preach to me about how to talk to these little hustlers out here. That's all they are," he grumbled, standing to his tall feet.

"I'm sorry, Sir. I don't mean to be rude, I just couldn't stand by and let you put down some helpless kid," I said, taking a lick of my ice cream.

The old man waved his hand, walking away. "Helpless my foot," he grumbled. "You two can have that bench. I don't have time to sit around and listen to some gullible female tell me how to talk to these little city slickers out here."

As the old man crossed the street, a tear ran down the little boy's face, which he quickly wiped away with his fingers. He took a seat on the bench, shaking his head. He looked up at me with puzzled eyes. "Why did you take up for me like that with that old man? I see that old man in this park all the time. He's always mean. I never should have asked him to buy anything." He shook his head. "He lied, you know. I'm not a thief."

Patting his back. "Of course you are not. You can't let people like that get under your skin. That old man has a problem. Next time you see him, just keep on past him. You don't need his money. There's more than enough people out here to sell your ice cream to," I said, trying to comfort him.

Still looking up at me, frowning from the sun in his eyes. "Lady are you an angel or something. You must be an angel. You are so pretty and nice. You remind me of one of those women who play angels on TV." He stood up and dug a banana ice cream cone from his cart. He ripped the paper off and flopped back on the bench. "I figured I would try a banana ice cream cone," he said, licking and biting into the ice cream. "It's the first time I have ever tried a banana ice cream cone, but if someone as nice as you like banana, then it must be good," he said, smiling up at me. "Are you an angel?"

"No, I'm not an angel. I'm just a regular person like you are." I licked my ice cream, noticing that it was melting down on my fingers. "Could I have one of your napkins?"

"Sure," he said, passing me two napkins. "Have as many as you want."

I took one napkin and wrapped it around my ice cream cone, then took the other one and wiped up the ice cream from my fingers. "What's your name?" I asked him.

"I'm Bobby. What's your name?" he asked, still looking up at me.

"My name is Paulene Dawson and I'm pleased to meet you, Bobby."

"Oh, yes. I'm Bobby Harris," he quickly relayed after I gave my name. "I'm pleased to meet you to Paulene," he said getting up off the bench, starting to push his cart.

"Paulene, if you're not an angel, you sure do look like one," he said, pushing his cart slowly. "I have never seen anybody as pretty as you are. Your hair is so long. I have never seen anybody with hair down to the waist like yours. How did you get your hair to grow so long?" he asked.

"Years and years of never cutting anything except my ends," I said, looking sadly at his malnourished looking little body as I walked alongside of him.

"My mother wanted her hair to grow," he said, still pushing his cart along. "But she gave up after nothing helped." He stopped in front of another empty bench. "She just wears a wig all the time now." He glanced his big clear eyes up at me. "The doctor's wife had long hair, but her hair wasn't as long as yours; and the two little girls with them had long hair too."

"You mean the young doctor that you were telling me about before?"

I asked anxiously.

"Yeah, that dude."

"Bobby, how do you know that the woman with him was his wife?"

"He said it was. He said, my wife and daughters will take strawberry ice cream cones and I'll have banana. That's how I know it was his wife."

My heart stopped racing, but now I knew for sure. The young black doctor that he was talking about wasn't Ben. One thing I knew for sure, Ben Drake was not married.

"It was nice meeting you, Bobby, but I'm going to take a seat on this bench for a bit then head back home," I said, reaching into my back pocket and pulling out a twenty-dollar bill. "Take this Bobby."

He stood looking at the money before he reached out for it. "Why are you giving me this? You can get almost fourteen ice cream cones with that? I don't even know if I got fourteen in this cart."

"Bobby, I don't want any more of your ice cream, but I would like for you to take this in payment for the time I took from you."

"That's okay. You didn't take my time. It's early. I won't have no trouble selling the rest of these," he said with anxious, yet sad looking eyes. He was being polite, but I knew he really needed the money.

"Here take this, Bobby. I want you to have it. Who knows I might see you out here again and you can buy me an ice cream, what you say?" I grinned.

He slowly took the money and put it in his money belt. "Thanks, Paulene. And you can get a free ice cream next time I see you," he said, pushing his cart away. "But I probably won't see you again, will I?" He mumbled sadly.

"Why do you say that, Bobby?"

He glanced over his shoulder, still pushing his cart. "Because you are an angel."

My heart was thankful for the time I had spend with that little boy. For a while, I wasn't focused on my own thoughts, my heart went out to him. Being in his presence somehow made my worries seem small to comparison. But now that Bobby was out of view and lost in the crowd, I sat there on the bench with my hair blowing in the breeze. The rubber band that had held my hair back in one ponytail had broken or slipped off.

While sitting on the weather beaten bench in deep thought, I glanced the landscape of the park, looking out at the people walking their dogs, jogging, having picnics and some couples walking hand-in-hand. Seeing the couples walking hand-in-hand made my heart ache for Ben Drake even more. I wondered if that would ever be him and I walking hand-in-hand. Someday I told myself, and then decided to flag a taxi and head back to the hotel.

Chapter Five

Sitting on the edge of the bed, staring out of the window, desperately thinking about Ben. I had counted every window in the building across the street. Now that I was consumed with thoughts of this man, all I could focus on was how lonely Saturdays were. The weekends had always seemed lonely since moving to the city, but especially this Saturday. Since, somewhere in this big city was a very special man who had stirred all kinds of feelings in my heart. Overwhelming feelings that had brought out a longing and a somewhat childish behavior. And if I was sure of anything, I was sure that my heart was surrendering to love. I knew I was falling in love for the first time.

Suddenly I had thoughts of home when it dawned on me how my parents would react to my lovesick behavior. It would be no end to the lectures from Aunt Haddie if she could see the state I was in and the reasons for it. Her preaching would be endless. Then suddenly as I sat there on the bench in disappointment of myself, her words sounded in my ears:

"Your father is all for it. But I'm not for you leaving here to go to that wild Chicago. School or no school! Just find one in the area and let that be it! I just don't like the idea of you in that big city by yourself. I guess you realize your father is trying to live his dream through you. It was his plans, at one point to relocate to Illinois. His plans fell through years ago, and now he's trying to push them in your lap. He's trying to make his lost dream your dream. You got to think for yourself, young lady. If you don't want to move to Chicago, then don't. Doug will understand. You know that deep down. So, think about it and don't make any haste decisions just to please your father. He really just wants the best for you and to see you happy. And if moving away is not going to make you happy, don't do it. But if on the other hand, moving to the city is what you want, despite how much I'm against it, I do give my consent, Paulene. You just turned twenty-one and you're very mature for your age. We know we can depend on you to do the right thing. You are very levelheaded just like Martha used to be. You are your mother's child, that's for sure. You are Martha all over again. We're very proud of you, and know you won't do anything to let us down or yourself."

"Well, Aunt Haddie, you wouldn't be so sure at this moment about that, not when I'm going out of my head in love with a man who doesn't even know I exist. A man who's family you loathe. If I could, right now at this very minute, I would call him up and have him come over so we could neck and kiss for hours. I would have him do all the things to me that I have daydreamed and fantasized about from the moment my eyes melted into his. So, Aunt Haddie, that's what your sweet, innocent little Paulene, so you call me, is thinking about here in the big city. The big city you felt would not penetrate my good girl standards and values. Think again, Aunt Haddie! It has. The wild thoughts that are running through my mind right now had never danced in my head before I bumped into Ben Drake. And, Aunt Haddie, just being in his presence my heart skipped a beat. But he didn't seem the least bit interested in me. So Aunt Haddie, that's what's going on with me. Yet, out of all of these things, the most shocking thing of all is I would never have guessed such passion was even a part of me. I had never thought of myself as a passionate person.

With both hands pressed on the bed on either side of me, I pushed myself off the bed. What could I do? It was too early to call Katie. Eleven-fifteen was way too early to ring her phone after the huge party she had hosted last night. She was sure to be exhausted after throwing such a huge party. And for the lack of anything better to do I curbed up on the sofa and glanced through a copy of *"Essence."* I read a few pages and then closed the book, shaking my head. I was still just as restless. The magazine did little to distract me, since reading the romantic articles only made me think of Ben more. I threw the book across the room. "Forget you, Ben Drake! Why did you have to be so different? Why couldn't you just ask me out? It's a man's place to ask out a woman. Couldn't you see it in my eyes that I wanted you to ask me out? No, you couldn't see it in my eyes because you were too busy working on your notes! You were so into your notes until you couldn't even look at me and say good-bye. Well, forget you! I don't need you! I'll just go back to my life as usual the way it was before you came into the picture! I'll just forget about you too!"

I went to the dresser and stared at myself in the mirror and I picked up a rubber band off the dressed, pulled my hair back in one ponytail and wrapped the rubber-band around it. I played with my ponytail and remembered what the little kid had said to me. He thought I was very pretty. But I was starting to have doubts about all the high praises of beauty that Aunt Haddie and my father had complimented me with so often. Because if that was the case, why didn't Ben Drake give me the time of day and ask me out?"

By eleven-thirty, I was climbing the walls and couldn't wait a minute longer. I picked up the phone and dialed Katie's condo with one thought in mind. I thought that maybe she could formally introduce me to Ben Drake. Ben had mentioned that she had invited him to her party, which meant she knew him, which meant maybe she could introduce me to him or something.

Almost embarrassed enough to hang up, my hand trembled with the receiver at my ear. But desperate to speak to her, I allowed her phone to ring eight or nine times and when she finally picked up, I said softly, "Katie, it's me, Paulene. I'm sorry I woke you. I know it's early and you probably had people at your house until sunrise! But this is so important." I paused. "Are you good and awake? Can you talk now, Katie, because I need your full attention about something?"

"You need my full attention about what?"

"So you are awake?" I asked anxiously.

"What do you expect, Paulene?" She yawned. "I'm about awake as I'm going to be." She yawned again. "After you let the phone ring a hundred times I guess I would be. What's on your mind little farm girl?"

"Okay, listen, Katie. I'll make this brief and I won't take away any more time from your sleep. I just want to ask if you're not busy later, could we possibly go out somewhere and have dinner together or get together for a glass of wine or something?"

After a bit of silence, she yawned again. "Paulene, you are kidding, right?"

"Why would you say that, Katie? I'm not kidding. If you are not busy later could we get together?"

"Paulene Dawson, seriously. Is that what you called me for? You don't have a crisis woman? You disturbed my sleep this time of the morning, knowing I was going to sleep in late, just to say you want to get together later?"

"Well no, not really. I really need to talk to you about something. It's a crisis to me. Otherwise, I never would have called you this time of the morning."

Jeff Burton, her long time boyfriend, who lived with her, was awake now and I could hear him in the background beginning to claim my attention.

"Who in the hell is that calling this early in the morning. It must be some jerk that wasn't at the party, because anybody who attended the party wouldn't be calling this darn early in morning waking us up," he barked. "I thought you said you were going to turn off that darn ringer anyway, Katie? Are you going to hang up the darn phone, Katie?" he asked in a sleepy, yet demanding voice.

"Listen, Paulene, I can't talk now. Jeff is very upset. This call is disturbing him. I'll call you back later around one." The phone went silent.

"Oh, God." I thought to myself. What was I going to do to keep from going nuts thinking about Ben until one o'clock? I hadn't felt so panicked and alone since I had first come to Chicago. And all because of a man who didn't even know I existed. I needed something to do to occupy my time until one pm. As quickly as I could, I dressed again and left the room. Instead of waiting for the elevator I walked downstairs.

Once outside the hotel I thought about taking a taxi back over toward Lincoln Park and maybe I would run into that little kid again who I very much enjoyed talking to. I enjoyed talking to him so much because he reminded me of the folks back home: Simple, genuine people with no hidden agendas.

Strolling aimlessly down Michigan Avenue, I stopped from time to time in front of a store window, but all I saw reflected in the glass was the face of a woman who was climbing the walls over a man that I had just had a brief encounter with. Brief it may have been, but I had thought of Ben and fantasized about him from afar. His presence had had an overwhelming impact on me. He hadn't seemed a tiny bit interested in me and it was ripping out my insides. Somehow he had gotten deep inside of me, unlocking all the special parts of my heart. He had somehow, in that little brief of time that we spent with each other, managed to open every secret room inside of me. He had opened all the parts that I had carefully guarded for so long, and also parts that I had no knowledge existed.

Finally I took the bus uptown, got off and walked toward the hotel, home.

It was twelve-thirty when I unlocked the door to my hotel room and let myself in; weary from my sleepless night and the emotional turmoil of the day. I undressed, sat on the edge of the bed and watched the clock. The minutes seemed like hours, as though they were standing still. Would Katie remember to call? With each passing moment my desperation built to such a point that I was more and more tempted to pick up the phone and call Katie back. It was five past one. Unable to control myself any longer, I was about to pick up the phone when it rang. For a moment I froze, my hands shaking as I took the receiver off the hook.

"Katie, is that you?"

"Yes, it's me. I'm wide-awake now and Jeff has left the house? Now tell me what you called for earlier," she said still sounding sort of sleepily. "And I'm sorry to rush you this time, but if you can make it quick, I really would appreciate that." She paused.

"You don't have time to talk right now?"

"Not that much time. I'm sorry. I have a full schedule ahead of me today."

"Oh, sure," I quickly replied, stumbling with my words. She had already knocked the wind and excitement out of me by making the statement that she couldn't talk long because she had a full schedule.

"Katie, you have a full schedule? Does that mean you won't be able to break away later?"

"What was that?" she asked.

"Remember, I mentioned to you when I called you earlier that maybe we could get together and do something. I was hoping maybe dinner." I paused and she wasn't saying anything so I continued. "Just the two of us. I really need to talk to you about something."

There was a long pause and I couldn't even hear her breathing.

"Katie, are you still there?"

"Barely, Paulene. I'm really beat," she stated with a somewhat icy tone.

"But you said you're wide awake now," I snapped, sensing a brush off from her.

"Yes, I'm wide awake, but I'm still beat. You throw a big party like I did last night and see how much energy you have the next day."

"I know. I can imagine how tired you are after giving such a large party last night."

"And that's not all."

"What you mean?"

"Well, the worse part was after the party ended."

"Why, what happened?"

"Well, after everybody cleared out and the last guest left, I had to put Jeff to bed. He could hardly stand up he was so wasted. I think he drank every thing in sight."

"That's too bad. I hope he wasn't too much to handle for you."

"No, he wasn't that bad. I got him out of his clothes and in bed without much trouble. But I can't really complain too much about Jeff because I wasn't that far behind him."

"So, you had too much to drink also?"

"That's right. But at least I didn't pass out on the sofa in front of the guests."

"Katie from what you tell me, Jeff gets wasted whether there's a party going on or not. Has he always been a big drinker like that since you two have been together?" I asked.

"Always, Paulene. He loves his booze, but he never misses a day of work and brings his pay home faithfully. Plus, better yet. The passion is high on his list. And the way I see it, as long as he can handle his work and take care of home, he gets no complaints from me about his drinking. Life is too short to nag someone about what they enjoy doing."

Hearing her talk like that was just making my heart melt more for Ben Drake.

"That was not cool," I said.

"Well, who cares? That's Jeff and he's not cool."

"Katie, I can tell by the way you talk about Jeff, he is the man of your dreams isn't he? You love him too death, don't you?"

She laughed loud. "Let's say one out of two isn't bad. He is the man of my dreams. But what love got to do with it?"

"Katie, are you telling me that you are not in love with Jeff? Haven't you guys been dating like forever?"

"Paulene, yes, we have been together for a long time. Almost five years off and on, but I stop falling in love years ago."

"I don't get you."

"I'm sure you don't. Because you haven't lived long enough and you haven't been through what I have been through."

"So, just like that, you just decided to stop falling in love and your heart listened?"

"That's right, when I woke up to the cold hard facts of life."

"And what's that Katie?"

"That love doesn't love anybody. You can fall in love and long for a person and lose sleep over them and they go right on with their life, because you are in love but they are not. So Paulene, that's why I have chosen not to get tangled up in love again, I have been there and done that. And I would prefer not to have that headache again."

"Katie, even though, it must be wonderful to be in love?" I mumbled sadly, knowing I was falling fast down that road for Ben.

"You'd better believe it, Paulene. But not so wonderful when someone pulls the rug from under you and you have to exist in pain until your heart heals again." She paused. "Now about this evening." She paused again. "I'm sorry, but I will have to take a rain check. I know I told you that I have a full schedule, but come to think of it, I'm not going to do anything to day. I'm just too darn beat for anything. I plan to just rest up tonight and tomorrow. I'll have to catch you at work Monday."

Tears came into my eyes. Much as I thought of Katie, I felt a resentment I couldn't deny. Sometimes she seemed like two different people: At times not able to do enough for me, then at other times, as if she secretly disliked me. Aunt Haddie had told me, that I only had myself to depend on in this city. Now I knew she was right. There really weren't any friends, not when you needed them. Not the kind of friends I was used to back home. How, I missed Aunt Haddie and Dad, maybe I should go home. People here were just too wrapped up in selfness for me, too self-centered, didn't really give a hoot when it came right down to it. Or maybe I was too much a part of Alabama, where neighbors were always willing to help, no matter what, or when. I'd thought that everyone was like the people I'd grown up with. But now I realized how unprepared I had been for Chicago after all. The curse words that seemed to roll out of everybody's mouth stunned me. I couldn't get used to all the swearing. And maybe I couldn't get use to it, because everybody used them so casually. Back home I wasn't around people who cursed a lot. Aunt Haddie could use a few curse words at times, but only when she was really upset. In this city everything was a curse word. After hearing people swear about everything under the sun, since coming to Chicago, it was just a part of the fixture in this city. I had also been shocked by Katie's choice of words. She didn't seem to mind rolling curse words out of her mouth. At first her choice words really bothered me, until I figured out it was just part of her very bold personality.

I sat now, trying to keep back the tears. "I understand, Katie. Thanks for inviting me to your party last night. I had a great time," I said, fighting back the urge to shout through the phone line. "Thanks for nothing."

At times I felt so close to her, just like she was the best friend in the world. But at times like this and the time when she gave me seven days to find a place of my own because her boyfriend was moving in, I can't help but get the feeling I'm just another person that she doesn't have time for.

After hanging up the phone, I gave in to the tears I had been holding back. After they subsided I merely sat. Maybe I could call Ben Drake and thank him for the ride. But how could I? I didn't know what hotel he was rooming in or if he had an apartment, or if he was in the phone book. I didn't know if he was living in Chicago permanent or if he was just in the city visiting? Paulene get a grip on your senses, I thought. You are losing your mind, going nuts over Ben Drake. You know that?

I took a seat on the sofa and held my face in my hands for a moment, and then I grabbed the phone from the end table, held it in my lap. Instead of trying to track down Ben's number, I called home instead. I needed to hear my parent's voice.

Chapter Six

In line with my regular workday routine, as usual it was seven o'clock that Monday morning when I stepped into the shower. I hadn't slept through one full night during the entire weekend and was worn out. Now, I wondered, was I going to make it through the day? But I would somehow. I needed the money, nearly every dime from my paycheck for my hotel bills. Seriously, I knew that if I was going to stay in this city I had to go apartment hunting.

Katie was not high on my list to socialize with, but I knew there was no way around it. She ran the place, avoiding her face would have meant not showing up for work. And when I walked into the boutique Katie looked up from the fragrance counter where she stood. "Paulene, why the long face?"

Trying not to show her how much she had hurt me and disappointed me by not showing me any consideration when I called her up on Saturday, I kept looking away from her, trying to avoid direct eye contact with her.

"I didn't sleep very well last night, if you must know," I snapped.

"Why not?" she asked, staring at me.

But I wasn't listening. I just wanted her to go on by her work and let me do mine. All I could hear was the voice inside of my head that said, where were you when I needed someone to talk to over the weekend?

Katie sensed my reaction and probably figured I was giving her the cold shoulder because she had brushed me off over the weekend.

"Paulene, I'm sorry about the weekend. What are you doing for lunch?"

"I'm not doing lunch today, but thanks all the same," I snapped.

"Come on, don't act like a spoil brat. Give this old chick a break," she teased. "I'm sorry about Saturday night. And don't even mention yesterday. I had so much stuff to take care of until you wouldn't believe it. I had to wash clothes, pay bills and buy grocery. You name it? Now, how about lunch? It's on me?" Katie asked, humbly.

Looking deep in Katie's eyes. I could see warmth. There was no doubt that Katie really was a very good friend, the only real friend I had made since coming to the Chicago. I was upset with her, but I wasn't about to lose the one friend I had. Besides, Katie was right, I was acting like a child and I had to pull myself together and get a grip.

My eyes met hers and I smiled. "Sure, if you are buying, count me in." I laughed. "And Katie, I want to apologize for acting like such a spoiled brat."

"Paulene, I was just kidding. You are anything but a spoil brat." She smiled. "Now where would you like to meet for lunch?"

"Anywhere that sells food. I feel like I could eat a cow about now."

"What about Bennigan's?"

"Bennigan's sounds good." I agreed.

At exactly twelve-thirty, the time Katie and I had made plans to meet at the restaurant, I was seated at a small square table near a window in a back rear corner. The restaurant was so crowded and noisy until you could barely hear the soft music in the background. I had kept my eyes glued toward the front of the restaurant, watching the door for Katie. I was sitting there at the beginning stage of getting upset, and I had a good mind to pay my check and leave when finally I glanced up and noticed Katie making her full-figured frame toward the table. She had finally arrived an hour late, but all smiles with her wind blown hair looking out of sorts on her head. My lunch hour was nearly up. I had been uncomfortable when the waiters began to look at me with fresh looks, one after the other, winking, smiling and debating among themselves who would get up the nerve to try and strike up a conversation with me first. Plus the place was crowed for lunch and the manager had given me looks as if I was taking up a table without ordering anything. So I had ordered a white Russian cocktail just to keep the table. I was now almost done with my second drink.

Katie took a seat at the table and sounded out of breath, as she said, "Couldn't help it, that useless meeting took longer than I thought. I didn't want to keep you waiting, but I couldn't get out of that darn office and away from that meeting to save my own soul."

I nodded. "I understand that you just couldn't get away."

"That's for sure." She agreed and then noticed my drink. "I see you're having a cocktail."

"Two." I held up two fingers, smiling.

"Well, Paulene, you've had your quota for the day," Katie said, then held up one finger for a waiter. The waiter rushed over and she ordered one for herself.

"Make that the same for me," I quickly added.

Katie didn't try to stop me. Maybe she felt the drinks would ease my mind and help me through some of the stress that was heavy on my shoulders.

After the drinks came, Katie asked me what I felt like eating.

"A slab of ribs with all the fixings." I grinned, feeling a bit tipsy.

Katie cut me off and slightly raised her voice. "Are you going soft in the head? Do you want to go back to your father and your Aunt Haddie looking like me?" She gave me a serious stare. "Do you know how much fat and calories are packed in those greasy ribs?"

"Who cares?" I waved a hand. "What good is my perfect figure if I have no one to look at it? I don't have a man in my life, do I?"

"Maybe you don't have a man in your life, Paulene." She shook her head and pointed her finger at me. "But that is definitely by choice. You could have any of these two legged-animals out here at the drop of a hat. And you know you could."

"Two legged-animals?" I shook my head. "Katie, please, why do you have to put men down all the time? What did they ever do to you?" I asked.

"If only you knew," she mumbled in a low voice.

"What was that, Katie?"

"Never mind, Paulene." She waved her hand. "But you can just forget those greasy ribs. I will not sit here and watch you eat something that you don't normally eat just to spite yourself." She stressed seriously.

"Lighten up, Katie. Like I said, who cares?"

"You want to know who cares?" She leaned forward, placing both elbows on the table. "I care and you do to." She sat back straight, taking a sip of her drink, while shaking her head. "You're just feeling sorry for yourself. That's what's going on."

After a moment of silence of staring at me as I kept my eyes downward toward the table, she stated in a demanding manner. "You are not going to louse up that five foot three, one hundred and four pounds of a perfect body with fat food like ribs." She paused and pointed her finger at me. "No way! If I have anything to say about it!"

"Well, you don't," I mumbled.

"I don't what?" she asked.

"You don't have anything to say about what I should and shouldn't eat. I can eat just what I please. And right now I feel like a full slab of ribs," I snapped.

"You can get huffy all you want Paulene, but you know you don't really want to order a full slab of ribs. I doubt if you have ever eaten a full slab of ribs. You wouldn't think of ordering a plate of ribs if you didn't have some kind of a problem."

"How do you know I have a problem?" I asked, stumbling with my words.

Katie laughed and shook her head. "It's written all over your face, Paulene. I don't need to be a mind reader to figure that one out." Katie paused as the waiter came to take our order.

"Two turkey breast sandwiches on wheat bread and two small garden salads with fresh ground pepper and vinegar and oil."

When she finished giving her order, I snapped. "You must be really hungry to order two sandwiches and two salads?"

"Don't be silly. One is for you, of course."

"I didn't ask you to order for me. I'm not a child! Remember, we had this discussion?"

"But, I thought."

"I know what you thought, Katie. And I know you mean well. But please…"

She held up both arms. "Excuse me for caring." She looked at the waiter. "Make that one sandwich and one side salad." And then she stretched her arm toward me.

"I would like to order a slab of ribs and a side of Cole slaw."

When the waiter left, I leaned toward her chair and whispered, "I have to go to the ladies' room. I'll be right back."

My trip to the ladies' room took longer than I thought. I didn't make it right back. Our meals were waiting by the time I returned.

"You took so long I thought maybe they had a party going on in there."

"No party," I slightly smiled. "I didn't feel too well. I threw up."

"Last night's dinner, Paulene? What in the world did you eat?"

"Nothing. I didn't have any dinner."

"Oh? Well, I think we should get down to a little girl's talk," Katie said.

Focusing, but really sort of in a daze. I watched as Katie picked up a small cucumber slice from her salad and sprinkled a tiny bit of pepper on it and pushed it in her mouth. Now that we were together it seemed difficult to begin. Yesterday the desperation would have poured out, but now I felt embarrassed, humiliated. Imagine going out and walking from one end of a park to the next for a man I didn't even know that well. It was all so childish. Katie was so worldly and sophisticated that she would probably laugh, and the one thing I was sure I couldn't stand at this moment was being laughed at.

Katie tapped her fork on the side of her salad dish, noticing me just staring down at my ribs and salad.

"Paulene, what are you waiting for? You were dying for those ribs. Do you plan to eat one bite of them? If not, start digging into your salad. You're not going to feel any better until you eat something. It will help to settle your stomach.

"Nothing is going to settle my stomach," I mumbled.

"Food will. It's all out of whack because you didn't eat anything last night. Not to mention having those two drinks on an empty stomach."

Poking in the salad with my fork, I mumbled. "Tell me about Ben Drake."

Katie finished chewing a portion of her sandwich, all the while looking at me very closely, before she swallowed and said, "He's smart, intelligent and drop-dead gorgeous."

I shook my head, still looking down at my food. "That I already know." I took a sip of my drink. "Can you think of something to tell me, besides the obvious? What about some of the things he likes to do? Some of the places he likes to go. Something I can stick my teeth into. Some real information about him," I smiled.

She sneered at me and shook her head. "You're barking up the wrong tree now."

"What do you mean by that Katie?"

"It just became obvious to me from that sparkle in your eyes that you are dead serious about Ben Drake," she said in a dry voice.

"Katie just tell me a little bit about him okay? Don't try to read too much into this. I just want a little bit of information about the man, that's all."

"Okay, stick your teeth into this. Ben Drake is a pleasure seeker." She threw a slice of pickle into her mouth.

"He's a what?"

"One who seeks pleasure from women," she snapped.

I narrowed my eyes and I frowned at her. "One who seeks pleasure from women?" I repeat, looking at her, but she was looking down at her food. "Katie, you can do better than that."

"You're right, Paulene, I can." She threw her napkin down on the table. "Let's see, what did I leave out. "He's also a stud, a Don Juan, and a skirt-chaser." She gave me a hard stare with a serious look in her eyes, taking a sip of her cocktail. "How did I do that time? Did I forget anything?" she asked.

By now, I was stunned to the point of being speechless from her reaction and the things she was saying about Ben.

She continued. "Oh, yes." She held up one finger. "He's also a Casanova, a make-out artist and a ladies' man who's tied to his mother's dress-tail. Now what else do you want to know?" She took a deep breath and grinned.

I didn't even smile the tiniest smile. I hadn't heard anything funny.

"Katie, what was all that about? Do you hate men?" I swallowed hard.

"Paulene, this is not about whether I hate men or not," she quickly replied, then paused and rolled her eyes toward the ceiling. "But come to think about it, that's not too far from the truth."

"Whatever, Katie. Just spare me all the rude remarks about the man. I'm just trying to find out a little bit about him. Nothing more than that."

"Well, that's what I was trying to do. Give you a little bit of insight about Ben Drake. You asked and I told you."

"What did you tell me, Katie?" I held up both hands. "Nothing that I can think of."

"Paulene." She shook her head. "I told you plenty. You may be a bit naive, but you're not stupid. You heard every word I said. And you knew what I meant. Ben Drake is a slut and a Mama's boy." She leaned toward me and stared me straight in the eyes. "I can't make it any plainer than that."

I covered my mouth with one hand and gave her a hard stare. Her put downs about Ben had me just about ready to get out of my seat and walk out of the place. I was excited about getting to know Ben and she was making him seem like the worst man in the world.

"Katie, I can't believe how you keep saying all these wicked things about Ben. How can you sit here and put him down like that?"

"Paulene, get with the program." She shook her head. "What I said about Ben Drake was not wicked. It was just the plain gossip."

"Well, Katie you could have fooled me. Where I'm from, saying something like that about a person is considered wicked."

"Well, Paulene, I'm from the same place you're from and if a man is a slut, he's a slut. Call it wicked if you want." She lifted her cocktail to her lip and drained it, sitting the glass back on the table heavily. "It's still not going to change the facts that Ben Drake is what he is!"

"Whatever Katie, you sure know how to spoil a person's lunch." I paused in her eyes. "Remind me never to ask you your opinion about some guy that I'm interested in." I sipped my water to clear my throat. "You can see I'm interested in the man and you're going to sit here and say the worst thing in the world about him." I pushed my plate aside; suddenly I was hungry anymore. Katie had painted such a discouraging picture of my dream man.

"I just call it the way I see it." She glanced at her watch.

"Maybe you do," I mumbled, frowning with my stomach turning in knots. "But, Katie, to say such things about someone who is supposedly a good friend of yours?"

"He's not a good friend. I just know the man! He's about as good of a friend to me as the rest of those phonies that attended my party."

"Katie, you invite people to your party and call them phonies? How would you like it if one of them called you a phony?" I shook my head.

"It wouldn't bother me one bit. Because they probably call me that anyway."

"Anyway, Katie, I was asking you about Ben because I thought you invited him to your party because he was your friend. And being your friend, I just didn't expect to hear you say such things about him," I mumbled in a low voice. "Plus, that's kind of two-faced."

"What do you mean two-faced?"

"You know! Saying those nasty things behind someone's back."

"I haven't said anything about Ben Drake that I wouldn't say to his face."

"But it's just not right to do that, Katie. He's your friend."

"Paulene, enough already! Why do you insist and keep singing that same old song? Calling Ben Drake my friends?"

"Well, if he's not your friend, what is he?"

"He's somebody I know." Katie laughed and shook her head. "But on the real side. I guess Ben Drake is what I consider a so-so friend. That's it. I would call Ben Drake a so-so friend: almost but not quite. If I have a party I invite him. If he has a party he invites me. That's about the sum of our friendship," she said in a more relaxed tone. "That's the reason why I can say what I said about him. I know him pretty well."

"You consider Ben a so-so friend. You invited him to your party, but you don't seem to like him at all," I pouted not pleased about what she had said about him.

She held up one finger for the waiter and ordered another drink. "We have fifteen minutes left, I might as well knock down another one." She looked at me and winked.

"Suit yourself. I'm done." I waved my hand, not pleased with her negative attitude toward Ben.

"I can see that you have drew an attitude. But just listen, okay?"

I nodded. "Okay, I'm listening and waiting to hear one kind thing about the man. Anything that would prove you doesn't dislike him."

"No, Paulene, you got that wrong. I do like Ben. He's a so-so friend who happens to be a slut! A slut I happen to be fond of," she said in a soft way.

My shoulders slumped and my stomach still somewhat hungry, my gaze stayed on the ribs and salad that I had pushed back in front of me. Not touching the food, I wondered if I should mention that I had heard of Ben Drake and his family and knew he was from Montgomery. But decided not to mention it.

"So, you're fond of Ben, are you? I thought you were so crazy about your live-in boyfriend, Jeff Burton?"

"I am, but there's all kinds of infatuations."

"Are you saying you're infatuated with Ben?"

"Not in that complete way. You see I've known Ben for a long time now. We are old so-so friends who have kept in touch with each other." She paused for a moment. "You had no way of knowing this, but at one time my Grandma Fanny used to work for the Drakes and that's how I met him and became associated with him."

"Okay. But I'm still waiting to hear the reason for calling him a slut."

"Paulene let me tell you something. If you're going to survive in this world that we live in today, you can't take everything so literally. I don't mean he's a slut slut. I mean…" She paused for a long moment, and as she continued, her face seemed to light up.

"At one time I was really infatuated with him, but he didn't feel the same about me." Another pause. "I guess I was about twenty-nine when I went home one summer to visit Grandma Fanny and ran into

Ben at that time." She gave me a serious stare. "Grandma Fanny was still working for the Drakes at that time. My Grandmother is a friend of Anita Drake. About as much of a friend as a worker can be." She pauses. "Just so you can know, Anita Drake is Ben's mother." She waved a hand. "Anyway, it goes like this. I was home visiting Grandma Fanny, and she was a server at a party Anita Drake was giving. I decided to help her out at the party to make some extra money. I met Ben Drake. We stayed in touch and have been associates every since. That's it." She waved her hand and paused. "The Drake family has a beautiful spread there in Montgomery, don't they? His family live in a dream house, if there ever was one?"

I nodded, but still did not mention that their big exquisite 9,600 square footage cream brick home, sitting on seven acres of beautiful landscape, was just a few miles down the road from my folk's farm. Which Katie already knew, of course? Thinking about that fact, suddenly, I felt anxious and didn't want her to tell Ben that I lived on a farm in the creek area. I had heard from Aunt Haddie how his family viewed the farmers who lived across the creek.

Katie continued. "During that time when I was twenty-nine, and I had went down home to visit Grandma Fanny, Ben and I were together more at that time than at any other time since I have known him. Well, to make a story short, I dropped off some ironing for Grandma Fanny and Ben was sitting out by their big swimming pool. He didn't give me a second look, but I couldn't take my eyes off of him. I knew he was much younger than me, but that still didn't stop me from walking over to him and pretending I didn't know who to drop the ironing off with. It was just one small basket of white bed sheets. He looked at me over the rim of his designer sunglasses and pointed to the patio's door.

"You can sit the basket over there and I'll see that my mother gets it," he said and stuck his head back into the textbook he was reading.

I didn't leave; I imposed on him and asked could I take a swim. He gave me a hard stare and nodded. "Why not? Help yourself." He grinned. "But are you going to swim in your clothes?" he asked.

"Yes, I am," I replied, getting into the water.

I was wearing a pair of black shorts and a black top. And after fooling around getting in and out of his pool for nearly an hour, he finally decided to join me. He mentioned that no one else was home and that pleased me. We swam in their big pool for awhile, and then got out of the water and sit in the lounge chairs, talking and laughing about things of that time. He was a kid at the time and at least I felt like a kid being with him. When we got out of the water and went upstairs to his bedroom, I was hoping he would make a pass at me, but he wanted to change into some dry clothes and give me something dry to put on.

I turned to him, looked in his gorgeous eyes and threw my arms around him. I held him so tight as we kissed until I thought I would knock him over. He wrapped his arms around me and we both seemed excited to be alone necking with each other. But just a few minutes after we started kissing, we heard someone come in downstairs. He seemed a bit nervous after that. I didn't want our kissing section to stop. So I kind of encouraged him to neck a bit longer. Then he pulled away and apologized for getting out of hand with me. He said he had shown me disrespect and hadn't meant for it to happen. He asked me if I would accept his apology and not hold the incident against him. I looked at him and said, OK. But that was the biggest joke of all times. Because I had came on to him. He was only nineteen at the time, a sophomore in college. And it didn't seem to dawn on him that I was the one who owed him an apology. And I must say, I didn't enlighten him. He thought it was his fault and I left it at that."

"You're still infatuated with him, aren't you, Katie?"

"Maybe a little. I suppose I am, but he's not and never has been infatuated with me." She paused, searching my face for my reaction. "It takes two to tangle, you know? Plus, let's face it, I was too damn old for Ben at that time and I'm too darn old for him now."

"My goodness, Katie, you are a bold woman to tell me all of this extremely personal information. More than I needed to know. You are not a shy woman."

"Believe it or not, Paulene. You remind me a little bit of myself when I was much younger," she said with serious eyes.

"I do? That was news to me.

"Yes, you do. I used to be somewhat like you. Not as much so, but somewhat. But that sweet, shy part of my life ended when I was seventeen years old. A real live one took care of that. "

"Katie, I thought Jeff Burton was your first love."

"Paulene, let me let you in on a little secret." She sipped her drink. "Jeff and I understand each other. Love is not part of the picture." She paused. "He keeps me happy enough. But I trust him about as much as I trust any man." She paused again. "But at least he's always there for me." She paused into space for a second and her eyes watered. "My first love was a fantasy that could never be and it took me a long time to realize that."

"A fantasy that could never be? What's that supposed to mean?"

"It means I had my head in the clouds believing in someone who loved me about as much as they loved this carpet beneath our feet," she said sadly. "I had to run through hell and back to get the picture, but I finally got it." She stared with distant eyes. "One day when we have more time, I'll tell you all about my first and only love, Shaun Parker."

"Yes, please do. It sounds like he was the one that you surrendered your heart to."

"Yes, but never again. Besides, Jeff gives me what Shaun never could. Or would." Her voice slightly trembled. "Let me tell you something, Paulene." She waved her hand with a sad look in her eyes. "It's nice to be wanted and loved. To have a man in your life that you can depend on to be there when you really need someone to lean on."

"But you don't love him, you just said?"

"No I don't love him. Being in love with a man is not apart of my agenda anymore. What counts is that Jeff loves me a whole lot. More than Shaun ever could. His love is enough for the both of us." She stared at me with water visible in her eyes. "Now what else do you want to know about Mr. Drake?"

"Nothing," I quickly replied.

"You don't tell lies very compellingly, Paulene." She shook her head. "So just stick with the truth and admit the obvious."

"And what's the obvious?"

"We both know that you have fallen hard for the guy."

I stared at her, not replying.

"So, why not just say it?"

I don't know why I was suddenly caught off guard that she had called me on my feelings. No need to be surprised that she figured it out. Of course it was obvious. It was like I had a sign taped to my forehead with Ben's name on it. From the moment she took her seat all I wanted to talk about was Ben.

"Paulene, I don't know who you're trying to fool."

"Why you say that? I'm not trying to fool anyone."

"Ok. If that's so, why did you give me that wide-eyed look when I suggested you had fallen in love with the man?"

"What look?"

She smiled. "You know what look? The one that's on your face right now." She pointed to my nose and shook her finger.

"You are just seeing what you want to see," I quickly snapped, not wanting to admit she was 100% right.

"No, Paulene. I'm not just seeing what I want to see. I'm seeing what's there." She kept smiling. "Why are you denying it anyway? I can see it in your eyes. You want Ben Drake like crazy."

"Do I?" I smiled.

"Yes. You do! Just say it, for Heaven's sake."

"Katie, maybe the shoe is on the other foot." I shook my head. "Maybe you still feel something for Ben yourself."

She lifted her eyebrows in surprise. "What are you talking about, Paulene? You want to run that by me again?"

"Well you just told me that you wanted Ben years ago and you had a necking session with him. And maybe you two were an item for awhile," I mumbled in a low voice. "And maybe you still want to be with him."

"You can't be serious." She laughed. "I'm sure this is your attempt to change the subject."

"I'm not trying to change the subject. It's the same subject. You said I have fallen in love with Ben and I'm trying to find out if you still have feelings for him. It sort of seem like you do."

"I see." She paused for a moment, shaking her head. "If what you said wasn't so ridiculous, I might be pissed right now!" She waved a hand. "Sometime I wonder about you, Paulene."

"I don't think it's ridiculous or so far-fetched."

"Believe me. It's very ridiculous," she quickly snapped. "And I want to make one thing crystal clear right now! Ben Drake and I were never an item." She sipped her drink. "I can't even believe you would think so."

"Why can't you believe it? It could of happened. You liked the man back then. Not to mention how the two of you seemed quite taken with each other in your story."

"Paulene, you got to be kidding? I never had a chance with Ben. He wasn't interested in me, okay? We didn't roll in the hay. I all but threw myself on the man and he said, see you! I was willing and ready to go to bed with him, but he never came on to me that way. I initiated that kissing session. I was infatuated with his good looks and that's the end of story. The emphasis is on the word "I" not "we." I was infatuated with him. He didn't give two nickels about me."

"But you said you are still infatuated with him," I uttered sadly.

"Why are you letting that bother you, Paulene? Of course, I said it. Ben Drake is the kind of man that a woman would have to be blind, crippled and crazy not to be able to be infatuated with." She paused, giving me a heated look. "Think about it? Look at yourself. You don't even know the man yet, and you are going out of your mind over him."

"I know what you are saying, Katie. But I just figured, if you are still feeling the same way about Ben, I didn't want to get in the way."

"Well, Paulene, I can assure you that you won't get in the way, because there's nothing to get in the way of. I thought I made myself clear that there has only been one man in my life that truly meant something to my heart." She held up one finger. "Just one. And there will never be another man that I will surrender my heart to. I'm just kind of out here coasting along."

"You know the saying, never say never. It could happen."

"That's impossible in my case," she said sadly.

"Don't be such a pessimist. Love can happen to anybody? We don't really pick or choose it? It happens! So, tell me how can it be impossible?"

"It's impossible because I can't love again." She paused and stared down for a quick second, and then looked at me with a brave put on smile. "Because it takes a whole heart to love," she explained with a hurt that seemed so deep inside of her that it would never leave. "My heart is broken." She tapped her chest. "It never mended. Shaun Parker broke my heart. I'll die with a broken heart."

The tears in my eyes were about to fall, which I quickly took my napkin and patted dry. I didn't know if they were for Katie or myself or both of us.

"What the hell are you crying for?" Katie asked.

"Because…what you said is so sad. You'll die with a broken heart."

"That's right. There's no hope for me. I gave up on love a long time ago?"

"Katie why would you do that as young as you are?"

"Well, Paulene, you take the hand you are dealt. I didn't want it that way, that's just the way it ended up."

"And of course, we're still talking about your only love, Shaun Parker?"

"That's the one." She smiled.

"Whatever happened to him, Katie?"

She shook her head. "I don't want to get into that right now. Now let's hear what happened with you and Ben Drake."

For a long moment, I sat there looking in her eyes. Her eyes seemed sadder than I had ever seen them after she mention her lost love, Shaun Parker. Finally I started to tell how I had bumped into Ben at her party, how embarrassed and tongue-tied I had been over wasting my drink on his fine clothing then how we had accidentally met downstairs and ended up in the same taxi. I repeated every detail and every event from that moment until now and ended with.

"Can you imagine anything so silly and childish as going to Lincoln Park and actually thinking I might run into him by chance? Katie, just say it, how childish can I get?"

"It's not childish and it's not silly. Every woman who surrenders her heart and falls for a man discovers things in herself she didn't know she possessed. Then she gets infatuated and preoccupied." She smiled. "That's a good word for it too," she said as if she was talking from experience. "She gets preoccupied with that infatuation and does all kinds of foolish things. After which, of course, she regrets them and hates herself for doing it. But she still proceeds to think of ways to attract him, catch him." She paused. "And for whatever consolation it may be for you, I have been right where you are."

"But Katie, I've never ever felt like this about anyone before. Believe me. I thought I'd lose my mind yesterday. I wanted to see him so badly."

"Oh, yeah, I have been there. You wonder if you can get through the next minute without climbing the walls. I have felt exactly the way you are feeling now." She stressed. "Don't look so surprised, Paulene." She paused and stared. "Why do you think I have been walking around all these years with a broken heart? Shaun Parker was the live one who dropped a bomb on me and burst my heart into a million pieces." She held up one finger. "Okay, enough about me. You said he didn't pay you any attention, much less ask you out, right? Well, we'll just take care of that."

"We will?" I grinned. "Katie you are like Dr. Jryke and Mr. Hyde. One minute you are telling me that Ben isn't worth my thoughts, now you're saying you'll help me win him over?" I kept grinning, pleased about her new attitude.

"Don't praise me so quick." She shook her head. "Cause if it was left up to me, you would stay as far away from Ben Drake as possible. You are a sweet, innocent young woman and I would like to see you stay that way." She rubbed her hand across the back of her neck. "But, you're a grown woman and it's your funeral." She paused. "So, like I said, if that's going to make you happy, I'll just have to get you two together."

"But how?" I asked as my eyes lit up at the thought.

"Simple. I'm having a small house party to celebrate Duane's big day."

"Duane's big day?"

"Yes. My brother's birthday."

My heart sunk deep inside of me for a second when she mentioned the word brother. Then it dawned on me that she had just said Duane. He was older than Casey and more sociable and talkative. And of course, she was talking about Duane, since Casey was currently locked up in a mental institution.

She looked at me and winked. "I'll make sure you and Ben are seated next to each other. That should help some." She smiled. "But just some. You need to make sure you open your mouth and talk to the man."

"Don't worry. I'll talk to him. I have plenty I would like to say to him."

"Sure you do, Paulene. But will you say it when he's sitting just inches from you?"

"Of course. Just put us in a room together and I'll talk to the man even if I feel tough-tied." I smiled.

"You sure sound brave right now, Paulene. But I know you are nervous about Ben."

"Some, yes." I paused. "But, Katie," I said, feeling suddenly anxious. "Are you sure you want to do this? I can understand inviting Ben to a large party, but to an intimate small one, won't it be sort of awkward for you, since he's just a so-so friend?"

"Awkward my foot." She stared at me. "Why would you say awkward? "Nothing is awkward to these skirt-chasers as long as they think they have a chance of taking you to bed," she said with a disgusted look in her eyes. "So-so friend or not, if he shows up, awkward won't be the problem." She assured me.

"I hope not." I smiled. "Anyway, thanks for the favor."

"I might not be doing you such a favor, you know. Even if he does ask you out."

"Why would you say that?" I asked, bracing myself for her reply.

"Like I told you once before, Ben is a one-nighter. A roll in the hay and that's it."

"You know this because?" I asked.

"I know it, because I know him. I have known him for several years now and I haven't seen one steady woman on his arms for more than a few weeks at best." She paused and held up one finger. "But Paulene, I'm going to tell you something else about Mr. good-looking that I'm sure you don't want to hear. He lets his mother pull him around by the nose. If it's what she wants, it's what she gets. He's a Mama's boy for sure."

I inhaled sharply. "Katie, you're extremely bitter toward all men. Aren't you?"

"Bitter?" She laughed loudly. "Damn right I'm bitter. If you had gone through the hell I went through over a lying, two-bit man, you would be bitter to."

"We're back to Shaun Parker, right?" I asked, glanced at my watch. "Katie it's five minutes past the time we were due back at work."

She waved her hand. "Don't worry about it."

"I'm not, I'm just letting you know. You're my manager and my immediate boss, so I can't get in trouble for coming from lunch late with you." I quickly relayed. "Now, you with your boss is a different matter."

"We'll go in a second, but let me finish telling you about Ben's mother. That woman has a lot to do with him not wanting to get close or seriously involved with any woman. That's why I called him a Mama's boy. From what Grandma Fanny told me, she hasn't let him breathe since the day he was so high."

"Is Ben's mother really that way with him? Ben doesn't seem like the type who would let anyone pull him around by the nose."

"No, not anyone, just his mother."

"Well, if she treats him like that she doesn't sound like the greatest person."

"But she is, Paulene. She's a nice woman. She paid Grandma Fanny well and also treated her fine and gave her money and clothes for me, Casey and Duane when our parents died in that crash. So don't get me wrong, she's a nice old woman. She just smothers Ben and tries to run his life. Even though he's a grown man of twenty-six with two younger brothers under him, she still considers him her baby. So there you are." She held up both hands. "I wouldn't spend too much time dreaming about a big fairy-tail church wedding and all the trimmings. I seriously doubt he's ever going to walk down the isle with any woman. Knowing him, I just can't see that happening. I know you don't want to hear this. From that look in your eyes, that old familiar look that I know so well, you probably couldn't forget that man now if your life depended on it. But on the serious side, Paulene, if my advice means anything to you at all, I think you should just seriously consider forgetting Ben Drake." She stared motionless in my eyes. "You two come from different worlds—looking for different things. You're looking for a Prince Charming to marry you, the beautiful wedding, the house and the kids, and Ben wants just the opposite. Just a fling and nothing serious."

Hearing her say the one thing I didn't want to hear was like a hard punch in the stomach. My eyes turned sad as I sat there quietly looking down. Katie was bursting my excitement bubbles one by one. When my eyes fluttered up at Katie and she shook her head, smiling.

"From the way you're sitting here with those sad eyes, you got it worse than I thought for the young doctor." She paused. "You know he's a doctor, right?"

"Yes." I nodded feeling like a balloon that had just lost all its air.

"I'm sorry to put a damper on your romantic thoughts about Ben, but I'm trying to head you off from a place I used to live: Heartache City. Take this tip from me and save yourself some pain. You are an exceptional beautiful young woman. You can have any man you want at the drop of a hat. It's your choice. So why not choose someone who wants the same things you do, a real relationship?"

"Katie, I know you mean well, but don't keep preaching to me like I'm your kid. I'm a grown woman and I think I can take care of myself where Ben Drake is concern. I know you are comparing Ben with that guy who used you years ago, but Ben is not him. I'll be okay, I'm really fascinated over him but I'll be okay." I touched her arm.

"Whatever, Paulene, but on the serious side, I am old enough to be your mother."

Shaking my head, not finding what she said the least bit funny. "Katie, come off of it. I get enough of this kind of preaching from Aunt Haddie. Just be my friend and be happy for me that I feel this way about someone."

She waved a hand. "Yeah, sure, but if you plan to surrender your heart to Ben Drake, be prepared for an adventure that's going to be like a fast trip around the world. That's how it was when I fell in love and became a woman at seventeen. It was the sweetest feeling I have ever felt. But all the candy in the world isn't worth the after taste of being dumped by the man you love."

"I just want to get to know Ben and spend time with him." I propped both elbows on the table to hold up my face. "I wanted to hear some creative ways on how to attract him, not the gloom and doom of staying away from him.

"Okay." She nodded. "I get that. But spending time with him means you'll be his bedmate, spending lots of time in his bed to keep him." She paused. "But sex is part of it all. And since you have never tried it, it's probably a good thing that Ben will be your first."

"Now, you think it's okay for me to sleep with him?"

"Well, I see it like this. After he takes you to bed, it goes no further, at least you can say you went to bed with a gorgeous man who happens to be a gentleman."

After saying everything she could to discourage me toward Ben, Katie wasted no time after work, when we arrived at her condo. She walked right in and picked up the phone to call Ben before removing her jacket or putting her purse down. She dialed his number and after a brief conversation with him, she hung up the phone. She was smiling.

"Ben said he wasn't sure he'd be able to make it, but that's what he always say whenever I invite him to one of my parties. He doesn't like to commit himself in case something better turns up. But mark my word! He'll be there. I haven't thrown a party yet that he didn't show up at. For the whole five minutes that he usually sticks around."

"Five minutes?"

"That's a figure of speech. But he's usually out of the door in less than 30."

"I'll take five minutes or thirty minutes, just as long as he shows up. Otherwise I'm back to square one."

Chapter Seven

My mind was in the clouds for the next five days, I could think of nothing but meeting Ben again, and by Saturday night my fantasies had become so real that I sat nervously next to him at Katie's dining room table and wondered if my feelings for him were written all over my face. I wondered if he could see the word "sprung out for you" stamped on my forehead or if he could read my mind and somehow knew I was sitting there thinking of him.

While lost in beautiful thoughts of what the evening could hold for Ben and I, I was jolted back to the gathering at the table when Katie slightly elbowed me.

I vaguely heard her said. "Jeff is killing us tonight, don't you think? If nothing else, the man is good for a good joke!"

I looked at Katie and she was beside herself laughing at a joke Jeff had just told. Ben leaned back in his chair grinning. He was carrying on as if the joke was hilarious. And then I glanced at Duane and his girlfriend, Olivia, and they were laughing as well. I was the odd one out as I sit there mute. I couldn't laugh because I had missed the joke, daydreaming of Ben.

After the laughing stopped and we were all eating and drinking and in conversations, Katie elbowed me again and pointed across the table at her brother.

"Look at that. Duane changed his hairstyle. He is sitting there looking just like Casey. Don't you think?"

"You're not kidding" I sipped my drink.

After Katie pointed out how much Duane looked like Casey, I sort of stared at him for a moment in a discreet way. It suddenly dawned on me that Duane looked so much like Casey it was creepy just looking at him. It was uncanny with his deep dark cinnamon haunting eyes and sandy brown hair, curly in the same fashion dangling thickly on his forehead, two inches from the roots. And suddenly, for a time that didn't leave any scars except sadness for Casey and his family, my mind took me back to that awful day two years ago when Casey Huntley tried to kidnap me.

For as long as I could remember, from the time we were both eight-years-old, I had always known Casey Huntley. He had been my neighbor, living with his grandmother, Mrs. Fanny Huntley in the pale green house across the creek only a block from us. We were the only two kids across the creek around the same age. We became best little buddies, always playing together and sneaking down to the creek to play in the water or sneaking off to Greenside Park to play on the swings.

After the horrible death of his parents in 1984, during the time he was about seven his grandmother took them in, Aunt Haddie said word got out that his father, Henry Huntley, who was the only child of Fanny Huntley, had went over the deep end and caused the crash himself with the intent of taking his life and his wife's, Fanny, life as well. But Casey never did say much about that rumor concerning his father, and his grandmother swore that it had no truth to it.

After middle school and around the time Casey and I started high school, he just changed toward me and started acting standoffish. He became somewhat withdrawn and started staying to himself. We went through four years of classes together, taking the school bus together to Montgomery High and he barely would say hello to me. But on my birthdays and Christmas, he would always give me a nice gift.

In high school, he had turned out to be a rather nice looking guy, 5'10 with wide shoulders, slender built with a smooth complexion and deep dark cinnamon brown eyes. But I never saw him dating anyone. He never had a girlfriend to my knowledge.

Right before we graduated, he approached me in the hallway with sad eyes.

"Paulene, I'm moving to Birmingham. I got to get away from this phony town. How would you like to come with me?" He said with a serious stare.

"I think I'll pass." I hit his shoulder and laughed, as I kept walking toward my class. "This town may be phony, but I'm not about to leave here and go anywhere except Chicago."

I could hear laughter in his voice as he hollered down the hallway. "Let's move to Chicago then! Anywhere beats here!"

I stopped in my tracks, turned around and held up both arms and shook my head. "Not we! Me!" I touched my chest and turned my heels to rush back down the hallway, smiling.

Casey stuck to his plans and immediately after graduation, he moved to Birmingham. He lived there for two years before moving back to Montgomery to accept a loan officer position. And then shortly after that he purchased a new house. He bought the place that everybody in the community used to call haunted. His grandmother, Fanny Huntley, told Aunt Haddie that Katie gave him the down payment for his new home.

Two months after Casey moved back to Montgomery, on a cold, windy Saturday afternoon in mid-January of 1996, I was napping on the sofa when I heard a vehicle as it pulled up to the edge of the yard. I slowly sit up on the sofa and yawned, to push back the fifteen-minute nap I had just enjoyed after helping Aunt Haddie with her canning of apple and peach jellies. My feet hit the floor and I hurried across the living room to peep out of the window after hearing the sound of an engine being shut off. Standing in the window, wiping my eyes with one hand and holding the long yellow curtains back with the other, I noticed him getting out of his shiny red jeep. He was wearing a long brown coat and a black hat. My heart pounded with excitement. I was happy to see him after all this time. I rushed out on the porch with my arms wrapped around me, shaking from the cold breeze.

He ran up the walkway smiling, holding on to his hat. We stepped inside and after I closed the door, we embraced and took a seat on the sofa together. While sitting there looking at him, amazed and happy to see him, suddenly he lifted my right hand and looked at me with serious eyes.

"Paulene, I stopped by to ask you something," he said without continuing.

"What? Casey?" I smiled.

"Never mind for now," he said, dropped my hand and glanced down.

After a long pause, he got off the sofa and stepped across the living room to the front door. He jerked the door open and stepped outside and closed the door behind him without saying a word. I thought he was behaving a bit odd, not even saying good-bye. Somewhat puzzled at his behavior, I quickly grabbed my coat out of the living room closet, threw it on and rushed outside behind him.

When I stepped outside on the porch, the cold wind sweep against my face and I immediately stuck my hands in my coat pockets.

"Are you leaving, Casey?"

"Not yet. I just needed some fresh air."

"Well, you'll get a lot of fresh air out here. It's cold out here, don't you think?"

"It's not cold. That's just in your mind," he said seriously, not smiling.

"No, believe me, it's cold," I said searching his face. "Are you okay, Casey?"

"Why wouldn't I be?" He snapped.

"I don't know. You just seem a bit."

He threw me a sharp, cold look, cutting me off. "I seem a bit what?"

"A bit different, maybe."

"Well, I'm not different. Maybe you are different," he said calmly, giving me a softer look. "Paulene, like I was saying, I stopped by to ask you something."

"What is it? Just ask me?"

"Okay, I will." He stared at me for a moment, and then blurted it out. "Is it true that you're moving to Chicago?"

"Yes, it's true," I grinned. "But I won't be moving until next year. It's wonderful isn't it?" I smiled.

"For you maybe. But not for me," he said in a low voice.

"What are you doing off work today?" I asked, walking down the old wooden steps into the yard.

"I could ask you the same thing you know?" He laughed.

I shook my head and rolled my eyes at him. He was acting peculiar.

"So tell me, Paulene, do you still read those steamy romances?" He laughed loudly. "If you do, let me borrow one?" He laughed loudly again, pulling a small bottle of gin from his coat pocket, turning it to his lips. He finished half of the bottle before snatching it from his mouth and then shaking his head. A moment after he lowered the bottle he looked at me and frowned.

"If this shit didn't make me feel so good, it would be obscene to drink," he said, putting the bottle back in his coat pocket. "So what's up, Paulene? You never did answer me. Are you reading one of those hot romances? Always reading romance, never living it for yourself."

I threw him a sharp look, not responding and after a bit of silence he laughed.

"Well, I was passing through and figured I would stop and say hello." He grinned, glancing around for Aunt Haddie and Dad who were usually outside in the front or backyard doing something.

"Where are your folks? Whenever I have stopped by in the past, I would always see them outside doing something like stacking wood." He pointed to the woodpile. "Fooling around at the pigpen, feeding the animals, chopping wood. Doing something outside." He kept looking around. He seemed a bit anxious.

I responded luke warm, not wanting to be bothered with him any longer. It was apparent that he wasn't being himself. Suddenly, his eyes looked foreign and distant to me. I didn't recognize the man I was talking to. The seventeen-year-old boy that had left town two years ago was not the man standing in my yard.

"I think Dad and Aunt Haddie are down the hillside gathering firewood." I gave him a quick glance as I stepped over to the clothesline to check the linen that I had hung on the line earlier.

"Well, I see you're busy, I should probably go," he said, glancing at his watch. "I got to get back to work anyway," he said and walked over to the edge of the porch, which wasn't that far from the clothesline and took a seat.

After a couple minutes of silence, I glanced over my shoulder and noticed him just sitting there—staring out into space as if he was in deep thought.

"Hey, what are you doing still sitting there?" I asked, removing a bed sheet from the line. "I thought you said you had to get back to work?"

He looked over at me, frowning from the wind pushing against his face but he didn't respond; he just kept staring at me as if some of that booze had suddenly made him tired. He rubbed his hand across his neck and forehead, just staring over at me with a daze like stare.

"Casey did you hear me? I said I thought you had to get back to work?"

He hopped off the porch and nodded at me, glancing at his watch again.

"Yeah, I definitely got to head back to work," he said angrily, then kicked the evergreen bush next to his foot a couple times. "I could kick myself for not saying something before now," he stressed with a sad tone as I was taking the last garment off the line.

"I have always cared about you. I was too damn stupid to tell you when I was working here." He paused. "Do you know what I mean, Paulene?" I just couldn't bring myself to say anything to you. Every time the thought entered my mind to tell you, I would lose my nerve just like that. I didn't feel fit, you know? That's why I left town. I was tired of people calling my father nuts! That's bullshit, you know? He wasn't out of his head. He was just tired, you know? He was tired of all the phony people and bull-shit you have to put up with on a daily basic."

After a long pause, he glanced at me, then back to the ground. "What I wanted more than anything was you. I wanted to marry you and I still do."

His words caught me by surprise. My eyes widened.

"You want to marry me? Casey what are you trying to say?"

"I'm not trying to say anything! I'm just telling you how I feel. I'm in love with you, Paulene. And I think you know that? I have always been crazy about you, Paulene. You do know that, don't you?" he asked with a strange look in his eyes. "Yeah, Paulene, you are the one."

Speechless from shock at his confession I just stared at him with a blank look on my face.

"Why do you look so surprised?" he asked. "If I hadn't been such a coward and had found the nerve before now, maybe things would have worked out differently." He frowned—hitting his fist against his hand.

Cold chills ripped through me while listening to him confess his feelings. It wasn't as much to do with what he was saying—it was how he was saying it and the odd look in his eyes and the sound of his voice.

"No! Casey," I shook my head. "Even if you had told me how you felt, it wouldn't have made a difference. I have always thought of you as just a friend."

He turned on his heels and walked away from me and headed directly across the yard and down the walkway toward his red jeep. He seemed ticked off and didn't turn to say goodbye, but as he reached the gate, he glanced across the yard at me and threw me a kiss. I couldn't bring myself to wave back. His confession and weird behavior had really thrown me. I took a deep breath, relieved to see him leaving. But as I had merely turned my back and headed toward the front steps, I glanced over my left shoulder and there he was hurrying toward me and calling my name, "Paulene! Paulene! Wait!"

Just as I grabbed the doorknob, his hand grabbed it at the same time, slightly squeezing my hand before I released the knob, allowing him to push open the front door. We walked inside and he seemed more anxious than before.

"Have a seat, Casey. Can I get you a glass of lemonade or something?"

"Sure." He nodded, taking a seat on the sofa. "Something sounds good. What about the something and forget the lemonade?"

He was giving me the willies with the way he was talking. I was trying to keep my cool, thinking that maybe the booze had him acting and talking that way."

A voice of alarm whispered in my mind and then became louder as I reached into the refrigerator for the pitcher of lemonade.

When I stepped back into the living room, Casey was standing in the living room window looking out. He looked as though he was a million miles away as I walked over to hand him the lemonade. "Here you are."

He immediately turned to face me, looking down at me with his rumpled wind blown chemically straightened sandy brown curls falling thickly onto his forehead. He stared at the glass of lemonade for a second, before grabbing his face and crying real tears.

"I don't want your darn lemonade. I want you, Paulene. I want you in my life. I'm not the same person I was back in school. I'm not your buddy or your pal. Why can't you see that? Would I be after you if I didn't love you so?"

"Casey, what's your problem?" I asked, looking into the eyes of a man who had always been kind and gentle to me. Now he was acting like a perfect stranger. "Casey, you can't blame me if I don't feel the same about you as you do about me." I shook my head. "I think you better leave! I think you're drunk anyway. Otherwise you wouldn't be standing here crying? You are acting like a little kid," I said, placing the tall glass of lemonade on the coffee table.

"I'm not drunk!" he said bitterly as his cinnamon brown eyes turned stone cold.

"Paulene, this is not about nothing but how I feel about you." He pointed his finger at me. "I have changed Paulene and I'm going to prove it to you! It's not about my father. If he was a nut, he was a nut and there's nothing I can do about it!"

My eyes widened and my heart skipped a beat as chills ripped through me, wondering what he meant by that statement.

Yeah, he had changed. He had changed into someone I didn't even know.

"Casey, you are not making any sense. Get real," I laughed.

"I am real! And I don't see anything funny about what I just said," he yelled—pushing me against the front door. And I started breathing pretty fast, as I could hear my heart pound. He had frightened me now, shaking in my tracks. Something had him rolled up into a ball and my rejection had affected him in a violent manner.

Lying there against the door with one hand on the doorknob and the other across my stomach, he had covered my mouth with his, before I could catch my breath—grabbing my face in a rough manner, trying to force me to kiss him. Thoughts of suffocation ripped through my mind, as he gripped my face between his hands and pushed his mouth against mine. He tried to penetrate my lips, but I kept them tightly shut. He bent my face back as far as he could, suffocating me with his thick lips. It was hard to breathe as I managed to rip from his embrace, only to give him strength to grab me more. He grabbed my shoulders and pushed me against the wall, knocking over a table lamp and causing a picture to fall from above the sofa. When my back hit the wall, my eyes flooded with tears and soon my face was covered with wet tears, but he wouldn't leave me alone. He stood before me grinning as he reached out and held my face with both hands, pulling me toward him.

"Please! Casey, don't! You are holding my face to tight," I cried out.

"I don't want to hurt you, Paulene. I love you and I just want to kiss you, honest. Just give me a kiss and I'll leave you alone."

"No! Let me go." I ripped from his hands. "No, you are going to leave me alone without a kiss. You can't make me kiss you."

My pleading didn't stop him. My resistance only made him more compelled to try and force me to kiss him.

"Paulene, I told you I didn't want to hurt you. But if you keep fighting me, I will!" He screamed right in my face, with his fist at my chin.

"Casey, do you think I'm stupid? You think I'm just going to be quiet and let you have your way with me? You better think again!"

"I said shut up," he yelled as he pinned my arms back and pushed his mouth against mine, spreading his lips over mine, trying to enter my mouth, but I kept my lips glued. I wasn't about to kiss him. I turned my head from side to side, avoiding his lips on my mouth, but he kissed and licked whatever was available: my neck, my head and face.

The more I tried to resist his kisses, the more force he would use. He pushed his body against me, as he wrapped me in his arms and I could barely move or breath lying pinned against the wall when I noticed the ripping sound came from the sleeve of my blouse. He had ripped a tear in it. Noticing it made me boil with anger and I pulled back my left hand and slapped him across the face with all my strength.

"Now get away from me, Casey Huntley!"

He rubbed the side of his face and grinned. "Hit all you want. It's not going to stop me if that's what you think, Paulene." He pressed his body against me, trying to kiss me.

In the midst of our struggle against the wall, the sound of a loud car engine passing down the road and the ringing of the phone took him by surprise and he quickly released me. His bottle of booze fell out of his pocket and spilled on the dark burgundy carpet.

"Damn! Damn! What am I thinking! I got to get the hell out of here before your old man and that big mouth Aunt Haddie gets back. See what you do to me? I love you in a crazy way!" He looked at me and grinned as if there was something to grin about. "The way I'm acting, I don't even recognize myself. And it's all your fault too."

My breathing eased as I stood against the pale blue living room wall trembling. It seemed every part of my body was shaking, but hearing him say he was leaving calmed my heartbeat. "You're right about that," I quickly replied. "And how do you plan to explain roughing up this place?"

He gave me a sharp look and shook his head, extending his hand to me. We're getting out of here," he demanded.

"What do you mean, we?" I asked, almost choking from his suggestion.

"Just that. You think I'm leaving you here, Paulene? No way! Come quietly or I'll get rough again. One way or another, you're leaving with me."

Water flooded my eyes and I noticed the small rip in my blouse. He had really flipped out of his head. I thought.

"You'll have to kill me first. Casey, Have you lost your mind or what? I'm not going anywhere with you! Why would I?" I screamed in his face.

As I eyed him with a straight face, he pulled a long butcher knife from inside of his coat pocket and pointed it in my face. I trembled at the sight of his knife.

"I'm not afraid of that darn butcher knife. I don't think you'll use it. Plus, since you claim to love me so much! I doubt you would stab me!"

He gave me a half smile, nodding up and down. "Well! You are right about that. I'm strung out, that's for sure. But the way I see it, you're leaving me no other choice. If you refuse to leave here with me I don't know what might click in me. I don't know what I might do. Just like right now, I think you can honestly say, you didn't think I would act the way I'm acting right now."

Stunned by how true his words were, I stared at him. It was plain to see that he was spaced out. He was dead on the money about that. I wasn't about to refuse leaving the home with him. I would just have to take my chances and hope against hope that he would come to his senses and show a glimpse of the Casey Huntley I knew.

"You see, Paulene. I have lived all my adult life dreaming about you. Now I guess my brain is fried from wanting you. Now I'm nuts like my father, I guess."

My head suddenly felt light and I grabbed my face with both hands, taking a deep breath. I looked him straight in the eyes. "Okay! Casey. I'll come with you. You give me no other choice. I can't believe you are doing this to me. I can't believe you are carrying on like this. What has happened to you, Casey? Why are you being this way and acting this way? Why? This isn't you Casey. If you leave now, I won't mention any of this to my folks or anyone else."

He looked at me and grinned. "And I'm suppose to believe that? I don't think so. You and I arc taking a little drive."

"A little drive where, Casey? Where do you plan to take me?"

"You'll know soon enough. Don't worry about it," he muttered with a frown. "But you can bear in mind, you'll be spending your life with me and not moving away from me to a big city like Chicago. Grab your things and let's go. We got to blow this place before your parents show up."

As I headed toward my room to grab a suitcase, he hollered, "Never mind! We don't have time for that. Come the way you are. We can think of clothes later."

"Okay." I nodded as he stretched open the door and pointed me out. My feet somehow put one before the other and I managed to walk outside as he rushed right behind me, pulling the door shut behind him making a loud slam. We stepped out on the porch, and noticed Dad and Aunt Haddie headed through the front gate with two armloads of firewood. It was a great relief to see my parents coming. They were looking down to their side, talking to our medium size white collie, Bud. They hadn't even noticed us standing there on the porch.

As we stood side by side, he stuck the long butcher knife back inside of his coat pocket. He looked down at me just as I glanced up at him. He smiled at me in an unsettling way, as I could see anxiousness written all over his pale face.

"Remember, Haddie and Doug showing up changes nothing. I have no beef with them, but I won't let them stand in my way. I still have nothing to lose, and can destroy them as well. They can't stop me, you hear? I'm just reminding you. So don't get any stupid ideas that by them showing up that it's going to make any kind of difference to me. One way or another, you'll be leaving here with me, if it's the last thing I do," he said sharply.

"What do you expect for me to say to them? They are not stupid, you know?

"He grinned. "Well, I know Mr. Dawson is a sharp man. But sometimes I think your Aunt Haddie is nutty as a fruitcake."

"Look who's calling somebody nuts? A guy that I thought was my friend."

"Put a sock in it! Paulene. You are gorgeous, but you talk too darn much!"

"I don't care what you say. They'll be able to detect something is wrong."

"You just better hope they don't detect anything." He gritted his teeth. "You got that? Just say we're taking a drive."

When Aunt Haddie and Dad stacked the wood against the backside of the house, we slowly stepped off the porch into the yard. I was anxious and a nervous wreck, biting my nails. Scared too death, hoping I wouldn't say the wrong thing to set Casey off. But I had to somehow pull myself together so they wouldn't get suspicious and figure out something was wrong. I had to act natural so they could figure his visit was just a friendly one. One mishap from me could upset Casey, and there was no telling what he would do, since he was so far off his rocker.

I felt a bit more relaxed when Aunt Haddie and Dad both smiled. From the expressions on their faces, it was obvious how pleased and happy they were to see Casey. They both walked up to him and shook his hand and patting his back at the same time.

"What storm blew you this way?" Aunt Haddie laughed. "Fanny told me about that good job you got for yourself since you been back in town."

"It's good to see you guys too," he said in a nervous manner."

"You look well, so I guess you are doing pretty good for yourself. I guess that's your nice jeep parked in the driveway?" Dad asked, pointing toward his jeep.

Dad was going on and on, while Aunt Haddie stood there all smiles. They had always thought a lot of Casey, giving him his first job of feeding the pigs.

In the midst of their warm welcome, he looked over at me with anxious eyes and I Knew what that look meant. I stepped closer and tapped Aunt Haddie on the shoulder. She looked around and smiled.

"Sweetheart, isn't it great to see this fellow again?" Aunt Haddie glanced at me and smiled. "When you two were little, you were inseparable! Always together! If you could find one, you could find the other one."

Dad nodded. "I remember. And I also remember how those two were always sneaking off and playing in the creek."

"And without anybody's permission I might add." Aunt Haddie laughed.

For a second the four of us sort of stared at each other, and then I broke the silent.

"I just want to let you guys know, Casey is taking me to see his new house."

"New house?" Aunt Haddie asked. She paused for a second looking straight in my eyes, and then she hit her forehead with the back of her palm. "Oh, yeah, that's right." She looked at Casey. "Fanny told me that you had bought yourself a house."

"I guess being a new loan officer must be bringing in plenty of dough for you," Dad grinned. "You're making big bucks now like your big sister. Here at your young age buying your first home. That was a smart investment to make."

"Yes, I promised to show Paulene my new place and we better get going so I can get her back before dark," he said with an anxious, wild look in his eyes.

"You didn't forget about dinner, did you?" Aunt Haddie asked. "You know that we always sit down for dinner at six."

"I know," I mumbled. We made a point of not missing any meals together.

"Well, I mentioned it, because it's almost four o'clock now. You kids won't have that much time. You sure you got time to see his house today? Maybe you should pick her up some other time, Casey. Some other evening when you'll have more time to show her your new place," Aunt Haddie suggested.

We stood there facing Aunt Haddie, motionless. We were both lost for words, and then Dad mumbled to Aunt Haddie. "Paulene knows what she's doing. If she misses eating with us, she misses eating with us. She's not a child anymore. Let the kids go."

Casey strolled quickly across the yard and down the walkway toward his red jeep, as I lagged slowly behind him, dreading each step. And the cold wind was pushing against my face, but I was burning up with fear, unsure what to expect once he drove off with me. I was wondering now could those rumors have been true about his Dad?

We left Aunt Haddie and Dad standing in the front yard smiling, as he pulled off with me. They were so thrilled about Casey being back in town, not knowing he was up to no good and it could be the last time they would ever see my face.

Suddenly Casey's hand clamped down on my left arm and triggered me back to reality.

During the drive I hadn't spoken or paid much attention to where we were headed, but now I could see he had driven deep into the woods, and we were headed down some narrow unpaved road, to some off-the-road forest preserve. He had the strangest look on his face and I was really terrified of what might happen. I had always thought of him as a pretty easygoing person who wouldn't harm a fly: A bit mysterious, but always harmless. It was plain to see—he was not being himself. Something had happened to his mind.

I looked over at him and he glanced over at me with a straight face. He had a cold, bitter look in his eyes. "I guess you can't stand the sight of me. Yeah, you probably hate my guts by now."

"I don't hate you, Casey."

"Well! You sure don't love me! You have made that pretty clear!"

"Just because I'm not in love with you, doesn't automatically mean I hate you. I don't hate you. I have never hated you, Casey! But I hate what you're doing!"

"So, in other words, you don't hate me, but you just would rather be in someone's else company. And dragging you out of your home against your will haven't scored any points for me, right?" he laughed.

My hand slapped his arm before I realized it. "You are talking and acting like someone I don't even know!"

"Don't kid yourself! You know me! You probably know me better than I know myself!"

"Well, I don't know the person you are right now. You are acting like a mad man. I feel like I'm having a nightmare," I stared at him, shaking my head in disappointment."

"Well, it's not a nightmare. It's life. It's happening." He laughed.

"What's so funny?" I asked, loudly. "I don't know what you find so funny about all of this, Casey? This is stupid, you know. Stupid! Stupid! Stupid! I never would have guess you would have pulled something like this, dragging me away from the house like this. Bringing me out here in these woods against my will." I wiped a tear. "And for what, Casey? Do you think being out here in the woods is going to make any difference about the way I feel about you, Casey? It's not going to change anything."

"Bitch all you want, but the way I see it. You're stuck with me whether you like it or not. For once, I'm getting what I want out of this miserable existence that I call a life."

Chapter Eight

It seemed like hours had passed, but it had only been twenty minutes since we left my house. Suddenly, he slowed down and turned off to a narrow gravel road that was lined with tall trees and weeds. After driving a good distance off the main road, he parked between a mass of tall pine trees and bushes near a small pond. I took my time getting out of his jeep and followed him through the bushes to the clearing near the bank of the little pond. After reaching the clearing, surrounded my tall pine trees and all kinds of bushes, a deep sadness came over me and disappointment ripped through me as I dropped down to my knees, covering my face with both hands and started to cry. And as I cried in silence and dried my tears with the hem of my skirt, I glanced at Casey standing against a tall tree with his hands on his head. I could see pain and deep sorrow in his red eyes. He threw his head back and took a deep breath before kicking the bushes all around.

"No! No! This can't be happening," he shouted, dropping to the ground, covering his face with both hands.

I slowly made my way up from my knees and stepped over to his side and dropped down to my knees in front of him. He kept his face covered so I couldn't see his tears as he took his shirttail and wiped his face before looking at me.

He looked at me, shaking his head as I patted his shoulder. "I can't believe you are trying to comfort me after the hell I just put you through? Why are you giving me the time of day? I drug you out here knowing you didn't want to come." He paused in my eyes. "And that's not even the worse part. The worse part was when I acted a even bigger fool and tried to make you kiss me." He looked up at the sky, grabbed his face, shaking his head. "God, I'm nuts!"

Touching his shoulder gently, I said. "Don't be so hard on yourself."

"Don't be so hard on myself?" he asked and paused in my eyes as a tear rolled down his face. "Paulene, how can you say that? Especially when I dread to think what may have happened if that phone hadn't rung? What if I had actually succeeded in making you kiss me? It would have meant I forced you, and that would have been wrong. Real wrong, you know?" He grabbed his head. "I was totally, all the way out of line. And I want you to know that I know that drinking is no excuse. Friends don't treat friends the way I just treated you. Friends don't even treat enemies the way I just treated you. How can you even look at me after what I have just put you through?" he asked humbly. "Grandma Fanny, Duane and Katie is going to hate me for this." He paused and looked at me with the eyes of a ten-year-old. "You know they are going to hate me, don't you?"

At a loss for words, I stared at him for a long time. So mad at him I wanted to spit in his face. But it was clear he was hurting and needed professional help.

"Look, Casey. We have our bad days. And today was your worse," I explained in a caring way. "It's what you do about it from here on out that counts."

"You don't have to tell me, I know I need to see a doctor," he uttered sadly.

Since his answer was what I wanted to hear, I didn't say anything. I didn't want to make him feel worse. We just sat there on our knees, looking at each other.

He reached out and touched my cheek. "Paulene, what's wrong with me? How could I have treated you like that? I'm so sorry. I never meant to hurt you." He touched my face, but quickly pulled his hand back. "I lost my head. I'm so in love with you. I know these feelings are over the edge. It's not right," he said, quickly standing to his feet, dusting the dirt and grass from his business slacks. "I'm going to pull myself together here and drive you back home." He looked down at the ground. "I hope and pray to God that there is some way I can make up for the way I just treated you."

Standing to my feet, I shook my head. "We'll just look at this as a bad dream sort of. Like a nightmare, okay? I won't mention this incident to anyone."

He stared at me with surprise eyes. "You won't? Not even Grandma Fanny?"

"Especially not Grandma Fanny. Look, Casey. I know what you did today wasn't really you." I have known you long enough to know that what happened here today was a freak thing. You're having a bad time. You have problems. Your head isn't on straight. That's life. You don't kick a dog when he's down. I'll live. I'll get over this. I just want you to seek some help for yourself," I said as he was looking at me nodding.

"I don't know why you came by the house and did those things, you did, Casey." I grabbed my face and paused for a second. "Dragging me out here in these woods. But listen, I forgive you. I know you won't do it again."

He gripped my shoulders and frowned with a sad pitiful look in his eyes. "How can you say you know I won't do it again?" He paused in my eyes. "You know more than I know. If I flipped out today and did something so darn stupid like this. Who can say it won't happen again?"

"I can say it." I touched his arm. "I don't think you'll hurt me or anyone else like this again, Casey. I can see the deep pain and sorrow in your eyes."

"You are amazing how you can see that, because Paulene I am sorry."

After we had buckled up in his jeep, he dropped his head on the steering wheel and cried silent, dry tears. I touched his arm.

"Casey what's really behind the way you acted today? I get this feeling that something else is really troubling you." I paused. "I wish you would share it with me."

He didn't look my way as he lifted his head and stared out of the windshield.

"Other than the facts that I'm crazy in love with you?"

I smiled. "Yeah, other than that."

He turned his head to face me. "I'm afraid Paulene," he said with a distant look.

I braced myself, almost afraid to ask. "What are you afraid of?"

"Life hassles. For years I have heard rumors and hurtful gossip that my father's father cracked up, so I guess this cracking shit runs in the family. It missed Katie and Duane and knocked on my door." After a bit of silence he continued. "I'm afraid the rumors about my old man years ago may have been true."

My nerves tightened at his confession. "The rumors that he was over the edge and purposely drove into that light pole killing himself and your mother?" I asked.

"Yeah, those rumors. They have haunted me all my adult life."

"You need to just let those thoughts go, Casey. You can't worry about what may or may not have been in your father's head at that time."

When I said that, he looked at me with boiling eyes and yelled in my face.

"Wrong answer! You won't see home now! The only home you're going to see is mine." He threw me a sharp look and gripped the steering wheel—stepping on the gas more. From the disturbed and confused look on his face, I knew I shouldn't say anything else that might be upsetting until we had reached his place.

Once we reached his big red brick home with black shutters, he pulled in front of his garage, killed the engine and hopped out quickly. He didn't look my way or invite me out of his vehicle, but I got out of the jeep and followed him across the yard toward his house. When we reached the front door, I grabbed my face with both hands, when I noticed a sign on his door that read, "Welcome Paulene." I just stood there for a moment before I slowly stepped through his front door. And when I entered his living room, it was even a greater shock to find his entire living room was wallpapered with my name! Seeing the extent of his crazy love—gone mad, a deep fear ripped through me and I covered my face and started crying hysterically.

"Please take me back home! I don't want you, Casey! I don't love you!

"Rant and rave all you want, Paulene. I'm never giving you up! I have waited too long for you," he said, and then stepped over to the fireplace and placed two logs on the low flame.

I glanced at the front door and it was cracked, but if I made a run for it, he would just catch me. All I could hope for was the clue I had left behind on the living room floor. I had managed to write a quick note, letting my parents know that he had taken me against my will to his new home on Church Road and Vine. But with such a wind day, the piece of paper could have gotten blown under a piece of furniture without them being the wiser. All I could do was hope as I stood there in the middle of the room shaking from nerves more than from the cold house.

He stepped away from the fireplace, slipped out of his coat and dropped it to the floor.

"It will be warm in here soon," he said, lowering the blinds in the living room.

"Casey," I yelled. "Are you out of your mind. How long do you think it will be before Aunt Haddie and Dad have the authorities after you? This is wrong! Why have you decided to just throw your life away like this? Why do you want to hurt your family like this? Have you lost your mind?"

"Listen, Paulene," he said, as he walked near me with a straight face and a calm voice, reaching out to stroke my hair. "I'm not out of my mind or anything. I'm just crazy in love with you. Don't you see that?"

"But, Casey, this is illegal! This is called kidnapping. You are going straight to jail for holding me here." I shook my head, realizing there was no getting through to him.

"Paulene," he said in a calm odd way, staring at the fire. "We grew up together. We were best friends. You loved me once when I didn't know how to love. Now I'm loving you, and you don't know how to love me back," he mumbled in a sad voice, and then he looked at me and grinned in a daze type of way.

From the look in his eyes, he needed more professional help than I had originally thought. He had slipped off his rocker for sure. I wanted to reach out and slap him across the face, but something wouldn't let me. I kept thinking if I did, I would be in worse trouble than I already was. Since I was trapped at his mercy. He had put away his knife and now had a big gun sticking in his pocket.

He looked at me and started stroking my hair some more. "Paulene, I want it to be like it was between us before I left town," he said in a whisper, grabbed me up in his arms. "You use to care about me then. Things were perfect," he whispered sadly in my ear. "I remember how good and soft you felt in my arms back then."

"Casey, wake up. Where are you getting these things you are saying? Things were never perfect between us," my voice trembled, desperate to get through to him. "I was never in love with you. You were just my friend. We didn't date or go together." I stressed. "We just hung out together! There's a difference you know?"

"You were nice to me, Paulene." His eyes widened. "You know you were, right?"

"Yeah, Casey. I was nice to you. You were my friend." I paused in his craze, red eyes and shook my head. "This is what I get for trying to be a good friend?"

Suddenly his eyes turned stone cold and he pulled out his gun and swung it around in the air for a few seconds, then put it back in his pocket.

"Paulene, you are trying to confuse me. But I know we were more than just friends." He kicked the coffee table over and looked back at me. "If we were just friends, what about that time you let me kissed you in Grandma Fanny's basement. And what about that time you let me kiss you in the school cafeteria? Those are not things that just friends do! You hear me bitch?" He shouted angrily.

I looked at him and shook my head. He had totally flipped and I was afraid to talk to him anymore. He screamed, "Answer me, now!" Then he pulled out his gun and shot through one of his living room windows.

My heart skipped a beat. "Please put the gun away! Please, Casey, put it away."

He placed the gun on the fireplace mantel, but kept his eyes on me. "Now answer me. "Why did you let me kiss and touch you if we were just friends?"

"Casey. Don't you remember? We were just nine years old. We were just kids. I didn't know what I was doing no more than you knew what you were doing. That doesn't count for anything, okay!" I grabbed my face and started to cry uncontrollably.

I didn't hear Aunt Haddie and Dad come in. I looked around and they were just there suddenly, and along with them were three policemen. The cops handcuffed Casey as he struggled to break free, but they over powered him and lowered him to the floor.

Chapter Nine

Shortly after allowing myself to relive the painful nightmare about Casey Huntley, I really wasn't in a cheerful mood for socializing, but then I wasn't in a jolly mood before that flash back. But, yet, I forced myself to join in the laughter, though I had hardly heard a word. We were all still gathered around Katie's dining room table eating finger foods and drinking champagne. On her counter top in her kitchen, she had a whole array of different finger foods to fit anyone's appetite. And they had all pretty much helped themselves to plenty. I was saving my appetite for the lemon birthday cake.

Ben was sitting there looking handsome as ever, but he had hardly given me a second glance. My evening was turning out thumbs down. I was remembering that Katie had advised me to come ten or fifteen minutes later than everyone else so I could make an entrance. She felt showing off my clingy chocolate dress and chocolate high heels would get Ben's attention.

"Let him see you in that dress with that figure to die for. He'll take notice. He'll eat his heart out. If that dress doesn't get his attention, nothing will."

"Well, maybe nothing was going to get his attention," I thought to myself. And whether he was eating his heart out or not, I had no idea. When Katie made the introductions he was in a conversation with Duane. He merely glanced at me and smiled.

"So, we meet again." Then he looked toward Katie and nodded.

"Paulene and I have met." Then he turned back to face Duane and they continued to conversant. If I had any hope that he found me attractive—his lack of attention and even less interest proved against that.

Now, sitting next to him, thinking how he looked drop-dead gorgeous in his charcoal blazer, black shirt and black slacks. I was uncomfortably aware of the huge chemistry effect he had on me, not only in my stomach but also all over my body. I wanted him to think of me as exciting and wonderful company to be around. But on the few occasions that he said something to me, I sat there with a fixed smile on my face, fumbling with my fingers over the table, with nothing much to say. He probably thought of me as a boring conversationalist. With anybody else, I had plenty to say, but when I was around him I couldn't seem to remember my own name or think of one sophisticated thing to say.

When the delicious looking yellow and white cake was finally brought in, Duane blew out the candles and Katie took up her glass of champagne in a toast. "To Duane, my wonderful brother who wears twenty-seven better than anyone I know."

We all raised our glasses and joined in the toast.

Then came the final disaster of the evening for me. As I was sitting there holding my saucer in my hand, enjoying a slice of Duane's birthday cake with extra whip cream on top, my saucer became detached from my hand and landed in the middle of Ben's lap. Jolted by the sudden dump in his lap, he stood up immediately and started raking the cake off of his suit with his hands. Bad choice. Then he grabbed a napkin and that didn't help much.

"My goodness, Ben, I can't believe I spilled my food on you." I grabbed my mouth with both hands and shook my head.

"No worries. The food just tops off the drink from before." He laughed. "What's a little drink with food?" He joked to make light of it.

"Thanks for being so kind."

"Accident's will happen."

"Yes, I know. But this is my second time dumping stuff on your clothes."

"It's really okay. This will wash right out."

"Ben, what can I say? This is so embarrassing. I'm so clumsy. Maybe you should walk the other way when you see me coming," I said jokingly to take some of the weigh of embarrassment off my heart.

"I wouldn't go that far." He grinned.

"I'm pleased to see you are smiling about the incident, because I really am very sorry about messing up your outfit," I said, wanting the floor to swallow me up from embarrassment. I continued to hold my mouth with both hands, shaking my head. Was this the end of what could be a beautiful relationship with Ben Drake before it even began?

"Lighten up, Paulene. It's okay," he said with a smile on his face. "But the look in his eyes said otherwise. He probably wanted to get as far away from me as possible.

His nice pants were smeared with yellow and white frosting. When he stepped across Katie's dinning room into the living room where she was standing near the stereo talking with Duane, he lowered his six-foot frame to kiss her on the left cheek. He glanced around in my direction where I stood near the dinning room doorway, but glanced right back at them and shook Duane's hand. I heard him say in a low voice,

"As usually you know how to throw a great party. Everything was great, but people are still coming in and I don't think I need to be in the spotlight right now. I'm going to take off."

She glanced down at the big spoil spot on his slacks and nodded.

"I understand. But thanks for coming." She showed him to the door.

"Drive careful," Katie said, and then closed the door and headed straight across the room where I stood. We took a seat at the dinning room table and I was lost for words—sitting there shaking my head, staring into space.

"What happened to his pants?"

"I happened with my clumsy fingers. I dropped a piece of cake in his lap."

She waved her hand. "So what? That's not why he left I'm sure."

"I don't think he left because of that," I mumbled.

"Of course, he didn't. He stayed his usually half an hour."

"But he probably would have stayed longer if I hadn't messed up his clothes."

"Paulene, forget it. A little cake on his clothes is not going to kill him."

"Forget it? Katie, come on. It's not going to kill him. But I feel just awful about it."

"I'm sure you do, Paulene. And I don't mean to sound insensitive but I'm sure he's not going to lose any sleep over you dropping a piece of cake in his lap."

He did smile and make a joke about it. But I'm still beside myself over it."

"Why are you beside yourself? I'm sure he doesn't plan to rip up your number over a little frosting and whip cream." She patted my shoulder. "Cheer up and have something to drink. It's still early and people are still coming in."

"Tear up what number? He didn't ask for my number. He didn't have time to ask me anything because the moment we were left at the table together I screwed that up real quick when I couldn't do without cutting myself a piece of cake. Which I didn't get a chance to eat anyway, since it landed on his clothes and your dinning room floor," I said disappointedly.

"I'm sorry, Paulene. I know you had high hopes about this evening. For your sake, I wish things had turned out the way you wished." She paused. "But tomorrow is another day." She patted my shoulder. "So how about another piece of cake and something to drink?"

"Thanks, Katie. But I think I'll take off."

"Okay, but take a piece of the cake with you."

"Okay, I think I will take a piece home."

I said goodnight to Katie and took a taxi to my hotel. So much for Katie's best laid plans to pave away for Ben and I to somehow make a real connection with each other. And it wasn't until five in the morning, as I lay in the dark staring up at the ceiling, that I finally gave in to the flooding ocean of tears that started pouring from my eyes, telling myself, over and over, that I had lost him. It was the most crushing, hopeless feeling deep down in my soul that I had ever experienced.

Chapter Ten

The following day, around one-thirty in the afternoon, the phone rang. I was lying back on the sofa, still dressed in my nightgown with a blanket thrown over me. I felt drained with no energy or determination to look forward to the day ahead. Even the effort to get in the shower or make myself a meal did not excite me. I was too disappointed and downhearted.

With a trembling hand, I picked up the phone knowing it was probably Katie.

"Hello," I said in a low, sad voice.

"Hello, Paulene, what are you doing?" She laughed. "That's a silly question to ask you, wouldn't you think? Because I can bet you're moping around with Ben Drake on your mind."

After a long silence, I replied. "Katie, I'm not doing anything. I'm just sitting here on the sofa in front of the TV."

"So you're watching TV?" she asked.

"No, not really," I mumbled. "I'm just sort of sitting here with it on."

"Listen, Paulene," she said in a sincere, concerned voice. "If you are just lying around in your room doing nothing, let's do dinner later? No, better yet. I'll treat you to a nice dinner. What do you say?"

"Katie, I'm really not hungry, but thanks all the same."

"Listen, Paulene. I know what you are over there doing. I can tell from the sound of your voice. You are lying around feeling down over that man." After a long pause, she continued. "I know I'm right. You better shape up and get your butt up and about."

"Thanks for being such a good friend, Katie, but I honestly don't think I'm up to going out to eat or anything else for that matter."

"I guess you feel pretty down in the dumps to turn down a free meal?" She laughed. "Just kidding. But that's too darn bad. You need to knock Ben out of your head. If he can't give you the time of day, I say forget the jerk. But I know telling you that is like talking to the wind." She paused and there was a rather long silence before she spoke. "Okay, Paulene, here's the deal. I have a few things I need to take care of and after that, I'll pick up a dinner for you and bring it to your hotel room around five."

My heart was too sad with an emptiness that only Ben Drake could fill. I didn't want to see her or anyone else. I just wanted to see the one person who didn't want to see me. And since I couldn't see him, I just wanted to be left alone in my blue mood.

"Katie, please don't bring me any thing over here."

"You got to eat something."

"I'll call for room service for a sandwich or something later. I just don't feel up for any company. I messed things up for good with Ben last night and I just need to mope by myself," I said sadly.

"Well, if that's what you want," she said in a snappy like manner.

"Katie, please don't think I'm being ungrateful but I just want to be alone to sort things out. I hope you understand."

"I can't say that I do. Because I don't get what you plan to sort out?" she paused. "You are assuming all these things."

"I'm not assuming I spilled my plate in Ben's lap."

"Get over it already. Who cares?"

"Katie, you don't understand how I feel."

"I think you are borrowing headaches and assuming things."

"If that's so! What am I assuming?"

"For one, you are assuming about Ben."

"Assuming what, Katie?"

"You are assuming that he's going to hold that little incident against you."

"Katie, it's not really the incident that has me in knots. It's really not about that. Not really deep down. Because whether he holds it against me or not, I just don't like the picture I have painted for myself with the man. That's it in a nutshell."

"No arguments from me there. I get it."

"You do understand, don't you?"

After a slight silence, she said. "Of course I understand. Say no more. Ben Drake specializes in breaking hearts. What absolute filthy animals they are!"

"Who?" I asked.

"Paulene, wake up. I'm talking about those two-legged animals that will rip your heart out and hand it back to you in the blink of an eye." She shouted through the receiver. "Men, of course." She paused. "Who in the hell else? They are no better than dogs. They'll do their thing with whatever and whoever wears a skirt. Then look you straight in the face and lie through their teeth!" She roared.

It made my stomach turn to hear her speak so negative about all men. Shaun Parker had worked one good number on her. "Katie, you can't just throw all men in the same category. Men are individuals just like the rest of us. My goodness you need to lighten up. And why are you jumping down Ben's throat, putting him down? I'm the one who keep pushing him away and sending him to the dry-cleaners with my clumsy fingers."

"Okay, Paulene, whatever you say. I still think you should let me drop you off a plate, but since you have asked me not to, I guess I'll just see you tomorrow."

"Thank you, Katie. I'm sorry if I put a damper on your party for Duane. Next time I see Duane, I'll give him my apologies."

"Come off it, Paulene. You didn't spoil the evening. And don't bother thinking you owe Duane any apologies. He had the time of his life. Dropping that piece of cake in Ben's lap didn't spoil his or my evening anymore than if you had dropped your napkin on the floor. Get the point. It was your Prince Charming—walking out of the party with his nose bend out of place over a few crumbs on his clothes. That's what spoiled your evening," she said.

"I really can't blame him. Not really. I mean, after all, it was the second time that I accidentally messed up his clothes."

"So what? A little spilled cake is nothing to get all bent out of shape over." She paused. "I tell you, Paulene, Ben Drake is just stuck on himself if you ask me. He could have easily dusted those few crumbs off of him and spent the evening with you. He would have to be blind not to have noticed how you kept looking at him with inviting eyes." She paused. "Anyway. Now get something to eat."

"I will, and Katie, thanks for everything. "

Chapter Eleven

Right at the stroke of midnight, when I finally collapsed in my bed, the warmth of Ben's incredible presence was still lingering within me. I wrapped my arms around myself savoring in my daydreams of being wrapped in his arms. I had never felt so wonderful and miserable and so hopeless and so alone. I rolled over on my side when I heard the faint sound of a kitten outside my hotel room window. I threw the sheet off of me, got out of bed and went over to the window to see could I spot some stray animal from eight floors up.

When I first pulled the long floral draperies apart, I only noticed the moon shinning bright, casting shadows across the tall buildings, then as I glanced down to my left, I spotted a small white kitten running across the street to the safety of some bushes. A smile overtook my sad face and soothed me as I watched the furry little animal peek his head through the bushes. I loved cats, but never was allowed to own one since Aunt Haddie couldn't stand to be around them. They made her sneeze and her eyes watery.

Standing there in somewhat of a daze looking at the little kitten and thinking of Ben, another smile curved my face as some short, thin lady who appeared to be a grandmother type reached into the bushes and gathered up the little kitten. She kissed the cat's face, rubbing its head and said in a clear voice that I could vaguely hear from where I was standing.

"Cookie, you got to stop sneaking out like this every time I open the door. You know they don't allow cats in this building. You are going to get us both in trouble if you don't stay put."

My smile widened, pleased to see that the kitten had been rescued by her owner and wouldn't be roaming the busy streets of downtown Chicago.

After the old lady and the kitten disappeared into the lobby of a tall building, I stretched my arms and yawned, but my eyes were still wide awake. What could I do? I needed some sleep to be able to free my mind of all the heavy thoughts I had centered on Ben. I stepped over to my small hotel fridge and pulled out a pint carton of milk, poured myself a small glass and heated it in the microwave. After drinking the milk, I hopped back in bed and lay on top of the covers with my head supported by two pillows, staring up at the ceiling.

Twenty minutes later, and I was still wide-awake. Ben was heavy on my mind. I couldn't shake the thought of him, and I was pleased that I couldn't shake thinking of him, and I was also pleased that I couldn't shake the beautiful feelings that thoughts of him left lingering in me.

Around one in the morning, my eyes were becoming heavy as I lay there on the two pillows, now under the covers. I could vaguely hear the sounds outside my window of a busy Chicago street.

My hotel room was dark and quiet and the only light that was still noticeable was the soft moonlight pouring through the window; and the only indoor sound I could hear was the clock on my bedside table.

It was a rather peaceful night, unlike many of the noisier nights when I had laid awake because of the sound of one fire engine after the next, one ambulance after the next, and the loud sound of squad cars sirens. Yet, there was nothing peaceful about the way I felt. By now I was drifting off to sleep with dry tears down the side of my face. I was feeling more and more relaxed from the warm glass of chocolate milk I had drunk earlier. I felt exhausted with desire for this handsome stranger from just the sensuous thoughts of him. As my eyes were becoming heavier and heavier, I was hopeful that Ben and I would meet again and one day be together. And just as I closed my eyes, I felt a smooth, cool hand cover my mouth.

My eyes lit up when I looked up and there he stood with his radiant eyes looking down at me. "It's me, Paulene," he said just above a whisper.

"Ben, I'm so glad you're here?" I smiled.

He dropped down to his knees beside my bed, looking directly in my smiling eyes. He pressed his lips against mine, and with the gentlest touch, gripped my face with both hands, giving me a breathtaking passion-filled kiss. He gently gripped a handful of my hair, propped my head back and smothered my neck with kisses, one after another.

"Paulene Dawson, I can't get you out of my head. How did this happen?" He lifted my hand and kissed the top of my palm. "Being with you is like reaching for the stars and touching them." He leaned in and kissed me again.

Within seconds of surrendering to his kiss, he pulled away and stood to his feet, standing over my bed looking down at me with the most wonderful look of desire in his eyes. And without saying a word, he slowly took a seat back on the edge of the bed next to me. He placed his lips against my neck and ran both hands through my hair, kissing me with great ease, barely touching my throat with tender kisses, as if I was a fragile flower that could easy bruise. And with each gentle kiss and every breath I took, my love grew for him more and more.

Sitting there wonderfully excited with tears slowly dripping from my eyes, he trailed tender kisses upward toward my face, and with the blink of an eye his mouth covered mine urgently with a gentle kiss. I was confused out of my mind in the sweetest way. He stood to his feet again and still hadn't said one word, as he looked down at me with desire in his sparkling eyes that lit up the room. He removed his jacket, his shirt, his slacks, and then pulled the covers back and got in bed next to me. He pulled me in his arms and we kissed passionately. Being in his arms felt like I was floating on a cloud high above a field of wild flowers on a warm summer day.

He sat up quickly, pulling me up in his crushing, gentle arms. Then just as quickly as he had pulled me up in his arms, he held my shoulders and placed me back on the pillow, bringing his mouth hungrily down on mine, covering my lips with a urgent grip as he kissed me deeper and deeper.

As his firm, smooth lips pulled away from mine, he smiled with desire ablaze in his eyes. "Paulene, you have been on my mind since you stepped out of that taxi tonight. You don't know how it drives me crazy to hold you like this. I want to hold you like this forever," he whispered breathless against my throat as he held me next to him.

Then moments later, with the sweetest contentment of being together, we lay in each other's arms. But as peace filled the room, I was wondering how was it possible that he was in my hotel room and in my bed. And as that thought dawned on me, immediately I told myself I was having another beautiful dream. It was similar to the one before, almost a repeat. He was wearing the same clothes as he wore in the first dream, the night of the party. And even realizing I was dreaming, I willed myself to continue the dream, hoping not to awake myself.

Ben raised himself on one elbow and smiled at me and whispered in my ear.

"Haven't you figured out how crazy I am about you, Miss Paulene Dawson?"

"No, I haven't figured it out, Ben. How can it be true? You don't even really talk to me. And you have never asked me out," I uttered tearfully happy.

"Paulene, I would like to ask you a question."

"Sure, Ben. What would you like to ask me?"

"I was wondering would you like to go out with me some time?" He whispered, his breath warm against my neck as he placed his lips next to my throat.

Just as I caught my breath to reply, I was interrupted by the sound of a squad car siren going off near my window. I jerked and my eyes blinked opened, staring up at my lonely dark ceiling. Once again, it had all been another beautiful dream. I rolled over on my side and smiled as I fell back to sleep.

Chapter Twelve

A couple days later, I awakened to a quiet peaceful morning with the sun beaming through my window. I could see through the small crack in my curtains that it was a clear day with a slight breeze moving through the trees. I rubbed the sleep out of my eyes and threw the covers off of me. I glanced at the clock on the wall above my small sofa, and it was barely ten am. I had overslept, tossing and turning most of the night with thoughts of Ben Drake. I was too sleepily and lovesick to go to work so I called in sick, complaining of stomach pains. It wasn't that far from the truth, since I really was having stomach pains. But they were the kind of pains that no medicine could help.

All day that Monday, I stayed at home and moped inside of my hotel room, not even answering the phone. And although I knew it was probably Katie trying to get in touch with me, I allowed each call to be picked up by my answering machine. I just didn't have the mind or the get-up to talk to her or anyone. I wanted to drown out my sorrows alone. What good was all the so-called glamour of wearing the right makeup, the right clothes and keeping my figure in perfect shape if I was so inept that I had driven Ben Drake the one and only man I had ever wanted away before I had even had a chance to get to know him? I felt out of my league in the big city and couldn't seem to get a grip. I was just another farm girl that should have stayed put in Alabama. The loneliness and depression I had felt when I first came to Chicago pounded down on my shoulders with even greater force now, and by that evening I laid in my bed staring up at the ceiling more convinced that my move to Chicago was a huge mistake. There were no more romantic fantasies and living *ever after daydreams* about Ben Drake. I was left with the reality of a sad fact that was pretty clear. As much as I wanted to be with him, we had no future together. I kept repeating that thought to myself. But by 6:30 that evening when someone knocked on my door, I quickly hopped out of bed wearing only my nightgown and rushed to answer it. The first person that came to mind as I headed toward the door was Ben Drake. Standing there yawning and rubbing my eyes, I knew it couldn't be Ben. He came to me only in my dreams, and since I wasn't dreaming, it most likely wasn't he. I peeped through the peephole. It was Katie, and she entered my room with sad eyes and a frown on her face.

While Katie stood facing me shaking her head, I took a seat on the un-made bed and covered my face with both hands.

"Paulene Dawson, I can't believe you. You look just fine to me. I was concerned about you," She propped her hands on her hips and shook her head. "You are no more sick than a cat on the moon."

Shaking my head in my hands. "Who said I was sick?"

"You did when you called in this morning complaining about your stomach." She paused. "Before I jump the gun, thinking what I'm thinking." She paused. "Were you sick this morning, but feeling better now?"

I glanced up at her and covered my face without answering.

"Well, I'm waiting."

"Waiting for what?"

"You heard me. I asked were you really sick this morning?" Or is this what I think it is?" She glanced about the room, noticing that I hadn't cleaned up the place. And it was unlike me to not have my room tidy at all times.

"I was sick and I'm still sick."

"You don't really look sick. What's the matter?"

"I'll tell you what's the matter! I'm sick of this place, that's for sure." I snapped.

"Are you referring to your room here at the hotel?"

I held up both arms. "This room! This town! I'm sick of it all! Just plain sick!"

"Yeah, you got that right. You are sick!"

"And what is that supposed to mean?"

"I'm just agreeing with you. You said you're sick."

"I know I said it. But it sounds as if you don't believe it."

"I believe it."

"So, you do believe I'm sick?"

"Yes, I believe it. But I just happen to think you're sick up here." She tapped her head."

"Thanks a lot for calling me loony."

"I didn't call you loony. I just think you're sick-in-the-head."

"Katie, please. What's the difference between loony and sick-in-the-head? It's all the same." I rolled my eyes at her.

"Well, what else do you call it? Here you are a grown woman lying in bed in the middle of the day." She shook her head. "Sitting around moping over some skirt-chaser who doesn't even know you are available for him to use!" She paused for a moment. "But I'm sure he'll know soon, if it's left up to you." She raised both arms. "I rest my case."

Still seated on the bed, I pointed toward the door. "Katie, just go! I can't deal with your preaching and yelling. How many times do I have to remind you that you are not my mother?"

"I know I'm not your mother."

"Well, stop treating me like your child."

"Maybe I will if you start acting like an adult and show more responsibility for yourself."

"I'll come in tomorrow and work overtime if you want me to, okay?"

"Paulene, this is not about that darn job. It's about you needing to pull yourself together." She looked toward the carpet at my clothes lying about on the rug. "Just look at this place. "You are a neat freak, so to have this room this messy can only mean you are moping around feeling sorry for yourself." She insisted. "And let me guess why?" She looked toward the ceiling and patted her right foot. "Could it have anything to do with the name: Ben Drake?" She said sarcastically.

"Oh, give it a rest, Katie."

"You're the one carrying on like your world has ended, and I should give it a rest?"

"Yes, you should. I'm okay. Don't make something out of nothing. I missed one day at work and I didn't clean my room. You act like the world is coming to an end because of that. What's the big deal, Katie?" I got off of the bed and stepped over to my small refrigerator and pulled out two bottles of spring water. I extended one to her and she shook her head.

"If you're okay, why are you still dressed in your nightwear and why didn't you show up at work or answer the phone when I called?" she asked sharply.

"Because I wanted to be left alone. Is that okay with you?"

"It's your life! But if you ask me, it seems you're trying to shut out the world, thinking that is going to somehow ease your longing for a man who don't even know you're alive?"

"That's enough, Katie," I snapped.

"You can get huffy all you like." She leaned against my dresser with her arms folded. "But you know I'm telling the plain facts. It's just the plain truth when I say you're trying to shut out people—thinking that's going to ease your longing!"

"No, I'm not shutting out anybody," I sipped my water and took a seat on the bed.

"No, did you say? Well, if you're not trying to hide inside of your hotel room and mope alone, just answer me one question. Why didn't you come to work this morning?" she asked in the same manner as Aunt Haddie.

"Because I didn't want to come to work," I snapped. "Does that answer your question, mother?"

"Now you listen to me and listen carefully." She pointed her finger at me. "I'm not your mother, but I'm damn sure old enough to be." She propped her hands back on her hips. "If you think I'm preaching at you, then I'm sorry. You are a grown woman and you can do whatever you please, but I'm just concerned about you. You are a beautiful and kind young woman. And Ben Drake is not worth driving yourself sick over. Neither is any other man, for that matter," she shouted and showed herself out.

Now that Katie had left, I could admit to myself that she was right. I was acting like a childish fool. But it also happened to be the first time I'd fallen in love. The rejection and humiliation was almost more than I could handle.

Chapter Thirteen

That next morning came just like any other morning. But a few hours of sleep did less than nothing to rid my longing for Mr. Drake. Yet, while getting dressed for work, I told myself that this would be the day that I would erase Ben Drake from my mind. But no luck of that! It was as if my heart had carved a permanent place inside of me for him to live. All day long at work he was in my thoughts. The radiant images of his face along with the overpowering feelings aroused by his presence were growing stronger rather than weaker.

When Katie saw me around ten o'clock that morning sitting alone at a table in the break room she tapped me on the shoulder but walked right past me as she was engaged in conversation with another worker. A short while later as I continued my break, sipping on a cup of coffee, she stepped back into the break room and over to my table. She was now alone. And from the look on my face she knew at a glance that I was still depressed. She stood there and smiled, but just as she opened her mouth to say something, I spoke first.

"Katie, I would like to ask a favor from you," I mumbled, looking down in my coffee cup, holding it with both hands.

"Sure, anything." She grabbed a chair and took a seat at the table with me.

Finally, the need to have some kind of contact with Ben Drake, just anything at all was so intense that I pushed my pride aside, looked up at Katie with sad eyes.

"Could you please give me Ben's number?" I looked her straight in the eyes.

She hesitated just looking at me for a second with a hint of irritation in her eyes. Obvious the irritation stemmed from me asking for his number and putting her in a position that she didn't want to be in. She thought he was no good for me, so she surely didn't want me to have his number. But after a moment of hesitation, she nodded and forced a smile.

"Sure. Why not?" She pulled a pen and a piece of paper from her purse and jotted his number down. "Here you are." She handed it to me.

"Thanks." I took the piece of paper and kept sipping my coffee.

"But Paulene, do you think?"

I held up one hand to cut her off. "I know I shouldn't call him, right? Is that what you were going to say?" I waved a hand. "Don't worry. I had the nerve to ask you for his number, but I don't have the nerve to dial it," I uttered sadly.

"Look, never mind what I was going to say," she said in a cherry voice, no doubt trying to cheer me up. "Do you know what I feel like doing, Miss Dawson?"

I shook my head at the least bit interest in holding a conversation at the moment.

"I feel like doing lunch at the Signature Room in the Hancock building. What do you say? My stomach is telling me to do just that."

"I'm sorry, Katie, but I don't feel hungry."

"I didn't mean now. I said lunch. I've got a meeting to attend with the owners in about fifteen minutes. I'll meet you there at twelve-thirty. Is that okay?" She glanced at her Movado watch and before I could object, Katie was gone. And the next time I saw her, I was sitting across from her at a small round table at the Signature Room. She wasn't saying much just kind of looking at me off and on, sipping her diet coke and nibbling off her turkey sandwich. I was being quiet, so she wasn't talking because she wanted me to take the floor and tell her what was the matter.

"Okay, Paulene, I promise, I'll try not to preach." She placed her white linen napkin in her lap. "But let's have it. I mean let's talk. What was yesterday all about? You lounging around in your night gown all day, not answering your phone, not cleaning up your room and not coming in to work?" she asked, humbly. "In your case it wasn't a Monday morning hangover! So what gives?" She said jokingly, trying to add some humor.

Looking down at my food, poking in my lime jello I couldn't bring myself to take one bite of my grilled cheese. When I finally looked up my eyes were heavy with tears. "I don't know what's wrong with me, Katie. I have done some really wacky stuff."

She waved her hand. "Haven't we all? Don't lose any sleep over it."

"I want you to know. You were right yesterday. You were right about everything. It's all about Ben Drake: me not showing up at work and not cleaning my room."

She nodded. "I figured that much."

"You figured right. I was so whacked out with thoughts of the man until I didn't have the mind to change out of my night clothes."

"Okay, but it's time to let all that stuff go and cheer up now."

"I know, Katie. But those are the kinds of things I never thought I would do."

"Paulene, life happens."

"But listen, Katie. I have been having these dreams about him and these fantasies in my head that the two of us are going to be together. That's really far-out crazy thinking, wouldn't you say? When the guy hasn't even asked me out."

Katie nodded. "So you call that crazy stuff?" She looked at me with distant eyes as if she was thinking of some other place and some other time. "Paulene, you haven't begun to know what crazy stuff is." She took a bite of her sandwich. "I wrote the book on doing crazy stuff for love."

Taking a sip of diet coke, I shook my head. "I've never done such things or acted this way in my life, never. Aunt Haddie would faint if she knew I was longing for some guy who hadn't given me the time of day. All my life I've been told by both my father and Aunt Haddie how levelheaded and mature I am. That's some laugh, wouldn't you say? I wasn't too level-headed to miss a day of work over a man."

Katie waved a hand and placed a slice of pickle from her sandwich in her mouth. She chewed the pickle, swallowed it and took a sip of diet coke.

"Paulene, get with the program." She shook her head. "Young lady, you got a lot of living to do if you think what you did was anywhere near crazy." She threw another pickle in her mouth, kept chewing and shaking her head.

"Katie, you got to admit that doing what I did was really kid stuff."

"So what if it was?" She grinned. "You don't think you're alone being silly, do you?" She placed another piece of sandwich in her mouth and took another sip of her diet coke. "Believe me when I tell you, there hasn't been a woman since the beginning of time who hasn't gone through all the crazy stuff and depression that's happening to you. Love can make basket cases out of the most leveled-headed among us all. Especially when it happens to be a one-way love affair and there's nothing you can do about it. This is still a man's world, Paulene. They still call the shots. They make the rules and only they can break the rules and still have their character intact at sunrise. If Ben Drake wanted you he wouldn't have to sit and wonder while he waited for you to dial his number. He would simply pick up his phone and dial yours. It isn't fair but those are still the rules of the game."

"So what do I do now?" I asked, finally taking a bite of my grilled cheese.

"I think you should go back to Alabama for a few days. Get away from this darn place and clear your head." She bites into a portion of her sandwich. "And don't worry about your job, it will be here when you get back. "

"I've thought about going home for awhile and I want to, but how will that help to get Ben out of my thoughts?"

"Well, let's just say, out of sight helps a little."

"It helps just a little?"

She nodded. "Yes. Just a little."

"So in other words, leaving town is not going to help that much?"

She shook her head. "Not really."

"No matter where I go, my thoughts of him will still be right with me?"

"That's about the size of it. There's no escaping love. Once you surrender your heart. You're all in."

"You sound like an expertise on the subject."

"Let's just say, I had a front row seat in that department."

I nodded. "I believe you."

After a long pause, she said. "I don't know what to tell you, Paulene. But I just think it's a good idea for you to go home for a little while. Because if nothing else, it's comforting to be with those who really love you when you're feeling down. It puts you in touch with a good reality. Home is where the heart is, they say. It's that perfect place to be when you're feeling in the dumps like you are now. You know what I mean?"

Thinking about Aunt Haddie, Dad and Bud and how secure and loved they made me feel. I nodded. "You're right. I think I'll stop at a ticket agency after work and buy a ticket for home."

"When are you thinking of leaving?"

"Probably this weekend," I mumbled.

"Are you coming back, Paulene?"

"I'm not sure. Once I get back home I might just stay there," I mumbled sadly.

"Wow, really?" She looked surprised.

"Will that be a problem with the boutique?"

"Don't worry about that."

"Are you sure? I don't want to leave you shorthanded."

"I know. But when you get back home if you want to stay there, then that's fine too." She assured me. "Just take care of yourself, Paulene, and never let a man get you down. You hear me?" She touched my arm. "Because if they can get you down, they will. I mean they will put you all the way down to the ground if they can. Walk on you! Chew you up and spit you out, like you were yesterday's trash!" She spoke with determination in her voice as if she really needed me to hear what she was saying.

Chapter Fourteen

Thursday after work with a calm, still blue-sky overhead, I left the boutique with my mind completely made up. I headed straight to a ticket agent, stopping at the first agency I spotted on State Street a few blocks from where I worked. I purchased a one-way Amtrak train ticket. The train offered great relaxation and lots of sightseeing along the way. Plus the train ticket saved me a hundred dollars at just $120.00. Around trip train ticket would have cost me exactly what a one-way plane ticket would have cost. But I only needed a one-way ticket, because if I was going home, I wasn't coming back. My date of departure was just two days away: Saturday morning at 10:30 a.m. It would be hard but I would just have to try to put Ben Drake out of my head.

After I stepped through the revolving doors from the ticket agent, I held the ticket in my hand and brought it up to my lips to kiss. Somehow, that ticket gave me courage and a peace of mind. I had finally made peace deep inside of me about my fading desire for city life. That peace gave me instant courage to feel free and indifferent about all the things that had happened to me emotionally since Ben Drake came into my life. But when I stepped off the curb to flag a taxi to take me to my hotel room, I waved the taxi on. In that quick instant, I made up my mind right on the spot to walk over to Michigan Avenue. I was now determined to pay a visit to the tall sixty-story building where Katie had told me Ben Drake worked. Since I was leaving town anyway, I figured what did I have to lose if I showed up at his office and he politely gave me the brush off. I had added courage now, and even the possibility of being ignored or having a door shut in my face didn't shake me.

My fear of rejection didn't seem to matter at the moment. All that mattered was to take a stand and go to him and extend my apologies. Soon I had made it over to Michigan Avenue and stopped on the corner, looking up at the tall, gray office building across the street. Standing there staring at the building, suddenly my brave heart had turned to jelly. My nervousness told me to head home and not set foot inside of that building to possibly get my feelings crushed. But without realizing what I was doing, something like a magnet pulled me across the street and inside the tall skyscraper where he worked. As I entered the building and walked across the thick plush red carpet, a voice said. "May I help you Ma'am?"

That voice knocked me out of the daze I was in. I looked to my right and the voice was coming from an attractive Chinese-American woman at the reception desk. She was smiling and looked to be in her mid-thirties. I walked in her direction, feeling uncomfortable because I had no idea what I was doing. Then just as I was a few feet from the information counter, she asked.

"Do you need a guest pass?"

"No thanks." I shook my head and started to walk straight ahead, but then I paused and sort of stood there in the middle of the lobby trying to spot the elevators. And apparently she knew what I was looking for. I glanced over at her again and she smiled and pointed to the right. "The elevators and escalators are straight ahead in the direction you are going—middle-ways the lobby to your left."

"Thank you." I glanced over my shoulders and smiled at receptionist as I walked farther down the lobby spotting the elevators and escalators within a few minutes. And to my relief and drained emotions, I quickly took the nearest seat on a long black leather sofa that was situated in front of elevators and escalators. I sat there and held my face with both hands for a few minutes as I allowed myself to catch my breath and relax. After collecting my nerves, I looked up at the large black clock above the bank of elevators. I noticed that some people were starting to come down in groups on the escalators to the left of the elevators. A few minutes later, I glanced up at the big clock again and it was 4:15, and I hadn't spotted Ben. But I would continue to wait. I had gathered the nerves to show up, and now I would gather the nerves to stay put, until the sun fell from the sky if need be. No matter what, I would wait to see Ben Drake on this Thursday before I left Chicago for good.

Katie had said earlier that it was a man's prerogative to do the pursuing, that those were the rules of the game. Well, maybe so. And maybe I was being unladylike. And without a doubt, I realized I was risking a flat out rejection from him, taking a chance showing up where he worked unannounced. What if he stepped out of the elevator with another woman on his arm? What if he didn't have another woman on his arm but looked my way and kept walking? The slightest rejection from him would crush me. But so be it. I couldn't eat and I couldn't sleep and my life had been turned upside down just thinking of him. I could no longer remain in a rut of just hoping. I had to take some kind of action and find out one way or the other once and for all if we had any kind of a chance together before I took that train back to Alabama. I would just have to deal with the consequences of those actions.

Keeping my eyes on the elevator doors, I tried to think what I would say, and how I would say it. Also how I would explain being in the building where he worked? A few thoughts came to mind. "All the different shops I had passed in the lobby: The photo shop, the camera shop, the candy store, the bookstore. I was shopping in one of the stores or I had an appointment to get my picture taken in the photo shop." I frowned and shook my head. That didn't feel right. And after thinking about what I was going to say to him, I decided against making up something. I wasn't going to act like a silly teenager. I was going to act like the full-grown woman that I was. I was going to be totally on the level with him even if it meant letting him see how vulnerable I really was. What I felt for him was too special to contaminate with anything less than the truth.

Sitting there squeezing my purse against my chest and holding my right knee to keep it from shaking, I glanced at my watch and it was four-thirty. Crowded elevator after crowded elevator began to pour out professionally dressed men and women by the bundle. And the escalator to the left of the elevator started rolling down groups of tired-looking workers. They all stepped out of the elevator and off the escalators, rushing like there was no tomorrow. Katie had told me when I first came to the city that a majority of the downtown workers lived out in the suburbs. Most likely, they were rushing to catch their bus or train.

Ten minutes later and things had calmed down a bit. Supposedly, all the 4:30 workers had clocked out and left the building. It was now 4:40. Hopefully Ben would show soon. But ten minutes later at 4:50 I was beginning to think I had missed him in the crowd, when suddenly there he was, coming down the escalators to the left of the elevators that had started pouring out groups of rushing workers again. I got up from my seat feeling nervous as I braced myself against the sofa for a moment, then took in a deep breath and started walking toward him.

"Hi, Ben." I smiled as my legs felt like jelly.

He looked toward me as he stepped off the escalators. "Paulene?" He smiled, with surprise written all over his face. "It is you?" He grinned, holding a black leather briefcase to his side with a second much smaller black briefcase under his arm. "I could see you from the top of the escalators, I didn't think there could be two beautiful creatures like you in this city," he said, smiling in my eyes, looking handsome dressed in a heather gray diamond weave double-breast suit with a crisp white shirt, solid gray silk tie with a pair of leather pinched tassel loafer brown shoes.

Looking straight in his eyes. "Ben, I'm glad I caught you," I said nervously.

"Yeah, me to," he said still smiling as if I wasn't taking up his time.

Still looking straight in his eyes, noticing my left leg shaking. "I know you just got off work, but I was hoping this would be a good time to buy you an ice cream cone or something," I said nervously, forcing my leg to be sturdy.

"Buy me an ice cream cone?" he asked with surprise in his eyes.

"Yes." I smiled. "That's what I would like to do to make up for my butterfingers," I said, pointing toward the door. "I know this little kid who sells ice cream cones."

"Is he outside there?" Ben asked.

"Oh, no, he's usually over by Lincoln Park." I was lost in his eyes hoping he wouldn't give me the brush off and say he had things to do. "If you don't have any plans we could go over to Lincoln Park and I could buy you an ice cream cone to make up for my clumsiness. Does that sound okay to you?"

He smiled, looking me up and down, as his eyes seemed to glow with delight. "It sounds better than okay. It sounds just splendid." He smiled and held up one finger. "But there's just one problem."

I paused and waited for him to continue. But he just smiled and then I asked.

"What's the problem? Are you tied up right now?" I glanced at his two briefcases. "I can see you got your arms full."

"The two briefcases? Typical workload." He smiled.

I smiled. "So then, you're not tied up?"

"No, I'm not tied up. But the problem at hand is, I wouldn't think of letting a beautiful lady like you spend a dime on me." He paused in my eyes and before I could feel rejected, he smiled. "Just lead me to your little friend who sells ice cream. The ice cream cone is on me."

It was incredible, I thought to myself as we headed out of the building. All the misery and anguish I had gone through for days could have been avoided if I had found the courage sooner to swallow my pride and come to where he worked.

We stood on the street corner in front of his office building for only a few minutes before he was able to flag a taxi that took us over to Lincoln Park. As we walked through the park looking for Bobby Harris, I said.

"Ben," I smiled and paused in his eyes.

He stopped in his tracks and looked at me as we both stood facing each other.

"Yes." He smiled.

"Thanks for being so gracious for offering to pay for the ice cream that I'm treating you to, but I insist on paying for it myself. It's my treat and my way of making amends for messing up your clothes. So when we finally locate Bobby Harris, I will pay for your ice cream. Deal?"

He narrowed his eyes and smiled. "It's a deal!" He nodded. "Under one condition." He held up one finger.

"And that is?" I smiled.

"You foot the bill for the ice cream cone and dinner is on me? How is that?"

He caught me off guard. "Dinner?" I stared at him.

He nodded. "That's my not so tactful way of asking you to dinner."

My heart started racing faster than it already was. But before I could answer and accept his dinner invitation, he pointed toward a beautiful bird on a bush. And the next thing I realized, we had walked through the park for nearly twenty minutes looking for Bobby Harris, without spotting him.

"Well, I guess my little ice cream friend isn't out here today," I said looking up in his eyes. "I'm sorry about that. I really wanted to treat you to an ice cream. Plus, I really wanted to try one of his banana favored ice cream cones."

"Did you say banana favored? I love banana favored ice cream," he stressed.

"You do?

"You bet."

"I do to."

He grabbed the back of his neck and rubbed it. "Come to think of it. I think I have bought an ice cream cone from the little kid you're talking about."

I looked at him anxiously listening.

"Isn't this kid short and thin as tissue paper? I mean a tiny little fellow?"

I nodded. "That sounds like Bobby," I said, smiling.

"I got an ice cream from him a few weeks ago. A banana ice cream cone."

"Was it on a Saturday morning?" I asked with my imagination going wild.

He nodded. "Yes, it was on a Saturday morning." He narrowed his eyes at me in a sexy way. "Why? Did you see me out there jogging around?"

"No, I didn't. But did you have a wife and two little girls with you?"

"I beg you pardon?"

"Believe me nothing." I smiled up at him, hoping he didn't think I was losing it.

"Well, since your little friend isn't out here. It's dinnertime and we both need to eat. I'm not trying to impose on you, but you never answered me before about dinner. Would you like to join me for dinner?"

I nodded and smiled, feeling overwhelmed by the opportunity. "I would love to."

"How about the Palmer House?" he asked.

With a big smile on my face, I nodded. "Sure, that sounds great." Thinking how any place would do as long as I was in his company.

We walked out to the street and he flagged another taxi. This time we sat a little closer in the cab and when we arrived at the upscale restaurant and was being shown to our seats by the hostess, my feet felt like they were walking on air as we stepped across the thick, smooth, Wedgwood blue carpet. My eyes glanced about the fancy restaurant, admiring the bright white tablecloths and bright white napkins sticking out of the tall, fine crystal glasses. We were seated next to each other at a cozy round table with a fresh array of spring flowers. After we were seated, the waiter took our drink order. We both ordered a glass of white wine and the waiter delivered it in three minutes flat. Now drinking our wine, I felt a sense of unreality about sitting at that table with him. The heightened awareness of his nearness, of what he might be thinking, of his eyes and voice, of the soft tingling feeling that danced in my stomach and washed me with a feeling of weakness was new to me, overwhelming. My entire being seemed tuned to his presence, as if nothing else existed, and yet it felt as if it might all be a fantasy, gone the moment I turned my eyes from him. Just like the dreams I had had of him.

"What would you like for dinner?" he asked, looking straight in my eyes, and then picked up his menu and glanced over it.

"Let me see what's on the menu?" I glanced at him quickly and glanced back at the menu. I felt like a high school kid on her first date, with my first crush, why couldn't I be at least a little more relaxed and talkative? I was afraid he was going to think that I wasn't sophisticated enough for a charming, outgoing guy like himself.

We were still looking over our menu when the waiter returned to take our orders. The waiter held out his pad and looked at me first. "For you Ma'am?"

"No soup or salad, just the Baked Scrod with mixed vegetables and rice," I replied.

"And you Sir?" Asked the tall, thin waiter.

"No soup or salad for me either. I'll take your Filet Mignon with pasta and mixed vegetables," Ben said, looking up at the bald forty-something waiter. I wondered if he was as nervous as me. If he was it didn't show on his calm, collected handsome face.

Somehow we found things to say and ended up having an enjoyable meal together, and by the time our desserts were served, in round crystal dishes, red jello for us both with whip cream on top, and a cherry on top of the whip cream, I decided that asking questions might be the best way to make myself feel more comfortable.

"Ben, Katie told me you're a doctor. What kind of doctor are you?"

"Internal medicine," he said taking a spoonful of his jello, but avoiding the whip cream and picking the cherry off with his finger, placing it in his mouth.

"What's internal medicine," I asked, eating only the whip cream.

"It means I'm a non surgical doctor."

"I see," I said, not knowing quite what else to say at the moment.

After a slight pause while sitting there eating our desserts, I thought I could hear my stomach making noises when he finally asked.

"Has Chicago always been your home, Paulene?"

I shook my head not sure if I should mention I was from his hometown or not. Or should I mention that I had heard of him and his family and knew he was from Montgomery too. But fear of tripping over my words, I just replied.

"I'm from Alabama," I said, looking down at my half finished jello.

"Where about?" he asked with a tad of excitement to his voice.

"Montgomery," I said, looking at him.

He looked at me for a second just smiling and pushed his finished jello dish aside. "You're from Montgomery? Well, I'll be. This is a small world. I meet the prettiest girl in Chicago and she's from my hometown. Well that beats all."

He was smiling and seemed pleased to hear that I was from his hometown, which made me feel more comfortable to be able to tell him that I had heard of his family and I had gotten a glimpse of him before.

"Ben, I already knew you were from Montgomery. I have heard of your family and I have seen you several times when you drove past my house. Your father is also a doctor and you have two younger brothers. Your parents live in a big brick three story house on what seems like a hundred acres of beautiful green hillside."

He reached out and touched my hand and my heart skipped a beat and I had to catch my breath at the touch of him. His gentle touch reached the depth of my longing.

"I can't believe you are from Montgomery and that you live close enough in the area to my folks that you would have heard of us." He paused for a second.

"Why haven't I heard of you and your folks?"

I was thinking to myself, I know you don't expect for me to answer that, do you? He hadn't heard of my folks or me because we were not in his circle. My parents were poor farmers living across the creek in a small frame house with one junk car after another lined up in the driveway and on the grounds, not to mention all the chicken coops and pig pens surrounding the place. But the inside of our home was still clean and comfortable.

Quickly I changed the subject. "So, Ben, this is your home now, I take it?"

"Yeah, for now. I'm here on a medical convention. It's been going on forever it seems. I have been here for the past three months and this damn thing is almost over. So I'm here until it ends."

"Ben, I have never heard of a convention lasting for months. I thought conventions only last for a week or two."

"That's true. This convention originally was only going to keep me away from my office in Montgomery for two and a half weeks. But I ended up with another project that stemmed from the original convention. Anyway, I have been stuck here every since. But like I said, it's almost over." He took a sip of ice water.

"What brought you to Chicago?" he asked, draining his wine glass.

"My father encouraged me to come here and attend college. Plus I wanted to get a taste of city life to see what the rest of the world was all about. I thought living in a big city would be something fascinating to write home about."

"You say you thought, past tense. Do you still feel the same?" he asked.

Shaking my head, I paused in his eyes for a second. "No." I smiled. "Not really. I think it lacks a lot of warmth."

He smiled. "Okay. I can agree to that."

"Ben, it's the people here. That lack of friendly faces and everybody willing to help everybody else types of people." I paused, hoping I wasn't boring him.

He nodded as if he was amused with me. "That good-ole southern hospitality that you run into back home right?"

"Exactly." I smiled. "I suppose when a person anticipates and expects too much the reality is always disappointing."

"Yes, maybe you were expecting too much."

"You're probably right," I took a sip of my wine and the waiter was placing another glass of wine in front of Ben. "I guess the truth of the matter, Ben, is I just really wasn't prepared for big city living and a lot of other things."

"A lot of other things such as what?" he asked, taking a sip of wine.

"I don't know, just things in general. It seems that a lot of the people in this city are so pushy and selfish."

"Yeah. That's big city living. Everybody trying to get ahead no matter who they step on to get there."

"Many times they just seem phony and shallow, as if someone's feelings doesn't mean too much." I took another sip of wine, feeling I was talking too much. "I guess I just wasn't raised that way."

His eyes narrowed and his smile widened as he placed his hand on top of mine again. This time his touch was like fire against my skin.

"Are we talking about men now?" he asked.

"Yes, I guess you can say that." I looked up at him with my heart in my throat with the touch of his hand making me melt right in my seat. "The men in this city that have approached me seem so into playing games. Being phony, that's the word."

"Have you dated a lot since you have been here?" he asked with curious eyes.

"No, not a lot, but I have gone on a couple dates." I sipped my wine. "But no repeat dates." I held up one finger, smiling. "The two times I went out, to see a stage play on each occasion, the man I was with felt he had a right to try to put his hand all over me just because I was sitting in a theater with him." I paused and he hadn't taken his eyes off of me. "I'm not saying that I think all men in this city are that way, but the two I went out with were less than gentlemen the way they tried to treat me."

"Sounds pretty typical." He smiled. "The men in Montgomery are no different."

I didn't comment because he was probably right. After a long pause, I said. "Ben, you must have thought I was pretty bold to show up at the building where you work?

He nodded. "It was a surprise."

"I bet it was, with me, waiting there in the lobby for you the way I did?" I glanced down and took a sip of wine.

"Believe me, Paulene. It was a good surprise."

"I want you to know that that was my first time taking the initiative and being that bold. But I felt so bad about being a klutz around you. I had to try and extend my apologies in a better way."

"I was knocked over with a feather while coming down the escalators, seeing you standing there. And when I got off the escalators and found out you were standing there waiting for me, I was floored. I mean how can one guy get so lucky as to have a beautiful woman like you waiting for him?" He grinned.

"Thank you for the compliment." I smiled, looking in his eyes.

"It's easy to believe you have never done anything like that. But I'm glad you were waiting there." He held his glass up to his lips and just kept it there, looking at me with amazement. "I got to admit, I'll never know why you even bothered. Each time I acted like a jerk. I acted as if a little spill was going to make me melt."

"You had a right to not be pleased about getting your clothes spoiled."

"I over did it the way I rushed out of the room."

"I didn't think you acted like a jerk. You rushed out because you didn't want to be in a roomful of people with a big wet spot on your clothes."

He sat there listening and smiling as if he was hanging on every word I had to say. "Believe me, Ben, I would have reacted the same and rushed home, not thinking I was being rude because I didn't want to be seen with a wet spot on my clothes."

He smiled, shaking his head. "Why do I seriously doubt that you could ever be rude?" He looked deep into my eyes. "Something tells me it would be impossible for you to be rude. Not even in your dreams." He smiled.

His smile made me blush sitting there looking at him. I took another sip of wine.

With overwhelming desire to know everything about him, I wanted to listen closely to everything he had to say about himself and his family. The story he told portrayed his mother, Mrs. Anita Drake, as nothing less than a loving and gracious woman who was always there for her family. He explained in a heartfelt way that while growing up, he could never remember a time coming home from school when his mother didn't have a hot meal waiting for him and his brothers. He said they always had housekeepers and someone to take care of the grounds, but never a cook. His mother made all their meals. He painted his father, Dr. Leonard Drake, as a dedicated, determined father who along with his mother pushed him and his brothers from the time they were so high to keep their eyes on the prize of education and what they really wanted to achieve in life. He described his father as a brilliant brain surgeon, as well as a humorous, understanding man who wasn't born with a silver spoon in his mouth. He shared with me how his father put himself through college and medical school by driving a taxi as a boy. He mentioned that his two younger brothers, Wesley, twenty-two and Calvin, twenty, were both living at home attending college. His younger brother, Calvin, plans to go to medical school and be a doctor like Ben and their father. Wesley plans are to be a corporate lawyer. Ben painted a beautiful picture of the closeness he shared with his family.

"So, Paulene that's a little bit of insight into my family," Ben smiled. "I haven't seen my folks in awhile, I've been here in this city for the past few months now. But I do my best to keep in touch and call home as often as I can." He sipped his cup of cappuccino that the waiter had just sat in front of us.

A smile was glued across my face listening to him, especially touched by his apparent selflessness. Coming to Chicago to attend a medical convention, not because he really wanted to, but because his mother really wanted him to. He could have refused and turned his back on the convention, but he wanted to please his mother. He said his mother had always been so supportive of him in every way that the least he could do was to make her happy by moving to Chicago for a while to attend the convention. A convention that his mother felt, more than he, that it would greatly benefit his practice.

"Ben, I'm impressed by your selflessness. Coming to Chicago to attend a medical convention that you didn't hundred percent want to attend just to please your mother?"

"Thanks, Paulene, but I don't feel that I have done anything so selfless, caring about my mother's wishes. To me it's just a matter of returning some of the love that she has showed to me. She felt that coming to this convention would be a beneficial move. I respect her opinion, so I came." He sipped his cappuccino.

I felt ashamed that only a short while ago I had thought that he was possibly insensitive and uncaring. When I had first met him I had been so swept off my feet that I hadn't stopped to wonder what kind of person he was. For all of Katie's sophistication, she had been mistaken about Ben, mistaken about his relationship with his mother. But then maybe Katie's feelings had been colored by her own disappointments with love. I was beginning to see that Ben was a man of some integrity, and his family had nourished that quality in him. I was also impressed with how understanding and loving his mother and father sounded.

"Your mother sounds wonderful," I said, draining my cappuccino cup.

"She is," Ben answered and swallowed the last of his cappuccino. "Now enough of the Ben Drake story. Where would you like to go?"

"Anywhere." What I wanted to say was, "Right smack into your arms.

Chapter Fifteen

The night was clear and warm with a fresh breath of wind here and there. After dinner we hopped a taxi to the Buckingham Fountain for a short period, and then to State and Madison Street to just look at the window displays. We walked slowly without really saying much, but at this point it seemed to me that words were not needed. I felt somewhat connected to him. A comfortable feeling like I got from being around Aunt Haddie and Dad. I felt warm in his presence, it was like I had been taken over by him and my heart wrapped up in his.

After walking a few blocks, Ben pointed toward the Lake Point tower. "I live in that building," he said. "On the thirty-fourth floor."

"That's a nice building?" I said, wondering if I would ever get the opportunity to see the inside of the building, especially his apartment.

We walked on, and much too soon he had walked me home. Now standing in front of the Westin Hotel, in front of the lobby door, for an awkward moment I stood silently looking at him. I was anxiously searching for the right words and afraid I would blurt out the wrong thing and never see him again. But he was the first to speak.

Looking down in my eyes, he asked. "Paulene, are you busy this weekend?"

I stared at him lost for words and he continued. "I know this is short notice. Tomorrow is Friday already. But I figured I would give it a shot. There's always a chance that you could be available." He smiled, waiting for my answer.

Suddenly, I remembered the one-way train ticket in my purse. My heart skipped a beat. I wanted so badly to see him over the weekend if that's what he was asking for. And it definitely sounded like he was asking me out. If I said no, would he ask me again? How many women were there in his life? It would be stupid to think for one moment that he was so taken with me that he would ever give me a second thought if I said no. I missed Aunt Haddie and my father desperately, and after Ben's story about how some of his patients just suddenly pass away on him and there's nothing he can do for them, I felt strangely compelled to see my folks even more. It was nonsense, I knew, but the urge to go home was almost as strong, in its way, as my desire to spend time with Ben.

"I was planning to take the train home this weekend to see my folks."

He nodded. "I see."

Maybe it was my imagination, but he at least seemed a little disappointed. And then before I had a chance to answer I found myself in a trance, looking up in his eyes, and I thought I would faint as he brought his handsome face down to my lips and covered them tenderly, with a quick feathery light kiss on the lips.

"It's just my luck. I meet the prettiest girl in town, and she's headed out of town," he said as he pulled away from my lips.

"I really miss my folks and thought I would pay them a visit this weekend."

He smiled. "I'm sure you miss them, and at the risk of sounding selfish. I wish you didn't have plans to go home this weekend. I was hoping you and I could get together." He held my face with both hands as we stood just inches from each other.

"Me too…but, I just picked up the ticket today." I paused. "Plus I called home on my lunchbreak and told my parents to expect me."

He nodded. "I see. So they know you are coming?"

"Yes. They know. Plus I feel I need to get away from here for a few days."

"A few days?" he asked, smiling. "So I take it, you'll be returning?"

My eyes looked at him startled at what he had just asked me. I had a one-way ticket in my purse and my intentions had been to take the train home and stay. But of course, now that he was talking to me, no way would I go back home and not return.

"Yes, I'll be back," I uttered softly.

He paused and glanced down for a split second and back at me. "I just want you to know that this was the best evening I have had in a long time," he said softly, looking at me with eyes that seemed to glow in the dark, ripe with desire as if he wanted to pull me in his arms and hold me forever. "I really mean it, Paulene," he said, reaching into his suit coat pocket, bringing out two small white business cards." Here you are." He smiled. "This is my card which include my home and work numbers. Give me a call when you get back to the city."

"Okay, I sure will." I took the card and just stared at it for a moment, admiring the design of his card; I was also admiring the thought that he had given it to me.

My eyes glanced back up at him and he was holding a Mont Blanc roller ball pen in his hand writing my name on the back of one of his cards. "May I have your number, Paulene?" he asked, handing me the card and pen.

"Sure." I smiled, and then took the pen and his business card to jot my number down.

"Here you are." I handed him the card.

"Thank you." He pulled out his wallet and carefully placed the card inside of it. He pushed his wallet back in his pocket, smiling. "Now I know I won't lose your number." He lifted my left hand and kissed it. "So, you have yourself a fantastic weekend and give me a buzz when you get back." He kissed my hand again and walked off.

Nodding, my feet felt glued in that spot and would not move until he hopped in a taxi and headed to his apartment. Only then could I leave that spot and quickly head inside. And as soon as I had closed the door to my room and sat myself down on the edge of the bed, I suddenly found myself sitting there holding my face and shaking my head. I knew I was probably strung out after the emotional drain of the last few weeks, hoping and praying he would ask me out, now when he does, I already have plans. But tonight had changed everything. Maybe there was a chance for us after all, but now what? I wanted to be with him but I had promised Aunt Haddie and Dad that I would be coming home for the weekend.

What to do? I stared at the phone for a moment, and then picked it up and quickly dialed Katie's number. "Katie? It's me, Paulene."

"What's up? You sound breathless," she said laughingly. "Paulene what have you been into young lady?"

"I just got in and I feel on top of the world, really." I laughed.

"You sure sound happy about something."

"I'm extremely happy, but I'm sort of miserable at the same time?"

"That's not out of character for you." She laughed. "All right, let's hear it."

"Okay, here goes," I said as I started relating the evening's events, beginning with how I had bought a ticket to go home for the weekend and had then felt the overwhelming urge to wait for Ben in his office building. Then there was the romantic dinner that Ben and I shared at the Palmer House, and how impressed I had been by what he had told me about his family—so much so that I summarized our conversation to her. "It just proves how people should never go by initial impressions," I paused. "Because I surely didn't picture him as someone whose family meant so much to him. The closeness he feels for his family is the same kind of closeness I feel for mine," I stressed. "He said he never misses the opportunity to mail home a birthday card or send gifts for an occasion whenever he's out of town on business as he is now."

It wasn't often to find Katie speechless, but she couldn't seem to find her voice. In her mind, maybe she felt Ben had presented himself in a false light.

Katie was brought out of her silence when she heard me say, "I suppose I found it all so surprising because of the things you had said about him."

"Like what?" she asked.

"You painted him out to be a selfish, Mama's boy who was only interested in feeding his own ego with one-night stands."

"I don't want to burst your happy mood, but you don't get to know a person from just one date. You have a long ways to go before you really know Ben Drake."

"I don't claim to know him. But I do know more about him. I spent an evening with the man and he seems to be a pretty super guy as far as I can tell. I'm really impressed with his devotion to his family, and I don't think he's a Mama's boy just because he wants to try and please his mother if he can." I paused. "You have totally misjudged him, Katie."

"Sure, you're right," she said it as if she was thinking quietly; if that's what you want to think, then suit yourself.

After a moment of silence, I laughed again. "Katie, we had such a great time."

"Okay, then, what's the problem?"

"Well, as I told you, Ben asked me out this weekend but I said I couldn't because I had to go home."

"But the reason for that is gone. You were trying to get away to get over him, but since you got up enough courage to take the initiative and the two of you have finally connected, why not stay? You can go home some other time."

"I guess I could, but I don't know. Something else tells me that I shouldn't put it off that I should go home to see Aunt Haddie and Dad now."

"Really? And what's this something else, Paulene?"

"My instincts and a little bit of fear. After Ben told me how suddenly some of his older patients die, immediately I started thinking about Aunt Haddie and my father."

"My goodness, Paulene, don't take everything to heart."

"I'm not taking everything to heart. But Dad and Aunt Haddie are getting up there."

"Not really. They are both under 60." She shook her head. "I'm beginning to think you're more afraid of spending time alone with Ben than you are willing to admit."

"How can you say that when you know how I feel about him?"

"I know how you feel, and I suspect that's why you're afraid."

"Honestly, Katie, that doesn't make any sense."

"I think it does. You want him and you know he's attracted to you, but you're afraid to put out because you want a commitment. The problem is that you're not in high school, waiting for some boy to go steady with you and carry your books before you'll let him hold your hand. When you deal with grown men, you play the games they play! And it's impossible not to end up in bed together if you want to stay in their circle! That's just the way it is! You wind up in bed, and take the chance that it's either the beginning or the end of what just started. You're a big girl, Paulene. It's time you learned you can't have it both ways."

Startling as it was, Katie had read it right. Yes, I was afraid that Ben would take me to bed once and then brush me off. Katie had warned me that Ben majored in one-night stands. Love them and leave them. But I had just told her I didn't believe that about him, or did I?

"So what do I do now?" I asked.

"That's up to you, Paulene. Just be sure you understand that if you get into a relationship with Ben, it may not turn out the way you're hoping. You need to be prepared for the possibility of being used. And if he takes you to bed, don't expect anything else from him. I'm sure you don't want to hear this, but when I told you that he doesn't allow himself to become involved. I was pretty much on the money with that. When a girl gets too into him, he backs off." She paused.

"Maybe he's not like that now."

"That's the Ben I have known all these years." She pauses again. "So don't say I didn't warn you if and when that happens."

"I know you mean well, Katie. But he didn't seem that way tonight."

"Maybe he didn't' seem that way. After all, it's typical for a man to be on his best behavior when he's trying to catch someone. But then, on the other hand, you're going to have to take that step eventually."

"Katie, why do your mind always end up on sex?"

"Because that's what Ben Drake is after. Not to mention it's the facts of life."

"Okay, already. Tell me something I don't already know."

"I'm sure you know enough. But if you take that step with Ben, just remember that he's a confirmed bachelor and may not want a commitment."

"We just had our first date. I'm not going to jump the gun expecting much more."

"Paulene, just remember to keep your head and play it cool. Treasure the time you spend with him, and be willing to accept things if it doesn't work out the way you were hoping! And if he suddenly walks away don't go through the rest of your life—bitter with all men!" She stared into space for a moment, and then looked at me with serious eyes. "So be careful and play it cool with Ben, Ok?" She nodded.

Katie knew even as she was speaking how ridiculous all that was. I was in love and a person in love didn't know how to play it cool. Well, at least I had been warned. Which was more than anybody had done for her when she was seventeen and in love with that Shaun Parker who has made her into the bitter woman that she is today.

There was a long silence. Then I asked, "Katie, I would love to see Ben but what can I do now? I told him I was going home,"

"Paulene, you have been dying to be with this man. You better take this chance and run with it. When you get off the phone with me, just call home and tell your folks you're not coming." She paused. "You can always use your ticket and hop on a train some other weekend. Give the man a call tomorrow and say you changed your mind about going home for the weekend."

Chapter Sixteen

After my phone conversation ended with Katie that Thursday evening, I took her advice and called my folks immediately. I explained that I wouldn't be home for the weekend, but I would make arrangements to visit soon. My conversation was quick and I retired to my bed with wonderful thoughts of my time spent with Ben. I didn't call Ben after I hung up with my folks because I didn't want to risk appearing too anxious. It wasn't easy but I waited and did not phone him until early that Saturday morning.

Ben sounded pleased with my call. "I'm glad you decided to stay. Now, what would you like to do?"

"Whatever you feel like."

"Great, we'll decide together. I'll pick you up at 7:30 this evening." He paused and asked. "What are you doing right now?"

"Talking to you and holding a dry piece of toast in one hand," I said softly.

"What about a picnic in Lincoln Park? I could pick you up at noon? I hear the weather is going to be perfect with clear skies and sun all day," he suggested.

"Okay," I said softly and swallowed hard at his invitation, biting down on my bottom lip to hold back my overwhelming excitement. Shouting time excitement.

"Okay, then. We are on for two dates in one day." He paused. "Sounds good to me," he paused. "Bring a blanket. I'll provide all the other goodies."

"Okay, and you won't have to ring my room. I'll be waiting in the lobby."

"That reminds me, what's your room number just in case?"

"It's 841. But you won't need it. I'll be downstairs waiting for you."

"Okay. Sounds good. See you later," he said, and then the phone went silent.

At noon on the head, I was waiting in the lobby for Ben with my black leather purse draped over my shoulder and a small blue blanket in my arms. I was dressed in a casual outfit: a pair of jeans and a white top and white gym shoes. He stepped inside the hotel lobby carrying a large wicker picnic basket. He was dressed in a casual outfit as well. He was wearing neatly pressed blue jeans and a neatly pressed purple shirt and white gym shoes. He escorted me by the left arm outside where he flagged one of the valet guys to fetch his car. When the valet guy pulled Ben's Jaguar in front of the hotel, he stepped out of the car, leaving the driver's door open and quickly stepped around to the passenger's side and opened the door for me.

Ben handed the guy five dollars and smiled. "You are quick. I was going to get the door for the lady," Ben said, handing the valet guy the picnic basket and the blanket. "Since you are so quick with service, I guess you wouldn't mind placing this is the trunk for us." Ben smiled, popping the trunk open with his remote.

Soon we were on our way. Sitting next to him, I felt both anxious and excited. He seemed happy as he drove at a comfortable speed, headed toward Lincoln Park. He appeared to have pleasant thoughts as a slight smile showed on his face as he looked straight ahead. Quick glances now and then in my direction told me that he was aware of me sitting there next to him. I wanted to say something, but I couldn't think of anything sophisticated to say. Soon the park was in full view as I stared out the window. The fresh outdoors and the idea of spending time outside always excited me. The park looked just as inviting as it did on the times I came without Ben. Its beauty just astonishing as before, but somehow more radiant since Ben would be sharing it with me.

Ben tapped my shoulders and pointed to a mass of shade trees off to themselves as he was turning off the main road into the park. "What do you think? Looks private enough?" He grinned.

"Sure," I nodded. "Wherever you like," I agreed, noticing all the people out and about having fun on the huge grounds: Some were playing ball, some were roasting food over the fire, some were sitting on blankets having picnics, some were sitting on grass reading, some were walking their dogs, some couples were walking around holding hands. Some couples were jogging around holding hands; some couples were walking with their kids. And as my eyes kept noticing all the people, I thought for sure I would spot that little boy, Bobby Harris pushing his cart and selling ice cream on such a beautiful warm day, but as far as my eyes could see, he was no where in the park.

At the park, what seemed like hours we walked hand-in hand through a mass of trees as the glowing sun radiated the entire park with warmth. Being in the outdoors, at mid-day felt romantic. My mind savored and stored everything about Ben. Every breath he took and every word he said, I listened as if I would never be able to listen again. My thoughts drifted with the soft breeze that felt soothing against my face as my thoughts reflected the brightness of the fresh outdoors. Being with him gave me a sense of completeness. Suddenly, I felt carefree as I threw my arms up over my head, turning around and around gracefully like a butterfly. Then I catch myself, not wanting to go over board and make myself look too playful and at ease. I glanced around and Ben chose a shady spot beneath the shimmering leaves and beautiful blooms of a tall dogwood tree. He hadn't noticed my carefree turns in the wind. I watched as he spread the cotton blend powder blue blanket on that spot, and then he glanced at me, patting the ground for me to come sat.

I grinned, unable to hide the urge to be playful. Overwhelmed about being on this picnic with him. Beside myself about being with him period.

"I'm not ready to sit." I said, teasingly. "Just try and catch me." I was laughing loudly as I took off in the direction of a clear landing of short grass.

Ben caught up with me within seconds, bringing me down in a playful tackle, right near a section of bright yellow flowers. I tossed and turned beneath him, trying to break away and run again. My struggle stopped when his smile faded and the look on his face turned serious. He became quiet; looking down at me as I thought my heart would stop from the pouring desire in his eyes. I wanted him to kiss me, but we both smiled and jumped up.

We stood to our feet quickly, laughing and grinning as we ran playfully back to our spot where he spread the blanket and left the basket. We lay back on the blanket, his hands under his head, and me on one elbow looking at him as he stared up at the endless space of blue sky.

"Paulene." He drew his breath in. "Being on this picnic with you, is just what the doctor ordered. I can't tell you how relaxed and comfortable it feels being here with you like this." He glanced at me and smiled. "It's a magnificent high to spend time with such an incredible beautiful woman like yourself."

"I'm glad to be here too. A picnic was a great idea, especially on a lovely day like this."

"The weather is lovely. But not as lovely as you." He touched my hand.

I smiled and didn't comment.

"I'm sure you know how beautiful you are." He smiled. "Spending time with someone as lovely as you is like paradise and heaven all wrapped up into one." He grabbed two bottles of spring water from the basket, opened one and passed it to me. "I don't really know how to explain it. You are so different from all the other ladies here in Chicago."

His words caught my attention and I didn't know him well enough to know if he was giving me a compliment or not. I immediately looked at him and slightly smiled. I was anxious to know what he meant by that. "Different in what way?"

"Well, just different," he said, taking a sip of his water.

I slightly lowered my head and my smile somewhat disappeared, hoping he didn't think I was too unsophisticated. After all I wasn't from his circle. I wasn't one of those rich, well-dressed types that I had seen at Katie's party. And that was the type that he was probably used too. It had to be. Someone with his prestige and wealth, I was probably his first date with an average working-class.

He reached out and touched my face. "I certainly mean different in a good way; a refreshing, sweet way. You are so refreshing to be around that's all I'm trying to say." He took another sip of water. "Paulene, other than being the most beautiful woman I have ever met. You're just a real delight to be around."

Whether he meant those words are not, hearing them instantly put the huge smile back on my face. I kept thinking over and over in my head how he had just said I was the most beautiful woman he had ever met. I wanted to scream from that. But I gripped my right fist real tight to hold back the urge to shout.

"There's that lovely smile," he said and slightly brushed my face with the back of his smooth hand and I had to swallow hard to keep from melting right before his eyes.

"I'm sitting here having a ball just sitting here. And I know you don't know me well enough to know this, but usually, at picnics I'm not having any fun until I break out the goodies. And when they're finished, I'm finished with the park."

My left hand covered my mouth and I had to laugh after that statement. "You mean you only come for the goodies? What about the fresh air and being outside of an office for a change?" I asked, shaking my head.

"I know." He grinned. "Go on and tell me how sad that sounds?"

"It's not sad. It's just you."

"So, maybe I'm sad." He teased and touched my hand.

"No, I wouldn't say that."

"Of course, not. Because you are so kind."

"You know who you remind me of Ben by saying that? You remind me of my Dad."

"Your Dad tells you how kind you are?"

"No, not that, but the part about picnicking just for the food."

"Really?" He laughed.

"Yes. My father is the same way. Whenever the family went picnicking, once the food was gone, he was ready to pack up and head home."

"Your Dad sounds like a smart man." He teased.

"Yes." I nodded. "After the food left, Dad was always ready to pack up the car and go."

He smiled and nodded. "But, the point I'm trying to make here,

Miss Dawson, is that my mind isn't even on the food," he said with a sensuous undertone that made my hand slightly tremble and my heart race. "Like I said, I'm having fun and I haven't even taken the first bite from one of the corn beef sandwiches that awaits us on ice in that basket." He pointed to the basket. "Not to mention the potato salad, and all the other goodies that's packed in there," he said, smiling. "The bottom line here is that your wonderful company trumps food."

We enjoyed the warm refreshing breeze sweeping over us as we lay on the soft blanket among the endless fields of fresh cut grass. And I kept hoping, since he said and seemed to be enjoying my company so much that he would at least kiss me or hold my hand. I wanted to be kissed by him so desperately, until. I would probably faint if he did. But I was dying more from just hoping.

Then suddenly out of nowhere as we lay on the comfortable blanket, he placed one arm around me and with one quick gentle pull into his arms, our bodies collided. As he held me next to him, he stroked my hair aside and sought my lips, pushing his mouth against my awaiting lips, kissing me in the most incredible gentle, passionate way. I thought my heart would stop as I had laid awake many nights hoping for his kisses, but just when I thought that, he pulled away from my lips, breathless as he lifted my left hand and kissed it.

"I could hold you like this and kiss you for the rest of the day, Miss Dawson. I can't think of any place I would rather be other than right here! Right now with you," he said.

"Being here with you, Ben, there's no other place in this world I would rather be right now than with you as well. It feels right," I mumbled breathless.

"Being with you feels more than right. It feels real," he said in a low, soft, sensuous voice as he kissed my hand again.

My eyes melted into his as we both lay there leaning on one elbow looking at each other. "Ben, there is so much I want to know about you. The things I want to know about you, it could take years to learn. But I want to know all of those things about you in this one day. I want to know what you looked like as a boy? Were you always this good-looking? How did you get through high school and college without being mobbed and stalked my hundredths of lovesick females dying for just one moment with you? What school did you attend? What were your favorite foods? How many friends did you have? Who was your first girlfriend? Have you ever been in love? Did you have your own room? How old were you when you got your first car? Did you have a pet? Did you ever play hooky at school? What was your favorite subject? Who was your favorite teacher? What was your grade point average? I want to know everything," I said as his mouth came down over mine, silencing my words with a breathtaking, lingering, but far too short kiss that made me want him to never stop.

He pulled away and looked in my eyes as if his desire for me was overflowing.

"In time, hopefully you will know all of those things about me and more," he said in a low, sensuous voice and gave me a quick kiss on the forehead.

Sitting up now, under those tall trees with the warmth of the sun and the soothing breeze filling the air with the sweet scent of the dogwood blooms. The touch of his hand holding mine drained me of all my strength. I felt like a feather that could just float in the wind as I sat there lost in his eyes.

"Ben, Oh, God." I thought to myself. "If you only knew how hard I have prayed hoping for a chance to be with you like this."

He smiled, looking in my eyes for a moment as if he would kiss me again. Instead, he reached for the basket. "Are you ready to dig in now?" Ben asked, busy opening and emptying the large wicker basket. The extra large picnic basket was perfectly designed for such a cozy picnic for two. It had enough room in it for nearly everything except the kitchen sink. It had separate compartments, securing two slender, gold trimmed, long stemmed crystal glasses, two white delicate China plates, a set of expensive looking silverware for two, two mint green cloth napkins fitted inside of two clear napkin rings. Beside the napkins, an interesting array of lime green and sky blue plastic containers and several bottles of spring water along with a tall plastic container of icy sweet lemonade.

My eyes lit up and my mouth began to water as Ben uncovered

the contents of the bright dishes. It was plain to see that he had gone through a lot of trouble to make sure our picnic was very special with every thing we needed as far as food was concerned. Containers of potato salad and coleslaw, thick sliced dill pickles, square chunks of fresh cucumber, celery and carrot sticks, tomato wedges, small cubes of American and Swiss cheese, black and Spanish olives. Sweet red and green grapes shared their container with ripe red strawberries. And wrapped within a large mint green linen napkin lay two corn beef sandwiches secured in plastic wrap.

Ben opened the lemonade and poured the delicate glasses half full.

"Dig in," he said as he passed one container after another.

I thought my nervousness might make eating impossible, but it didn't hinder my appetite as I filled my plate with three strawberries, three chunks of cucumbers and four cubes of American cheese. It was very unusual that I was able to eat, I realized. Ordinarily, in a nervous situation, I was quite incapable of consuming even the tiniest piece of any food. When anxious, I was in the habit of refusing anything except, perhaps, water or a glass of wine. But somehow, this situation was different. How so? I wondered as my teeth sank into the moist coolness of a chunk of crisp cucumber. Was it the perfect setting, the perfect weather and the perfect man?

Chapter Seventeen

Ben pulled in front of the Westin Hotel and double-parked by 4:00 o'clock that evening. When the doorman waved his arm trying to stop Ben from double parking in front of the place, Ben ignored the tall, pencil thin, thirty-something doorman who was dressed in a blue and red uniform and parked there anyway. But by the time he killed the motor, the angry looking blond hair doorman had stuck his head in the car on the passenger's side where I was sitting.

"Sir, you can't park here," the doorman snapped. "This strip is only for cabs and express mail. Didn't you see me waving you on?" he asked sharply.

"How you doing, Sir?" he asked the doorman politely. "My name is Dr. Ben Drake and I'm here in town on a medical convention." Ben extended his hand and the doorman shook his hand. "I'm here to drop off my friend, Miss Paulene Dawson, and I would like to see her to her door. I would only be a minute."

The blue eyed, smooth skinned doorman frowned hard at Ben, then shifted his eyes to me and smiled, giving me the kind of look a man gives a woman when he lust after her. "Do you room here, Ma'am?" The doorman asked me.

"Yes, Sir, I do." I nodded, hoping he would allow Ben to see me to my door.

The doorman glanced about, and then stuck his head back in the window. "Okay, here's the deal. You can park here for no more than ten minutes, but you have to keep your engine running. Otherwise, I'll get chewed out by my boss," the doorman frowned.

Ben nodded and started the engine, then pulled his burgundy leather wallet from his back pocket and pulled out a ten-dollar bill. He threw me a smile as if it pleased him a lot to be able to walk me to my door, but not as much as it pleased me. He stepped out of the car and walked around to the passenger's side and escorted me out of the car like a gentleman. As we headed inside, he handed the doorman the ten-dollar bill.

"Thanks for your trouble," Ben said.

"You're welcome, Sir." The doorman smiled at the money. "Just don't get me in hot water by leaving your car parked there for more than ten minutes."

"You got it," Ben assured him.

Ben held my hand as we got on the elevator to the eighth floor. When we got off the elevator he held my hand as he walked me to my door. Once in front of my room door, I looked up at him and I could see a look of desire in his eyes.

"Okay, it's a quarter to four, so I guess I'll see you in about three hours," he said, leaned down and kissed the side of my face.

"Okay, I'll be ready. I'll be waiting downstairs in the front lobby," I said.

He waved good-bye as he walked quickly toward the elevator. I stood there at my door and watched as he stepped four rooms down to the elevator where four other people were standing and waiting. He didn't look back toward my door as he and the group of people stepped on the elevator and then he was gone. Now I could catch my breath. His overwhelming presence was breathtaking.

With beautiful butterflies in my stomach, I quickly took my room key and let myself in. Once I was behind closed doors in my small hotel room, the wonderful realization of it all hit me. And suddenly I felt weightless as I threw myself across the bed on my back. My mind was filled with so many happy thoughts as I lay there staring up at the ceiling, savoring our afternoon together. But I couldn't savor too long. He would be picking me up for dinner at seven, which gave me three hours to make myself as stunning as I could for our first real date: Our first private, at night romance. And by seven o'clock I was a nervous wreck. In the last hour I had changed six times and was still not sure I was wearing the right thing. I knew the look I wanted. I wanted to look charming, sophisticated and sexy. But what could I wear to get that look? Katie would know, she was good with fashions and was usually dressed to the nines everyday at work. I needed one of those drop-dead gorgeous dresses of Katie's. But I had to face it, I didn't have Katie sophistication about fashions and either did I have her bank account to be able to buy those kinds of clothes. Realistically, I had to do the best with what I had, deciding on one of my favorite dresses. Something inside of me told me that Ben would like the dress. A long ankle-length silk and cotton blend light peach dress that enhanced the delicate coloring of my fair honey complexion and brought out the radiance in my chestnut brown eyes. I had just finished up my makeup and was now standing in the mirror combing my hair when the phone rang.

"Hello," I said.

"It's me. I'm waiting here in the lobby for you," Ben said.

"Okay, I'm ready. I'll be right there," I said, hung up the phone and grabbed my head. For a moment I couldn't think. I looked in the mirror and suddenly the dress that I thought looked so nice just minutes ago, didn't look nice. My hairstyle that looked okay minutes ago, somehow suddenly didn't look okay. Nothing about me looked good enough in my eyes. Then I started laughing and told myself to get a grip. "You are just experiencing the signs of falling in love," I told myself. "You want to look and be your best for that person." After calming down, I glanced at my watch and five minutes had passed since Ben phoned the room. I grabbed my purse and wrap and left the room in a rush. When I walked over to the elevator it was just opening on my floor.

Apparently, I had guessed right when I decided on the peach colored dress. When he saw me coming toward him his sexy smile told how much he approved of how I looked. He took me by the arm and before I knew it, we were sitting side by side in a taxi again just like before.

Sitting there in that elegant Palmer House restaurant having dinner with him yet again was like heaven on earth. The food and wine was great, although it seemed that neither one of us ate or drank that much. We were too busy just sort of looking at each other. He seemed to be looking at me as much as I was looking at him. I probably took two bites from my green salad and no more than two bites from my salmon and green beans while he finished his garden salad and nibbled on a slice of the French loaf of bread that was served with our meal, pushing his white fish with lemon sauce aside altogether. We were too busy gazing into each other eyes to eat much. And real conversation passed us by too. We hardly said that much of anything to each other.

Sitting across from each other in the soft romantic candlelight I was thinking only of what lay ahead of us that evening. Ben seemed eager to get dinner over with as if he was having difficulties keeping himself from taking me by the hand and walking out of the restaurant before we had finished our meals. It seemed to me there was now no doubt that he would take me home to his apartment.

Walking out of the restaurant, I was hoping he would reach for my hand, but he only opened the door for me, and briefly placed his hand on my shoulder as he guided me toward the end of the street. He flagged a taxi and once again we were in a cab, this time sitting closer to each other and only now did he hold my hand. His soft hand wrapped around my hand instantly made my heart melt and I wanted to throw my arms around him and jump on his lap. But as usual I was too reserved to let out my emotions. And he seemed a bit more reserved and not as relaxed as he had seemed at the park. But just that wonderful romantic gesture of holding my hand made everything perfect.

"Where would you like to go?" he asked in a loving, gentle way as if my every wish was his command. "There's a club on Rush Street that features a live jazz band every night and I hear the music is really good." He nodded.

"If you like," I said, smiling, hoping deep down he would suggest his place so we could be alone together. I wanted him all to myself just to sat and look at him and lose myself in his gorgeous eyes. "Wherever you decide is fine with me."

He smiled. "Hearing you say that is music to my ears." He paused, still smiling.

My heart raced when the taxi dropped us off at his apartment building, but before I could wonder if we were going up to his apartment, he informed me that we were just stopping to pick up his car from the parking garage.

When we got to the jazz club, while sitting in the darkened parking lot, he turned the engine off and propped his elbow on the steering wheel just staring at me, smiling. Nerves and not knowing what to say, I glanced at my watch. "It's getting late, Ben. Maybe we should head in there and stay for a little while then you can take me home."

"It's still early. Is it okay if we sit here and talk for a while? I want to know all there is to know about you, Paulene. You take my breath away." He whispered, moving his smooth, handsome face closer to mine, and before I had time to respond, he had placed his lips against the side of my face, gripping my face with both hands, turning my face toward his, and then kissed me passionately.

After not much struggle on my part, I managed to softly push Ben's face away from mine, figuring we shouldn't keep necking in his car. People were coming and going into the club. Sitting on the front seat of a car smooching just didn't seem right, but within seconds of his lips abandoning mine, he reached back out and grabbed my face gently, bringing his face back down on mine. My head laid against his car window as his hungry kisses owned me. His mouth captured mine and I was delighted as he kissed me urgently. His kiss released emotions in me that left me breathless.

He pulled from my lips and looked me in the eyes as if he adored me. I was motionless looking at him, almost trembling as I tingled all over for him to kiss me again. Slowly, inch by inch, with a look of great desire in his eyes, he brought his lips closer and closer to mind; and I thought I would die in his arms when he grabbed my face and urgently kissed me once more, caressing my hair with his fingers in a wildly manner. I couldn't take it, thinking to myself how my body seemed to just melt against him. How I couldn't seem to find the strength I needed to say no. But I had to say no before things got out of hand. I had to make sure I was strong around him and not let my guard down, since Katie was so sure that he would just take me to bed and toss me aside afterward.

Somehow ungluing my lips from his. "Ben, I really think we should get inside," I whispered.

He released me and rubbed one hand over his hair, giving me a wicked smile with a glow of desire in his eyes.

"Okay, sure." His voice said full with passion. "But, I was thinking, you had mentioned that anywhere would be fine with you. So actually, instead of the jazz club, I would rather we go to my apartment." He paused again, looking in my eyes, this time not smiling. And as I looked at him out of my head with excitement of his suggestion, I had to hold my stomach to keep from shouting, yes. But I only looked at him without saying a word as he continued. "Paulene, I'll understand if you would prefer not to. I just figured we could relax and have a glass of wine."

With my eyes melting in his, I nodded. "Sure, I would love to see your place."

He started his engine and the drive to his apartment was mostly in silence as Ben sort of glanced over at me off and on and I sort of looked out of the window. I was staring out at the city, bracing my back against the seat, holding my excitement inside. Finally we were at his building. He pulled into his parking garage and turned off the engine. My nerves seemed to tighten more and more with anticipation of what awaited us during the evening. As we stepped out of his car and walked through the garage to enter his building, I was in a daze. I was conscious only of the comforting feel of his hand wrapped around mine. I felt like I was wide-awake in a dream that I didn't want to end. I wasn't fully aware of the sirens from an ambulance in a distance, or the airplane overhead, or the noises from running cars on the street, or the hello from the doorman dressed in all black that opened the door for us, or the click of our footsteps across the exquisite marble floor on the way to the elevator. I snapped out of my trance when he spoke to the three people that were already in the elevator.

"34th floor," he said and squeezed my hand gently.

When we stepped off the elevator, it seemed we walked forever to reach his apartment at the end of the hallway. The beautiful floral cranberry colored carpeting went on and on with expensive looking paintings on either side of the hall. My stomach flipped over excitedly when he unlocked his apartment door and held out his arm for me to step inside. Suddenly my feet felt like they weighed a ton as I stepped inside and stood in the foyer. He stepped in right behind me and flipped on the lights as I stepped on inside of his large apartment.

It was spacious, beautifully and elegantly furnished. The walls of the living room were sandal wood beige. The plush thick carpet on the floor was a deep cedar green color. The long draperies at his living room window were striking to the room in a shade of green identical to his carpet. Two tiebacks parted the draperies, revealing a pale yellow sheer, which gave the room a touch of romance. An assortment of four expensive paintings hung over his beige leather sofa and a huge round solid oak coffee table with a glass top sat in front of the sofa. A bright bouquet of yellow, white and green silk flowers sat gracefully on his coffee table. There were two large chairs in stripes of cedar green and pale yellow plaid on either side of the fireplace. Built-in bookshelves covered a portion of one wall with a built-in stereo and bar occupying the remaining portion of the wall. The dining room and kitchen area was large as well and neatly furnished with pale green appliances and a round solid oak dinette set which seated six. The dinette set was finished off with six cedar green plate mats and matching napkins inside of napkin rings. The dinning area and the kitchen looked out onto a balcony from which you could see a lavish view overlooking the vast blue sparkling waters of Lake Michigan.

When I heard the soft music coming from his stereo, playing the romantic song by Barry White *"I Can't Get Enough of Your Love,"* I turned from the breathtaking scenery of the fabulous view from his 34th floor apartment.

"What will it be," he asked, holding a silver tray of four glasses or wine. "I wasn't sure what you would like so I decided to bring out a glass of everything I have. And if you don't like any of this I can run out and get more." He winked, and then placed the tray on the coffee table.

"Okay, what do you have over here?" I asked all smiles.

He pointed to the glass of deep red wine. "This is blackberry Merlot. Give it a sip."

My hand was sturdy when I picked up the delicate glass and brought it up to my lips. I took a sip and frowned. "Not this one. Too bitter." I grinned, placing the glass back on the tray.

"Okay, not to worry. We got more over here," he said, laughingly. "Here you are. Try this one." He suggested, passing me the glass of rose tinted wine.

"Okay." I smiled and lifted the glass to my lips. "Not bad, but not to good either." I looked in his eyes and smiled, slightly shaking my head.

He touched the side of my face and smiled. "You are a tough lady to please…"

Before I could reply, he held out both hands. "Just kidding." He smiled, passing the glass with the bubbles on top. "Here you are. Try the champagne?"

"Champagne?" I grinned, reaching for the glass. "Now this should taste good." I took a sip and smiled. "I'll keep this one."

A big smile spread across his handsome face as he took a deep breath. "Okay, something the lady likes," he said in a teasing manner, laughing.

Now that I had my drink in hand, suddenly excitement flooded my stomach as it dawned on me that I was alone with my dream man.

He touched the side of my face as he looked into my eyes as if he was amazed with what he could see staring back at him. "I'm glad you're here," he said.

"I'm glad to be here." I looked at him as I held my champagne glass with both hands.

He took the second glass of champagne off the tray and raised it in a toast to me.

"I'm glad you changed your mind and decided not to go home this weekend."

"So am I." I smiled and then took a sip of my drink.

"Everything is decorated really nice. But this is just a temporary…?"

He cut me off. "Yes." And stretched out one arm. "This is my temporary home away from home. None of these furnishings belong to me. All the apartments here come completely furnished."

"Furnished or not, it suits you and it's fabulous."

He smiled. "Thank you, Paulene. I'm glad you like it."

"Of course." I nodded, looking at the place. "I'm sure anyone would."

Being alone with him in his apartment, I didn't feel quite as at ease as I had felt in the park earlier. The complete privacy made me feel over anxious. And there was a moment of awkward silence. More out of embarrassment than curiosity as I wandered across the room to look at the paintings. I had taken the last drop of my champagne when Ben was standing beside me pouring more sparkling liquid into my glass. I watched as the bubbles danced, then looked up at him. Only a few weeks ago I had been sure I would never see him again. If this was a dream, I didn't want to ever see the light of day.

Taking the glass from my hand, he placed it back on the coffee table and pulled me in his arms in a tender embrace—holding me tightly, yet gently. He slowly, never taking his eyes off of mine, brought his mouth down on mine and kissed me gently on the outside of my lips, and just when I thought I would melt through the floor, he wrapped his arms around me even tighter and started kissing the side of my neck, my throat, and then he pulled away and smiled down at me.

He inhaled sharply. "You are so beautiful," he whispered in a low, sensuous voice, smoothing my hair back off my face. He held his hands on both of my ears, slowly lowering his mouth back on mine, kissing my lips tenderly and at ease. When he sensed my willing response, he kissed me more urgently. Being in his arms felt right.

"Oh, Ben," I moan in delight as he kissed me as if he needed my kisses to breathe.

Seconds later he pulled away from my lips smiling, taking my hand, leading me over to the long sofa. We took a seat and he reached out and grabbed our wine glasses from the coffee table, handing me mine. We sipped our wine and looked into each other eyes. No words seemed necessary. All I wanted was to be near him. Being with him felt like my heart had reached that perfect place. A place my heart had searched for all my life. A place so comforting and so secure that it could surrender itself to love.

After we finished our drinks, Ben clicked on his big screen TV. We were both relaxing, sitting back on the sofa with his left arm around my shoulder. Within seconds he had covered my lips with his as all my strength just somehow melted away. I fell back on the arm of the sofa, stretched my arms around his back, totally lost in his arms as he swept me up in his arms and headed toward his bedroom.

He kept walking toward his big queen size bed until I said convincingly. "Please! Put me down."

In the middle of the room, he slowly let me down and stood back with his eyes ablaze and much confusion on his face.

"What's the matter? Paulene? I feel you want me as much as I want you."

"You're right. I do want to be with you, Ben," I said as we stood there in the middle of the floor just a couple yards away from each other. My heart was racing and I couldn't look in his eyes.

My desire and need for him was overwhelming. I wanted him with every breath I took, but how could I make love with him? I didn't even know him yet and he didn't know me. I didn't want my first time to be just a one nightstand.

Before my eyes lowered to cover my expression, I glanced up at his face and noticed a sparkle in his sexy eyes, and a warm feeling dashed through my stomach. The deep passion and desire that spoke through his eyes made me weak in the knees for him as I did all I could to keep from trembling before his eyes, to keep from throwing myself at him. I knew he wanted to grab me in his arms again just as desperate as I wanted him to grab me in his arms. I wanted him to pull off everything I was wearing piece by piece and adore and kiss my skin as he pulled off my clothing. After he had stripped me naked, I wanted him to make passionate love to me for hours and hours and yet more hours. I loved him with all my heart and soul and as I finally gazed into his dreamy eyes, my heart was screaming for him to grab me in his arms again, but my mouth betrayed me as I looked at him and shook my head.

"I think I should leave, Ben," I said anxiously, using all the strength I had to force those words out of my mouth.

My hands-off behavior seemed to have had him puzzled to the point that he probably wanted to just shake some answers out of me.

"What's the matter, Paulene?" he asked.

"I don't know. I guess I'm just nervous, Ben," I mumbled sadly.

"You are nervous?" he asked and paused in my eyes. "Paulene, you don't have to be nervous with me, ever," he said, holding out his arms to me.

"Come here," he said in a sensuous whisper as he stepped just inches from me. He wrapped me up in his arms and I thought my heart would explode from the sheer sweet sensation of being next to him.

"It will be okay," he said, holding me tighter and tighter next to him as a tingling sensation erupted throughout me as I felt his excitement and the sound of his heart racing in his chest.

He lifted my face with one hand and cupped the back of my neck in his palm as he passionately kissed me. He took his free hand and pulled the satin peach-colored ribbon from my long flowing hair and smoothed it down my back and shoulders. I felt sexy in my new soft, flowing peach-colored dress that was buttoned down the front and was being held together by only eight large buttons, and I inhaled deeply as he unbuttoned the second button. By the time he unbuttoned the third one, I knew that was it, and I wouldn't have the strength to push him away this time. He slipped both hands inside of the open top portion of my dress and caressed my bosom and I thought I would scream from the pleasure of his hands touching me.

He pulled away, then gripped my shoulders tenderly and sought my lips with burning passion, kissing me deep as if he needed my kisses to breathe. He softly whispered in my ear. "Please don't push me away."

How could I stop him? My need to be with him seemed as strong as my desire to breathe, but I had to stop him. I wasn't ready for that step. I just wanted to be with him and get to know him better. I didn't want to be used. I pulled away from his embrace, but he pulled me back in his arms and kissed me once more. We were standing in his room kissing some more and I didn't have the strength to stop him. My level-headedness couldn't seem to overshadow my great want and need for him. I was like a feather in his wonderful arms as we kissed. And then suddenly the entire front of my dress was open. He slid it from my shoulders to the plush thick-carpeted floor. There I stood in my white lace slip.

"Paulene," he whispered, curving one arm around my waist and kissing me against my neck. His voice was sending tremors racing through me. "You don't know what it does to me, to hold you this way. Do you want me as much as I want you?"

Hypnotized by his voice and his electrifying touch, I slipped my arms about his neck. I knew I had surrendered my heart to love.

"Yes, Ben," I whispered, unable to stop myself. "I want you," I said breathless, holding tightly to him with my face against his shoulder.

"I want you more," he said as his mouth covered mine. "Paulene, let me place you on the bed, where I can see all of your incredible beauty. I want to lie next to you and never stop holding you," he whispered.

When I did not refuse, he swept me up in his arms again and placed me on his bed. Lying beside me with his face close to mine, I looked at him, my hands unconsciously tracing up and down his left arm.

"Paulene, you are perfect," he whispered the words filled with passion. "I have been lying awake in bed, going out of my head, thinking of this moment."

Hearing him say that, suddenly, I realized I couldn't let him. Not yet, maybe not ever. It dawned on me why I had pushed him away the first time. I was probably just another body to him.

"Ben, I can't. Please let me up," I uttered sadly as I pushed both hands against his hard chest.

"Paulene, what's the matter?" Ben asked in a stiff, but calm voice, rolling off of me to sat on the side of the bed. Deep disappointment showed in his eyes.

"I just can't, Ben," I mumbled, feeling miserably, still laying there on my back as he looked at me.

My answer probably wasn't the answer he expected. But no matter how much I wanted to, I couldn't go all the way with him when it was apparent that my body was all that he wanted from me.

There were tears falling down my cheeks. Ben automatically reached over to wiped them away with his fingers as his sparkling eyes, full of disappointment, searched my face. "I thought it was something that we had both agreed that we both wanted. Was it something I said or something I did?" he asked humbly.

Shaking my head, looking in his eyes as my insides still ached for his touch. I touched his arm softly.

"It was nothing you said or did," I said, getting control of myself, sitting on the edge of the bed beside him. "I'm just sorry."

"You're sorry?" He rubbed the back of his neck and inhaled sharply. "You have nothing to be sorry about. But if I'm wrong tell me, but I was under the impression that we were both enjoying each other. You even said you wanted me, otherwise, I would have never pushed it this far." He touched my cheek.

Feeling awkward suddenly, I stood to my feet and walked over to his bedroom window. Leaning both hands on his windowsill, I glanced around and watched as he stood to his feet and leaned his back against his dresser with his arms folded. He was looking directly at me with deep desire still pouring from his eyes. I turned back to the window and pulled the curtains back, staring out into the darkness trying to catch my breath as my heart kept racing for his touch. A few moments later, I walked back across the room and dropped down heavily on the edge of his bed, covering my face with both hands.

"I'm having the time of my life being with you, Ben." I paused. "But, I'm just not ready for this," I uttered softly and somewhat shyly.

He stood back in silence for a second, and then walked over and took a seat on the bed beside me and gently rubbed my shoulder. He didn't say a word. Feeling suddenly embarrassed, I hopped up and rushed to his bathroom.

Chapter Eighteen

When I stepped out of his bathroom, Ben was sitting on the small green sofa in the corner of his bedroom. The half bottle of champagne and two fresh glasses sat on the oval mahogany coffee table in front of him. He had his head propped against a bright yellow throw pillow and his bare feet propped up on the coffee table. He beckoned for me and patted the cushions next to him. Glancing about the room, I noticed that it was decorated with the same colors as the rest of his apartment. But his bedroom contained light greens instead of dark greens. Long spring green curtains hung from his two bedroom windows with a matching comforter and shams. Directly over his bed was a huge 30X30 painting of a rain forest that consisted of light and dark greens and bright yellows. His bed, dresser, chest and two nightstands were made of deep dark mahogany wood.

As I headed across the huge bedroom to where he was seated, he looked quite handsome sitting there and I wanted to fall in his arms, but suddenly halfway across the room, I felt shy When it dawned on me that I was wearing only my ankle-length white slip. Quickly I glanced about the room for my dress and I noticed it over by the side of the bed, almost under the bed. Anxiously, I rushed to the garment, reached down and picked it up off the carpet.

"You don't have to put that back on right this minute, you know?" He said in a sexy manner. "You look lovely in what you're wearing." He winked.

I looked down at my slip and then held out both arms. "Which is barely nothing."

"What's wrong with nothing?" He teased.

"Ben." I stared at him.

"I'm kidding, okay? I'm just trying to let you know I think you look just perfect in what you're wearing, you know?" He said with desire in his voice.

Looking straight at him I answered softly, "I think I should leave, Ben."

My words caught him off balance it seemed and he hopped right off the sofa and walked over to me where I stood with my back leaned against his dresser.

"I'm sorry I made that comment. I was just teasing."

I nodded. "I know, but I should probably head home."

"Why do you want to leave his early?" he asked with anxious eyes.

Taking a deep breath, I said, "I just think I should. I have had quite a bit to drink."

"You are fine, Miss Paulene Dawson." He grinned. "The night is young and we're just talking and having a few drinks, getting to know each other better." He paused with an anxious look in his eyes. "You don't really want to leave, do you?"

"Not really, but I feel I should."

"Ok. You feel you should. But it's still early." He stressed.

"Maybe, you're right. It is still early." I hit his shoulder in a playful way. "Now do me a favor and turn your back while I put my dress back on."

"Turn my back? Why do you want me to turn my back?" He stared me up and down with longing in his eyes. "What do you think I'm going to see?" He ginned. "You are just going to take that dress and slip it back on over your slip, right?"

"Right, right, right, but just turn your back anyway," I stood in front of him, my eyes glued to his, and from the look of deep desire in his eyes it seemed as if it took all his strength not to try to get me in his bed again. He took a deep breath and nodded.

He turned his back, stared up at the winter white ceiling and patted his foot on the thick cedar green carpet, laughing as if he was enjoying me. "Miss Paulene Dawson, you are something. You got all your clothes on basically, but I still got to turn my back before you can put on another layer," he said teasingly.

As he stood with his back to me, I quickly slipped back into my dress. When I was finished, I tapped him on the shoulders. He turned around, smiling, and then took both hands and smoothed my hair off my face. He brought his face down to mine and kissed me achingly for a second. After the kiss, he stepped across the room and got the bottle of champagne and two glasses, placing them on the nightstand. He poured a glass for each of us, and then held out his hand and I went to him.

We sat on the edge of the bed and sipped on our bubbling drink. Suddenly I became nervous realizing I was sitting on his bed beside him, yet again. But I sipped once more, and then drained the glass. "Ben, I got to admit that this champagne is delicious. It's nothing like those ten dollar bottles like Aunt Haddie used to buy," I said, handing him my glass to be refilled.

The champagne began to work its way to my head, and I felt more confident and at ease as we sat beside each other making easy conversation in low voices like we had in the park. So what if I had acted like a scared teenager and said no to him? That was my right. But suddenly he seemed more cool and reserved not saying as much as if he had lost a bit of the interest that he was pouring on me before. I was wondering if he was going to react as Katie had predicted and send me walking since I had turned him down. But as we sat there talking, he kept smiling at me. He hadn't given me a brush-off and sent me home after saying no to him.

"More champagne?" I said, smiling, holding my glass out to him.

He grinned. "If the lady wants champagne, the lady gets champagne. But you know this bubbly isn't diet coke? You could wake up with your head feeling like a balloon and your stomach feeling like a train wreck."

"I wouldn't care if it was diet coke. I happen to be very fond of diet coke, and even more fond of your expensive sweet champagne."

With trembling, nervous hands, I lifted the drink to my lips and only took one sip before I stood to my feet and then took his hand in mine. I lead him out of the bedroom, through the kitchen and dinning room to his living room where we sat closely. He pulled me in his arms and held me close. I responded eagerly, allowing him to kiss me without restraint as he ran his hands along my arms and shoulders pressing me to him. Then suddenly I felt I shouldn't let him touch me and I pushed him away thinking he was trying to take me to bed. Seconds later we had fallen asleep in each other's arm.

Chapter Nineteen

My eyes blinked opened and I was startled to find that I had spent the night at Ben's apartment. I was laying flat on my back on his living room sofa with a thin blue sheet over me. I was feeling slightly not here or there. My head was pounding and the bright morning sun pouring through his living room window painfully bothered my eyes. I had poured down too many glasses of his expensive sparkling champagne last night. What a foolish thing to have done. I was sure I had made a complete fool out of myself. Getting drunk on our first real date was no way to impress him. How would I ever be able to face him, much less explain why I drank so much? When it dawned on me that he was no longer on the sofa with me, I grabbed my face and shook my head, feeling even more foolish.

"Good morning. Did you rest okay?" he asked, stepping into the room. Now standing over me, I could see there was nothing disappointing in his voice or eyes. In fact, if anything it was a voice that sounded content. But how could he be content? I had said no and pushed him away all night? Content or not, still, I couldn't look at him.

I quickly covered my face with both hands. "Ben, don't look at me. I must look awful cause I sure do feel awful." I peeped through my hands at him standing there.

"What are you hiding that beautiful face of yours for?" He smiled.

"Because I can't believe I lost my senses."

He kept smiling. "Believe me, you lost nothing."

"Nothing but my mind."

"It was a fantastic evening, wouldn't you agree?"

I nodded. "Yes, it was nice. But I can't believe I had all that champagne."

"I know how it looks, but we just fell asleep." He smiled.

"But I ended up staying all night here and sleeping in your clothes." My hands left my face and grabbed my head.

"Are you okay?" He stood there smiling with his arms folded.

"No, I'm not okay. I feel lousy about my behavior from last night."

"You feel lousy about your behavior?" He bend over me looking straight in my face, smiling. "Believe me, you have nothing to feel lousy about."

"Yes I do. I was raised to be a lady at all times."

"Well, you are still on track."

"How can I be on track when I'm lying here on your sofa—wearing your clothes."

He held out both arms. "They look better on you, than they ever have on me." He teased.

"Don't tease me right now."

"Come on, Paulene. Lighten up. We both had a bit too much to drink and fell asleep on my sofa. What's the harm in that?"

"The harm is that I should have kept my head and stayed a lady."

He shook his head and smiled. "I don't get you. You did stay a lady. Any more of a lady and you would have been Mother Teresa." He teased.

"Ben I'm serious."

"I believe you are serious." He held out both arms. "I'm serious too when I say, you couldn't be anything but a lady. Take it from someone who had his share of non-ladies."

"Is that statement suppose to make me feel better, Ben?"

"Sorry, wrong choice of words. But you get my point."

"After a long silence, he asked.

"Can I get you a glass of orange juice or coffee?"

My head nodded up and down as I searched his face to see if I could see anything of last night in his eyes. His eyes revealed nothing. I asked softly, "I had too much to drink and I suppose I said a lot of things last night that I shouldn't have said or acted in some way that I shouldn't have acted?"

"Not that I can remember," he said seriously with no smile to his face.

"It was my first time having that much too drink. Honestly, Ben. I hope you know I've never been that way before," I said in a low voice. "I don't want you to think I hit the bottle like that all the time.

He shook his head and smiled. "You're kidding, right? You don't actually think I would think that of you, do you? No way would I think that."

When he left the room and headed to his spacious, cozy kitchen for the juice, I sat up too quickly. I was feeling as if my head was pounding from all four corners, like it was going to explode. I inched myself to the edge of the sofa and stood unsteadily at first. After a second I was okay. I took a deep breath, and then walked to the bathroom, where I used an extra toothbrush that Ben had laid out on the vanity for me. After brushing my teeth with Ben's ultra brite toothpaste, I slowly got out of the clothes I was wearing. A soothing shower would make me feel better, but I didn't have the time, the strength or the mind to blow dry my hair, so I wrapped it in a bath towel, then stepped into the shower, letting the soothing warm water pour against me.

Turning the shower knobs off reluctantly and reaching for a towel, I dried myself off slowly, and dressed into my yesterday clothes just as slowly. Doing things in slow motion kept my head from causing me more agony. I pulled the towel from my hair and came out of the bathroom looking more refreshed and awake, but my stomach was still boiling and my head was still pounding from all the champagne.

He was standing there waiting with two tall glasses of red something in his hand.

"Here you are," he said, passing me one of the drinks. "I think you'll like this. It's one of my mother's recipes."

"Oh, yeah." I smiled up at him, reaching for the glass. "Your mother's recipe? A homemade breakfast drink?"

"Fresh ingredients from scratch." He smiled, nodding.

"All fresh ingredients from scratch?" I asked and paused for a second.

"I'm quite impressed. Cause that means you took the time to put this drink together, all from scratch, while I was in the bathroom?"

"You got it." He took a sip from his drink and winked at me. "Did you hear all the noise I was making with the blender and the ice crusher?"

I shook my head, holding the tall, crushed iced drink up to my nose, admiring the deep red color and the fruity scent. "I couldn't hear anything in the shower."

"I'm pretty sure you will like it. Come on and taste it." He took another sip of his. "Yeah" He held the half empty glass out and looked at it. "This is the drink my Mom used to serve for breakfast after one of their big parties." He grinned. "It always did the trick to soothe the stomach." He smiled. "In other words. It's the perfect hangover remedy."

With slightly nervous hands, holding the glass with both hands, I took a sip.

"This is good," I said, taking another bigger sip.

I held the glass out and looked at it, and then glanced back at him. "What kind of drink is this? It taste like…I don't know what it taste like, but it's good."

"It's strawberry-watermelon with a hint of cherries. I'm glad you like it." He stood there smiling, looking perfect in the morning with his eyes glued to my face.

"So I take it, you approve of my mother's after party breakfast drink?" He reached out and smoothed one long curl out of my face, looking in my eyes admiringly.

"Yes, Ben, I do." I took another sip. "I want this recipe."

We sat on the sofa side by side sipping on the fruity drink.

"Did anyone ever tell you that you look like an angel?" He touched my hand.

"Oh…a few times," I answered, teasingly.

"I can believe that," he answered seriously.

"Ben, I was just kidding."

"Are you sure," he teased.

Then suddenly, my mind focused back to the little kid, Bobby Harris that I had met in the park who gave me the greatest compliment of calling me an angel. But to me, he was the angel. He had in some way touched my heart, but I had a feeling that I would never see him again.

"Well, did they?" he asked with a serious tone.

"Yes, once," I mumbled sadly.

"Oh, yeah, who?" He grinned, holding up one finger. "I bet I can guess."

"I doubt that."

"You doubt that? Well, doubt no more." He smiled. "I'm sure it was some male, fascinated with your good looks and your sweet nature."

I nodded. "It was a male. A little boy," I quickly laughingly replied.

"A little boy?" he asked.

"Yes, a little boy. That little kid I was telling you about that sold me the banana ice cream in the park." I looked at him with serious eyes.

"Oh, yeah." He nodded. That little kid?"

"Yeah, I thought he was pretty super. Out there all by himself pushing that cart in the hot sun trying to make himself a few dollars," I said in Ben's eyes.

"He'll grow up not being afraid of hard work that's for sure." Ben paused. "In about twenty or thirty years, he's probably own his own company," Ben predicted.

"That's a nice thought." I smiled. "Because I don't know if you noticed when he sold you the ice cream, but I noticed his torn clothes and shoes. I gave him twenty dollars the day I met him."

He grinned. "You did? I gave him ten."

"Good hearts think alike." I touched Ben's hand. "Anyway, Ben there was something about the way he called me an angel. Something inside of me tells me that he really meant it." I paused. "When he said it, chill went up and down my spine."

"Of course he meant it. Why would that amaze you to think he meant it?" He touched the side of my face with the back of his palm and stroke it a couple of times. "I mean it to." He wrapped his finger around one of my curls and sort of focused on the hair wrapped around his finger. "If I could paint or draw, and had to come up with the vision of an angel, it would be your face," he said as his eyes melted into mine. He took the glass from my hand and placed it next to his on the coffee table. "You look like someone I have seen in my dreams, but could never reach."

He took my hand and lifted it to his lips. Then a second later he leaned my head over on the arm of the sofa and wrapped his arms around me, kissing me passionately. I felt myself melting into him listening to his heartbeat.

Chapter Twenty

Later that morning, while Ben was in his bedroom dressing, I sat on his sofa and thought of my life and all the stress I had experienced just a few weeks earlier. My weekends had been spent in the worst sort of emotional turmoil. I had been desperate, walking through Lincoln Park like some lost soul looking for a place to call home. And I would still be walking around wondering what if and waiting and hoping for Ben to call me, if I hadn't pushed aside what Aunt Haddie had once told me. If I hadn't taken a chance, throwing tradition out of the window, to follow my heart. I would never have been in Ben's life. Being with him now was all credited to the bold initiative I took by stopping at his work place. Now I felt content and incredibly excited to be in his company.

Still sitting on his sofa some minutes later, while Ben continued dressing, I figured I would head into his guest bathroom and get myself together. While I was in his bathroom looking at myself in the floor length mirror against the bathroom's door, I wondered how I was going to walk into the Westin Hotel where I lived wearing the same dress that I had left there in yesterday. Even though I had good odds in my favor that no one would notice or pay my attire any attention, there was always a chance that I would be noticed. And if that were to happen, everyone would know I had been out all night. And of course, they would get the wrong idea.

Ben stepped out of his bedroom, smiling. "Are you ready?" he asked.

"Not really," I mumbled sadly.

He stared with confused eyes. "What's the matter?"

"Ben, you have to give me something to wear back to my room. I can't walk into that hotel wearing what I left there in. Everybody will know I didn't sleep in my own bed last night. I live there and I don't want people getting the wrong idea. Especially Miss Becky at the front desk. She likes to gossip."

He grinned and waved his hand. "Paulene, don't worry about what those people at the Westin Hotel thinks." He looked me up and down. "You look beautiful."

"Ben, Miss Becky doesn't care how pretty I am. She just likes to talk."

"So let her talk." He replied.

"I just don't want her talking about me."

"I'm sure she probably will not."

"Ben, you don't know Miss Becky. She is sweet. But she is very into other folks' business. And believe me, if I walk in there wearing the same dress, I'll hear about it again."

"Okay, so you did have on the same dress last night, who is to say you didn't stay at a relatives or whatever?" He stressed. "Just don't let that bother you."

Ignoring what he said as if he didn't even say it, I asked. "Seriously, Ben do you have a pair of shorts and a pullover shirt or something I can put on?"

Noticing the seriousness in my eyes, he didn't change a word. "Sure, no problem. Wait here and I'll grab something for you." He rushed to his bedroom.

He returned moments later with a pair of white shorts and a white T-shirt. He handed them to me. "T-shirt will look okay on you, but I don't know about those shorts. You are so tiny." He smiled.

"Thank you, this will work out just fine." I smiled, feeling more at ease now that I had something to wear back to the hotel. I took the clothes and rushed to his guest bathroom to change.

Shaking my head as I stared at the lousy results. The shirt wasn't too bad on me, but the over sized shorts made my legs look like they were pencil sticks. Yet, still wearing his shorts and top was a safer bet than walking in the hotel with yesterday's clothes. Feeling awkward, I slowly stepped out of the bathroom and went back to the living room where Ben was waiting. He passed me a J.C. Penney's shopping bag to place my dress into, but he seemed in such a hurry to get me home that he didn't even notice how his clothes looked on me until we stood in front of the elevator. I wondered if his rushing was due to the fact that he was through with me, since I hadn't given in and shared his bed.

"I guess my shorts are a little big on you?" He grinned.

"Yeah, they are." I grinned. "But, I could hardly go back to my hotel room wearing what I left there in. I didn't want that woman at the front desk thinking naughty thoughts of me." I pulled up the elastic waist of the shorts.

"Naughty thoughts of you? I don't think so." He shook his head.

"See, Ben, that's one of the problems of living in a hotel. Everybody notices you. They want to know who you are coming and going with."

He was still grinning. "Beautiful woman, this is not Montgomery, Alabama. People here are too busy trying to get ahead to worry about somebody's attire, "he said seriously. "Believe me." He grinned. "In this big city, people are too busy and caught up in this rat race to nosey around in other people's affairs that much."

"Maybe you are right. But they are not too busy at the Westin to nosy into your affairs," I quickly replied.

"At least Miss Becky isn't too busy."

"I'm not sure about Miss Becky, But I think you could have walked right in that front lobby wearing your own clothes and nobody would have really paid you any attention," he said. "No let me reword that. Everybody would have noticed you, but not your clothes." He winked at me.

"I would have tried to convince you to wear your dress back to the hotel." He touched my nose in a playful way. "But I don't know what good it would have done, because if you're anything like my mother, once you make up your mind about something that's it." He leaned over and kissed my forehead.

"I know what you are saying, Ben, how I shouldn't worry about what other people may think or say about me, but I do. That's how I am," I explained.

"I know." He smiled with an understanding look in his eyes. "By-the-way, did I tell you how desirable you look in that outfit you're wearing?" He teased.

"Don't tease me about your clothes I'm wearing. I already feel awkward enough."

"Who said I'm teasing. You could be wrapped in newspaper and still look good."

"You really think so?" I blushed as we stepped into the elevator.

He answered by lifting my hand and kissing it. He was just releasing my hand when the doors opened. We took the elevator down to the first floor and then walked out of the back lobby to the garage across the street and Ben helped me into his silver Jaguar.

"I meant to tell you how much I like your car, Ben. This is about the nicest car I have ever seen," I said as he stood there holding the passenger's door open.

I took a seat inside his car and he closed the door. And a proud smile curved his face and a look of admiration showed in his eyes for his car. "Yes, these are my wheels." He patted the hood, smiling. "That I hardly get a chance to drive in this city. It's just easier to call or flag a taxicab instead or fighting with the traffic in this city." He opened the driver's door and got in, looking at me smiling.

Riding in Ben's car felt smooth and comfortable. A far difference from how it felt sitting in my father's old black truck or Aunt Haddie's old blue Plymouth. Before I knew it, Ben was stopping at the curb in front of the hotel and turning off the motor. He stepped out and paid the valet guy, then escorted me out of the car.

When we stepped into the lobby of the hotel and walked past the front desk, I glanced at the customer service counter and Ben had been right. Miss Becky didn't even notice us. She was too busy helping the hotel guests.

When Ben and I stepped on the elevator to go up to my floor, something inside of me told me that he wasn't going to visit me. He seemed anxious about something as if something else was on his mind and that he couldn't wait to drop me off.

In front of my door, he leaned over and kissed me on the lips, then stared in my eyes for a second. "I can't do this. I can't think when I look in your eyes." He smiled, looked away and glanced at his Rolex watch. "I'll call you," he said.

"Okay," I nodded. "I'll wash your clothes and give them back to you when I see you again, okay?" I smiled.

He turned and walked quickly toward the elevator, shaking his head. Before he reached the elevator, he turned around and threw he a kiss. "I'll call you."

My ears heard him, but my heart didn't believe him. I felt he was just saying that to be polite and as I unlocked the door and stepped into my hotel room, a wave of loneliness swept over me. It was as though I had suddenly been set adrift in an unfamiliar world.

My face turned red with anxiousness as I thought I would never get to see him again. I threw the shopping bag, my purse and shoes across the room. And then I pulled off Ben's shorts and shirt and sat on the bed blowing my nose and wiping my eyes. I felt incredibly alone. Being in love was like a roller coaster ride. Your emotions are up and down. When you're happy nothing can top it, but when you're sad, nothing can feel worst.

I reached over, grabbed the phone from the nightstand and placed it in my lap. My fingers nervously dialed my home number.

"It's me, Aunt Haddie," I mumbled.

"Paulene, I'm so glad you called." She laughed, pleased to hear from me, then she paused. "Are you okay? Is everything all right?" she asked.

"I'm fine. I just miss you and Dad so much Aunt Haddie."

"We miss you also, sweetheart." She paused. "Do you have a cold?"

"No, I'm fine. I haven't been sick with a cold since I have been here."

"Well, that's good. But, you sure sound like you do. Are you feeling okay?"

"Aunt Haddie, I just said I'm doing fine. How are you and Dad doing?"

"We are both doing just fine."

"Could you and Dad come to Chicago for a few days?"

"Paulene, you know I'm not one for big cities." She paused. "But, I guess a few days up that way couldn't hurt. But we can't come anyway. Your father hurt his leg when he tripped in the chicken coop last week. His leg is going to be fine. But he just isn't up to a trip right now."

"I see, well, then I think maybe I'll come home next weekend. I want to see you and Dad. I'm sick of this place, Aunt Haddie."

There was a silent moment. "Paulene, are you sure you are all right?"

"I'm sure. Just a little homesick, that's all."

"Well, Doug and I will be there to pick you up when your train pulls into the station. Just make sure to let us know when you're coming."

"I will."

"We'll need to know what time your train is scheduled to arrive."

"I know. I'll let you know." I paused, and then asked. "Is Dad there?"

"He's here, but he's outside fooling around with that old truck of his. You want me to get him to the phone?"

"No, that's okay. Tell him I said hello. And Aunt Haddie…I love you."

After hanging up I sat with the phone in my lap with my hand on the receiver. I couldn't shake the rotten feeling I had, thinking Ben wouldn't call me again. He must have thought I was an old-fashioned little girl instead of a grown woman from the way I chickened out on our romantic evening. I protested like a frightened child when he started unbuttoning my dress. The thought of him thinking less of me made my flesh crawl. I went into the bathroom, let the water run in the tub and lathered myself with the sweet scent of *Wind Song* perfume soap. Then I lay back in the soothing bubbles wondering if Ben had even given me a thought.

After my bubble bath and going stir crazy for a few hours thinking of Ben, I dressed for dinner. And the moment I hung up after talking to Katie, I took up my purse and headed out of my hotel room to meet her. I locked the door and was no more than a few feet down the hall when I heard my phone. I hesitated for a moment and thought of rushing back to my room to answer it, but I kept walking toward the elevator. The call would have hung up by the time I reached the phone anyway. Standing at the elevator, a smile came to my face and a ray of hope came to my heart when it dawned on me that the caller could have been Ben. The only other possibility was Katie, and I was on my way to meet her for dinner. And if it was him calling, I hate I had missed his call, but I had to face the facts. If he really wasn't just about getting me in his bed and was interested in seeing me again, he would call again.

Chapter Twenty-One

When I met Katie at the Signature Room, she had gotten a table for us and for once, I had kept her waiting. She didn't seem bothered by my tardiness as she was sitting there all smiles.

"You look cute," she said, looking me up and down admiring the blue pantsuit I was wearing.

As I took a seat at the small round table, she held up one finger to get the waiter attention. She ordered us both a glass of white wine and before I could take one sip of my drink she noticed a tear that had rolled from my right eye.

"Oh, no, what's going on now? I thought you would be on top of the world smiling from ear to ear. Didn't you have a date with Ben last night?"

"Yes, I did have a date with him, which will probably be my last." I sipped my wine.

"What happened?" She downed half of her wine. "Did he turn out to be the dog I said he was just like the rest of these walking sluts? Did you at least get a dinner out of the man before you dropped your skirt for him?" she asked, assured I had slept with him.

"Katie, you were right. He wanted sex. Our first romantic time alone and he only wanted to get me in his bed. He claimed he wanted to get to know me, but he seemed more interested in just getting to know me under his sheets first."

She shook her head, smiling. "And that surprises you, Paulene?

Did you listen to anything I was trying to tell you about Ben Drake? Anything at all?"

"Well, yeah, but I'm so in love with him, Katie. I have never felt this wonderful before in my life. You know that. I just want to be with him. I miss him already. He dropped me off this morning and I haven't heard a word from him since."

"This morning?" She lifted an eyebrow, staring hard. "I was teasing when I said you dropped your skirt for him? Don't tell me you did?" She finished off her glass of wine.

"Hold on, Katie. Yes, I stayed all night with him, alright." I sipped my wine, trying to block out some of the disgust I felt for myself for having too much to drink at his apartment. "But there's no need to look at me like that."

"Are you sure? All night alone with Ben Drake?"

"Yes, all night alone with him. But I'm telling you nothing happened."

"You are a grown woman. If you slept with the man, that's your business."

"If it's my business, why are you looking at me like that?"

I shook my head and stared at her for a moment and then leaned in toward her a bit. Then she said, "I guess I was hoping you wouldn't be the fool I had once been."

"I guess everything boils down to you and that guy!"

"What guy?" She quickly snapped.

"Do you need to ask?" I shook my head. "The one you can't forget!"

"Oh." She smiled and nodded. "I think you hit the nail on the head," she said with distant eyes as if she was remembering something that she lost.

"But Serious, Katie." I held up both hands. "Nothing happened."

"Is it because you didn't want it to happen?"

I shook my head. "No."

"So you did want it to happen?"

I nodded. "Yes."

"So, why didn't it? I'm sure Ben wasn't a boyscout with his hands to himself."

"I didn't have the nerve to sleep with him. I wanted to. I really wanted to, but I don't want to be just another woman that he sleeps with." I paused, taking another sip of wine. "I want to be that special woman in his life," I said as another teardrop sneaked down my face.

At that moment, the short, slender waiter stepped over to take our orders. I ordered a small garden salad with ranch dressing, baked chicken, wild rice, broccoli and cherry jell-o for dessert. Katie ordered a small green salad, a chopped steak, well done with a baked potato, corn, rice pudding for dessert and another glass of wine.

"Very well," the waiter said and stepped away from the table.

"Katie, before the waiter took our order, you understood what I was saying, didn't you? I couldn't sleep with Ben because I want to be someone special in this life."

She laughed. "Yeah, I got that, Paulene."

"Well, what's so funny?"

"What's so funny is what you got to do in order to be that someone special in his life."

"And what's that? Sleep with him?"

"No not that." She kept laughing. "Something much more difficult to pull off."

"Katie, I don't have a clue to what you are talking about."

"Well, allow me to enlighten you." She paused as the waiter placed her fresh glass of wine in front of her. "First of all, you need to gain about forty extra pounds, dye your hair salt and pepper gray and buy yourself a pair of bi-focus."

"What are you talking about, Katie?"

She held up one finger. "And don't forget to tack about 40 years to your age and add about three inches to your height."

"Katie?"

"Don't you get it, Paulene? The only special woman in Ben's life is his mother. The rest of the female population is just a piece of meat to him."

"Katie, don't say that." I waved one hand at her. "Whether it's true or not, I just don't want to hear anything like that about him, okay?"

"Oh, grow up, Paulene. Get your head out of the sand, for goodness sake. Why shouldn't I say it, it's true? Ben Drake may be my so-so friend, but make no bones about it. I pretty much know what he's all about." She took a sip of wine. "Just like I told you—before you even went out with him."

"And what did you tell me?"

"I told you how he's just after one thing from you, and it's not your sweet nature." She paused, giving me a hard stare. It's your body! Consider yourself lucky that you didn't sleep with him last night."

"Katie, what am I going to do? I love him so much. But I would die if he used me and threw me away."

"Of course you would." She touched my hand. And by this time, our meals were being placed in front of us. She continued. "Paulene, I know you love Ben, but you deserve to be with someone that respects you and love you back. Someone who won't use you and destroy that sweet innocence nature you have. A man like Ben Drake who might be the most handsome man you have ever seen, is only going to use you and break your heart. And when he's finished, you'll feel used up and that innocence glow won't be in those eyes of your." She took her knife and fork, chopping her steak into small pieces. "Do yourself a favor and just let that man go on by his business." With her fingers she picked up a small cube of steak and put in her mouth.

"Katie you are starting to sound like my mother again," I snapped.

"I'm not trying to sound like your mother. I'm just trying to be your friend: a good friend. Paulene when you were a toddler I met and fell in love with a guy that I just had to have! The bastard used me and kept using me. It got to the point, that I didn't mind being used just so I could be near him." Her eyes watered.

"Are we back to that guy you can't forget? Shaun Parker?"

"That's the one. I was addicted to him, but he was bad news for me. He chewed me up and then spit me back out! So, if it sounds like I'm preaching it's because I have been where you are." She shook her head. "And how? I would hate to see you take the same trip and come out on the side of being tough and hard with no trust or respect in men or the word love." She touched my arm. "So take it from me Paulene, forget Ben Drake. Get your education and forget all about love! You are still very young with your whole life ahead of you. You will have plenty of time for all that stuff later. Don't throw your innocence away on a man who probably won't even look back after he gets what he wants. Go back home to Alabama while you still have your pride intact." She stressed.

"I can't do that, Katie. I can't forget Ben. Deep in my heart I feel that we were meant to be together. It was fate that brought us together. How else would a back-creek young woman like myself, end up meeting a Prince like Ben?"

"You are supposedly upset with him for trying to get you in bed, but yet he's still a Prince in your eyes, Paulene? You are so far gone until I doubt if hearing how Shaun Parker used and wrecked my life will do any good. But if my sad story can save you some heartache I will give it a shot." She held up one finger. "But know this, you will be the first that I have ever told this story to. The story that shaped my life."

"You have never told anyone else about your relationship with Shaun Parker? Not even Jeff?"

"Specially not Jeff." She shook her head, sounding a bit tipsy.

"One day Paulene, you will learn that the less you tell a man the better. I just wish you would listen to me and go back home and forget Ben Drake. "

"Katie, I have thought about going back home. And I'm sure I would have moved back there permanent by now if Ben hadn't came along. It was crystal clear in my mind that I wanted to move back, and then I met Ben. Now I don't want to lose him."

"Lose him?" She waved a hand. "You can't lose what you don't have. I doubt if you will ever hear from Ben Drake again. You didn't put out last night so he's on to the next pretty face who will." She stared. "Paulene, don't you know that's all he's about?"

"Katie, you didn't see how he looked at me and how nice he talked to me."

"Of course, he talked to you nicely and treated you fine. Why wouldn't he? If nothing else, he has a lot of class and smarts to boot. He knows you can't attract bees with vinegar. Cut your loses Paulene and go back to Alabama. Forget the man!"

"I'm not saying I'm going back home," I mumbled toward the table,

"But if I do decide to move back, will you do me a favor?" I asked, looking straight in her eyes.

"What's that, Paulene?"

"If Ben asks for my phone number or address, please give it to him."

"If you're trying to get away from the man, why give him your information?"

"Because I'm still hopeful that one day he'll feel about me what I feel for him."

"Whatever Paulene. It's your funeral." She waved both hands. "But can Mr. Drake rest for a minute while I attempt to enlighten you about Mr. Parker?"

"Sure, Katie." I nodded. "I want to hear about what broke you two up."

"Okay, here goes." She frowned. "It was a clear afternoon in early June, what seems like ages ago, of 1981. I was down on my knees picking wild flowers down by the duck pond behind the barn, when suddenly I heard the sound of footsteps in the grass. I looked around expecting to see your old dog, Bud, but spotted a tall, trim, bronze complexion guy with broad shoulders coming out of the tall bushes. I stood straight up dropping all the flowers I had gathered. His sudden appearance startled me as I stood there looking directly in his deep dark caramel brown eyes. A thousand words rushed to the tip of my tongue, but I couldn't seem to manage a single hello. This man was like an angel walking. His short wavy, low cut black hair and deep dark caramel eyes glowed in the radiant sunlight. He wasn't a drop-dead gorgeous type, but good-looking he was. To me he looked like a real live Prince Charming.

Noticing his trim figure, I wondered did he find plus size women attractive. He stood there at arms' length and smiled as he raked one hand through his hair and wiped his forehead with the other. He had a tired look on his smooth face as sweat rolled down his brow. He appeared to be about twenty-one at the time and I was right. He was twenty-one. Four years older than me. He looked drained as if he had walked a long ways. If he had walked all the way from down town Montgomery he had walked nearly seven miles and was probably hot and thirsty.

"Good afternoon," he said, tipping his cap to me as he walked on past me. After a few steps, he turned around to look back and my heart started beating faster.

"I'm looking for the Huntley's farm." He smiled.

I still couldn't seem to open my mouth, but I managed to point up the hill.

"Is the Huntley's farm up the hill there?" He smiled with glowing white teeth.

I nodded. "Yes."

"All right, thanks a million." He smiled at me, as he just stood there looking at me. He had an anxious look on his face and seemed as if he wanted to say something else, but turned his back and rushed up the hillside toward my house.

My hands trembled as I quickly picked the long stem flowers off the ground one by one and then headed right home. I was anxious to know why he was looking for our farm.

When I reached the edge of the front yard, there he stood, talking to my mother.

"My name is Shaun Parker, I'm here about the painting job."

"Okay, yes. I'm Fanny Huntley. The job is still available, and it's yours," Mama replied, extending her hand to him. "But I must say, young man, I didn't expect any callers until tomorrow. Showing up here today was pretty prompt on your part. I just placed that ad yesterday." Mama grinned as they shook hands.

"Yeah, I know. I grabbed the paper this morning and spotted your ad and decided to rush right out here before someone else could beat me to it." He wiped his forehead.

A slight frown came to Mama's face. "You're not from out this way?"

He shook his head, "No, Ma'am, I'm just passing through."

Mama wouldn't let him finish his statement, rudely cutting him off.

"I'm sorry, Mr. Parker. But it now appears I spoke too soon. I'm not going to be able to give you that job after all. I didn't know you were from out of town."

"I really need the job, Mrs. Huntley. I'm a pretty good painter to. What difference does it make where I'm from?"

"Pretty good." Mama shook her head. "I'm sorry, Mr. Parker, to give you a ray of hope just to pull the plug. But I just can't use you. Now I think you should leave."

He didn't say another word. He shook his head and headed across the yard with his white baseball cap in his hand. He hurried straight down the walkway toward the highway. Mama stood there with her hands on her hips and watched until he walked through the gate before she headed inside.

As he headed toward the highway, something inside of me cried out for him. I couldn't let him walk out of my life. I had to stop him somehow. I threw the flowers on the ground and ran after him, calling out his name. "Mr. Parker, Mr. Parker."

He looked around and stood in place until I reached him. "So, we meet again." He smiled. "You're the pretty young lady who directed me to the Huntley's farm. But how do you know my name?" he asked.

When I looked up at his face, it seemed every word in my head vanished. Just being around him touched me in some magical way. After a deep breath, I managed to speak breathless. "Hi, my name is Katie. You can't leave."

"I beg your pardon?"

I stared up at the sky for a second, and then placed my eyes back on his. "I'm Katie Huntley; and I was just coming up the hill when I heard my mother offer you that painting job, then rudely refused to let you keep the work when you said you weren't from around here."

He pointed toward my house. "Oh, that's where you live?"

"Yes, that's our farm. And what I'm trying to say, is if you'll give me a chance to talk to my mother, I think I can convince her to let you have the job."

He smiled and extended his hand to me and we shook hands. "Thanks a million. But why would you go out of your way to get me that job?" he asked.

We looked at each other for a second and he smiled. "Don't think I'm not grateful for your willingness to help me. I'm very grateful; but I was just wondering why. You don't even know me."

I looked at him and smiled. He was right, what could I say? I didn't really know him, but my insides tingled from being near him. All I knew was that I couldn't let him walk away.

"I guess I'm doing it, because you have such friendly eyes."

"So, it's my eyes?" He grinned.

We headed down the highway, then up the walkway to the house and just as we walked inside the fence, Mama turned the corner of the house. From the expression on her face, she didn't seem too pleased to see the stranger walking beside me. She stopped in her tracks and stood where she was. I left Mr. Parker standing at the gate as I ran toward her. When I faced her, I thought she would explode from anger.

"Katie, what are you doing with that man? Did he ask you for the painting job? He was just here a few minutes ago. I told him I couldn't use him." She held up both hands, shaking her head. "So before you say a word, there's nothing you can say that's going to make me change my mind," Mama shouted.

"Mama, could we just please step inside for a moment?"

We stepped inside and I rushed to peek out of the living room window to make sure he was still standing against the gate where I left him.

"Mama, come on and give the man the job," I suggested humbly.

"Did he send you in here to plead his case?" she asked sharply.

"No! Mama. It was all my idea." I paused in her eyes. She stood there shaking her head as if she didn't believe me.

"Honest, Mama. It was my idea. He was on his way back to town."

"And you stopped him, right?" She propped her hands on both hips and shook her head. "Why in the world would you do that, Katie?"

"Because he's cute," I said laughingly.

"Because he's what?" Mama asked, not finding my answer funny.

"I'm just kidding, Mama," I said laughingly, and then grabbed my mouth with both hands and collected myself. "He is cute, but the real reason I stopped him, is because I overheard you offer him the job, then you refused him after he said he wasn't from around here."

"That's right, I did refuse when he said he wasn't from around here! That's the point. He didn't volunteer to say where he was from," Mama said loudly.

"So he isn't from around here. What's the big deal? What difference does it make where he's from? He seems all right. He'll do a good job on that old barn and fence. Isn't that what really counts?"

"Katie, he seems all right, true enough. But you heard him say, he's just passing through. And passing through from where? Town is seven miles away, and each neighbor is within a few blocks or no more than a mile of us. So who in the hell is he?"

"He's tall, good looking, neatly dressed...", I said, but Mama cut me off.

"Yes, he's tall and halfway decent looking," she said, staring at me hard, shaking her head. "And that's all you can see is how good looking he is. You better wake up young lady, looks are not everything."

My stomach started turning in knots. I couldn't convince her to let him work.

"Katie, trust me on this. You heard on the news about that escaped rapist.

Good-looking men are not exempt from bad deeds! I'm not taking any chances!"

"Come on, Mama. I know you don't think that man out there is dangerous." I pointed toward the window. "He's just a regular guy. Can't you see that? His jeans and red shirt looked fresh from the dry-cleaners." He's no escaped rapist."

Mama had a frown on her face as she walked away from me, headed toward the kitchen, waving her hand. "Look Katie, I don't want to discuss this any longer. I have said what I have to say! He can't work here and that's that. Just let that man go on back where ever he came from."

"But Mama, if you're afraid to hire him because you think he's some bum, you know he isn't. He's dressed too neat and talks too proper to be anything less than just an average guy." I pleaded, following her into the kitchen.

She looked at me with an indifferent look on her face as she headed back into the living room. "Anybody can throw on neat clothes! Clothes don't make a man! And if he's so average," she stressed, propping her hands on her large hips. "Tell me, why is he here on some farm, looking for a painting job? He should already have a job."

She made a point, but none of it seemed to matter. I wanted him to stay.

"Just give him a chance, Mama."

"Look, Sweetheart, I can not give him a chance and that's that! OK? I'm not trying to be a jerk. The young man said he needed the job and I wanted to hire him." She paused. "And I would have hired him if he hadn't been from God knows where! The point is—we have to watch who we give a job to around here. We can't take any chances with strangers. We don't have your father here right now to protect us. He's going to be out of town at that clinic for the next week. We got to look out for ourselves. And I know you should be able to understand this decision I'm making. Don't you?"

My hopes were fading as I looked deep into Mama's eyes, she was dead set on not giving him the job, but I was hoping she would change her mind.

"So that's it, Mama? You won't even consider giving him a chance?"

"A chance to do what, Katie? A chance to rape or rob us! He's from God knows where. He's doesn't seem to own a vehicle, walking down that long hot highway proves that. He could be running from the law or anything! My answer is still no, I cannot let some drifter stay here and work! Just forget it!"

I couldn't accept her answer and kept pleading with her. "Mama that man is okay, just give him the job!"

"Katie, what has gotten into you? Why in the world are you pleading for that stranger? You don't know anything about that man or what he could be up to!"

Suddenly a hopeless, draining feeling ran through me, a feeling that all the words in the world wouldn't change Mama's decision. I stepped over to the sofa and dropped on it, shaking my head. "What's the use? You don't understand."

Mama walked over and sat down beside me, smoothing her hand down my ear-length black hair. I looked at her. She was sitting beside me smiling.

"This is silly, Katie, but if you feel that strongly about him being okay, then he probably is. The job is his. Go tell him he has the job."

Her words stunned and excited me at the same time. She had changed her mind. She just stared back, giving me a pat on the shoulder.

"Well, what are you waiting for? Go on and tell him he has the job."

I hopped off the sofa and rushed toward the door, stretched it opened and looked back at my mother. "Thanks, Mama. I have a good hunch about this guy. He's okay, you'll see," I said, hurrying out of the front door.

When I stepped outside he wasn't waiting at the gate. My heart skipped a beat. Suddenly I felt weak from the thought of never seeing him again as I stood on the walkway looking straight toward the highway.

Seconds later, I figured that he couldn't have gotten too far and hurried down the walkway, outside of the fence, to the edge of the highway. I looked to my right and there he was, headed toward town again.

"Mr. Parker, Mr. Parker, the job is yours. You got the job!" I called out.

He turned and paused for a second, and by the time he realized what I had said, he headed toward me, walking quickly. When he reached me, he grabbed my 5'4, one hundred and thirty-five pounds up in his arms and circled around with me in the middle of the highway. When he released me, I thought, "Wow, this guy is strong. He lifted me like I was light as a feather.

"Thanks, Katie. You have done me a much needed favor." He held out both arms. "And please forgive me for grabbing you like that, but I was so excited about getting this job, until I lost my head for a moment."

"No problem with that. I'm excited also." I laughed. "Because believe me, it wasn't easy changing my mother's mind."

"But she did, thanks to you." He smiled.

We headed back toward the house and my body still tingled from being in his arms. I was falling for him and didn't even know him. But something inside of me told me that he was going to be an important part of my life."

"Katie, you two meet in such an usual way. It feels like fate to me."

"Paulene, everything feels like fate to you. I'm not buying that. If it had been fate, he never would have treated me so cold and cruel," she mumbled sadly.

"You are right, of course. I'm sorry I said," I apologize. "Now go on and finish your story. What happened after he got the job?"

"Well, that evening he had dinner with us. It was just a simple Spaghetti dinner that I prepared. Then around 6:30, I showed him to his quarters. The one-room white storage house behind the barn that my father had fixed up into a living quarters for part time helpers on the farm.

"This is where you'll be staying for the next few days, until you finish your work here. I'm sure you'll be pretty comfortable here. It's not the main house. But it's not too bad. Mama keeps the place fully accommodated for comfort and convenience. I'm always out here reading or just relaxing."

He wasn't saying much, but he was smiling. And as I swung the door open to the little cottage his smile grew.

"Fully accommodated, I would agree," he said, stepping inside.

He seemed pleased with the accommodations, but the little one room storage house was nothing to write home about. It contained a small black and white TV, a throw rug over a wooden floor, a twin-size bed and a small dresser and a half bath.

"So you like it?" I asked.

"Sure. I would have been pleased bunking in your barn for the next few days. This is more than I could have hoped for."

"Well, I'm glad," I said opening the door and stepping outside.

"Wait up," he said, walking toward me.

We stepped outside together and he grabbed my hand and slightly squeezed it, sending tingling chills dashing through my stomach.

"How about sitting here on the steps awhile and keeping me company?"

"Sure, Mr. Parker; I would love to."

He pulled a white handkerchief from his back pocket and wiped the dust off the old steps. He turned to me and smiled, slightly shaking his head.

"It would please me a lot if you would just call me Shaun."

"Okay, here goes. Shaun. I like the sound of calling you by your first name."

"I like the way it sounds too, Katie."

He looked at me and smiled, as his eyes seemed to sparkle with a hint of desire. That hint of desire in his eyes made me feel a bit anxious, and quickly I turned my back to him, looking up at the stars.

"I was just wondering, how long will it take you to paint that old fence and barn?"

"Well, let's see, probably a couple weeks. Why would you ask?"

"No special reason, I just wondered."

"You just wondered." He looked in my eyes as he grabbed my face, bringing his face close to mine, kissing me urgently.

He pulled his lips from mine and we smiled at each other and stepped into the storage house. Standing in the middle of the room, he kissed me passionately. A hot flood of warmth was building up from my feet, slowly flowing through every part of me. I gripped both fists as I thought I would explode from the heat that had spread throughout me. He slowly pulled away, uncovering my lips.

"I'm sorry, Katie. I didn't mean to come on so strong. I just couldn't seem to help myself. You're one of the finest women I have ever laid eyes on. So just push me away if I get too touchy feely," he said, smiling.

"There's no need to explain. It's okay," I assured him, smiling.

"Maybe, but I don't want to give you any false notions about me, like thinking I'm trying to take advantage of you. I just wanted to kiss you," he explained.

"It's okay, Shaun. I wanted to kiss you to."

We grinned at each other and headed toward the door. I gripped the doorknob with my back against the door.

"Well, thanks again for talking to your mother. This job is going to give me the dough to get my truck out of the shop."

My eyes lit up at the mention of him having a truck, only because Mama had made an issue of him showing up on feet.

"You have a truck?"

"A Chevy. It broke down on me about five miles out of town."

"Where are you from, Shaun? Are you here visiting someone? You don't really have to tell me, if you would rather not. I'm not trying to pry."

"No, it's okay. I don't mind telling you. You have gone out of your way to help me out; the least I can do is tell you where I'm from and why I'm in these parts in the first place. I'm from town, Montgomery that is. And it's plain and simple as to why I'm out here in this farm country. I'm out of work and I read the ad and came for the job. I knew my old white pickup wasn't in the best shape, but I figured it would make the trip here and back. It made it half way between here and town."

"I'm sorry about your truck."

"Thank you, Katie."

"Well, if it's going to take you a couple weeks to do the painting, I guess you'll be calling your folks."

"No folks, just me. He smiled and reached out to touch my shoulder.

"Do you work, Katie?" he asked and searched my face. "Or should I ask you what high school do you attend?" He grinned.

I looked at him and smiled. "I just graduated in May." I held out both arms. "This is it, helping my parents with the farm."

He smiled and lifted my face toward his. "Well, I guess helping your folks with the farm is enough work within itself."

"Yeah, I know you're right, and Mama needs my help more than ever since my father is having a few mental problems." I paused. "But I don't want to get into that subject about my Dad."

"Then don't," he said in a gentle kind way.

"Anyway, Shaun, it seems as much as I help out, we still can't keep this farm running smoothly. Now that my father is having problems, my mother has talked about selling, but I doubt if she ever will. So right now I don't really know what Mama may decide on doing about this place. But I know one thing for sure. I'm tired of working in fields. It's not the way I pictured my future."

As I went on and on about being tired of farm work, he never looked away from me for one minute. I figured I was boring him and he was just being polite.

"I'm sorry for going on and on. I'm probably boring you." I paused. "I hope I'm not boring you. I'll leave now and let you relax."

As I turned my back to him and headed toward the door, he gently grabbed my left arm and released it just as quickly as he grabbed it.

"No, please, you are not boring me. I'm enjoying your company. You're so different from all the ladies I know in town."

His words caught my attention. I immediately looked at him and smiled. I was anxious to know what he meant by that. "Different in what way?"

"Well, just different," he said, smiling.

My smile disappeared, hoping he didn't think I was too country or too chunky.

He reached out and touched my face. "I certainly mean different in a good way: A bold, refreshing, cut to the chase kind of different. Other than being so fine, you're just fun to be around," he said, placing his lips against mine, kissing me in the same passionate way. And when his lips released mine, he smiled.

"Katie, what are you doing to me? You better run along while I still have the strength to release you."

He didn't try anything with me that evening. I went to bed that night with the sweet impression that he was being a gentleman, not wanting to come on too strong. But timing was everything to him. And he came in for the kill, the night before his departure. He took me out for dinner and dancing but before the meal and the dance hall, I was in his bed. The feel of Shaun Parker's body pressed against me was the closest thing I have ever felt to pure happiness. Sweat rolled off of our bodies as we held each other as if we were holding on to a cliff for our lives. His muscular arms held me tight. I could hardly believe I had just surrendered my virginity to him, let alone with such enthusiasm. As he trailed kisses into the side of my neck, my body shivered with sweet satisfaction of the way he was making me feel. Wrapping my arms around his neck, I stretched with exciting delight. I was only seventeen and I wasn't ready to sleep with him yet, but he swept me off my feet and blew all rational thoughts clear out of my head. He charmed me and kept me so off balance with his touch—moving his hands up and down my back, gliding them over my arms, caressing my shoulders, my neck and every part that he could touch with his smooth hands. I had told myself it didn't matter, but deep down it was the only thing that mattered.

After lying in each other's arms for about an hour, we showered and dressed and headed out on the town. We enjoyed a light meal of hamburgers and milk shakes, and then headed to the dance hall. When the lights went low and the music turned slow, he wrapped me in his strong arms and held me so closely that I felt like I could melt right into his body and die of pleasure. The next thing I remembered, the evening was over and we were in this room again, on this bed, and my heart was pounding and my pulse was racing from the bottom of my feet to the top of my head.

Now that we were back in his room on his bed, I totally surrendered to him. Being with him felt so right. The touch of his hands made me want him more and more. His hands were warm and soothing, as he smoothed them all over my back and hips, and while lying there wrapped in his arms, he slowly started sliding his hand up my dress, rubbing up and down my legs. He gripped me tightly against him, desperately kissing my neck, journeying back over to my lips, and just as I thought I would scream from the pleasure he was giving me, he pulled away, looked down at me and smiled.

"Katie, what are you doing to me? I can't stop kissing you for a minute before I want to kiss you again. The feel of you in my arms, is simply out of this world. I think I'm falling in love with you, Katie. I know I am."

With trembling hands he slowly begin to unbutton my blouse. As he removed each button from its socket, he kissed me. When he threw my blouse to the floor something in the back of my mind was telling me to stop him, but my heart wouldn't listen.

"Shaun, it's so special being with you like this. I'm falling in love with you too, Shaun."

After my confession of love, his kiss was demanding. It was as if he had been waiting all his life to kiss me. We held each other tenderly and made love as if it was helping us to breathe and as we held on tight to each other, we gripped on to each other as if we were holding on for our lives. All the things I had heard my mother and Grandma Fanny say about love finally made sense.

I breathed in his after-shave as he slowly pushed up on his elbows. He looked down at me smiling. "Are you all right?" he asked.

"Yes." I was more than all right. I felt like a new woman.

"Good." He rolled out of bed, and I propped on one elbow to get a glimpse of his beautiful figure in the dim light of the room. He was not just good-looking, but he was built like a permanent brick house. He had wide shoulders, hard biceps and lean muscles that defined his chest. And he had lots of body hair all over his chest and legs. My heart skipped a beat when I noticed that he was now dressing.

"What are you doing?"

"I got to take off for a minute."

A moment before I'd felt at ease with letting him see me without my clothes on; now I suddenly felt uncomfortable. I started looking around for my dress and then I noticed it balled up at the foot of the little bed.

"Why? Where are you going? You don't have a vehicle remember?" I watched as Shaun put on his jeans and shirt and didn't bother to fasten them up.

He pulled a pack of Winston cigarettes from his shirt pocket and looked over at me. "I'm just going to take a quick walk and smoke a cigarette." His dark brown eyes softened, the corner of his mouth crooked up with a slight smile, and then he took a step toward the bed.

"Okay, let me get dressed and take that walk with you?" I said, wrapping the sheet around me—grabbing up my clothes off the floor.

"No, Katie, don't bother. I sort of like to take my smokes alone," he said with no pep to his voice.

"Okay, I'll be right here in your bed when you get back." I smiled, not seeing the writing on the wall. That he wanted me gone now that he had gotten what he wanted.

"No, Katie. I don't want your mother coming out here looking for you. Legally you are under age. You are only seventeen and I'm a twenty-two-year-old man."

When he said that, I was out of his bed in the blink of an eye, throwing on my things. I was slowly getting the picture. "Shaun, why are you saying that to me now? It didn't seem to matter to you before. Did it?" I shouted with tears coming to my eyes.

"Katie, it's been great. But it was just sex." He held up both hands. "Nothing more and nothing less."

"Just sex? It was my first time, Shaun?"

"So, what? It was going to be your first time soon or later?" He barked with an attitude.

"But, Shaun."

"No, butts!" He threw up his hands. "You knew when I took this job that I was only going to be here a few days, and then I would be leaving. I didn't make you any promises little girl. Now get out of my bed and run on up to your house! I need to get some rest." He pointed toward the door.

A heavy sad feeling overtook me. Moments before I was happier than I had ever been, now I was sad enough to just die.

"Shaun." I grabbed my face in shock. "You said all those sweet things to me and said you wanted me."

"Katie, you may be young, but you know how it works. We say what we have to say to get what we want to get." He stared at me and just for a split second I thought I could see a reflection of care and regret. But he shook his head and that reflection was gone. I felt like such a fool as I stepped into my shoes, now fully dressed.

My eyes sneered at him and I wanted to throw something at him as I walked out of the door. He didn't look back at me. He stood there with both hands pressed on the dresser, leaning forward toward the mirror with his head lowered.

Then early that next morning before I had even gotten out of bed, he had taken his pay and left. I felt my whole heart go with him. I would never be the same or know that wonderful magical feeling that being around him gave me.

"Katie, I don't mean to interrupt you, but that was awful what he did to you." I touched her hand.

"Yeah, Paulene. He got me good. He said all the right words to get me into his good graces then he took my virginity and treated me like a piece of trash afterward."

"Katie, what happened after that? Did you ever see him again?"

She didn't answer. Her jaws were sucked in and suddenly she looked deeply sadden as she sat there staring down in her drink.

Chapter Twenty-Two

The silence was broken when a waiter walked up and poured more ice water in our glasses. After the waiter stepped away from our table, I touched her on top of the hand and asked again.

"Katie, can you tell me what happened after that?"

She nodded in silence as she continued to look down in her drink.

I reached out and touched her hand again. "If you would rather not right now. That's Ok. You can tell me some other time. I'm just curious. Your story is so heartbreaking."

"It's okay." She sipped her drink, but still staring down at nothing.

"So, did you ever see him again?"

She nodded. "Oh, yeah. A few years later in 1984, he was back to stick it to me again."

"So, it didn't get better between you two?"

"Better? It was never even alright." She waved a hand.

"Okay, so tell me."

"He showed up after he had heard about my parents being killed in that crash. Somehow he had heard that their death could have left me a nice sum of life insurance. By now, Casey, Duane and I had moved in with Grandma Fanny. And it's crystal clear in my mind just like it happened yesterday. It was a rainy, Friday evening. Not long after I got in from my job at K-mart where I was a cashier. Duane had left a note lying on the coffee table that said Shaun Parker had called and he had left his number. Later after having a snack and changing out of my work clothes, while relaxing with my head propped on two throw pillows and both legs resting on the sofa with the phone sitting on my lap, against my better judgment, I dialed Shaun's number."

"What in the world made you call him after the awful way he had treated you, Katie?"

She shook her head. "I can't tell you why I called him. I just know I wanted to talk to him and see him again more than anything I could think of. But when I called he wasn't home."

"So, you didn't get to talk to him that evening?" I asked.

She smiled. "Oh, yes. I talked to him. It was no more than five or ten minutes later after I tried calling him that he called me again. The phone was still sitting on my lap. I quickly picked up the receiver on the first ring.

"Hello," I said.

"Hello back to you," he said and became quiet. He was probably wondering to himself, the reason behind my willingness to return his call. After all, he had used me and left town without saying goodbye.

"Shaun, I'm glad you called and left your number."

He grinned. "I couldn't ask for a better greeting than that."

"Well, a lot of time has passed and I have had a lot of time to think."

"And what were your thoughts?"

"Just mostly about if I had the chance." I paused in silence for a moment not wanting to sound too over anxious.

"Continue." He laughed. "If you had the chance to what?"

"To be friends again."

"Sound fine to me." He laughed and paused. "You want to start tonight?"

He caught me off guard and I didn't answer.

"Are you still there?"

"Yes. I'm listening."

"Well, can you try answering? I said what about tonight?"

"I heard you, Shaun, but I guess you sort of caught me off guard. I just got home from work and I didn't expect to go back out."

He grinned. "Work is a drag. But if you want to get out of the house for a few drinks, I know a pretty cool place we could go."

"Okay, sure. Why not?" I agreed, jumping at the chance to be with him. It would give us an opportunity to mend fences and try again.

"Needless to say, I was on top of the world to be asked out by him, but Grandma Fanny wasn't pleased to hear I was going out with Shaun. She had heard all the negative things about him, being lazy, not keeping a job and being into heavy drinking and using women and throwing them away like yesterday's newspaper."

"I can understand why your grandmother felt that way," I said.

Katie waved a hand. "Yeah. I knew she was right about Shaun. But none of that really mattered to me. I just wanted to be with Shaun Parker again and I wanted him any way I could get him."

"Did your grandmother have much to say?"

"She said plenty when I announced that he was picking me up for the evening.

"Katie, young lady. I sure hope you know what you are doing? I think you are making a big mistake to start taking up with that man again," Grandma Fanny shook her head. She was sitting in her wheelchair near the fireplace as I was peeping out of the front window waiting for Shaun to pull into the driveway.

Noticing the fire getting low in the fireplace, I looked around at her, smiling.

"I know you are right, Grandma Fanny, but something inside of me is telling me to try and be friends with him. I want to at least give it a try," I said stepping out on the porch to get a couple logs for the fire.

While placing the logs on the fire I heard a car engine pull into the driveway, moments later a knock on the door. I rushed to open the door and it was Shaun dressed in a black outfit, looking like someone with their head on straight instead of the loser I thought he was.

We went straight to the dance club and while sitting anxiously and excitedly across from him at a small round table, he reached across the table and touched my hand. "I'm really pleased that you decided to take my call. I have wanted to call for awhile but I didn't want to get hung up on."

I quickly smiled. "All the hard feelings are in the past."

"I like your attitude a lot, the willingness to give us a second chance at this thing." He stared.

"Well, we are both a little older and hopefully a bit wiser."

He nodded. "Yes, older we are. I don't know how much wiser. I guess time will tell."

"You got that right."

"That sounded like maybe you are not sure about me being any wiser."

"I just agreed with you that time will tell if we are wiser."

"Whatever? Have you landed yourself a job yet?" he asked.

"Yeah, if you want to call it that. I'm working at K-mart at the moment."

"No more farm work?" he asked.

"No. We lost our farm when my parents were killed in that accident."

"That's too bad. I'm sorry to hear about your folks. You had a real swell mother."

"Thanks, it's been pretty rough these past few months."

"Yeah, I bet it has. I thought you would be a teacher or something about now. Like a math teacher?"

"Why would you think that, Shaun? I didn't go to college and I'm not in college now. But now that you mentioned it, I do have to start taking some classes. I got to get an education and get myself a better job than what I have."

He shook his head. "School books are for the birds. You can't make any real money doing a nine to five. If you want some real money you got to be a darn movie star or a sports icon, anything where your work is fun and your pay is big."

"So I take it, you're not working?" I asked him.

"No nine to five for me." He winked. "But I have a few irons in the fire."

"Well, if you are so against 9 to 5, why did you think I would be a math teacher?"

He narrowed his eyes at me and winked. "Let's just say, you should be into figures, cause you are built." He grinned and winked, holding up one finger. "Just kidding, but on the real side. I thought you were pretty book smart when I first met you." He paused. "That's why I thought you would have gone to college or something."

During the middle of our conversation, a slender, very pretty lady who looked to be about my age walked up to our table and grabbed him by the arm, taking him across the floor. She had shoulder length black hair and was dressed in business attire with a briefcase in her left hand. I couldn't hear what they were saying, but she seemed upset from the look on her face and her hand expressions in his face.

He returned to the table, smiling. He immediately got the waitress attention and ordered a double scotch on the rocks. I had a glass of water sitting in front of me. He glanced at my glass and didn't ask me if I wanted anything. Plus, maybe he figured if he offered me a drink that he would have to pay for it. And he figured I was loaded since my parent's death, so he wasn't about to buy me one thing. But, I couldn't believe he was being that rude and somewhat cold toward me as if he had suddenly drew an attitude. It made me even more determined to reach him and try to be friends. Because I really wanted him in my life whatever way I could get him. But what I didn't know at the time was that he was still the same jerk that had treated me badly.

"Did you ask him who was his friend in the business outfit?"

"No, I decided not to go there. I asked him about his rude manner instead."

"Shaun why did you rush the waitress away without giving me a chance to order anything? That was quite rude of you, wouldn't you agree?"

He grinned, rubbed one hand across his hair and pulled his black blazer jacket together, as if he knew he looked fine.

"I'm sorry. Did you want a drink?" He pointed at my water. "I thought you had one. What's that, lemonade?"

I knew he was being funny, because he was sitting right there when the waitress walked over with a tray of water, I accepted a glass and he declined. I didn't make anything of his reply; I just pretended he wasn't the wiser, trying to focus on the purpose of getting together with him.

"Shaun, do you think we can try to get along and bury the hatchet from 1981?"

"If you want us to be friends, then I guess we can be friends, Katie," he said, giving me a curious stare.

"Why do you say it like that? You called me after all this time because you wanted to try again, right?"

He very boldly changed the subject. "I'm in a tight way at the moment. Think you could do me a favor?" he asked, grinning. "If you do me this favor, I'll know you are serious about trying to mend fences with me."

"Shaun, I'm serious. You think I would have taken your call and agreed to come here with you, if I wasn't serious about trying to develop some kind of friendship with you?"

He stared at me hard and narrowed his eyes. "You really got a thing for me, don't you, Katie?" he asked with a sexual undertone to his voice.

It offended me that he could see through me.

"Don't get so full of yourself, Shaun," I snapped at him in a huffy manner. "I haven't forgotten how you treated me."

He drew an instant attitude. "What you mean that you haven't forgotten? You come out with me and say you want to be friends, but you bring up some old garbage?"

"Look, Shaun, I'm just telling you that I haven't forgotten how rotten you treated me. But I have forgiven you. I want this to be a new beginning for us."

The waitress set the drink in front of him and he grabbed it up and drained it in one swallow. After he finished the drink, he looked at the waitress and shook his head.

"That little drink didn't even wet my tongue! I know you don't expect me to pay for that, do you?" He waved a hand.

She didn't smile or raise her voice. "Yes, Sir, I do expect for you to pay for it."

"Well, let me think about it while you run along and get me another scotch on the rocks and this time make it taller and bring something for the lady too."

The waitress didn't move. "Sir, you owe me for the drink you just finished."

"Miss, your money is good, now could we please get our order?" I snapped.

The waitress nodded and rushed off to get our orders.

He looked at me and grinned. "Thanks for setting that bitch straight." He ripped the plastic from a package of Winston cigarettes and lit one up.

"Do you mind if I smoke," he asked after he had already very rudely blew his smoke across the table in my face.

"No, go right ahead." I shook my head, fanning his smoke.

"Thank you. Now back to the business at hand. You want to be my friend for old time sake," he said and winked at me. "Damn! Katie, you are fine. I wish you had the hots for me the way you did back in 1981. Why not ditch this friendship thing and give me another chance. I have had my eye on you for a long time. A good woman like you is what my father always wanted me to have. Someone like you could straighten me out." He reached across the table and touched my hand. "What you say, Katie? You need someone in your life just as much as I do."

Looking down at the table, I knew there was still that chemistry between us.

"I don't know Shaun. I think we need to work on being friends before we can be anything else. I got to get to know you better and learn to trust you." I looked up at him, becoming aroused from the sparkle of lust and desire in his eyes.

"Katie, nobody cares about that shit. What does friendship have to do with two people trying to find their way back to each other? I don't mind being your friend, but I want to be your lover too. You are a fine woman, Katie." He shook his head. "And you look very desirable from where I'm sitting." He touched the top of my hand. "Please come home with me, Katie. We both need each other. Let me show you how much I want you."

"What about the woman that's already at your house? Don't you live with some woman?" I asked, wanting to be close to him in the worst way.

He grinned. "That's ancient history. She left. I'm all by my lonesome."

"Well, what about that woman who was just in here? She seemed upset with you?"

"She's history to. You are it, Katie. You are the only woman I want in my life and in my bed. Is that plain enough for you?"

It was plain enough for me. All I could think about was how wonderful it had felt to be in his bed years ago. That one time was branded in my heart. I couldn't wait to get another chance to be alone with him.

My car trailed his to his apartment, and when we parked in his driveway, I was touched and impressed when he quickly got out of his car and walked over to open my door for me. But the moment we stepped into his apartment, he fell across the bed.

"Since your folks left you all that bread, could you please lend me this month's rent? I'm about to get kicked out of this darn place, but if all goes well, I should be pretty well set after next week. I got a job interview downtown with this big insurance company. The name of the company is Towne Insurance. My interview is set for next Wednesday at nine-thirty in the morning. Keep your fingers crossed."

"So you are going to try the nine to five?"

"A man got to do what a man got to do? Don't think I like it."

"I hear you. Whatever you need. Come over tomorrow and pick it up."

After I promised him that money, he reached out his hands and asked me to join him, as if my words had boosted his mood.

"Why are you just standing there? Are you going to join me? It's no fun lying here admiring your fine body if I can't touch it. Did I ever tell you that I have a thing for women who has a little meat on their bones?"

Standing there slightly smiling down at him, I still hadn't figured him out or what he was really up too. As he lay there on that queen size bed with his legs crossed and both pillows propped under his head, before I could answer, he had rolled out of bed to give me a hand. He quickly started unbuttoning my top as he kissed my neck and ear, and with his other hand caressing my waist. Then suddenly with full force he pulled me in against him, completely taking my breath away.

"Katie," he whispered in my ear. His voice was sending sensations racing through me. I needed the warm feelings his touch and voice was stirring in me.

"If only you knew what you do to me. You feel too good. Holding you like this—drives me nuts. Tell me you want me. Say it now. Say we can be lovers. I have ached to touch your body since that first time years ago."

Somehow his voice hypnotized me. He was smoldering my neck and face with such delight from the warmth of his kisses. Being next to Shaun had made me feel light as a feather. The anticipation was burning me up. I guided his anxious hands to unzip my skirt, and as it slipped to the floor, he reached for my blouse, unzipped it and slipped it off my shoulders. Then sweep me up into his arms, placing me across the foot of the bed and fell right on top of me.

He breathed hard, kissing me tenderly and urgently, whispering in my ear.

"Say you want me. Say you have always wanted me. I can tell you want me now. Admit it, Katie. Tell me you want me."

He had figured me right. I did want him. Every muscle within me had relaxed and surrendered to his passion and his urgent longing for me.

"Yes! Shaun. Oh, yes, I do want you. Take me now," I moaned out to him with every bit of longing within me. And as his fierce passion erased every trace of thought in my head, I wrapped my arms around his back and clung to him. I couldn't think of any of the negative things about him—just that I adored how he was making me feel.

So later that evening, when we got dressed and left his apartment, I sneaked Shaun into the house. We walked softly down the hallway pass Duane's and Casey room, two doors down from Grandma Fanny's room. My insides were screaming out for him. Making love with him had totally overwhelmed me and I couldn't wait to get undressed and back in bed with him. All I could think about during the drive home was a repeat of how he had made me feel earlier.

After we undressed and slid beneath my sheets, being careful not to be noisy, he grabbed my face kissing me deep and demandingly. We were lost in each other's embrace. I rubbed my hands over his back as he held me close. His rapid breathing sent heat flowing throughout me.

"You feel out of this world, Katie," he breathed hotly against my neck.

Overcome with the thrilling passion that he had stirred in me, I felt so loved and wanted laying next to him. My whole soul had surrendered my heart to love for only him.

Much later, he rolled over on his back and pulled me on top of him.

"Katie, I'm going to give you this kind of loving always. This is the kind of loving you deserve. The kind no other man but I can give you." He reached up and pulled my mouth down on his and we kissed passionately. When he uncovered my lips, he smiled.

"Katie. You are driving me crazy woman," he mumbled between our kisses.

"You thrill me beyond words," he said breathless as his lips wrapped around mine in a deep passionate kiss.

We snuggled there on my bed wrapped in each other's arms and fell asleep elated with lingering sensations. And when my eyes blinked opened, we both were lying at the foot of my bed still completely nude. Shaun's arm was stretched across my stomach and one of his legs was stretched across one of my legs. I glanced toward my bedroom window, and noticed the sun shinning brightly through the curtains. We had over slept. The hands on the clock, which sat on my nightstand, read 10:00 o'clock. Seeing the time immediately reminded me that I had to drop Grandma Fanny off at the hair stylist at ten-thirty. Minutes later, just as Shaun opened his sexy eyes and squeezed me next to him, we heard a soft knock at my bedroom door. I grabbed my mouth with one hand, and then quickly grabbed my nightgown, which was lying on the bed beside me, with my other hand. I was trying to cover myself.

He looked at me and smiled. "Don't worry, Mrs. Huntley isn't going to walk in on us. The door is locked. Isn't it?"

Nodding, anxiously. I couldn't let Grandma Fanny catch Shaun in my bed. She would have a fit. "Wait here," I said in a whisper, getting out of bed and hurried across the floor to the door.

"Who's there?" I asked, sounding kind of silly, knowing it could only be Grandma Fanny or her nurse, Diana Banks, since Casey or

Duane never knocked on my door.

"It's your Grandmother, who else do you think it is?"

"What is it Grandma Fanny?"

"Are you about ready? I got to get to my appointment, you know?" she asked. I got a whole floor filled with vegetables that I got to can later."

"I know Grandma Fanny, but give me a couple minutes. I over slept."

Chapter Twenty-Three

Katie seemed so distant and sad and didn't say anything for five or ten minutes. She sat there at the table in silence tapping her right fingers on the table. She was slightly shaking her head, and then suddenly she got the attention of a passing waiter and ordered us both another round of drinks: Scotch and soda for her and a glass of white wine for me. She waited until the waiter returned with drinks, and after she had nearly finished it off in one swallow before she continued.

"So, I took Grandma Fanny to her appointment and Shaun stayed in my bedroom until I got back. He was still in bed when we returned."

"Did your grandmother ever warm up to Shaun Parker?"

"Not really and I didn't expect her to. I was a fool to even be with the man but I couldn't help myself. So, I didn't put any pressure on Grandma Fanny to get along with him."

"Was he polite to her?"

"Yes, he was. But she let him have it with both barrels." Katie smiled and paused. "But I didn't stay in Grandma Fanny's house long after we got back together. Just two weeks after starting a new relationship with Shaun, I found and moved into my own apartment. Moving out was fine with Grandma Fanny, but since she had hurt her hip and was in a wheelchair, she had to stay at my apartment for awhile until the doctor released her from the wheelchair. She didn't get released from the chair until two more weeks down the road. That was all fine and dandy with her, but she hit the ceiling when she found out I was having a thing with Shaun again. Shortly after the dust settled between me and Grandma Fanny about me dating Shaun, three days before the doctor would be taking her out of the wheelchair with a clean bill of health, Shaun got kicked out of his apartment and had no place to go.

While sitting at the dinner table trying to enjoy our meals that evening, Grandma Fanny and I were both too upset with each other to touch our food.

"Katie, it was one thing when you decided to start going out with Shaun Parker again, knowing what a loser he was, but now to consider letting that good for nothing bum to move in here with you. Have you completely lost your mind? That boy is trouble! You hear me, Katie? He's all trouble!" She shouted, staring at me with disbelief in her eyes. "You keep telling me that you are going to make something of your life and live high on the hog one day! Well, if you are planning on doing it with that Shaun Parker next to your side, you might have another thought coming!" She grumbled. "I don't know what happened to you, you were such a smart student, making straight A's in your classes. Where is your brain now when you need to use it for yourself?" She shouted, hitting the table with her fist.

The nurse, walked in—in the midst of Grandma Fanny hitting the table.

"Fanny, I noticed that it's getting a bit late. After you finish dinner, do you still want the hip massage?" Diana Banks asked.

"Yes, Diana, I do. And I don't consider 8:30 PM late! Now if you could please excuse us?" Grandma Fanny snapped.

Diana nodded and stepped quickly out of the kitchen.

Looking straight across the table at my grandmother, I didn't blink. "Grandma Fanny, Shaun has changed. He has grown up just like I have. We were both kids back then." I sipped on iced water. "He's not as bad as everyone makes him out to be. He's not into all that drinking and smoking grass anymore. I haven't seen him with any drugs. He doesn't talk about drugs around me, so as far as I'm concern, he's no longer into that stuff."

Grandma Fanny nodded, and then shook her head in disgust. "And you believe that?"

"Yeah, Grandma Fanny. I believe it. Shaun cares about me and I care about him. It just happened. Now that he has someone who really cares about him, he's not into all that mess anymore." I paused and wiped my mouth, placing the napkin on top of my leftover spaghetti and garlic bread.

After a moment of silence, while Grandma Fanny finished up her meal, and drained her iced-tea glass, she looked at me and pointed her finger across the table.

"I tell you why it just happened. It happened because that man wants the money he knows your father and mother insurance policy left you and your brothers! I'm sure that's what he's up to."

"Whatever, Grandma Fanny. Could we please not talk about this anymore?

Shaun and I are together and that's that. He's moving in here tomorrow. Is that okay with you, Grandma Fanny?"

"No, it's not okay!" She rolled her eyes. "I won't live under the same roof with some guy who's into using or dealing drugs and God knows what else."

"Grandma Fanny." I swallowed hard. "What are you saying?"

"I'm saying you can suit yourself. This is your apartment, Katie." She stared at me hard, shaking her head. "But I'll be damn if I stay here with the likes of your no-good man!" She shouted and wheeled away from the table.

"I'm going to pack, and if you could be so kind to take me and Diana back to my house, I would really appreciated it."

So, the next day, before Shaun moved in, I took Grandma Fanny and her nurse back to her house. I wanted to back down and not allow Shaun to move in, but I couldn't. I wanted to be with him, it seemed more than anything. I promised to continue paying for her nurses' care from the insurance money I had, which was in my care. It wasn't that much, just $10,000. But that seemed like a lot of money to us at the time.

Then toward the end of four months into our relationship, Shaun showed his true colors. They came to the surface. I thought things were moving along rather smoothly. I had started taking a couple classes at the community college. Shaun supposedly was still working for the Towne Insurance Company down town. I thought we were becoming closer and closer, but in actuality I was becoming the biggest fool that had ever lived. I was blinded by his charm and good lies. He had a spell over me.

One week before Labor Day, on a Tuesday evening after one of my classes around 3:30, I removed the mail from the mailbox, and as I stepped inside, I noticed a white envelope that had been pushed under the door. It had been hand delivered by someone. I closed the door, placed the mail on the coffee table and picked up the envelope. It was addressed from the apartment complex to me in big, red bold lettering. I quickly ripped open the envelope and found an eviction notice, effective immediately it read.

Standing there in the middle of the living room, I dropped the notice. I was stunned, wondering why had I received such a notice. I always paid my rent every month and on time. After a few seconds, I pulled myself together, grabbed my coat and left the apartment. I drove straight down town to Paxton Apartment Management. I was fit to be tied, boiling angry, burning rubber in the parking lot. And when I stepped inside the office I insulted the first person I saw, which was some older man sitting at a desk in the corner.

He held up one finger, looking at me over the rim of his glasses. "I thought I locked that door. Ma'am, I'm getting ready to close the office."

What did he say that for? It made me boil even more. I rushed over to his desk and pointed my finger in his face.

"I don't care if you're getting ready to die! You are going to tell me why your office mailed this damn eviction notice to me?" I held the notice up to his face.

He stared up at me and frowned. "Well, Ma'am, if we mailed the notice apparently you haven't been paying your rent."

"I pay my rent every month on time!" I hollered in his face, so mad I couldn't think straight. "Check your damn books and you'll see."

"That's exactly what I plan to do Miss," he mumbled nervously, grabbing a black ledger from a nearby bookcase behind his desk. He flipped through it for a second then looked up at me with a permanent frown on his face.

"What's your name?"

I held up the notice again. Upset that he was taking his time. "It's Katie Huntley. Didn't you read it on the notice?"

He shook his head as if I was really getting on his nerve, and started flipping back through the ledger, stopping on page sixty-eight, which read evictions.

"Yes, your name is here on this list all right," he said, nodding up and down.

"I didn't think we were trying to established if my name was on the list, but why it's on the damn list in the first place, Sir?"

He held up one finger. "Just hold on, I'm getting to that next," he said flipping pages again, stopping on page thirty-four, which listed my name across the top. And I read along with him, June, July, August and September all had a zero where four hundred and seventy-five should have been.

He looked up at me, passing the ledger to me. "Here you are Miss Huntley. It appears you haven't paid your rent in the last four months," he said and paused up at me for a second. "Apparently, before that, we didn't have any problems. You always paid on time."

I shook my head. I had no reason to read again what I had just read. Now all of a sudden, I wasn't angry anymore. I was crushed, in a trance standing there looking at the old man. Tears started to pour down my eyes. I grabbed my face and started crying right in front of him. He rushed out of his seat and handed me a facial tissue.

"Look, Miss Huntley, maybe we don't have to kick you out, if there's any way you can bring us the money for the four months you are behind." He scratched his head.

"Okay, that's the deal. If you can bring those months you are behind to us by the end of the week, then we won't evict you."

Drying my eyes with the tissue, I nodded. "Thank you," I said humbly as I made my way out of his office. When I reached my car, I noticed him standing in the window looking out at me, probably wondering why was I being such a big baby. He had no idea what was going through my mind, and it had nothing to do with being kicked out of the apartment.

As I started up the engine and headed out of the parking out, I noticed the tall building next to the Paxton Apartments Complex. The sign read, Town Insurance. It was where Shaun worked. A conversation we had came to my mind.

"I can drop the rent off the first of each month. The place I work is right next door to Paxton Apartments Complex. It will save you the stamp."

There was no doubt in my mind that he had ripped off the rent money for four months straight, the entire time he had lived with me. Those thoughts choked me up as I was driving home, crying and stiffing, barely able to see the road for my tears. So angry, there was no limit to what I might do to Shaun.

Like a zombie, I walked inside of my apartment, not bothering to close the door behind me as the cold air filled the room. I was numb, feeling like a knife was sticking straight in my heart as I dropped to my knees in the middle of the living room floor, crying. I had allowed Shaun Parker to rip out my heart again.

After crying for ten minutes straight with the door stretched opened, one thought told me: "Get up off the floor and pull yourself together. Not all is lost. You still have what's left of your parent's insurance money in the bank. Plus, you got nobody to blame but yourself. You knew Shaun Parker was trouble, but you had to have the pretty boy, a snake that had bitten you before."

Standing to my feet, I dried my eyes with my dress-tail and walked over to close the door. Boiling inside, I took a seat on the sofa, still in thought: "So that no-good bastard took nineteen hundred of your rent money, you still have money to pay the Apartment Complex. You can still keep your apartment. Pay your rent and kick that jerk to the curb, and never have anything else to do with the loser." I told myself.

Wiping away the last tear, I grabbed the mail off the coffee table, sunk back on the sofa and decided to try and calm myself by reading the mail. Sitting back reading through my mail had calmed me a bit, until I ripped opened the last letter on the stack, which was my checking account statement. My hands went limp and the statement slipped to the floor. I grabbed my face and screamed.

"No! Not my darn money! I didn't read it right! I couldn't have!" I shouted.

Trembling, I thought I was going to faint as I inhaled deeply a couple times, then bent over to pick up the statement. My heart beating loudly as I stood there staring at it for a few minutes before my sore eyes flowed with more tears. Sharp shooting pains ripped through me. The ending balance read: $9.30, which was $7,500 less than what it should have read. Then I noticed twenty-five withdraws, all for the month of November of $300. Each withdrawal was made at the automatic teller machine. Every dime I had in my checking account. Quickly, I called the twenty-four hour automatic teller to check my savings. It hadn't been touched. He wasn't aware of my savings. The balance was still $4,200. As far as he was concern he had totally left me penniless. I knew exactly what I would do.

I pulled out the pink shoebox from under my bed, opened it slowly and pulled out the small silver pistol that used to belong to my father. I checked and it was filled with bullets. I took a seat on the sofa knowing he would be arriving at eight o'clock. As soon as he walked through the door I would shoot him once in each foot, making him a cripple for the rest of his sorry life. I waited, and by mid-night I was still waiting. By daybreak I was still waiting, and by sun down the next day, I realized I wouldn't be able to take any revenge on him. He had what he wanted, my money. He had no reason to return! Leaving me with a tough bullet to swallow." Katie shook her head. "If you think I was a love struck fool then, think twice. I was a bigger fool when I took him back just a short two weeks later."

"Katie." I shook my head. "After all of that. In just two weeks you took him back?"

"Yes. I did, and if he came knocking on my door right now. I would do the same!"

"What excuse did he have for himself for hightailing out of town with your money?"

"He lied as usual and said he was sorry. Some song and dance about how he had to take the money to pay off some drug dealer to stay alive, so he claimed. He could have told me he needed to pay off King Hong and I would have believed him. I was so foolishly in love until I couldn't see past by nose as far as Shaun Parker was concerned. He moved back in and asked me to marry him. I was all set to marry him, but a few days later while he was out drinking with some friends, I packed a couple suitcases and took a cab to Union Station. My destination was Chicago. That happened on a cold, rainy evening in November of 1984. I didn't know what I was going to do when I got there, but I knew I had to get away from Alabama and the life I was tangled up in with Shaun. I wanted better for myself."

"Had you planned to leave him in such a dramatic way as you did?" I asked.

"No, Paulene. I had no intentions of leaving Shaun, ever. It just popped in my mind that evening that if I wanted to better my situation, I would have to leave him cold turkey."

"And that's what you did. But it's clear to me Katie, that you still love Shaun Parker."

She nodded. "Oh yes. That's for sure." She paused as water filled her eyes. Then she looked at me with a deep serious look in her eyes. "If the truth be told, I love the man more than anything or anyone! I just cannot help myself. He's all I think of and all I want. It's like a thirst I cannot fill a hunger I cannot satisfy. All the money and things in the world cannot replace this empty feeling inside of me—living without him. He treated me like dirt when we were together but all I want is the man. The only thing I have to hold on to is that, in my heart, I feel he loved me once!"

"Katie, it amazes me how you can still love a man who treated you so bad."

"I'm not proud of these feelings. I'm ashamed to say I still have these feelings for the jerk, but I do. I'll go to my grave in love with the man."

Chapter Twenty-Four

Katie looked at me as she nodded up and down. She was smiling but she had a sad distant look in her eyes. "I know what you are wondering, Paulene? You probably are wondering did I ever see him again after that?

I nodded. "You are absolutely correct. I was just about to ask you, did you ever run into Shaun Parker again?"

She stared straight ahead, looking at nothing and then slowly a smile curved her face. And then she looked at me. "I think you know the answer to that one."

"So you did run into him again?"

"Oh yeah." She nodded. "When I saw him again it was seven years later."

"Seven long years?"

"Yes. Seven years and it wasn't planned. I had no idea I was going to run into him. I was home for the summer visiting Grandma Fanny, just taking a stroll in Greenside Park. You remember Greenside Park where we used to play?"

I nodded and smiled. "Yes. I remember Greenside Park. How could I forget? When Casey and I were little we played in that park all the time."

"Well, I was just looking around the place and taking delight in all the little kids playing and having fun. I also noticed how much had changed. Then suddenly, out of the blue, I saw him coming across the park toward me. He was smiling and walking quickly in my direction. He was waving one arm over his head.

"Katie. Katie. Wait up," he said.

He was telling me to wait up. But I was frozen and couldn't move if I wanted to. I thought to myself. "Shaun Parker! My Shaun!" But quickly it dawned on me that he wasn't my Shaun and had never been except in my dreams.

"And, Paulene. Just as quick as the blink of an eye, I knew that all the things I'd been telling myself for all those years were lies. I had told myself that I had forgotten him and that the sight of him could no longer touch my heart. His presence still held the same brightness in my heart as always. Grandma Fanny called him a pretty boy, but he wasn't really a pretty boy. Ben Drake is what I call a pretty boy. Shaun was just an attractive man who knew just how to charm the pants right off of any female. And once he did, he knew exactly where to touch you and make you feel like you had just been to heaven and back. The way he made me feel, I have never felt that way before or since." I grabbed my stomach. "After all those years. He still had that same effect on me. Anyway, he spotted me and stopped. Then I saw the warmth and shock in his eyes. He had a torn look as I had imagined he had when I had left town and mailed his ring back.

Then I heard his voice, "Katie is that you? Katie?" And then I stood frozen like a school girl with her first crush. I couldn't answer because my throat felt tight from the mere thought and nearness of him.

"I can not believe it's really you, girl! You look really good. Time has treated you well, that's for sure." He smiled as he walked closer.

As we faced each other, I stood with my eyes glued to his with every thought in my mind a sudden blank.

He continued. "You live in Chicago, right?" He extended his hand to me. He was looking older and more stable. That unsettled, on-the-go look was out of his eyes.

I looked down at our hands gripping tightly to the other and managed a shaky smile as I looked up again, slowly releasing my hand from his. Finally I spoke in a rather nervous voice.

"Yes, I do live in Chicago. I'm just here visiting my Grandmother.

He smiled. "How is Miss Fanny?"

"She's doing real good. Thank you for asking," I said, stumbling with my words. "Do you still live downtown. What brought you out here in these sticks, to this old park?"

"I moved out this way a couple years ago. Bought myself a little two bedroom house up the road there," he said with pride in his voice.

"I'm glad to hear you're doing well," I said.

"Katie?" He touched my face and his touch was like an electric shockwave through my body. All I could think of was how much I still loved him after all those years. One touch from him brought it all flooding back.

"Seeing you and looking at you, is like seeing a ghost," he slightly laughed. "I have hoped for years that I would run into you again, but I didn't really think I ever would."

What he said was so close to the truth that it brought chills to me. I couldn't smile back. Because that's exactly what we were to each other now—ghosts. And since nothing is sadder than two ex-lovers meeting on formal and polite terms the meeting was almost unbearable. He had once and still meant everything to me. I felt my self-control cracking. I couldn't stand and make small talk with Shaun. I knew I was going to cry or say the wrong thing. Plus my overwhelming need to be touched by him was hard to bear.

"I'd better get back to Grandma Fanny, I guess," I quickly said. "It's been really nice to see you again. Well, good-bye and take care of yourself, Shaun."

And I would have taken to my heels and ran, but he caught me by the arm.

"Please, you can't run off this way without telling me anything. Can't you spare a few more minutes? Let's go to that ice cream shop across the street?" He pointed.

I mumbled unsure, "I really should get going. Grandma Fanny will wonder what's keeping me."

"I promise not to take up much of your time." He held my arm and led me into the little ice cream shop.

"Remember when we used to come here?" Shaun smiled as he pulled a chair out for me to be seated at the table the hostess had showed us.

Within minutes, the waitress had taken our order for two hot fudge sundaes. And as the short, thin waitress walked away, Shaun looked at me with one eyebrow higher than the other and said. "Well?"

"Well what, Shaun?"

"Everything." He held out both hands. "How long will you be here? What about yourself? Are you happy? Healthy? Rich the way you always wanted to be? Married to some rich guy maybe?"

I looked down at my trembling hands that lay in my lap out of his view and said, "Another week. Healthy enough. No husband, rich or otherwise. As the rest." I stopped. "How about you?" I asked quickly. "Should I ask how is your wife, your health and so forth?"

He didn't answer for a moment, and then he said slowly, "I'm doing just fine Katie. I'm a graduate from Montgomery University a year and a half ago with a Bachelor In Science. I teach third grade at Montgomery Elementary. I think you told me that you went to school there when you were a little girl, right?" Pride showed in his eyes.

"Yes, I did go there and both of my brothers to." I was smiling from ear to ear. "Well, that beats all, who would have ever thought that you of all people would have end up getting yourself a college degree?"

He pointed to his chest, shaking his head. "You are not asking me are you, because for the life of me, I don't know how it happened? All I know is that one-day I wake up and I couldn't stand my own company. I couldn't stand to be around myself. Therefore, I had to change my present company. I cleaned up my act, took out grants and got myself an education." He held out his hand. "And the rest is history." He put a spoonful of ice cream in his mouth. "Thanks to you, Katie, for leaving me high and dry," he said with a tad of bitterness to his voice. "I deserved a lot better than I got."

My words stormed out in a hot rush before I could stop them. "That isn't fair to say that to me, Shaun," I snapped, pushing my ice cream to the side.

He shook his head. "Oh it isn't? Is it? Well, get this Katie. It wasn't me that turned away from marrying you—it was you who turned away from marrying me." He looked toward the ceiling then back at me.

"How you think I felt when I found out about your decision to leave for Chicago instead? Nothing had prepared me for that kind of hurt."

Shaking my head before he could finish talking. "Maybe, I did back away from marrying you. But I think I had plenty of good reasons where you were concerned, Shaun. For one, the first time you took me to bed. You were my first time and you treated me like a common tramp and never called back." I pointed my finger, anxious to say these things that I needed to say to him years ago. "And if that wasn't enough treating me like dirt, we get back together and try living together and you empty out my bank account to pay off some drug dealer who was after you. So you claimed, that could have been a lie too. I thought my heart would break into a million pieces." I paused, biting my lip.

"Should I go on?" My eyes burned a hole into him, as unpleasant memories of our past made me feel sad inside.

"But your heart didn't break, did it, Katie? You are still in one piece."

"Maybe hearts don't really break. Maybe we just grow harder and unhappier and tougher and more cynical," I said sharply.

He leaned on the table toward me. "Katie—if you really felt like that, then why? Spell it out to me, why did you accept my ring and said you would marry me? You looked me straight in the face and lied to me." He pushed his ice cream aside and strung the spoon on the table. "So I guess we both are liars."

"I did want to marry you. Even after all the garbage you did to me."

"Then tell me why did you jump up and move to Chicago without even telling me that you were calling off our engagement? I had to figure it out on my own after I never heard from you again."

"I had to leave suddenly and couldn't get in touch with you," I mumbled.

"Bullshit." He snapped, tapping his fingers on the table and looking toward the ceiling, he replied sharply. "I'm still waiting for your answer. Are you going to tell me why?" he asked looking straight in my eyes.

"You know why! You know it was Grandma Fanny."

He said bitterly. "If anybody on God's green earth could keep you from marrying me, then it simply meant that you didn't love me."

"You can't say that—I won't take it." I shouted. "I did love you, you bastard. No matter what you put me through, I always wanted you back. Maybe it meant I was weak, but it didn't mean I didn't love you."

"If you'd waited Katie and not jumped up and moved so quickly."

"I didn't jump up and move so quickly! I had been waiting for you, Shaun for years," I said between my teeth.

"It's not too late for us, Katie. I still love you and from the look in your eyes, you still love me, too. Marry me now. I've been nuts about you for all these years and that's never going to change. I was a fool back then and full of myself. But even back then, I loved you."

I shook my head. "I never knew you loved me, Shaun."

"That's because I was such a jerk and never treated you with the respect you deserved. But yes, I loved you then, and I love you now. I will always love you, Katie. Don't you know that? I'm serious about getting marry."

"Are you really?"

"Yes, I am. You must know by this time, if you are ever going to, whether you care enough about me to marry me. Listen, sweetheart, I have the ring in my pocket right now. Do I put it on your finger, and do we get married next week, or is it good-bye?"

"Next week?" I mumbled, looking at him. Shaun had set his lips against mine, then pulled them away and looked me deep in the eyes and answered.

"Yes, next week. Why not? The sooner the better! We have wasted too much time already! I'm tired of climbing the walls wanting to be with you."

I looked deep into his eyes and decided that he meant what he was saying. "Where's the ring, anyway?"

"Right here in my pocket where I always keep it." He pulled the ring from his pocket and put it on my finger.

He leaned over and his eager lips pressed passionately against mine. At that very moment I was happier than I had known I could be. I was all set to marry, then out of the blue two little twin boys about the age of five were standing at our table tapping on his shoulder. "Daddy, we are ready to go. Mommy is in the car. She sent us in here to see if you were in here. Are you ready?"

"Run along, I'll be right out."

His two sons ran out of the ice cream shop and I wanted to just die. I didn't think he could hurt me any worst than he already had, but dropping a bomb on me by asking me to marry him when he already had a wife and two kids—took the cake."

"Katie, before you say anything. Yes those are my boys and yes I am married to their mother. But it's just in namesake only. We are trying to raise our sons. Nothing more. Please, Katie, please keep my ring and give me your number so we can keep in touch. Don't disappear out of my life forever again! Please! Once my divorce is final then we can start our life together. I promise you Katie. I am on the level! I love you, Katie! I love you!" He pleaded.

Shaking my head, holding out both hands, I couldn't say a word to him and I didn't have the strength to throw his ring back to him. He walked out of that ice cream shop and that was the last that I saw of Shaun Parker. And the end of me ever giving my heart to another man." She held out her hand and pointed to the little ring on her pinkie. "That's the ring. I wear it to feel that I didn't walk away from that relationship empty handed. It fits my pinkie now because I have put on ton of weight since then."

She was trying to sound brave, but deep down I could tell that Katie would still give her heart and soul to be with Shaun Parker. She leaned both elbows on the table and gave me a big forced smile. "There you have it, Paulene. Now you see why I have such little respect and trust in the male species. The one man I truly loved and thought I could respect didn't tell me nothing but one lie after another. And after all he put me through, I will go to my grave loving the man!"

Chapter Twenty-Five

Three miserable, confused months later, the second week in August, on a warm, windy day, while Aunt Haddie and I were standing near the side of our small pale green frame three bedroom house getting ready to hang the wash on the clothes line, our big white collie, Bud, who was laying on the grass near the walkway started barking. We looked toward the road just in time to see Ben driving up in his silver Jaguar. He stopped at the end of the driveway and stuck something in our mailbox. He looked at us and smiled, threw a wave and drove off. This was the second time he had stopped at our mailbox.

Aunt Haddie looked at me with a not-so-pleased look, but before she could say a word, Daddy called out for her from the back yard.

"Haddie, where's my lunch? I'm ready to head down to the bean field."

"I'll be right there," Aunt Haddie yelled back.

The moment Aunt Haddie walked around the back, I ran to the mailbox to see what Ben had stuck inside. It was another letter addressed to me. I looked around and when I didn't see Aunt Haddie, I sniffed his letter and kissed it. Thinking to myself. "If only he loved me and wanted me in his life. I would be the happiest woman alive. If only he wanted me. Really wanted me the way I want him."

Dear Paulene,
I still would like to take you to that dance, next Friday night. You never did give me an answer to the first note I left you. I'll stop by this evening after work and find out your answer.
Yours Truly, Ben.

Before I could finish reading Ben's letter, I looked around and there stood Aunt Haddie slightly smiling, in a disgusted like manner and shaking her head, while continuing with the chore of hanging laundry out to dry. She had that look on her face that said she was steaming inside.

"So, I guess Ben Drake left you another note in the mailbox. I hope you know what he's after. A fancy well-off young man like Ben Drake can only be interested in one thing from a poor farm girl like yourself. I can't even believe he's pursuing you, and then again I can. He's only interested in you because you are unobtainable. If he could have you at the drop of a hat, he wouldn't want you."

"Why do you say I'm unobtainable, Aunt Haddie? What in the world do you mean about a statement like that?"

"I mean just that. There is no way Doug and I will ever let that Ben Drake have his way with you."

"Have his way with me?" I smiled. "Aunt Haddie, I don't know what you are trying to say, but you are making it sound as if I have no say so in the matter. Has it ever occurred to you that I might be as interested in Ben Drake has he seems to be in me?" I paused with a serious stare. "I know you mean well, Aunt Haddie," I said calmly, not sounding upset. "But if I decide to date Ben Drake, that will be my own choice. I'm a grown woman and I make my own decisions about who I will and will not go out with."

Aunt Haddie gave me a look of disbelief, shaking her head in even greater disgust. "Paulene, what are you trying to say? Do you have a crush on Ben Drake? If you do, there is going to be some trouble. Because, if you don't know by now, I will tell you, the Drakes consider us to be beneath them. Or should I say, any family that lives across this creek."

Aunt Haddie walked away from me. I could tell she was pretty worried about the possibility of me going out with Ben. She would be fit to be tied if she knew I had had a brief encounter with him while staying in Chicago when he was there on a medical convention. It was my secret, I would never tell her and my Dad how Ben Drake tried to get me in his bed and after that he never called me again.

Now sitting on the edge of the porch holding Ben's letter tightly in my palm, my mind drifted back to the reason I left Chicago. I made my decision after my last dinner with Katie. She dropped me off and I waited in my hotel room all evening hoping Ben would call. By ten o'clock, I fell asleep on the sofa with wet eyes. The next evening the same thing, and by the end of that week I couldn't bear waiting for my phone to ring any longer. Deep down I knew I had blew my chances with him. I had my chance and blew it. I was too afraid of not pleasing him—to try and please him.

My thoughts were interrupted when I heard Aunt Haddie call my name from inside the house. "Here's the snack you wanted to take to the field."

While visiting Dad in the cornfield, during a snack break, I decided to ask him a couple questions about the Drake family. No matter how I tried to deny it, I had very strong feelings for Ben. I still loved him. But I was so afraid that he didn't really have feelings for me, just the way Aunt Haddie had mentioned.

Daddy was a reasonable more understanding, more easy-going and laid back person—different from Aunt Haddie as night and day. I knew he wouldn't be so quick to judge Ben as she had been.

While sitting on a long log under a big oak tree, Dad and I had just finished sharing and eating half of a meat-loaf sandwich. Dad peeked at his watch while standing to his feet. He looked at me and smiled as he picked up his hoe from the ground and started back to chopping weeds from around the beans.

"It's almost four o'clock. Isn't it about time you get going up to the house to help Haddie start supper?"

"There's time. Are you trying to get rid of me? You always say you don't have enough help with the fieldwork. I wondered if I could give you a hand until I start back to college. And you try to run me off."

He shook his head. "Paulene, I might need help with some of this work, but I sure don't need your help. You know I don't want you down here in these fields for no reason. It's okay if you want to come down here and have lunch with me sometime, but I really don't want you to spend too much time in these dusty fields." He glanced at me. "Girl, watch your hair, sitting on that old dirty log. Your hair is sweeping up leaves and everything." Dad frowned.

"Daddy, why do you always do that?" I asked, wrapping my hair around my right arm and placing it in my lap.

"Always do what?"

"Always call me a girl? You always do that."

"Because that's what you are."

"I mean, why can't you just call me a young lady, because when you say girl, you make me feel like you think of me as a kid, and I'm not a kid anymore. You know. Not to mention I'm a twenty-one-year-old woman."

"So, that makes you a woman?" Daddy smiled.

"Yes! It does." I smiled.

"Daddy, you know what I mean. I just don't want you to think of me as a kid."

"Paulene, I can see that you are no longer a kid. I have known that for some time now. You have grown into a beautiful young woman." He pulled out his wallet and looked at an old photo of my mother. "And with each passing day, you look more and more like your mother. Martha was around your age when we fell in love and got married. Your mother was an angel, Paulene. A living angel with a big heart."

My father peeked at his watch again. "Okay, young lady," he said, looking at me with a more serious expression. "Are you going to head to the house or stay here with me in this dusty field for the rest of the evening? Seriously speaking, Paulene, if you don't like the big city life, and don't plan to move back up there. I think it's about time you start looking for something to do here."

"Something to do here?" I mumbled without excitement.

"Not out here." Dad shook his head. "I'm talking about downtown for one of those elite office jobs like you had in Chicago."

"Daddy." I shook my head. "You know I didn't work in an office. I worked in a fragrance boutique. You know that." I smiled.

"You know what I mean, Paulene. An office job or a job in one of those fine stores like where you worked." He paused. "If I have mentioned this to you once, I guess I have mentioned it a hundred times, a smart, pretty young girl like you, or should I say, a smart, pretty, young lady like yourself shouldn't be trying to spend any kind of time in these hot fields." He looked out across the field. "When Martha and I first got married, we got caught up in these fields and couldn't do any better. But I promised her that you would have a better life. Through you and your children—your mother and I will live the dream we couldn't have," he said with a sad look in his eyes. "Martha will always be with me as long as I'm alive!"

"Daddy, some time you talk as if my mother is still alive."

He smiled. "Yeah, I guess I do." Then he pointed to his chest. "She'll always be alive in here."

"I wish I could have known her," I said sadly.

"Just look in the mirror and you're looking at her."

"I look that much like her?"

"You don't just look like her, you talk like her and smile like her." He paused. "I promised your mother that you would never see what a field looked like."

Laughing, I grabbed my mouth. "Daddy, how could you promise her that I would never see what a field looked like—when we live on a farm?"

He laughed. "I know you are being funny, young lady."

Still laughing, I nodded. "Yes. I am. But I couldn't resist the urge to crack a joke on that one. We live on a farm and I would never see a field?" Another big laugh, then it was out of my system.

"Daddy, I know you meant I would never work in the fields, but seriously, I just like to come to the fields to visit with you. You know I don't do anything when I get here." I smiled, but he kept a serious expression on his face.

"Daddy, why are you giving me that serious look? You know I don't do anything except sit on a blanket under a shade tree or on some log like I'm doing now when I come to visit you."

"Yeah, Paulene, I know. And I enjoy your visits. But I guess I just don't like seeing you in these fields under no circumstances." He paused, wiping his left eyebrow with the back of his hand. "I didn't allow Martha in these fields. She never got her delicate hands dirty doing this kind of work. Haddie is another story. I couldn't keep her out of these fields if I tried. She's a born farmer. Her heart is in this farm a lot more than mine. I'm an old man now, and I'm stuck here working this land. But you know I want better for you."

"I know, Daddy."

He glanced at his watch again. "So shouldn't you be heading out of this out sun? He asked.

"I guess you're right. I should be going, but first I would like to ask you, why is it that everybody look down on those of us who live across the creek?"

Daddy slightly laughed as he propped himself on the hoe and rubbed one hand down his short thick grayish black hair.

"Everybody did you say? What everybody?" He put his cap back on. "The only people I know that look down on those of us across the creek are the Drake family; at least, that's what I have heard. And that's because everyone across the creek are hard-working farm hands or farmers or whatever and the rest of the families on that side have big houses, new cars and cushy jobs. The Drake family is probably "the everybody" you're speaking of. So you probably better stay your distance from them."

"But, Dad, are they really that way? Do you think they really look down their noses at everybody who lives across this creek?"

"Well, Paulene, I have heard that for years, but I can't really say if they do or if they don't, but your Aunt Haddie is sure convinced."

"Yes, I know how convinced Aunt Haddie is, but I'm not really quite sure if they are really the way she thinks they are."

Daddy looked at me with a concerned look on his face. He pulled off his cap again and wiped his blue shirtsleeve across his face.

"I guess you're asking these questions because Haddie tells me that

Leonard Drake's son been coming around?"

Gazing at Daddy, I nodded yes with a frown. I wanted to confide in him that I had met Ben in Chicago, but something wouldn't let me, I was too afraid he would mention it to Aunt Haddie. I merely turned my back to him and headed to the house.

Chapter Twenty-Six

It was almost 4:30 in the evening when I made it to the backsteps. I didn't go right inside. I took a seat on the steps. I was thinking about the letter from Ben and the things my father and Aunt Haddie had said to me about his family. I had stayed longer in the field, because I knew Ben would be stopping by and I wasn't sure if I should talk to him or not.

Then, suddenly, I heard a knock on the front door. My heart started beating faster and faster with each second, because I figured it was he. I felt glued to the back steps. I wanted to greet him, but something wouldn't let me. Then I heard Aunt Haddie.

"Paulene isn't here. I'll tell her you stopped by."

"Yes, Mrs. Dawson, the same way you told her I stopped by last week; if you don't mind, I think I'll just stand out here and wait for her."

A sudden quick, tight feeling dashed through my stomach as I grabbed my chest then my mouth. Aunt Haddie hadn't mentioned his visit.

"Look, Son! It's not going to do you any good to wait. She's down in the cornfield with her father; and I don't expect them for supper until around six o'clock. So if you wait, it will no doubt be a long one!" She shouted.

"If it's all the same to you, I would still like to wait."

"No! I think you should leave. I really don't like your attitude at all."

"Mrs. Dawson, I'm only here to see Paulene and maybe my attitude isn't what it could be, but I'm reacting to the cold way you are treating me. And the cold way you treated me when I stopped by last week. I know you don't like me and your attitude is very cold toward me. So if I'm not bubbling over to be polite—that's why."

"Okay, I see your point, but I can't erase the facts," she said sharply.

"What facts are you referring to?" he asked humbly.

"I'll tell you what facts," she shouted. "The fact that your family looks down on everybody who lives on this side of the creek. None of them would be caught dead across here because we are all too common. We don't drive the right cars and wear the right clothes! We don't fit in with you blue bloods."

For a moment I didn't hear them talking anymore, then suddenly I heard Ben speak in a louder, somewhat irritated tone.

"Well, of course that's not true Mrs. Dawson. That's a bunch of nonsense. But I guess you are going to say you dislike my family because we have a little money. You can't blame me because I was born into a wealthy family."

"No, I don't blame you for being born into a rich family, but I darn sure blame you for looking down on those of us who wasn't! You think we are all beneath you."

"Mrs. Dawson, I don't feel that way. Would I be interested in your daughter if I felt that way? I really like Paulene and I would love to take her out and spend some time with her now that I'm back home. It doesn't matter to me where she lives. She could live across the moon and I would still think she's the prettiest girl in Alabama."

"So, you really like Paulene, I see."

"Yes! I do. Why would I be standing here if I didn't?"

"Well, I'll tell you why. You don't care anything about my daughter. You are only interested in using her. You have no intentions of taking her to that big brick house you live in and introducing her to your high and mighty, high society folks. She doesn't have the right address, remember?"

Sitting there anxiously waiting to hear Ben's response, I was nervously biting down on one of my fingers. But he never said another word.

"Yes, that's right! Walk off. You know I'm right. Stay away from my daughter. I'm sure Leonard and Anita Drake would skin you alive if you were to bring the likes of Paulene in their midst."

When I heard Ben's car door slam, I walked through the back door. I didn't know what to say to Aunt Haddie. I had heard their entire conversation. In a way, I felt it was wrong to just sit there and listen to their conversation, but I was just too afraid and embarrassed about what had happened between us in Chicago to greet him. I was confused about what I would say and what my answer would be. Deep down I knew I really cared for him, but I kept wondering if maybe Aunt Haddie could be right about him not really being interested in me, but just after what he could get. That's what Katie had said, and since I didn't sleep with him in Chicago it appeared that he had lost interest. Now that he was back home, I was wondering if he was sincere about a relationship with me or figured he would just try getting me in bed again.

With my head lowered, boiling inside from Aunt Haddie's behavior toward Ben, I walked in the kitchen and took a seat at the table. Aunt Haddie was fixing beef stew and biscuits. She seemed to be in a fighting mood, slamming the cabinets and being noisy with the pots and pans. Then she looked at me and yelled in a very nasty tone.

"Your boyfriend stopped by. You just missed him. I want you to tell that piece of trash to stay away from here."

"But, Aunt Haddie."

"Don't Aunt Haddie me! You should have heard the way that stuck up bastard spoke to me! He has no respect for his elders."

"What I know of Ben…."

She cut me off. "What you mean, what you know of Ben? How can you know any thing that much about that man? You haven't set foot in his big house have you?" She roared as if she would have fainted if my answer were yes.

"Of course, I haven't."

"And you never will! Because he can run over here to see you with one thing in mind, but see if you'll ever be good enough in his eyes to take to his big house? No, you won't because he's a piece of trash just like his damn folks," she said with water-filled eyes.

Why did she hate the Drakes so much? I wondered, not pleased that she was taking her bitterness out on Ben.

"Like I said, to you young lady, you should have heard the way that high class spoiled brat spoke to me?"

"Aunt Haddie, I don't think Ben is the way you seem to think he is," I said, jumping out of my seat, because I had heard the way he spoke up for himself and I had heard the way she spoke down to him. "Maybe his family is that way, but I think he is different."

"And what makes you think he's so different? He's cut from the same cloth. I think you better think again!" She said bitterly, making it apparent that she really had no heart where the Drake family was concerned.

"No, Aunt Haddie, I don't think he's that way."

"So, you think he just loves you and plans to introduce you to his high and mighty family?"

"I'm not sure if he really cares for me or not; but I don't think he's as rotten as you think. He seems okay. I'm seriously considering going out with him."

"Okay, Paulene, if you don't want to listen to me, go right ahead and go out with Mr. Drake I guess you want to find out the hard way. Once he uses you and throws you aside, you can forget about any other nice men coming across this creek to take you out. Once Ben finishes with you, nobody else will want you."

Aunt Haddie's words frightened me. I was confused. I wanted to go out with him, and give the relationship we started in Chicago another chance, but her words had destroyed my courage again.

"Okay, Aunt Haddie, I guess you might be right, but the sad thing about it is that I really do like him. I have had a crush on him ever since I have been old enough to remember seeing him drive by in his new cars and always dressed nice. He is the best-looking man I have ever laid eyes on." I paused. "You got to admit that much about him. He's very fine looking, isn't he?"

"Paulene, of course, he's tall and good-looking with not one ounce of fat on his bones, with nice dark brown wavy hair, styled like a movie star, and he dresses well and talks fine and drives new cars." She paused, shaking her head. "But let me tell you something young lady, if I had all his money, I could do the same. I could wear the best clothes and go to the better salons."

"You're not being fair, Aunt Haddie."

"Okay, okay, what do you want me to say? You want me to tell you that—yeah, I can see that Ben Drake is an extremely good-looking young man? Is that what you want me to say, Paulene? If it is, even though it may be true, it still doesn't change the fact of who he is and how he will surely hurt you."

"Oh, Aunt Haddie," I cried, desperate for a sign that he loved me. "You really don't think there's a chance that he could really care about me?"

Rubbing my back, she uttered in a stiff voice. "No, sweetheart. I'm sorry, but I think you should just forget him." She gave me a serious stare.

"You know, it's not impossible that he could really care for me. I may not wear real expensive clothes and drive a new car, but I'm not the worst-looking person in the world," I said and stormed out the back door into the backyard.

Aunt Haddie ran out behind me and grabbed my arm. "Now, you listen to me, Paulene. Of course, you're not the worst looking person in the world. You are the prettiest girl across this creek or in this whole darn town if you ask me. And as Ben Drake said earlier, the whole darn state of Alabama for that matter."

"Okay, Aunt Haddie, I get the point," I said, taking both hands drying the tears that were dripping from my eyes. "So you do think I'm pretty?"

"Of course! Don't be silly to even ask such a question! And you need to wake up to the facts that this isn't about how pretty you are. It's about how rotten he is." She paused. "I couldn't love you more Paulene, if I had given birth to you myself." She touched the side of my face. "I know you take pride in being this independent, brave woman that you call yourself. And I know you think you can handle the likes of Ben Drake." She paused and held up one finger. "And don't think for a minute that I'm trying to call you a push-over." She glanced down at the ground and when she lifted her head and looked at me, she had sad water-filled eyes. "But to me you are as fragile as Martha was. My little sister was so much like you, until it's almost like I'm standing here talking to her." She touched one of my long curls. "You see, Paulene. You have the same tendency she used to have. I mean identical. You are just too good-hearted and trusting for your own good."

After a slight paused, she continued. "So you hold your head up and don't let me see you shed no tears over the likes of that piece of trash," she said angrily as her eyes seemed ablaze with bitterness. "Because I'm sure you're the last thing on his mind."

Hearing her say those words made my stomach turn over in knots as another tear dropped from my left eye. I wiped it quickly. Because if by chance her words were true, I had to somehow accept them and accept the fact that he would never be mine.

"Paulene, I can see that sad look in your eyes, and what I'm about to say will probably make you even sadder. But I'm going to say it to you all the same. Because I couldn't protect my sister and I probably can't protect you, but I'm damn sure going to try harder with you than I did with Martha." She paused looking at me as I waited for the next shoe to fall. What was she about to say that would make me even sadder?

"Paulene, when Ben Drakes comes back around, I think you should just flat out tell him that you are not interested. If you do that, he'll stop bothering you."

"Okay, Aunt Haddie, I'll tell Ben to stay away from me, but it's going to be so hard. I really care a lot for him."

"But you know he doesn't care, and will sweet talk you as long as you let him. And once he gets you in his bed he's history."

Chapter Twenty-Seven

The wind was calm and the air was warm that evening at shortly past 7:00 PM. We had just finished dinner when I heard a soft knock on the front door. I was in the kitchen placing the dishes in the dishwasher when I heard Aunt Haddie call my name.

"Paulene, Ben Drake is here to see you."

As fast as my feet could carry me, I zoomed out of the kitchen and found Aunt Haddie standing there holding the doorknob. She hadn't even asked him in. I was drying my dishwater hands on my apron while rushing across the living room floor toward the front door to greet him. Aunt Haddie was giving me a look that could kill. I knew she wanted me to tell him to get lost, but I had to do it in a nice way, if I could find the strength to do it at all.

Stretching the door open, I had to brace myself as I looked into his eyes to keep from falling into his arms. I was so hopeless in love with him.

He stood at the edge of the porch with his back propped against the porch railing. He smiled at me and his eyes seemed ablaze with desire as he moved them slowly from my waist-length hair to the long soft yellow angle-length dress I was wearing. Then his eyes moved discreetly from the hem of my dress down to my white sandal feet, and swept upward. The tightness in my stomach moved to my legs and turned them to jelly, as I didn't think my legs would have the strength to stay sturdy. I didn't want to appear nervous in his presence.

"Hi, Paulene," he said, smiling. His gleaming smile seemed to make an already bright moonlight evening even brighter, standing there on the porch wearing a nice gray suit and tie.

"Hi, Ben. I heard you stopped by earlier," I said, making a sandwich between the door, to keep Aunt Haddie from listening to our conversation and myself.

"Yes, I did. I'm sorry I missed you."

"Me too. Would you care to come inside?"

"Well, I thought that maybe we could talk outside in this beautiful moonlight," he said, smiling, pointing toward the sky.

"Okay, sure," I agreed with a smile.

Aunt Haddie, who was sitting on the sofa by now, had her big hazel eyes glued toward us with a big frown on her face. I glanced around at her, and then pulled off my long white apron and threw it to her.

"I'm going to step outside and talk to Ben."

She nodded, but I could tell she didn't like it.

The moment we stepped off the porch he grabbed my hand and led me to the flower garden near the edge of the yard. He pulled off his nice suit coat and spread it on the lawn so I could sit. I felt somewhat uncomfortable. I felt as if I wasn't high class enough for him. I didn't really know what to say, but I had to find a way to tell him to stay away since Aunt Haddie and Katie had convinced me that he wanted to use me, painting him as a man looking for a one night stand and nothing more.

While sitting there in the moonlight, he reached out and touched my face, lifting it toward his. His hands felt so warm and gentle.

"Paulene, I could stare in your beautiful brown eyes like this forever," he said in a low soft voice and winked at me.

His voice made me feel happy inside, thinking about the first time he held me in his arms.

"So, what's the answer? Will you go to that party with me or what?" He smiled.

Smiling, I wanted to say yes. I wanted to go but I knew I couldn't. I didn't want to be used. Even though he seemed sincere, unlike the way

Aunt Haddie and Katie had said, I still wasn't brave enough to take a chance.

"I'm sorry, Ben, but I can't go to that party with you. I'm sure the sophisticated ladies here in Montgomery are in line to go out with you. Just ask one of them."

"I asked you, Paulene. I'm not interested in taking out every woman in Montgomery. I'm only interested in you."

I jumped up. I couldn't believe his words.

"Don't tell me you're only interested in me." My voice trembled. "Because I know better. I'm not as naive as you think."

"I don't think you're naive. I just want to be with you the way we were. Is that too much to ask? I thought you wanted the same thing. Am I wrong in my assumption? Would you like to go to the party with me or not?"

While he was standing there facing me, I dropped my head. I couldn't answer him. I really wanted to say yes. I knew I couldn't. He took both hands and grabbed me around the waist forcefully, yet gently. He gathered me in his arms and held me tenderly. I could hear his heartbeat and for a split second I felt as if I was standing on a cloud. Being in his arms felt so right, but just as forcefully as he pulled me in, I tore from his embrace.

"Don't do that," I said, looking toward the ground, then looked up in his eyes melting from his touch.

He looked toward the sky and shook his head. "I don't get this. You seemed interested in Chicago. What has changed?" He raised both arms toward the sky. "Why now that you are back home you are giving me the brush off? Did I do something to offend you the last time we were together? If I did, tell me. We had a beautiful evening together. It was something so special that I haven't experienced it before or since. One minute you were in Chicago and the next minute you were gone." He reached out to touch my face, but pulled his hand back when he noticed me tremble at the thought.

"Paulene, talk to me. Why won't you give me a chance now that you are back home? I think you care for me as much as I care for you, but you are afraid of something. Tell me what?"

"Yes, I'm afraid!" I screamed. "I'm afraid that you just want a repeat of our last time together. You only wanted to get me in bed and after I didn't, you didn't even give me the decency of calling me back."

"Paulene is that what you thought that evening was all about." He shook his head. "Well it wasn't. Plus, I tried to call you all that evening after I got home but your phone was busy and after that I got no answer. I had just gotten word that I had to leave for Springfield the next morning. I left you a message with the front desk that I was leaving town for a week and would call when I got back." He paused. "I guess you didn't get the message. Is that why you left without a word and told Katie not to tell me your number or address?"

My mouth felt glued, I didn't reply. Those had not been my instructions to Katie, I thought to myself, still standing there looking toward the ground as he continued.

"I stayed in Springfield on business for six days, returning late that Saturday night. I called as soon as I got back in Chicago and was told you had checked out of your room and left no forwarding address. I called Katie and she all but acted as if she didn't even know where you had moved. It wasn't until sometime later that I finally got her to tell me that you had moved back home. And it was hard as hell getting her to give me your address. She never did give me your phone number."

Even more confusion swept across me, thinking to myself, why wouldn't Katie give him my number? I was upset with him, but I hadn't really confided that to her. I hadn't asked her not to give him my number or address. Actually, she knew I wanted him to have my number and address. And was actually depending on her to give it to him if he had happened to asked for it.

"That's the whole story. I wanted to see you again. I thought you didn't want to see me. Not to mention after getting back home and you haven't as much as given me the day of time, Paulene."

Standing there looking in his beautiful eyes, melting away, his words sounded sincere. But how could I know?

"Ben, if all that is true and you were so interested in me, why didn't you get in touch with me before now? You could have called or written and explained the way you just did. It's been three months since I left Chicago."

"Yeah, I know. But like I just said, Paulene. I didn't have your number or address. I was only able to obtain your address from Katie two weeks ago when I left Chicago. I tell you, she wouldn't give it to me. She didn't think you wanted me to have it. She told me so herself that you precisely told her in no uncertain terms to not give out your information to me. And she just followed your wishes." He paused. "So that's why I couldn't get in touch with you before now. And luckily after I got home, I asked my folks had they heard of any families around here by the name of Dawson and they told me exactly where you lived. My parents know your folks pretty well, and knew exactly who I was talking about and where you lived."

After a long pause of him standing there looking at me and me standing there looking at him, he broke the silence and smiled.

"Now that you know I have been going crazy to get to see you again after that one evening in paradise with you, what do you say? Can we start over? There's nothing to be afraid of and there's nothing stopping us." He reached out and touched my face and held his hand against my face for a second, enjoying his beautiful touch before he pulled his hand away and before I lost myself in him.

"Ben, I think I should be afraid. Just look at me. Look at my clothes compared to your clothes. Look at my hair compared to your hair. Look at my life compared to yours. You shopped at Neiman-Marcus in Chicago on Michigan Avenue when you lived there. Now you drive all the way to Atlanta just to shop at Neiman-Marcus. The bare minimum you can pay for a man's suit and a pair shoes in that store is twelve hundred dollars and up." I paused. "You visit a salon once or twice a week. My family and me shop wherever we can afford to and I visit a salon once a month, if that. You are a twenty-six-year-old doctor. And I'm a barely 21-year-old farm girl who hasn't even finished college. You live a fancy life in a big mansion and I have an ordinary life in a section of the community that you don't even visit, and you think I should think that you are interested in me? Aunt Haddie opened my eyes. I know you are only interested in getting me into bed and nothing more! I haven't forgotten how you tried to get me in your bed on our first date in Chicago."

The tears inside of me felt like a broken damn that was getting ready to pour. I could feel my tears building in my eyes, but I couldn't let him see me cry.

"So just go and get out of my life and leave me alone forever!" He grabbed me and shook me. I could see the anguish in his eyes. My words had apparently ripped at him.

"No, Paulene, your Aunt Haddie is wrong. I'm not out to get you in bed. That's not what I'm after. You should be able to see that. I could swear it's your mother I'm standing here talking to. She has, without a doubt, filled your head with all that nonsense about my family and me. I thought you knew better. Can't you see, I'm not just out to get you into bed. I have been after you for months now. I knew you were the only woman for me when we spend our first evening together in Chicago just walking around. And did I notice you at both of Katie's parties, yes? You were the prettiest woman at each event and the only one I noticed. And did I want to sleep with you in my apartment in Chicago, yes? But is that all I want from you? No way!" He paused. "And, yes, I see your clothes and I don't see anything wrong with what you are wearing. As a matter of fact, I like the way you dress, I like everything about you." He paused.

"A price tag doesn't always determine how nice an item is," he said examining the sleeve of his suit coat, and then pointed toward the long yellow floral dress I was wearing. "It wouldn't matter to me whether your dress cost two dollars or two hundred dollars. What counts is that you are in it. You'll come to see that I'm not wrapped up in that kind of stuff." He paused again. "I'm wrapped up in you. You are so beautiful, Paulene. You hear me? Beautiful, beautiful, beautiful." He reached out and slightly touched my hair with the back of his left hand. "And yes, I see your hair and what I see is lovely, those long light brown curls hanging down to your waist like ropes of pure gold. Your hair is too naturally beautiful to be touched by a stylist. It's folks with hair like mine that need to run to the salon every week." He raked a hand through his gorgeous hair. "It may look okay at the moment. But to make a story short, let's just say that's why my salon bill is so much each month."

Slowly, I lifted my face to look up at him and my strength somehow vanished. He took both hands and held my face. The next thing I knew, he was slowly bringing his smooth handsome face down to mine, gently covering my mouth with the softness of his. I wanted so much for him to kiss me. His hands moved slowly with a slight tremble down the side of my face and on down to the bottom of my neck and accidentally he touched the top button on my dress and I thought I would die from the electrifying touch of his hand. My body shivered from being within inches of his. The magic of his touch was the sweetest feeling I had ever known. My body was awake for the first time since the last time I was in his arms. I was experiencing enormous sensations just as I had before. And when his mouth met mine, pressing tenderly against my lips, I thought I had left this world and entered some other magical existence like a place that only he could take me to. A place that's like a wondrous land, where one can surrender their heart to love.

My heart flooded with excitement as he kissed me tenderly, swallowing me up urgently. Sensations of delight rushed from me one after another as he kissed me deeply and hungrily. We kissed and held on to each other faces as if we needed each other's kisses to breathe. Our arms were wrapped around each other as we held each other tight—savoring the relaxing comfortable feelings that we were giving each other.

"I'm so filled up for you, Paulene, until I explode just from the sweet scent of your beautiful hair," he said as he buried his face in my Vidal Sassoon scented curls that swept down my back thickly. "And the feel of you next to me," he said breathless against my lip as his mouth seemed to own mine, but in the midst of my undeniable need to kiss him and to be kissed by him and to melt in his arms, I ripped out of his arms and ran across the yard toward the house. I stopped mid-way to turn and look at him as I held my stomach from the strength his touch had drained me of.

"Ben, please! Just please leave right now. Don't confuse me anymore."

"But, you wanted…I could feel you melt in my arms. I know you care for me too. I could feel it! Damn! Paulene, why do you keep fighting it? Why are you trying to convince yourself that you don't care for me when you know you do?"

"Just leave, Ben. Please! Go and live in your high society world and let me live in mine! Don't try to convince me that someone like you from a filthy rich family could fall in love with a dirt-poor farm girl like me. I know it's not possible. You are trying to use me, Ben Drake. If I let down my guard and give in to you—you'll use me and throw me away. I know you will!"

As I was running up the walkway toward the front door, he didn't chase after me. I heard him yell, just as I reached the front steps.

"Paulene, for heaven's sake! Why can't you get over thinking that way about me?"

"Maybe because I don't know of any other way to think of you," I glanced over my shoulder breathless and weak with emotions.

"And how can you say it's not possible?"

"Because it doesn't seem possible to me."

"But it is possible," he stressed. "I love you. You got to know that, and I know you love me too." He paused.

"Paulene, I'm not playing games with you. I really adore you, and not even a thousand words could say how much. I could live forever and never find a single thing on God's green earth as lovely as you. I fell in love with you the first evening I laid eyes on you. It was that first evening you spilled champagne on my white suit. I took a quick glance in your eyes and as my heart registered your beauty, I had to run from that darn party. I had to run for my life, Paulene. You took my breath away."

His words may or not have been true, but I thought I would melt right down to the porch when he said that. Especially, since I had felt exactly how he had just mentioned he had felt. He was talking fast, as quick as he could as if to say everything he wanted to say before I stepped inside.

"You were standing there in a roomful of beautiful women, but you were the only light that penetrated my heart. That quick glance into your clear brown eyes and I had to catch my breath. It was as if I could see right through your eyes, into a precious world, where only someone like you could live. I know a lot of attractive women? But when I look at you I see more than just your good looks. And even though, you are stunning beyond words! I feel a deep connection with you. It's deeper than anything I have ever imagined. All I know, Paulene, is that you are the only woman I want in my life. It feels like I have loved you all my life."

When he said those words it took all the strength I had to hold on to the doorknob and not run back in his arms. Holding back my overwhelming urge to give in to him and scream out how much I loved him was causing me the greatest pain I had ever felt. I couldn't have felt more pain from a razor sharp knife being pushed into my heart.

Pausing at the front door with my head lowered, I still held my stomach with one hand. My heart was like a magnet. It kept pulling me toward him, but my head kept my hand gripped to the doorknob and I kept thinking about what Aunt Haddie had said, that his words were a means to an end, and that "end" was to get me into bed and throw me away.

Then suddenly while standing on the porch facing the front door, I released the doorknob and gathered enough strength to turn myself around and face him. He was standing at the end of the walkway with the most tortured look on his face, as if his heart had been crushed. He seemed so sincerely hurt, until I didn't know whether to run inside or run back into his arms. Just as I caught my breath and inhaled, Aunt Haddie yelled.

"Paulene, is that you?"

"Yes, I'm coming right in."

And that was my answer. I looked around at Ben, after turning the knob and cracking the door to step inside. He called out to me.

"Paulene, please! Wait!"

His voice faded away as I stepped inside and shut the door behind me.

Closing the door on Ben that night made me feel as if my life was over. It made me realize how deeply in love I was with him. I loved him more than anything or anyone. All I could think of was being with him. But every time I had good thoughts about him, sad thoughts would follow, thoughts of him only wanting to use me. Then other thoughts would follow: Could I be wrong? Could Aunt Haddie be wrong? Could he be right? Could he truly love me too? It seemed as if my heart and mind were having a constant battle over which way I should turn, and neither one was winning out.

Chapter Twenty-Eight

Two long, painful, miserable weeks had passed and Ben hadn't knocked on my door anymore. He had left me alone. Aunt Haddie was pleased that Ben hadn't been around and kept trying to take my mind off of him by suggesting I have my old blue 1970 Chevy Nova that was parked in the yard towed to a shop for repair so I'd have transportation until I was able to purchase a better car. The old car was twenty-eight-years-old, which Dad had purchased new and gave to me on my sixteenth birthday. Aunt Haddie also tried to encourage me to get motivated about starting college in Montgomery. She also wanted me to call up old friends and get my social life back on track, like going to the movies every Friday with Linda Payton and going downtown to window shop and out to eat with her on Saturdays, the way it was before I had moved off to Chicago. But I had called Linda as soon as I got back home and was informed by her folks that she had moved away to Huntsville. After I told her Linda Payton had moved out of town, she then encouraged me to call Katie sometime.

"We'll pay the dime. Feel free to call Katie in Chicago whenever you feel like it. Because that Katie turned out to be just as nice as Fanny said she was. Giving you a good job and a place to stay for all that time proved that. And best of all, she didn't hold it against you about her nutty brother ending up in that institution."

Aunt Haddie was right, Katie had been very good to me upon my arrival and stay in Chicago, but it seemed that after I met Ben and told her how I felt about him, she cooled toward me. Or it could have been that I cooled toward her, feeling that she still secretly loved him.

There was really nothing Aunt Haddie or my father could do to lift my spirits, because I could care less about socializing or getting my old car fixed or getting ready for college again. But they were determined to cheer me up. My father had my car repaired that Friday morning and that Friday night, he and Aunt Haddie invited me to come with them to Mrs. Fanny Huntley's 78th birthday party.

After I dressed for the party and stepped into the living room where my father and Aunt Haddie were waiting for me, Aunt Haddie grabbed her mouth and shook her head.

"Where did you get that dress?" she asked me, stumbling with her words.

"I got it out of that old black truck in the attic. Why is there a problem?" I asked looking down at the dress. "You told me I could have whatever I wanted out of that old suitcase," I said, stepping across the room to sit on the sofa to buckle my sandals.

"Yeah, that's fine. I saved those things for you anyway," she said. "It's just that."

I cut her off, smiling, looking her broad overweight figure up and down. "Aunt Haddie, I guess you were my size when you were younger?" I asked with one foot propped on the footstool to buckle my sandal.

Aunt Haddie shook her head, grinning. "Paulene I was never your size, not even when I was in diapers." She glanced at Dad who was standing at the back door gripping the doorknob, ready to head to Mrs. Huntley's party as soon as we were.

Dad quickly uttered while adjusting his tie. "Those things in that old truck use to belong to your mother, Martha. It fits you well just like it was made for you," he said.

"It sure does, Doug." Aunt Haddie looked at Dad. "Have you ever seen such a beautiful sight?" Aunt Haddie pointed from my head to toe. "Paulene wearing that old white dress of Martha's. I think that's the dress Martha wore to her high school prom." She stressed and looked back at me. "That's why I grabbed my mouth like that when you stepped into the room. You are a split image of your mother wearing that dress." Aunt Haddie eyes watered.

Seeing the looks on their faces, something touched me inside. It was obvious that they both had loved my mother very deeply. It made me feel sad that I never knew her and that I couldn't feel that special bond that they felt. The only real mother I had known was Aunt Haddie. I felt a bond for her. She had raised me and all my birth mother was to me was a beautiful image in my head of a very special person who had died too young. "I wish I had known my mother. The way you two talk about her, she had to be something special," I said standing to my feet, grabbing my purse from the coffee table. "I'm ready if you two are," I said as they kept looking at me in that dress.

My father finally broke his stare and shook his head. He pulled the door open and headed on out before us. "There's a God up there. There's a God up there," he said under his breath.

"What's with Dad, Aunt Haddie?" I said, looking through my purse for my house key.

She patted my back and held up her door key. "I'll lock up. You can go on to the car," she said.

I stood there on the back porch as she locked the door. "So, what's up with Dad? Why did he make that statement on his way out the door?" I paused, looking down at the ankle length pale white dress that had a yellowish tone to it, not from manufacturing, but from years of being stored away in a plastic bag.

"Well, I'll tell you like this, Paulene. Martha was your father's soul mate and life. She was also my life to. And seeing you in that old dress just makes us both realize how blessed we are to have that portion of her that's a part of you." She patted my back as we stepped off the porch, down the four steps into the backyard.

"Aunt Haddie, I wish I felt that closeness for my mother that you and Dad feels."

"I know you do, Paulene. But you never got to know my sweet sister." She touched my face. "And you look so much like her. But I tell you what, when we get to the party, we'll sat down together and I'll tell you a little bit more about your mother," she said, now opening the passenger's door of her old blue Plymouth.

She took a seat on the front seat of her old car and held her seat forward as I scooted on the back seat. Dad was seated behind the wheel dressed in a crisp white shirt and a pair of neatly pressed pale blue dressed pants. He was also wearing a dark blue tie. He always dressed up at whatever occasion possible; since he took pride in every opportunity that he could to wear a tie. He would probably be the only man at Mrs. Huntley's birthday party dressed in a tie, but that was fine by him, since his line of work kept him in overalls and casual clothing too much for his liking.

Driving along, Dad and Aunt Haddie were in a low conversation among themselves. They were discussing property taxes and something about the fieldwork. I interrupted and tapped Aunt Haddie on the shoulder.

"Aunt Haddie, you said you would tell me a little bit more about my mother when we get to the party," I mumbled sadly, twisting the tiny gold ring that I was wearing on my pinkie finger. "Dad has told me tons about her, but I guess what I really would like to know is more about her illness. How she got sick and died so young," I said, still twisting the ten-karat gold ring that contained a small ruby setting. It had belonged to my mother. Dad had given it to me on my fourteenth birthday.

"Paulene there's not much to tell about your mother illness," Dad said with a tightening to his voice. "Martha wasn't sick."

"What do you mean she wasn't sick?" I asked.

"I mean just that. Your mother was not sick."

"If she wasn't sick, Dad. How did she die?"

"I'll tell you how she died," he said sadly and paused.

Aunt Haddie patted his shoulder. "Try not to get too excited, Doug. Just tell her what happened."

"Haddie, if you'll let me finish. That's what I'm trying to do."

"Dad, if you would rather not talk about it," I quickly said, sensing a little tension. "You can tell me later."

"It's Okay, Paulene. I can tell you now," he said and paused. "Your mother went to the doctor for her yearly examination and after which, was told she had a lump in her breast. That was it. She wasn't sick until those darn doctors at Montgomery Memorial made her that way. She didn't want to be cut, but those damn doctors convinced her that they would remove the lump and she would be fine."

"Your father is right." Aunt Haddie quickly added. "They filled our heads with a bunch of garbage about research and modern medicine and way too much talk that we just didn't understand."

"Haddie is right. I definitely didn't understand those procedures and what they were explaining to us. And Martha didn't understand any of it either!

"But how could you expect to really fully understand? You guys are not doctors."

"We are not doctors, but we have a choice over our bodies and whether we want to chance being cut or take our chances." Dad shook his head. "The bottom line, Paulene, is that they talked your mother into that surgery. "

"But Dad, if they found a lump in her breast she had to have it removed. What other choice did she have?" I asked.

"She had a choice to say no and not go through with it," Aunt Haddie snapped quickly before Dad could reply. "She was happy and full of life and nothing was hurting her. She didn't want to leave her young infant to go lay up in some damn hospital bed with doctors who wanted to cut the life right out of her," Aunt Haddie barked bitterness toward the doctors at Montgomery Memorial.

"Well, if I had been in her shoes, I would have made the same choice. Doing nothing, it was sure to kill her. Doing so could have saved her life," I explained.

"Well, it didn't save her life." Dad shook his head and threw up one hand. "She walked into that darn place with a smile on her face. She was trying to comfort me that everything would be alright, but she never walked out of that place," Dad said, now turning into the gravel driveway of Mrs. Huntley.

Aunt Haddie turned toward the back seat to look at me. "That's right, Paulene. They did that surgery on Martha and in three weeks she had left us. I had just lost my job at the dress factory where I was working at the time. I told Martha I would stay and take care of you while she was hospitalized. We had no idea that she was walking into that place and would not be returning."

"That's right," Dad mumbled sadly, turning off the engine of the old Plymouth. He had parked behind three other cars that were parked on Mrs. Huntley's grass.

Opening my door and getting out of the back seat to follow them inside, I mumbled. "Well, I'm glad to hear that my mother wasn't really sick and didn't suffer long." I touched Dad's back, comforting him as the three of us headed across Mrs. Huntley front lawn toward the front door. It was obvious from the strain sound of his voice that talking about the time my mother passed brought back deeply sad memories, unlike the happy memories he always talked about.

After saying our hellos, Aunt Haddie and I took a seat on one of the long black leather sofas in Mrs. Huntley's family room where the party was being held. She had music coming from an antique looking stereo. It was all 1950's, 60's and 70's music. The Supremes, Tom Jones, The Drifters, Fat Dimino and Elvis Presley. Not one single song that I wanted to hear, except "Love Me Tender" by Elvis Presley.

While sitting next to each other we were both sipping on a glass of red wine that Mrs. Huntley had handed to us. Dad was standing in the corner of the semi-large room talking to some old man he knew. Aunt Haddie touched my shoulder. "Paulene, since you want to know about when your mother died, I want to tell you about that day." She took a big swallow of her wine. "It's a day that is forever embedded in this old brain of mine." She leaned forward and placed her glass on the long square coffee table in front of us. "It goes like this. When your mother died, a light went out in me and one went out in your father to. Something died in both your father and me. Apart of me and Doug was buried right along with your mother. Paulene, to know Martha was to love her. And we both loved Martha with everything we had. She was the most understanding, caring person I have ever had the privilege to know. Doug and I both needed her in our lives desperately. She was pretty much his only family and definitely mine. As we told you earlier, your mother had been hospitalized for three weeks suffering from the aftermath of her breast cancer surgery. Anyway, day-by-day she just got weaker and weaker. Her doctor said she needed another operation, but in the next breath, he told us that performing another surgery would only make her even weaker and that it really wouldn't do any good." She waved her hand, looking around the room at the couple dozen of guest that were there attending Mrs. Huntley's birthday party. They were all too busy drinking and mingling to hear our conversation. She turned back to me. "Martha was the sweetest, prettiest thing in the world and she had to die."

"Aunt Haddie, those three weeks that she was in the hospital, how did she seem to you? Did she know she was going to die?"

"She seemed in a good mood, smiling and talking every time we visited her. Doug and I were the two who looked broken down. It was only on that last day did she seem a bit sad."

"Did she know at that time that she was going to die?"

Aunt Haddie nodded looking out into space. "Yeah, she knew it from day one after her surgery. Somehow she knew and tried to tell Doug and I, but of course we wouldn't listen, because it wasn't what we wanted to hear her say. But she was trying to prepare us."

"So, she knew?" I took my first sip of wine.

"Yes she did, but she never did stop smiling," Aunt Haddie said.

"So, she knew, but she still smiled and didn't seem crushed over it?" I asked, as I was amazed at what I was hearing.

"That's right. There was always a smile on that pretty face of hers and she never once shed one tear until that last day. And the tears she cried were not for her, but for Doug and I. She could feel our pain and she felt helpless that she couldn't do anything about it." Aunt Haddie reached out and fumbled with the collar of the dress I was wearing.

"Aunt Haddie, my mother's untimely death changed your life and Dad's life forever. Suddenly you became a new mother with a baby that you never expected to raise and Dad was suddenly a young widow with a new baby that he probably didn't even know how to change a diaper for," I said sadly, sipping on my wine, holding the wine glass with both hands, somewhat in a daze thinking about their lives as she was telling me.

"It changed our lives alright. For the worst!" She touched my arm.

"Don't get me wrong. "I have enjoyed every minute of raising you up. You are my daughter in my eyes. And the years with Doug have been great. But I would trade it all in the blink of an eye if it meant Martha could have raised you herself and lived to be an old woman with your father." She looked at me with water in her eyes. I had never remembered seeing Aunt Haddie look so humble or speaking so touching about anything or anyone.

"Paulene, I never will forget that night," she said, interrupted by a tap on the shoulder from Mrs. Huntley.

"Haddie, can I get you another glass of wine?" She took Aunt Haddie's empty glass from the coffee table.

Aunt Haddie nodded. "Sure, Fanny. That sounds fine to me."

Aunt Haddie looked at Mrs. Huntley as she walked her short, thin, fragile frame across the room to the refreshment table. She poured Aunt Haddie's glass to the rim and strutted quickly back over to the sofa and handed it to her.

"You and Paulene can help yourself to that food over there any time you like. The both of you have been glued to this sofa since you got here. Everybody is dancing. When are you two going to get out there and break a leg?" Mrs. Huntley asked, smiling.

"Maybe after another one of these," Aunt Haddie held out her wine glass.

Mrs. Huntley smiled and headed back across the room.

But Aunt Haddie was teasing. As far as I knew, she didn't dance and didn't really drink much. If she finished that second glass of wine it would be a miracle. They never had wine with dinner, because Dad didn't drink at all.

Aunt Haddie leaned forward and placed the glass of wine on the coffee table without even taking one sip. "Hopefully I can continue telling you about your mother's last day without anymore interruptions," she smiled.

"I hope so to. I'm really enjoying hearing about it." I glanced across the room and Dad was still standing in the same corner talking to the same man.

Aunt Haddie held her face for a moment, and then took a deep breath.

"Okay, Paulene here goes. It was a hot summer night in mid-July, 1977. You had been born on February 8th of that year. You were now only five months old. I was down the hallway in the nursery changing your diaper. It was almost seven o'clock. I had just made dinner for Doug and I had given you a bottle. You were now tired and sleepy and just as soon as I changed your diaper I would put you to bed. The moment I placed you in your bed, the phone rang. I knew Doug was sitting on the living room sofa looking at his and Martha's wedding album. All while Martha had been sick and in the hospital—that was his daily chore to sit on the sofa and look at their wedding pictures. That's the only thing that would make him smile when he wasn't around her. That and spending time with you." She paused to wipe a tear.

"Well, after four rings I knew Doug wouldn't be answering it. I strolled down the hallway quickly and found him sitting there on the sofa with both elbows resting on his knees with his hands covering his face.

"Don't answer that, Haddie. Please just let it ring. I can't take this! I just can't take this!" He uncovered his handsome, broken face and looked over at me with real tears rolling down his face."

Hearing her say that, my heart sunk deep inside of me. "Oh, my goodness, Aunt Haddie. How sad to hear that Dad sit crying."

"Well, he wasn't the only one crying," she said and pointed across the room in the direction where my father stood. "What you have to realize, Paulene, is that at that time your father wasn't that almost sixty year old man standing over there. When he lost Martha he was just thirty-six years old: A young man with his whole life ahead of him. But after Martha passed, he didn't care about anything except taking care of you and raising you up right. He just kind of existed day by day, eating, sleeping and working, but not really enjoying the fullness of life. It took years before he really smiled again." She paused and patted my hand.

"Like I was saying, the phone was ringing and he was sitting there crying.

My soul went out to him because I knew his heart was breaking minute by minute into a hundred different pieces. But I couldn't save his heart because my world was shattered to. We both knew who was calling. The doctor and nurses had informed us earlier that morning to expect a phone call before Martha passed. They had pulled Doug and I to the side telling us that she probably wouldn't make it through the night.

Like him, I was afraid to answer the phone to, but I had to answer it. We had to know what was going on with Martha. Anyway, with my heart in my throat, I answered the phone and just like we thought, Martha's nurse was on the other end of the receiver. "Is this the Dawson's resident?" The Nurse asked.

"Yes, it is?" I replied.

"May I please speak to Doug Dawson? It's about his wife."

When the nurse said it's about his wife, the receiver slipped out of my hand and I grabbed my face with both hands. I couldn't listen to anymore that nurse had to say. I couldn't bear to hear what I thought she was about to say.

"Haddie what did they say?" Doug found the strength and sprung from the sofa. He gripped my shoulders. "What did they say, Haddie?"

"Nothing," I cried. "I wouldn't let them tell me anything. I couldn't. I threw the phone down."

When I finally dried my eyes, Doug seemed more collected. He hung up the phone and grabbed his car keys off the coffee table.

"That was Martha's nurse. Martha is asking for us. They want us to hurry," he said trying to sound brave as I followed him into the kitchen.

"Is she?" I asked, sniffling.

"Is she what, Haddie?" he asked with an agitated edge to his voice, reaching for his glasses on the kitchen counter. "She's dying okay? She's dying and they want us to come say our good-byes. Does that answer your question?" He shouted as water filled up in his eyes.

My hands trembled as I pulled the back door open for him. I patted his back as he headed down the back steps. "I'll call Fanny now and ask her to let Katie come over and look after the baby."

He nodded as he stepped around to the front, hopped in his car and started the engine. He burned rubber out of the driveway. In the meantime, I rushed to phone Fanny and within fifteen minutes, Fanny was dropping Katie off to baby-sit you. I told Katie where your bottles and diapers were and stormed out the front door to get to your mother.

The air was calm and warm, but I felt like I had a blazing inferno going on inside of my chest. I had never felt so much pain before or since as I did that night driving to Montgomery Memorial to see my sister. My foot felt like lead as I broke every speed limit all the way. It didn't matter whether a cop stopped me or not. Nothing mattered except getting to Martha's bedside. I wouldn't be able to live with myself if I didn't get to her bedside to say good-bye. I drove quickly through the narrow roads in the neighborhood. Although, on one side road that lead to the main freeway to downtown Montgomery, I hit red light after red light, and even though the streets were nearly empty because of the dinner hour, I stopped lawfully at each one of them. I couldn't chance getting stopped for a ticket. Not this time!

Martha had shown more guts and courage than she had received from us. She had asked that we bring her no flowers and make no fuss over her illness. Just show her love through preparing ourselves for her passing. Although Doug agreed with her when she said it, he still couldn't resist beautifying and brightening her hospital room with flowers from her own garden. That seemed to cheer her up. And although we knew what the doctor had said, we were still hoping for a miracle. He wasn't ready to lose his beautiful wife and I wasn't ready to lose my sweet sister. His relationship with her was the most perfect relationship that I had ever witness two people on this earth to share. When she turned thirty-three two weeks after she had been hospitalized, Doug's gift to her was that portrait that hangs over the fireplace. That painting came directly from his heart. He breathed life into that one portrait. He said to her as he held the portrait up for her to look at: "You will always be with me and Paulene. This portrait will hang on the wall over the fireplace and we will be able to look at your beautiful face for the rest of our lives."

"When I pulled into Montgomery Memorial, only a few cars were parked in the visitors' lot, and I found a spot close to the hospital entrance. Inside, the lobby, standing there for the elevator to take me up to the 6th floor, I was praying to myself, trying to prepare myself for what lay ahead. I knew I would find Martha with the same calm, uplifting attitude she always had. Because she wasn't afraid of dying, and knowing that gave me a tad bit of comfort, but not much. Because even though she wasn't afraid of dying, we didn't want to lose her."

The moment I stepped into Martha's room my heart sunk inside of me. Martha seemed calm, lying there beautiful as a picture on that hospital bed. Doug was sitting on the bed beside her. It was obvious that she was trying to hold her pain to herself to keep us from feeling bad. She seemed much weaker than she had that morning.

With trembling hands and eyes filled with water, I stepped over to her bed and rubbed her beautiful hair. "Martha, it's me, Haddie. I just want you to know that I'm here," I said holding back my tears.

She looked up at me with her eyes half opened and smiled. "Hi, Haddie. I see you are wearing pink. You look cute in that color. I'm so glad you're here."

"I'm glad I'm here to, Martha."

"How is the baby?" she asked.

With my back now turned to her to keep from showing my tears, I said. "Paulene is just fine. Everyday she looks more and more like you," I wiped my tears with my fingers, stepping over by the window.

Doug held both her hands in his. She had a peaceful look on her face, but an anxious look in her eyes, what you could see of them. And the anxious look did not leave her eyes until she said. "Doug promise me," She tried to speak, the words coming out between her gasps for air.

He leaned close to hear her. From that angle, he could see the bright moon through the hospital window. "Don't try to speak, Martha." He smoothed a long curl of her hair away from her face.

"Promise me," she said with her eyes half opened, smiling up at him.

"Promise you what, Martha?" he asked gently.

Slowly she managed to turn her head in my direction, and then back toward Doug. "That you will make a life for yourself." Her lips trembled from the strain of speaking. "You are still young and good-looking."

Doug touched the side of her face and smoothed his hand down her hair. "Martha save your strength. Please don't try to talk, sweetheart."

"This is my only chance to tell you this. I really don't have much time left." Her soft, weak voice tightened with frustration as she struggled to get the words out.

"Martha, I will promise you that I will always love you," he said holding his tears.

She let go of his hand to reach toward the night table, her arm trembling as if it caused her great pain. Doug saw the note pad she was reaching for and picked it up himself. Martha had written my name on that pad.

"Haddie." Doug read. "Your sister, Haddie, standing over there?" He pointed toward the window where I stood in tears.

"Yes, my sister," she said. "Please look after her. She has no family." She swallowed and breathed with much discomfort. "Promise me," she mumbled.

"She wanted Doug to look after me. Why? I can't answer that. That was just Martha's way—good as the days are long. Sweet as honey itself."

"But…why, Martha?" Doug asked. "Haddie is just fine. She doesn't need me or anybody else to look out for her. She is one tough cookie, you know?" He paused. "Can you tell me what you want me to do for her?" he asked.

"Let her move into the house with you and the baby."

"Let her move in? Sure, if she wants to move in, that's fine with me. But, Martha," He looked toward me with sad eyes. "Haddie has her own place."

"She can't afford that rent anymore. You know the dress factory let her go. She can move into that second bedroom and save some money."

"I promise you. It's fine by me, Martha." He kept caressing her face. "If that's what Haddie wants to do."

"Yes, that's what she wants. I know she will not speak up and say these things to you, Doug. That's why I'm telling you. And that's why I want you to promise me that it's alright with you."

Doug nodded. "I'll promise you anything, Martha. Don't you know that? So, if it's what Haddie wants, it's all fine by me!" He assured her.

"She wants to help take care of Paulene. She told me that. Let her help you take care of Paulene, please."

"Haddie is already helping me take care of Paulene. She is doing a good job. You don't have to worry about that my precious. We will both take good care of your baby."

"My baby." The tears poured from her weak looking eyes. "My little precious girl will never know me! Please, tell her about me, Doug. Please tell her about me."

He squeezed her hand and nodded. "You bet I will. I will tell her everything about her wonderful, precious mother." He paused to collect himself. "Haddie and I both will." He reached into his pocket and pulled out his wallet and showed her the picture of herself that she gave to him when they first met. "You see this picture? It will stay right here in my wallet until the day I leave this world. When Paulene grows up, I will show her this picture of you and tell her everyday how much you loved her and wanted her."

Martha's bright eyes were barely open, as she lay there barely alive but as radiant and beautiful as ever. "Promise!" she said. She made a motion with her hand to try and lift it to reach for his, but she couldn't seem to move it. He grabbed her hand with both of his and brought it up to his lips kissing it repeatedly as tears poured from his eyes like water from a rooftop. He cried harder than I have ever seen a grown man cry before and since.

Doug and I were similar in a way. Martha had been our life. His mother had died when he was fourteen and his father had raised him on his own. Like me he felt alone growing up. Meeting and marrying Martha seemed to somewhat complete him. He sat there at her bedside holding her hand as it grew limp and cooler in his.

He looked toward me who was bent over in tears with my hands pressed on the window sill, and between my crying noise and his silent pain, it was a minute before we realized that our beautiful, special Martha had closed her eyes for good. Sitting motionlessly, he held her lifeless hand in his. And suddenly the room filled with a silence as still as the tallest peak of a mountaintop.

Chapter Twenty-Nine

Early Saturday morning, after the party, I was up and about at the crack of dawn. I usually stayed in bed until at least after nine on weekends. But that red wine from Mrs. Huntley's party had my head sort of out of sorts. And just as I walked into the kitchen, I spotted the back of Dad's head. He was headed out of the back door to feed the animals. Aunt Haddie was sitting at the small round solid pine kitchen table that seated four. Sitting in the middle of the table, a platter of steaming hot pancakes and a dish of fresh strawberries. Rubbing my left eye and yawning, I pulled out a chair and took a seat across from her.

My stomach wasn't hungry, but Aunt Haddie passed me a plate. I proceeded to place one pancake on the dish and placed two fresh strawberries on top of the pancake. She passed me the maple syrup and I poured a bit over my food. Then she passed me the pitcher of icy cold fresh squeezed orange juice and I proceeded to pour myself a small glass of juice. After she stopped passing me things, I looked at my food, shook my head and pushed my plate aside.

"Aunt Haddie, I figured I should eat something, but I'm really not that hungry."

"You're not hungry?"

"Not much. It's probably because I have a pounding headache, like crazy. Not to mention my stomach feels like it's boiling inside. What kind of wine was that Mrs. Huntley was serving?"

"Paulene, you need something in that tiny stomach of yours," Aunt Haddie insisted. "If you have a headache, it surely won't be stopping if you don't put some food in your stomach. At least eat those strawberries," she said, sipping her coffee, holding the cup with both hands with a serious look in her eyes.

"College woman or not. You are still my baby." She grinned, cutting a piece of pancake with her fork, placing it in her mouth. "You may not feel like eating, but try and nibble on your food. It will make you feel better."

A slight smile curved my face. But I wished she wouldn't fuss over me and call me her baby. "Okay, Aunt Haddie. I'll nibble on the berries. But, will you please do me a favor and stop calling me your baby." I sank my teeth into the coolness of a sweet strawberry. "I know you like calling me that. But I'm a grown woman and I just don't like hearing it anymore."

Aunt Haddie was silent for a moment, but not too pleased about what I had asked her to stop doing. She broke the silence.

"Paulene, you didn't mention to us if you enjoyed yourself at Fanny's birthday gathering last night. You thought it was okay, didn't you?" She sipped her coffee.

"Aunt Haddie, I meant to tell you and Daddy last night that I thought the party was okay," I said, sipping my orange juice.

"I wasn't sure after you planted yourself permanently on Fanny's living room sofa with your head buried in some magazine. You could have stayed in the family room and mingled with her guest a bit longer. Fanny kept asking me if you were okay? She wanted to know if you were enjoying yourself? We looked around and you were no where to be found until I spotted you sitting in her living room all alone with that book in your lap. If you don't get out and enjoy yourself around here, you might take a notion to want to head back up to that darn Chicago. Or even worse, get yourself back tangled up with that Ben Drake." She shook her head. "I don't see how you could have enjoyed yourself sitting in some stuffy old living room by yourself with nobody to talk to. Did you?" Aunt Haddie asked.

I nodded. "Yeah, I did. I enjoyed it a lot better than being around all that booze and smoke that was polluting up that room the party was in."

"You're right, Paulene. It did get pretty smoky in there. And it doesn't help that Fanny is a chain smoker, one cigarette right after the next. At one point, she had three cigarettes lit on different ashtrays with one in her mouth," Aunt Haddie took a sip of coffee. "But go figure. She never coughs and looks healthy as an ox. Apparently, cigarettes haven't penetrated her weak link."

Aunt Haddie, like I said, the party was okay. But Mrs. Huntley's birthday party was no place for me. There wasn't one person my age at her party. And I didn't expect there to be. She's a seventy-eight-year-old woman. She's your friend and Dad's friend. She's not my friend. She's a nice old lady and I like her. But, I just feel too uncomfortable around Mrs. Huntley. After all, she is Casey's grandmother."

"Well, Paulene, you know, Fanny doesn't hold what happened to her grandson against you. She's my best friend for crying out loud. You think I would still be hanging around her if I thought she was holding a grudge against you?"

Shaking my head, I looked at Aunt Haddie with sad eyes. "I know she doesn't hold a grudge against me. I just feel uncomfortable around her because I know she misses Casey so much." I touched Aunt Haddie's hand. "But I thank you and Dad for asking me to come along. It was okay. But that red wine she was serving didn't agree with my stomach. Maybe, I would have mingled in the party room longer if the wine hadn't bothered my stomach."

"Is your head feeling any better?" she asked.

"Yes, a lot better." I held up my juice glass. "Thanks to this cold, fresh glass of home squeezed juice, no doubt."

"Aunt Haddie." I touched her hand again. "The best part of the evening was when you shared my mother's last day with me. It was deeply touching. Thank you."

"I'm happy to tell you anything I can about your mother, Paulene." She looked straight in my eyes. "But I can't say that it was touching to relive that day. But I did it for you and for Martha Jean. I'm sure she would have wanted you to know how she died a brave woman, thinking only of others as she took her last breath."

"My mother had a middle name?" I asked. "Martha Jean." I smiled. "That's a pretty name."

"Maybe to you, but not to Martha Jean. She did not like it when I called her that. She did not like her middle name," Aunt Haddie assured me.

"Out of all these years, I have not once heard Dad mention her by Martha Jean."

"And you never will. Mama and all the kids at school called her Martha Jean and she just hated that. When she and Doug started dating, she asked him to never call her by that name. And he never did while she was alive and he never has since she died."

"After breakfast, do you feel up to being my fishing companion? Maybe you'll catch your first fish?" Aunt Haddie laughed.

"I'm not sure I feel up to fishing," I mumbled.

"That's your problem, young lady. You don't seem to feel up to anything lately."

Aunt Haddie was right. My life didn't feel connected to anything. I loved Ben so much and wanted to be with him so much until nothing else seemed to matter. And because my heart and soul felt that way, I was slowly dying inside because of it. I needed to see him and be in his presence. I felt as if I needed his presence to breathe. I wasn't really living. I was just alive, existing somehow, through each long heartbreaking day.

"You might enjoy it. Think about it. I'll probably go down to the creek in the next hour. I need to change into a pair jeans and a shirt first. I'm not about to head down there in this dress that will catch every weed around." She got up from the table and put her dish in the sink.

"So, what's the word? Do you think you want to catch your first fish?"

I looked at her and shook my head. "Thank for asking me to join you, and I probably would if I knew anything about fishing."

"There's nothing to know. I'll show you. You put the bait on the hook and you throw your line in the water. You catch the fish. If it's big enough, you keep it and cook it. If it's too small you throw it back in the water. It's just that simple."

"I still think I'll decline." I laughed. "I don't think I would have much fun taking a hook out of a helpless fish mouth."

Chapter Thirty

Mid-week of the third week of not hearing from him, he knocked on my door. It was a clear, warm Wednesday, right around noon. Aunt Haddie and Daddy were both down at the creek fishing. When I opened the front door and stared in his face, I almost lost my balance. Seeing his face awakened every part of me and made me feel completely alive again. But what could I say? I wondered why he was at my door, and what did he want and was it possible that he had missed me too.

"Hi, it's a beautiful summer day; isn't it? The birds are singing. Everything is beautiful." He pointed to the sky. "Have you ever seen a more perfect day?"

Apparently he was in a very good mood for some reason. He was smiling with a look of excitement in his sparkling eyes. He was dressed wonderful as usual as he stood there near the bird fountain wearing a dark burgundy suit with a light rose-colored shirt and burgundy and rose colored tie with one hand behind his back.

Being in his presence felt right as I stepped off the porch and into the yard near him. I noticed my attire and I was pleased that I was dressed in one of my nicer dresses with my hair pulled back tightly in one neat ponytail. I was wearing a cotton and silk blend long cream colored casual dress that I had purchased at Marshall Fields while living in Chicago. I couldn't think of anything I wanted more than to be near him. Then, suddenly he pulled from behind his back a big radiant, bouquet of flowers.

"These are for you, Miss Dawson." He handed me a beautiful bouquet of fresh cut flowers that had the sweet aroma of a field of wild flowers.

A smile curved around my mouth as I was trying to keep my composure to see what his visit was really all about. I lifted the array of flowers up to my nose and breathed in the fresh clean fragrance of the bright bouquet.

His expression showed that he was pleased to see that I adored the flowers and hadn't thrown them back in his face.

"Paulene, thanks for accepting the flowers and thanks for stepping outside to hear what I have to say. But before I go any further." He glanced about the yard. "And get into why I'm here. Let me ask you, are your folks around?"

"No, Ben, Daddy and Aunt Haddie are both down at the creek fishing."

He slightly smiled and gave me a curious look.

"I hope I don't put my foot in my mouth here, since I'm here today humbly at your service hoping you will hear me out before you tell me to get lost, yet again." He grinned, with both hands in the pockets of his suit jacket. "But I have always wanted to ask you—why do you call your mother, Aunt Haddie?"

A big smile spread across my face at that question, as I stood there almost trembling from his gorgeous presence.

"Because she's my aunt and my mother. She's my real mother's sister, and when my real mother passed away a few months after my birth, Daddy asked Aunt Haddie to move in with us to help out with me, a new baby. They became good friends sharing their grief for my mother and eventually fell in love and got married, and they have always had me call her Aunt Haddie."

He nodded. "Oh, I see, but back to the reason I'm here. I'm here because I haven't been able to eat or sleep or concentrate on anything since you ran away from me three weeks ago. You finally opened my eyes to a lot of things that were mainly my feelings for you. I love you, Paulene," he said with love pouring from his voice as his eyes melted into mine.

"But I guess we didn't get started on the right foot. For starters, I pushed you away by leading you to believe or wonder if I was really interested or if I had noticed you on the two occasions we first met. Both times being at Katie's parties." He paused. "The truth is I did notice you, Paulene. Who couldn't or wouldn't? You were the only woman I did notice. But I felt I had to run from you for dear life. I felt I wanted to keep my life just the way it was: single. Deep down I wanted you and I knew you were the woman, the only woman I could lose my heart over. And I didn't think I wanted to lose my heart," he said in a lower tone with his eyes still focused.

"But whether I wanted to or not, you had my heart in the palm of your hands from the moment I looked in your radiance eyes. I didn't want to believe that and I tried to push it out of my head. But all I could see every time I closed my eyes were you: the incredible vision of your beautiful face. Coming down the escalators and seeing you standing there, time stood still. I couldn't believe it was you. And that one evening we spent together can never be topped. I can't even put into words what it felt like just being alone with you, and kissing you and touching you were like something out of this world. Something so special that I can't even began to describe. The closest word that can describe how I felt being with you is paradise. It was like one evening in paradise. And after that one unique evening with you, no matter where I went or what I did—it was all lacking something compared to the time I had spent with you," he said with a hint of water in his radiance eyes.

He paused up at the sky for a second and shook his head, then focused back on me, smiling. As he continued, my heart pounded with warmth just listening to him. I wanted to reach out and touch him. I wanted to throw myself in his arms, but I just stood there melting from his words.

"I could kick myself for not giving in to my feelings back in Chicago, but when I was there, Paulene, I was so damn unsure and afraid to give in to my deep feelings for you. I was trying to understand and accept the feelings I had for you. Feelings I had never had before for any other woman in my life. And I must admit, they were feelings that I didn't welcome. Feelings that I felt I wasn't ready for. Feelings that I had told myself would never own my heart. Because I had no plans to ever surrender my heart to love." He paused. "But I had to face it, there was something about you. Something that was deeper and larger than life." He paused with watery eyes. "Whether I wanted to surrender it or not. You had my heart from the start. And you on the other hand." He smiled. "Besides all the misunderstandings that derived from our meetings and first couple dates, listened to the tales of the Drake family not associating with anyone across the creek, and I'm sure your Aunt Haddie hasn't put in too many good words for me either." He paused as we both looked toward my front door at the ringing phone.

He looked at me and I looked at him and when I made no move to rush inside to answer the phone, he seemed pleased and continued.

"I know I live in a big house, the biggest in the area and come from a wealthy family, but it doesn't change how I feel about you. You will probably continue to think that until you know how I really feel. Well, here goes. I have fallen deeply in love with you, Paulene, and I swear, if you can't accept me because of the world I live in, I will give it all up for you. Whatever it takes to have you a part of my life, that's what I'm willing to do. My life will not be complete without you." He paused with water visible in his eyes. He reached out and touched my face. His touch was gentle and soothing.

"I see the big picture. You are the woman I want and need in my life. Will you please be my wife?"

By then tears were rolling down my cheeks. I could see love pouring from his eyes. My dream had just come true. He loved and wanted me as much as I loved and wanted him.

Standing there lost in his eyes, several seconds passed as I struggled to find my voice. At last I said. "Yes! Yes! Oh! Yes! Ben, I'll marry you. I love you, too. I have loved you from the very beginning." I glanced around for a spot to place my flowers.

He kept his eyes on mine as he slowly took the bouquet out of my arms, and with great ease, placed the bright flowers on top of a nearby evergreen bush. With the same great ease, took my left hand, brought it up to his mouth and kissed it.

"Now that you have said that, let me represent you with this." He reached his free hand into his shirt pocket and slipped on my finger a three-carat diamond.

My eyes lit up, I was speechless and before I could gather my thoughts, he gently pulled me next to him. He wrapped me in his arms and lifted me off the ground in a sensational embrace. As my feet landed back on the ground, I could feel my body melt against his. He lifted my face with one soft, strong hand and cupped the back of my neck in his palm, and then it happened. His head came fully down to mine. My heart skipped a beat when all at once his lips pressed down on mine and he urgently kissed me. And very gentle to the touch, he took his free hand and pulled the peach satin ribbon from my hair as my thick curls sweep down my back. He kissed me in such a passionate manner that left me breathless. While gripped in his arms, he softly whispered.

"Paulene, if only you knew how happy you have made me at this very moment. I had sleepless nights that this day may never come. Now it's here and I feel complete."

Ben stood at the opened door as I quickly stepped into the kitchen with my big bouquet in hand. I placed the flowers on the kitchen table as I looked in the cabinet beneath the sink to find a vase. No luck. I pulled out a tall glass pitcher, filled it with water, placed the sweet smelling array of flowers in it and placed the bouquet in the center of the kitchen table. Then quickly as my heart raced and my skin still tingled from Ben's touch, I wrote a short note for Dad and Aunt Haddie, letting them know Ben was taking me to meet his family, I taped it to the refrigerator. When I returned to the living room, he was standing there quietly, looking up at the sixteen by twenty painting of my birth mother, which hung over the fireplace.

He took his eyes off the painting and glanced at me smiling.

"That's my real mother. My Dad did the painting of her right before she died over twenty years ago."

"He's good," he said, stilling looking at the painting, rubbing his chin.

"Yeah, I know. But he never got a chance to do anything with his talent. Aunt Haddie never understood his secret love for painting." I looked toward the carpet for a second then back at the painting. He said my mother didn't have to make an effort to give him the understanding he needed toward his passion for painting. She was the embodiment of an understanding person. A good-hearted soul who took lovingly from life with both hands and invited my father to do the same. She wanted my Dad to follow his dreams. He has never forgotten her, Ben." I paused. "And just between us, I don't think he has ever loved another woman."

"But your Aunt Haddie and he are."

"Yes, I know they are married. And he does love Aunt Haddie in his own way. But, Ben, the way I have heard him talk about my mother, I know deep down that he has never stop loving her."

"I can see why. She was very beautiful." He looked at me and smiled. "But as beautiful as she was, her beauty doesn't come within miles of yours."

"My father says I look just like her."

He nodded. "Yes, the resembles is overwhelming. That's why I couldn't help but to stare. But, Paulene." He paused in my eyes. "Nothing or no one could never compare to your breathtaking beauty. You are one of a kind. Believe me."

Chapter Thirty-One

When we pulled into his driveway, his parents and his two younger brothers, Wesley and Calvin, were all standing on the front porch as if they were waiting for us? I felt so nervous, but I felt anxious and filled with complete happiness. All I wanted was to be with Ben, the man of my dreams.

Before he could get out to open the car door for me, his mother had beaten him to it. She was so beautiful and refined with friendly green eyes and perfect styled grayish black hair hanging to her neck. She was dressed lovely in a beautiful gold and black print dress. She pulled open my door and extended her hand to me.

"Welcome, Paulene. Ben has told us so much about you. My son loves you deeply, and he said today he was going to ask you to be his wife. We couldn't be happier for him. You are such a lovely young lady. A split image of your mother."

Shaking her hand, a big smile covered my face. "You met my mother?" I asked, excited that she had shared that with me.

"Yes, I knew Martha quite well." She nodded, smiling. "You look just like her."

"Thank you. That's what my father always tell me."

Just as we all were headed up the walkway toward their big lovely home, we all looked around and there was Aunt Haddie and my father pulling up at the end of their driveway. Aunt Haddie stormed out of the car, opening the door almost before Dad came to a complete stop. She left Daddy sitting there shaking his head. I couldn't imagine what she wanted as she strutted quickly across their huge lawn toward us. She had a mean look on her face with yesterday's attire. A pair of khaki shorts that seemed two sizes to large for her with an oversize brown T-shirt. She just brushed past Dr. Leonard Drake and Mrs. Anita Drake in such a rude manner.

"I'm here to see my daughter," she said in a cruel, angry voice.

She walked over and grabbed my arm and pulled me halfway across their front lawn. "What in the hell are you doing over here? Paulene Dawson? I thought you told Ben Drake to go on his way!" She yelled in my face.

"Well, I did, but now it's different. He really does care about me. He loves me as much as I love him. He asked me to marry him and I accepted." I held out my hand to show her the ring. "Isn't it beautiful?"

She stared hard at the ring with more of a shock look in her eyes than a look of admiring the flawless round diamond. She looked up at me and her eyes spoke volume. They were filled with disappointment.

"Aunt Haddie, why are you looking at me like that? Can't you see there's nothing to worry about? He's not trying to use me or embarrass me the way you thought, and his family has made me feel so welcome. They don't seem cold and looking down their noses at me, the way you described. They seem very warm and caring. So please, don't make any trouble or embarrass me in front of these people. Can't you see it in my eyes, that I love him more than anything else in this world? He makes me happy. Don't you want me to be happy?" I cried, wiping my tears the moment they fell.

Aunt Haddie arched an eyebrow and just stood there looking at me with such bitterness in her big hazel eyes as if I had given her the shock of her life. The fact that he meant well by me didn't seem to change her attitude.

My feet nervously walked back over and stood by Ben. He held my hand and softly squeezed it, then curled an arm around my waist as I looked up at him and smiled. He looked down at me smiling as well but I could see that look in his eyes, the obvious concern on his face. I could tell Aunt Haddie's presence was making him nervous.

"Is everything okay?" He mumbled softly as he bent over to kiss my forehead.

"Yes, everything is just fine," I uttered, but I wasn't sure about Aunt Haddie's actions. I was hoping she would just head back to the car where my father was waiting. He was sitting behind the wheel looking our way. The passenger's door was stretched open and he was sitting there shaking his head with a frown on his face.

"Are congratulations in order?" Asked Dr. Leonard Drake, dressed in a dark blue suit, white shirt and a berry red tie. He was looking toward Ben and I.

"Yes, Dad. This beautiful woman has agreed to be my wife, and I…"

But before Ben could finish his statement, Aunt Haddie rudely cut him off.

"Over my dead body will I let my daughter marry a Drake?"

Incredible disbelief poured from me—I knew Aunt Haddie didn't like Ben and his family, but not even I thought she would have embarrassed me the way she just had. I couldn't believe my ears. Aunt Haddie had just poured water on the second most precious day of my life. My first date with Ben was the first happiest day of my life.

"Aunt Haddie, please don't. We love each other. Why can't you just accept that? Why are you trying to stand in the way of our happiness? I thought you would be happy that he wanted to marry me and not use me as you thought he would?"

"No, Paulene, I'm not happy about this engagement and your new Drake family knows why."

By then, my father had stepped out of Aunt Haddie's old blue Plymouth and was walking across their huge front lawn in the direction of Aunt Haddie. From the look on his face, he seemed moments away from exploding with Aunt Haddie over her rude behavior. It was very obvious that he didn't share her opinion and didn't approve of what she was doing.

When he reached the spot where she was standing, he addressed her sharply.

"Haddie, let's go! Paulene is a grown woman. She has the right to pick and choose her own friends and make her own decisions," he said sharply, almost yelling. A tone I had never heard him use before. He was usually easy going and would go along with Aunt Haddie just to save an argument. But not this time! He felt she had crossed the line by embarrassing and upsetting me.

"No, Douglas! I'm not leaving here without Paulene. I will not let a daughter of mine marry into a family that killed Martha," she pointed her finger at Daddy.

Her words stunned me. I needed to know what she was talking about. I looked up at Ben and he shook his head.

"That's right, Ben, just deny that you know anything about Martha's death!" She shouted with bitterness in her voice.

"Who's Martha?" Ben asked.

His parents looked at each other and shook their heads. A hint of annoyance showed on both of their sixty-something faces. His father spoke out.

"Martha was Paulene's birth mother. She passed away when you were just a little boy," he said as he raked one hand down his short gray hair.

Aunt Haddie yelled, looking toward Dr. Leonard Drake.

"But did you tell him how she passed away? And did you tell him that she would still be alive if you had done the right thing, instead of being such a tightwad. You refused to make a loan to Doug for the money he needed for Martha's operation? The money that could have saved my sister's life would have only been a mere drop in the bucket to you heartless people! You don't care about nobody but yourselves!" Aunt Haddie yelled angrily with sparks shooting from her eyes.

"Haddie, be quiet! Let's go! You know just as well as I do that I didn't tell Leonard what I needed the money for. I just went to him and asked to borrow four thousands. He's a businessman, Haddie. People don't just go around dishing out thousands from their bank accounts if they don't know why? And if they don't know how that person plans to pay them back. The farm wasn't doing that well at the time. And besides that, I gave him no explanations why I needed it."

"He didn't need an explanation. Why would he? You were doing some work for him at the time. He could at least have helped out one of his workers!"

"You don't know what you are talking about, Haddie. I wasn't one of his workers. I was repairing his roof. And how many times do I have to tell you that he didn't know why I needed to borrow the money. I had too much pride to tell him I couldn't pay for my own wife's medical bills."

"Nevertheless, my sister died because these big shots wouldn't lend you the money. They couldn't spare a few thousands from all of their millions. And damn me! If I let..." she shouted and stomped her foot.

"Look! No more! Okay!! You either get in that damn car or I will grab you and throw you in it. I have had enough of your nonsense. Because you know as well as I do, what Martha's doctor told us? He said Martha's breast cancer was in the last stage. The operation was not going to save her. Now face it and let's go!"

Dad reached for Aunt Haddie's arm and she slapped his hand away.

"Get away from me Doug."

"I said I'm not leaving here without Paulene."

That did it. Aunt Haddie had embarrassed me and shamed my family in the presence of Ben and his family. Suddenly my face was covered with tears and I was choked up with disappointment and humiliation! I couldn't take anymore. I tore from Ben and ran across the lawn to the gravel road at the end of their yard. I started running down the road, hurt and embarrassed. Aunt Haddie had so disappointed me. She had let me down. I didn't know where I was headed, I just wanted to run somewhere and hide.

"Paulene, Paulene, no! Wait! Don't run away!" Ben called out for me.

Running as fast as I could in the middle of the road, when I looked up I didn't have time to get out of the way as a car was headed right toward me. I froze and grabbed my mouth. I didn't have time to scream or run out of the way.

Lying in the middle of that road, I was wearing my long pretty cream-colored dress with blood pouring from my left side, but that didn't frighten me. I was too much in love. All I could think of was the joy I had found in loving Ben.

I vaguely heard voices from the driver who hit me. "I'm so sorry!" A woman's voice cried. "I didn't see her. I looked up and there she was in the middle of the road. I turned the steering wheel as quick as I could to miss hitting her, but the car still bumped her!" She cried. "She just got to be okay! I could never live with myself if she doesn't pull through!"

I could hear this unfamiliar voice going on and on about how sorry she was that she had accidentally hit me with her car, but I didn't hear anyone responding or saying anything to her. Of course, everyone was in shock and the driver of the car that had hit me wasn't at fault. I was totally at fault for losing my head and running into the middle of the road. Now, laying there flat on my back, just the trace of a movement gave me unbearable pain. By now everyone had made it over to the roadside and gathered around me. Ben dropped to his knees and ripped out of his suit jacket and with great ease, placed it under my head. He then touched my face with his left hand that trembled with each beat of his heart. We looked at each other and our tears were pouring at the same rate. He leaned down and kissed my lips and the side of my face over and over as the tears in his eyes were dripping on to my face.

"I love you, Paulene," he said with the sweetest, yet saddest voice. "I love you with everything I have and everything I am." He placed my limp right hand in his and lowered his head to kiss it. "Don't be afraid. The deepest part of my heart is telling me that you will be fine. And I know this like I know the sun will rise tomorrow." He pointed toward the sky. "And the reason I know this, is because fate is on our side. We are destined to be together forever." He paused and gently raked a bit of dirt and gravel from my dress. "Until at least my hair turns the color of this beautiful dress you are wearing."

A slight smile came to my face from what he said about his hair turning the shade of my dress, but the pain was so unbearable that it hurt to smile and what was meant to be a smile turned into a frown.

"The ambulance is on the way," Ben said with sad, watery eyes.

"Ben, I love you so much until my heart is overflowing," I said in a low voice, making sure not to move my face or any other part of me as I spoke.

"There is so much love in my heart until there's no room for tears as I lay here not wanting to cry. But I'm crying for me, and I'm crying for you, and I'm crying for all those precious days that we tore our hearts out wanting to be together, but we couldn't find our way to each other," I said in a low, weak voice and had to pause when a sharp pain caused me to frown and breathe rapidly.

When the pain eased up, I lay there staring up at him wishing I had the strength to reach out and touch his handsome face. I knew I would be fine, because I was looking in the eyes of an angel.

"Ben, you made me the happiest woman alive when you asked me to marry you," I managed to utter between the waves of pain.

"You are going to be fine, Paulene. The ambulance is on the way. Just save your strength, sweetie. Don't try to talk."

Sad tears were falling from Aunt Haddie's eyes, as she and my father stood there frozen with fear. I could see the hurt and the fear in their eyes, but I could feel the love in their hearts as they were all looking and waiting for the ambulance. Only my deep love for Ben would keep me holding on until it arrived.

Chapter Thirty-Two

Half asleep when I looked around and noticed Aunt Haddie pulling my long lacy bright yellow curtains apart, I just wanted her to close them back and leave.

"Paulene, I just don't know what to say. It's a clear, sunny day and you're lying up in this room with all the curtains pulled." She fussed. "You need a little sunlight in this room," she stressed. "Don't you think?"

"I guess. Did the mail come yet?"

"You just asked me about the mail when I was in here fifteen minutes ago. It hadn't come then and it hasn't come now." Shaking her head, staring at me. "Paulene, you know that carrier never usually gets here before noon."

"I know, Aunt Haddie, but I guess I'm just so anxious to get a letter from Ben. You know I have been home from the hospital for a whole week and he hasn't called me once. He hasn't visited, nor has he written," I mumbled, twisting my engagement ring.

"Well, Paulene, you know my views on Ben Drake and they haven't changed. I tried to tell you not to get tangled up with that rich bastard in the first place!"

"But, Aunt Haddie, you know as well as I, that during my entire three weeks in the hospital he came to see me every single day and he called me every single night. I know there has to be some kind of explanation for why I haven't heard from him. He's probably out of town on business. I know I'll hear from him soon."

Aunt Haddie looked at me and rolled her eyes, propping one hand on her hip.

"Well if you know that, you know more than the rest of us. Your father and I think he has given you the brush off, since you are laid up on your back," she said and strutted out of the room.

After lunch, still lying in my bed downhearted, restless and bored too death, my eyes lit up when Aunt Haddie walked in my room looking through a stack of mail that she had just gotten from the mailbox. I was hoping for something from Ben.

"Well, here's a piece of mail for you." She glanced at me over the rim of her reading glasses. "Nice handwriting, but no return address on it." She handed me the letter and stood there for a second waiting for me to open it, but I held it to my chest and just stared at her—giving her a look that said, I'll read my letter after you leave. She shook her head at me and walked out.

Dear Paulene:

So you finally made it home from the hospital. Tell me how does it feel to be lying flat on your back while Ben and I are having the time of our lives? If it hasn't finally sunk in that Ben has dumped you, I'm writing to let you know, without a doubt that he has indeed dumped you. So you can now stop wondering why he hasn't visited or called. And you don't have to run to the mailbox, if you could run. I'm sorry; it's silly of me to mention running. I forgot you can't even walk yet. I guess running is out of the question. Ha! Ha!

Yes, I know how he visited you every day while you were in the hospital, but he only did that because he felt sorry for you. You know, Paulene, I'm surprised that you even thought Ben was serious about you in the first place. Were you really stupid enough to believe he was really going to marry you? In case you didn't know, I'm going to tell you, Ben never had any intentions of marrying you. For your information—Ben is deeply in love with me and he always has been. If there is a wedding it will be between him and I and not you and him. Paulene, if this is all coming to you as such a big surprise, why don't you just ask yourself one question. Why would a classy Drake want someone from across the creek? You are somewhat beautiful in a simple kind of way. But I'm here to tell you that looks are the only thing you do have. And believe me, just good looks are not enough for Ben. He needs more than looks and believe me what he needs you can't give him. Because you don't really know anything about anything.

Try not to cry too hard. I just hope you learned your lesson to mingle with your own kind. Find yourself some poor farmer across the creek, and stop dreaming about being with a high-class guy like Ben Drake.

Forget what I said about not crying too hard. Because I could care less if you cried forever. Yeah, I know, for even me, that was a lousy thing to say to you, but it's also lousy for you to try to take my Ben away from me. So don't bother writing back; just stay away from Ben.

Signed: Anti-Creek

Immediately after I read that cruel letter, deep down I knew that the letter had to come from some heartbroken ex-girl of his who had probably read our engagement announcement and just wanted to be mean and hurt my feelings, yet I couldn't keep myself from screaming out, "Oh! No! Lies! Lies! I know they are lies!"

Aunt Haddie rushed into my room with a concerned look on her face. She took a seat at the foot of my bed with a dishcloth in her hand.

"What's wrong, Paulene? Why are you crying now?"

She hopped off the bed and rushed toward me, "Let me dry your tears. You got to pull yourself together."

"Not with that dishcloth," I held up my hands.

"Of course not, Paulene," she said, shaking her head, then passed me the box of facial tissues from my dresser.

"It's nothing. Just leave me alone, please."

"No, I'm not leaving this room until you tell me why did you scream out like that? I want to know what has you in tears."

"Okay, if you must know, it's this nasty letter I just read. Who would write me such an awful letter? Who would hate me that much? Who Aunt Haddie? Who? I could try and think until I'm blue in the face, and I could never think of one person that I would think would write me such a nasty note. A note to purposely bring me pain. But there's no doubt in my mind that it's a flat out lie. That I know for sure. It can't be true, Aunt Haddie. It just can't be."

"Well, what did it say?" she asked.

"It's too nasty to repeat. Here it is, just read it." I handed the letter to her. Aunt Haddie threw the dishcloth across her shoulder and stood reading the letter and shaking her head the whole time. After she finished reading it, she looked at me with a straight face and an "I told-you-so look" in her big hazel eyes.

"Sweetheart, how can you be so sure that this letter is a lie?"

"Well, of course it's a lie. How could you even think otherwise?"

"Well, you know, Paulene, if it's all a lie, just tell me how can you explain the facts that he hasn't visited or called since you returned home from the hospital?"

"What you mean—how can I explain it? I don't have to explain it. I know Ben loves me and wants to marry me."

"Paulene that was before your accident. I tell you that man has forgotten about you, young lady. Now you need to forget about him and get yourself well. He has gone on with his life and you won't see him across this creek again."

I wiped a tear from my right eye as her discouraging words made my heartache even more.

"Aunt Haddie, I tell you, there is no doubt in my mind, or in my heart. Not the tiniest bit of doubt." I pointed to my chest. "I know this deep down in the depth of my soul. I know this with everything that I am."

"If there's no doubt in your mind, Paulene, then please tell me why are you all upset and crying over this letter?"

"You're right. I am upset, but not because I believe one word in that note, but because it's such a cruel, nasty letter. Someone must really hate me to write such filth."

Aunt Haddie glanced over the letter once more and immediately crushed it in her fist. There was a bit of silence as she looked at me with concern written all over her face. I merely turned my back to her and threw the covers back over my face and head.

"You know, sweetheart, you just can't totally disregard that letter."

"Aunt Haddie, just forget you even read that note. I have. Now, if you don't mind, I'm still a little sleepy." I mumbled while still buried under the cover.

"Paulene, you are not that sleepy. I don't want to hear it. You are lying around hiding under the covers, moping over Ben Drake. You better wake up and smell the coffee. Hasn't this past week taught you anything? You know that boy who claims to be so head-over-heels in love with you has not called or visited you once and you plan to just disregard that letter we just read."

With all the strength I could manage, I threw the covers back and grabbed my robe from the foot of the bed. I threw it on and had the hardest struggle trying to get out of bed. Any weight on my left leg caused me so much pain. Aunt Haddie passed the walker over to me.

"Take it easy. You're going to hurt yourself, Paulene."

As I made my way down the hallway and through the living room, Aunt Haddie never left my side. When I finally made it to the kitchen, my face was covered with tears. I was still very weak and couldn't seem to regain my strength. It was so frustrating not being able to walk or do a simple thing like washing my hair or fixing myself something to eat.

Softly and carefully, I took a seat at the kitchen table as Aunt Haddie fussed over me, trying to make sure I didn't hurt myself.

"Are you okay? You can't keep crying over that boy."

Aunt Haddie was starting to really get on my nerves. She always had to say something against Ben. She was never willing to give him the benefit of the doubt. Always blaming him for the beef she has with his parents.

"I'm fine. Don't worry so much about me and my feelings for Ben."

"I'm your mother. I'm supposed to worry. Besides, if I don't worry about you, who will? You don't seem to be able to open your eyes about that man. You are willing to just totally disregard that letter."

"Yes!" I had shouted before I realized it. "I am willing to disregard that letter because I happen to know that Ben loves me. He loves me! He loves me!" I dropped my head on the kitchen table and began to cry uncontrollably.

Aunt Haddie walked over and smoothed her hand down my hair and spoke in a calmer voice. "Sweetheart, you got to stop crying over that man. You're making yourself sicker than you are." She paused. "I know you say you believe he loves you. But maybe deep down you really don't. Because just think about it for a moment, if you were so convinced that Ben loved you, you wouldn't be in all those tears."

Slowly I raised my head and pulled a napkin from the holder. I dried my eyes. I couldn't allow myself to break down in front of Aunt Haddie. And I knew she would take it for weakness and think I didn't have faith in Ben's love for me.

Aunt Haddie stood back looking at me as I grabbed the walker that was standing next to my chair.

"Where are you going?"

"I'm going back to my room."

"Paulene, you know Dr. Carr made it very clear that you should get up and about as much as possible. But ever since you have been home from the hospital, you have just been moping around—lying around in your room, as if you have no mind for anything and I don't care what you say. I know you are in this mood because you haven't heard from that man."

Easily, I just dropped my body back in the kitchen chair and caught my breath before I spoke. I looked straight at Aunt Haddie with a straight face.

"Okay, you are right, I miss him so much. I can't believe he would let an entire week go by without visiting me. He has to be out of town or something."

"So if he is out of town, are you so convinced there are no phones where he is? Paulene, I just hope you realize that there is no excuse for him not getting in touch with you; especially since you just got home from the hospital."

"I'm going to my room, Aunt Haddie," I said in a snappy manner. I had gotten pretty irritated with her for being so pessimistic, as usual, where Ben was considered. "Maybe I'll eat something later. I'm just not hungry right now."

Aunt Haddie didn't fuss over me as I collected myself from the kitchen table and headed to my room, and she didn't lag behind me to help me into bed.

The moment I reached my room, I crawled back into bed and buried my head under the covers.

All during the night I kept waking up drying my tears. I couldn't stop crying, but I didn't really know why. Because deep down I knew Ben loved me. It was the waiting and the helplessness that was making me sad.

Chapter Thirty-Three

The next day, about an hour after Aunt Haddie had tucked me in for my afternoon nap, I couldn't close my eyes. I felt too restless and stressed from my situation. I was wide-awake lying there looking through the window. My curtains were pulled apart and I could see the beautiful blue sky and a slight breeze making the leaves dance on the trees. I could see the birds flying about from one tree to the next. Looking out, everything appeared quiet and peaceful, but somehow, through my eyes, the clear skies seemed cloudy because there was a storm inside of me: a storm that was destroying all of my strength.

Ten minutes later and now I was just lying in bed staring up at the ceiling, feeling weaker than ever. Aunt Haddie stressed how much a nap would help me, but I couldn't seem to fall asleep no matter how I tried. I kept struggling to turn from one side of the bed to the next. Ben was heavy on my mind. My thoughts were wrapped up in how he had forgotten me.

Dr. Carr had just checked me over before lunch and told Aunt Haddie to check me back into the hospital on Saturday if I hadn't shown signs of improvement by then. What they didn't know was that I was weakening from the absence of Ben and not my illness. It was the middle of the second week that I hadn't heard a thing from him. It was killing me alive.

Then, just before my eyes became heavy, I heard a knock on the front door.

"Didn't I tell you to stay away from here?"

"Yes, you did Mrs. Dawson."

"Well, why are you back?"

"Because the woman I love lives under your roof, and I will never stop trying to see her, even though for the last couple weeks you have prevented it. But I don't believe your story about Paulene being finished with me; and I don't believe your story that she has decided we don't belong together. I didn't believe it when you told me last week and I still don't believe it, that's why I will keep coming back and knocking on your door everyday, just as I have done every day since she was released from the hospital. But I'm sure you have probably avoided mentioning my visits to Paulene."

"You're right. I haven't mentioned your visits because it would only upset her needlessly. How many times do I have to tell you that she's over you? Why can't you just accept that and stay away from here?"

"It doesn't matter what you say, Mrs. Dawson. I mean there is nothing you could ever say that would make me believe that Paulene doesn't love me. We have a unique special connection that even I can't explain. If she didn't love me anymore, I would know it. I happen to know Paulene loves me."

"Are you calling me a liar?"

"I'm just stating a fact."

"So you are calling me a liar."

"No! You're putting words in my mouth. I'm not calling you a liar. I have too much respect for Paulene to disrespect her parents. All I'm saying is that I don't believe Paulene is finished with me. I believe she still loves me as much as ever."

"Call it what you may, but it still sounds like you are calling me a liar. Because I just told you she wants nothing more to do with you. The accident opened her eyes and made her realize that the two of you really have nothing in common and that your relationship would never work. But telling you this, of course, it doesn't faze you, because of your ego, no doubt! You just can't accept the fact of being rejected. So you refuse to believe me because you refuse to believe that especially a simple little Creek girl could reject the high and mighty Ben Drake.

Well, believe it! It's true! Now get off my damn property."

"Mrs. Dawson, as I stated before, I will not leave here without seeing Paulene. You can fuss at me, scream, throw things or say anything under the sun, but I swear I will not set foot off your property without first seeing the woman I love."

"Well! If you refuse to leave, I'll just have to make you leave."

The front door made a slamming sound, and then I heard Aunt Haddie hurrying to the kitchen, rambling through the kitchen drawers. Then she ran back out, slamming the front door very loud behind her; how did she think I could sleep through all that noise?

"Now do you still refuse to leave, Mr. Drake? Get off my property and don't you ever come back around here trying to see my daughter!"

"I'm not afraid of that gun and I still refuse to leave without seeing Paulene. The only way you could stop me from seeing her is if you were to shoot me down in cold blood, and I don't think you would do that. I don't think you would shoot anyone, not even a Drake," he said with an even tone.

My heart pounded in quick pumps at the thought of what Haddie was trying to do. Apparently she was trying to scare Ben away at gunpoint. I struggled in my weakness to somehow make it to the front door. I was too weak to use my walker. I easily rolled myself out of bed and onto the floor. I managed to crawl down the hallway, reaching the front door and just before I pushed open the door, I heard a shot and a scream.

With sore arms and barely any strength, I pushed open the door and there stood Aunt Haddie in tears, bending over Ben, who was on his knees at the edge of the front steps. His white shirt was covered with blood. Before I could catch my breath to say a word, I saw Daddy running up the hillside from the side of the house with an ax in his hand. He threw the ax on the lawn and ran to Ben's side.

Shock overwhelmed me to the point of being speechless. I couldn't believe my eyes. My own mother had shot the man I loved. I was on my hands and knees, struggling to get to the edge of the porch to be near him.

Daddy pushed Aunt Haddie aside.

"Get the hell out of my way, Haddie, this beat all! Have you lost your mind completely, Woman, shooting this boy? Ben are you okay? Can you stand up? I'm going to get you in my truck and rush you to the emergency room."

Ben managed to stand with the help of Daddy, while Aunt Haddie stood there shaking with her face covered in tears.

"Oh, my goodness, what have I done? I didn't mean to harm you, Ben. I only meant to scare you away. I'm deeply sorry. I didn't pull that trigger. I wouldn't try to shoot you or anybody."

Daddy yelled with boiling anger on his face and in his voice. He was madder with Aunt Haddie than I had ever seen him.

"Well! You should be Haddie. What you have done to this young man is unforgivable! You have just topped your own foolish behavior."

Daddy leaned Ben up against his old black truck as he opened the passenger's door of Aunt Haddie's old blue Plymouth. "Ben, get in."

From the expression on Ben's face, I could tell he was in a great deal of pain. He had not looked toward me. He was in too much pain to notice I was on the porch. And just as he went to be seated, he refused.

"No, not yet," Ben said as if each word caused him unbearable pain.

"Son, we can't waste any time here. You have lost a lot of blood."

Ben had a painful looking frown on his face as he held his wounded left arm with his right hand. "I don't care. I'm not going anywhere before I see Paulene."

"There she is sitting on the porch." Dad pointed toward me. "Haven't you seen her already? The only person you need to see is a doctor."

"I am a doctor. And I know what condition I'm in. I'm in a great deal of pain from the gunshot that went straight through my shirtsleeve and grazed the edge of my upper left arm. I will survive this wound but I will not survive without seeing Paulene's beautiful face, and knowing she still loves me."

"Here I am Ben. I do love you."

Daddy walked Ben over to the old wooden porch and up the steps to sit beside me. He found the strength to grab me with his unwounded arm and kissed my face and hair repeatedly. I put my arms around him and kissed him back. We were both wounded and in pain but our love were greater than any pain we could ever endure.

"Oh! Baby," he said breathless. "All I want is to hold you forever. I love you so. I cannot be without you, not ever." He inhaled deeply as I could feel his heart pounding at the same rate as my own. "I have tried to see you, every single day. I swear I have. It was sheer torture not being able to see you and hold you." He took a deep breath. "I thought I knew pain when you left Chicago. And I thought I knew pain when I moved back home and you wouldn't see me. But I didn't know pain until these past two weeks of not being able to see you: Calling and not being able to speak to you. Not knowing if you still loved me." He paused to catch his breath. "Not knowing if you still wanted to share your life with me."

"Ben, I do. Oh, I do," I said breathless as his lips covered mine. And his kiss felt so wonderful and so precious.

"Paulene," he said as his lips pulled away lingering inches from my mouth. "I'm so filled with happy to know you still love me. Because the remote idea of you not loving me was more painful than any wound I could ever suffer. Because holding you in my arms are like spending an evening in paradise."

"I love you, Ben. I love you with all my heart and with every ounce of blood running through my veins. There is nothing living or dead that could destroy my love for you. I have loved you forever!"

While sitting there in his arm, I felt a sharp pain in my left side. I grabbed my side and bit down hard on my bottom lip to try and hold back the stinging discomfort of the shooting pains that had over taken my left side. But I couldn't. "Oh, my side is hurting," I said louder than I wanted to. Dad and Aunt Haddie ran to my side and Ben was breathing hard as his eyes watered. He was apparently in as much pain as I was.

"Paulene, you need to be in bed." Ben glanced at Aunt Haddie and she nodded with tears streaked down her face.

"I know, and you need to let my father rush you to the emergency room."

"As soon as they put you to bed, I'll let him take me."

"No, let him take you now. I'll be okay. Please, let him take you," I begged.

Tears started pouring down my face faster.

"Okay, sweetheart, whatever you say. I'll go with your Dad. But don't worry. My arm is going to be just fine. It's just this blood from the tear of my skin and the pain from the open wound that makes it appear worse than it is." He glanced at Aunt Haddie as if he was trying to comfort her. To let her know she hadn't really hurt him as bad as she thought.

He rolled up his shirtsleeve and showed me. "See, it's just a flesh wound that I could bandage up myself."

Quickly turning my head, I looked away as I got a quick glimpse of his arm covered in blood. It hurt me deeply to look at his wound. Flesh wound or not, I couldn't bear to see any kind of wound on him. As I turned my head, Aunt Haddie slowly stepped near him and he held out his arm for her to see.

"Mrs. Dawson, it's just a flesh wound. The bullet barely grazed me."

Aunt Haddie's hazel eyes looked humble. She touched Ben's shoulder.

"You got to believe that I am deeply sorry about what I just did to you. I only meant to scare you away with the gun. I didn't pull that trigger. The damn thing went off by its self," she said humbly.

"Haddie that's because that's my hunting gun and I never leave the safety on it," Daddy said angrily. "You never should have had the damn thing in the first place. You know you don't know anything about guns."

"I know, Doug. I said I'm sorry. And I truly am."

"Well, maybe you are Haddie. But it was just plain wrong and downright stupid what you did. You know how Paulene and Ben feel about each other. But could you put your own beef aside and stop interfering in their lives? No! Now look what has happened. You got a lot of making up to do woman!"

With a slight frown on his face, Ben reached out his unwounded arm toward Aunt Haddie. He wanted to shake hands with her. As they shook hands Daddy shook his head in disbelief. It was amazing that Ben could be so forgiving.

"Mrs. Dawson, I'm not claiming to not be upset about what just happened here or what has taken place over the past two weeks. But your heart was in the right place. You happened to love Paulene just as much as I do. You thought you were doing what's best for her. I'm not one to hold a grudge. I just want your blessings, because I love your daughter more than life." He grabbed his wounded arm in pain.

"You have my blessings," she said as a slight smile curved her sad face.

"Ben, I see the pain on your face. Daddy, please take him to the emergency room now. I don't care if it is a flesh wound it's causing him pain. It needs to be patched up and bandaged up."

"She's right, Ben. I better get you on to the hospital."

"Aunt Haddie helped me up in her arms and Daddy helped Ben up in his arms. Ben and I looked at each other for a few minutes one last time before Daddy helped him to the car, slammed the car door and pulled off. Ben threw me a kiss; and just as they backed out of the driveway, I fainted and when my eyes blinked opened I was lying in my bed looking up at Aunt Haddie.

"It's okay, sweetheart, you just fainted from all the excitement. I'm sorry for putting you through all this pain. I'm totally the blame. But you have my word that I will never stand in the way of your happiness with Ben again. I didn't mean for that trigger to go off. But by that happening, it really opened my eyes to reality. And it's like Doug said. I was trying to discourage your relationship with Ben, not because I didn't think he was good enough for you, but because I didn't think I was good enough for them." She shook her head. "What a fool I have been living in the past. "It is now crystal clear to me that Ben Drake loves you more than life itself. He was willing to die, just to be with you. Pulling that gun on him didn't scare him the least. And that's why I ran and got the gun in the first place. I was trying to scare him." She paused. "Of all the foolish things I have ever done, that takes the cake. But anyway, he didn't make one step out of that yard. And even after what I did to him, he never got angry or said a nasty word to me, which I would have deserved, to say the least." She wiped a tear from her eyes. "I especially want you to know sweetheart, that just as soon as he is patched up and Doug brings him back here, I will throw myself at his mercy and beg his forgiveness some more."

"Aunt Haddie, you don't have to do that. He doesn't expect that. He has already accepted your apology." I pointed to the half pitcher of ice water that sat on my bedside table.

"I know, but I feel like I should do something more," she said, pouring water into my glass sitting there. "I have been so hard on that young man, who has turned out to be the Prince that you have always told me he was." She handed me the glass of water. "Well, if you don't want me to make a fuss over him…"

I cut her off, smiling and shaking my head. "Please, don't make a fuss over him. You'll make him feel uncomfortable." I took a sip of water.

"I know what I can do, I'll do everything in my power to see that your wedding to him is the most beautiful, precious wedding that ever was. Because, Paulene, I know within my heart that you have picked a winner. May God bless you both?"

"Aunt Haddie, I forgive you, and Ben has forgiven you too. We both love you and all we ever wanted were your blessings, and now that we have that—we have everything." I held out my arms and we embraced, our faces covered with tears.

CPSIA information can be obtained at www.ICGtesting.com
Printed in the USA
BVOW05s1819040115

381727BV00001B/14/P